RIGHT AND GLORY

MAX ADAMS, who worked in covert operations
for a time, now lectures on diverse historical subjects
and divides his time between the UK and Andorra
with his wife.

Also by Max Adams

To Do or Die

RIGHT AND GLORY

MAX ADAMS

First published in 2011 by Pan Books
an imprint of Pan Macmillan, a division of Macmillan Publishers Limited
Pan Macmillan, 20 New Wharf Road, London N1 9RR
Basingstoke and Oxford
Associated companies throughout the world
www.panmacmillan.com

ISBN 978-0-330-51034-9

1 3 5 7 9 8 6 4 2

A CIP catalogue record for this book is available from
the British Library.

Typeset by Ellipsis Books Limited, Glasgow
Printed by CPI Mackays, Chatham ME5 8TD

Visit **www.panmacmillan.com** to read more about all our books
and to buy them. You will also find features, author interviews and
news of any author events, and you can sign up for e-newsletters
so that you're always first to hear about our new releases.

To Sara, as always

ACKNOWLEDGEMENTS

I must thank my agent, Luigi Bonomi – who was awarded the title of Literary Agent of the Year 2010, which just confirms what I've always thought about him! – for his unswerving support and friendship. Thanks also to Jeremy Trevathan, my editor at Pan Macmillan, for his incisive editing and comments on the book, despite the technical problems he experienced and the disruption caused by moving his office twice in the same year. You can always rely on a pencil, Jeremy! Finally, I must again thank Ronald Fairfax, author of *Corky's War* (Mutiny Press, ISBN 978-0-9559705-0-4) for his invaluable assistance in the vital field of research. He did a sterling and thorough job, just as he did with the previous book. As always, any errors of fact are mine and mine alone.

AUTHOR'S NOTE

This is of course a novel, but it has been built upon a basis of fact. Fort Eben Emael was the strongest and most powerful defensive fortification in Belgium, possibly in Europe, and was popularly believed to be invincible. At the very least, that fort, and the numerous other armoured structures in the area, were expected to be able to hold up a German invasion for several days, long enough to allow for French and British reinforcements to be sent to the Dyle Line, the Belgian fall-back position.

There are a variety of estimates for the time it took the German troops to effectively neutralize the fort, ranging from about fifteen minutes to around half an hour, but certainly within sixty minutes of the first of the German gliders landing on the roof of the structure, Fort Eben Emael was a spent force. Some of the guns continued firing for a while, but from that point onwards surrender was inevitable.

Interestingly, the plan was conceived and organized by Adolf Hitler personally, and was a triumph, perhaps the single most successful German operation of the entire conflict. The attack was carried out as I've described it in the novel, the German troops landing in camouflaged gliders, to avoid the sound of aircraft engines being detected by the Belgian defenders, and with tiny swastikas painted on them so that the aircraft couldn't be identified visually until they were almost on the ground.

It could be argued that the fort fell due to simple incompetence on the part of the Belgian defenders, and this is a difficult argument to refute. All the events I have described in the novel relating to this attack are as accurately portrayed as is possible so long after the event, and show clearly that mistake after mistake was made, leaving the fort woefully unprepared to meet the attack that the Belgian troops actually *knew* was coming.

Perhaps the most unbelievable error was that the two heavy machine-gun positions on the roof of the fort – Mi-Sud and Mi-Nord – were unmanned and didn't fire a single shot during the attack. If they had been ready for action, these weapons could have riddled the gliders with bullets the moment they landed, and killed or incapacitated every German attacker. That was what the two posts had been constructed to do, and it's still something of a mystery why this didn't happen. But whatever the reason, the mistake in not having *every* position manned when the German gliders landed led directly to the capture of the fort.

One of the more bizarre aspects of the fall of Eben Emael was that the Germans had no need of spies or secret agents to ascertain details of the interior layout or the construction methods used, because the structure was actually erected by a *German* building firm – perhaps not the best idea the Belgian government had in the tense years leading up to the Second World War.

The concept of a hollow-charge weapon, named the *Hohlladung* by the Germans, was first described by an American named C. E. Munroe in 1888, and became known as the 'Munroe Effect'. It utilized a shaped charge of TNT which produced a convergent shock wave and consequently created a directional explosion. An inner core of copper made the detonation even more effective, and the combination of the explosive gas and jet of molten metal was able to penetrate armour plate and reinforced concrete.

I've slightly altered the timescale of the German advance, for dramatic reasons.

A note on terminology: the name 'Schmeisser' was used by British troops throughout the war to refer to the German MP 38 and MP 40 sub-machine-guns, but this was actually a misnomer. Hugo Schmeisser produced ground-breaking designs, including the first successful such weapon, known as the Bergmann MP 18, back in 1918, but had nothing to do with the design of either the MP 38 or the MP 40. The German army funded the development of the MP 36 by Berthold Geipel of the Erma-Werke company. This weapon was in part based on the VRM 1930 designed by F. J. Vollmer of the Erma-Werke company. Vollmer himself then redesigned the MP 36 to produce the prototype MP 38, which was adopted by the German army. The MP 40 was a mass-produced variant of the MP 38 which utilized stamped steel components rather than machined parts wherever possible. Both the MP 38 and the MP 40 were manufactured by Erma-Werke.

MAX ADAMS
Monpazier, France

CHAPTER 1

9 MAY 1940: GAP OF VISÉ, BELGIUM

'Not another bloody fort,' Eddie Dawson muttered, staring across the heavily wooded landscape towards a massive, slab-sided grey concrete structure, the huge and almost level top of which was covered in grass.

'Well observed, Dawson,' Major Sykes replied, striding along beside the corporal. 'But this one might actually do the job, as long as Adolf hasn't got any clever ideas up his sleeve.'

Sykes had requested Dawson's assistance two days earlier, but it had taken the corporal all that time to get across Belgium from Lille, just over the French border, where he'd been helping erect a series of anti-tank defences, to the Gap of Visé, the strip of territory that lay between Liège and Maastricht, close to Belgium's eastern border with Germany.

'So what am I supposed to be doing here, sir?' Dawson asked.

'Just the same as before. When you looked at that Maginot Line fort in France things didn't go entirely according to plan, but the requirement's still there. We still need to assess the strength of the static defences against a German invasion – which is coming very soon, mark my words.'

'I heard Hitler wanted peace,' Dawson said, glancing at the major. 'A piece of Austria, a piece of Czechoslovakia, a piece of France.'

'Funny, Dawson,' Sykes replied, without a smile. 'And unfortunately true.'

'You think the Jerries would invade Belgium as well?'

'I think Adolf intends to take over every country he can – certainly everywhere in Western Europe. He's already doing his best to isolate Britain with his U-boats and surface raiders in the Atlantic, hitting merchant ships.'

'I thought the Royal Navy was doing OK in the Atlantic. They sank that bloody *Graf Spee* back in December, didn't they?'

'That was just one ship, Dawson. A powerful and important ship, I grant you, but just one ship. Our cruisers were hopelessly outgunned, so we were very lucky the battle ended the way it did. We could easily have lost all three ships. And don't forget we did lose the *Royal Oak* in Scapa Flow, of all places, a supposedly secure anchorage. In Europe, the German land forces walked into Denmark with barely a shot fired. Within a few months they'll take Norway as well. Hitler will want Sweden's iron ore resources as well, and I doubt the Swedes will give him much trouble. Soon his forces will be heading for Belgium and France. And then Britain, unless we can find a way to stop him.'

'You almost sound like you admire him, sir.'

Sykes stopped beside the track and stared to his front, looking at the few sections of the massive grey concrete fortress that projected above the ground.

'It's not a question of admiration, Dawson,' Sykes said. 'Adolf Hitler is, without the slightest doubt, a genius. An evil genius, but he's a genius none the less. How else could an Austrian corporal and third-rate watercolour painter have managed to become the leader of Germany?'

'Somebody told me he was a house-painter, not an artist,' Dawson said. 'Two undercoats and one gloss.'

'Yet another myth that's been circulated about him,' Sykes said. 'Did you know he fought for Germany in the Great War? And he was decorated twice for bravery.'

Dawson shook his head.

'We underestimate that man at our peril. He may not have had the classic background and training that makes a great military leader, but his record so far in this conflict is really impressive. All you have to do is look at what he's achieved.' Sykes ticked off the points as he spoke. 'In 1936, he reoccupied the Rhineland. Two years later, he did the same with Austria and the Sudetenland area of Czechoslovakia. Last year, he annexed the rest of Czechoslovakia. All without serious opposition because of his political acumen.'

'And then he marched into Poland,' Dawson said.

Sykes nodded. 'Exactly. He'd been planning that move for long enough. Between you and me, Dawson, we – the intelligence bods, I mean – believe he orchestrated the timing perfectly.'

'Hang on, sir. I heard that some Polish soldiers attacked German troops near the border, and that's why the Jerries invaded.'

'Not quite. The Germans claimed their radio station

3

at a place called Gliewitz near the Polish border was assaulted by a Polish army patrol. That was the story. But now we think that it was just a ruse. The Poles have no record of any troops in any action with German forces in that area at that time. Latest intelligence suggests the Germans took a group of men out of a prison camp somewhere, dressed them in Polish army uniforms, faked an attack on the radio station and then shot them. That provided the excuse Hitler needed, something he could show to the world as an act of unprovoked aggression. And it's difficult to argue with because the only people who can prove they weren't Polish soldiers are all dead. That's why we're here now – the invasion of Poland finally brought Britain and France into the war.'

'And the Jerries smashed the Poles in a month,' Dawson said. 'That *Blitzkrieg* thing.'

'Yes. It translates as "lightning war", which is a very apt description. The Polish armed forces were tiny and ill-equipped. Their army numbered about three hundred thousand, and they faced two and a half million German troops. They sent cavalry units out to face Panzer tank divisions. Their aircraft were old and obsolete. The conquest of Poland only took so long because the Poles refused to surrender until they had absolutely no other choice. They're a very brave people. And you can see that in the figures. In that short campaign, the Germans lost about fifteen thousand men.'

'You think Belgium might be next, sir?'

Sykes shook his head. 'That I don't know. But if you look at a map of Western Europe, you'll see that if the Germans want to conquer France – and I don't think there's any doubt that walking down the Champs-

Elysées is high on Hitler's list of objectives – they really have no choice but to go through Belgium, and they'll have to subdue Holland as well. The French did get one thing right. The Maginot Line down to the south of Luxembourg is simply too tough an obstacle for an invading army to crack. I've no doubt the Germans will break through it eventually, but the open plains of Belgium and Northern France are the obvious route for his forces to take. So sooner or later he'll send his troops this way. And there's another reason as well. Before Hitler can tackle us, he'll have to conquer Belgium and France at least – he must get control of the Channel ports on the Continent if he wants to launch an invasion of Britain.'

'Kind of domino effect, then. First Holland and Belgium, then France, and finally Britain?'

'Exactly. Anyway, Dawson, we've been sent here to take a look at this fort – it's called Eben Emael, by the way – and the other defences in this area, so let's do that.'

The two men stopped and stared down the lane. Directly in front of them, to the north, was a massive, near-vertical, concrete wall. The wall looked to Dawson as if it was around 400 yards in length, and clearly formed one boundary of the fort. At each end of it was an armoured circular observation post, with machine-gun ports and openings for heavier weapons as well. Beyond each observation post was a further massive length of reinforced concrete wall, linked to the main section at an angle of about forty-five degrees to enclose the heart of the fortress. Above the walls, a rounded grassy mound extended well to the north, a couple of what looked like steel cupolas for heavy weapons set into it.

'A bit different to that last place we looked at,' Dawson muttered.

'That's something of an understatement,' Sykes said. 'Eben Emael is probably the strongest and most powerful fort ever built. It's certainly the most powerful fortification in Belgium. It's shaped like a triangle or a wedge of cheese, with the point aiming north, towards Maastricht. We're looking at the base, at the southern end. Overall, it's about eleven hundred yards from north to south, and eight hundred yards from east to west. It's a huge structure, built into the rock of this plateau, and it carries a formidable armament.'

Men wearing unfamiliar uniforms strode around outside the fortress, and, as they looked over towards it, an officer spotted them standing there and headed in their direction.

'Do they know you're coming this time, sir?' Dawson asked innocently, recalling what had happened in France the previous year, when the two men had been on a similar mission.

'I think so, yes.'

The Belgian officer stopped in front of them and snapped off a crisp salute that Sykes returned somewhat casually.

'I'm Capitaine Verbois, sir,' the Belgian officer said, his English reasonably fluent. 'Are you Major Sykes?'

Sykes answered the question with a nod. 'Yes, and this is Corporal Dawson. He's my explosives expert.'

Verbois looked at Dawson with interest. 'I understand you are here to assess the tactical situation, Major, and the ability of Fort Eben Emael to guard this section of the border, but I do not understand what for the corporal is here.'

'He's here to see how easy it would be to blow the place apart.'

For a few moments Verbois just stared at Dawson. Then his mouth curled into a smile, and then he laughed out loud.

'Blow it apart?' he said. 'Blow it apart? You obviously have no idea how strong Eben Emael is. Nothing can "blow it apart", as you put it. This fort is invulnerable.'

'That's a very impressive claim,' Sykes said. 'Can you justify it?'

'Of course, sir. Let me explain. This structure takes four years to build. We do not even start work on it until 1931, when it was clear Germany was going to be again a problem.'

'That's one way of putting it, I suppose,' Sykes murmured. 'Germany's quite a big problem now, though, isn't it?'

'Of course, which shows that our government is absolutely right to embark on this huge project. Our country has a problem: if Germany ever chooses to invade France, the route most obvious for the invading army would be through Belgium.'

'Just what I was saying to you, Dawson.'

'That happened in the Great War,' Verbois continued. 'In 1914, we faced an army that outnumbered us ten to one. We had only two defences – our neutrality, which was ignored by the Germans, of course – and the line of defensive forts we had built along our eastern border to protect Liège and Antwerp. When Germans invaded in August, they used heavy artillery, specially designed heavy mortars, to pound these forts into submission in a matter of days. We had badly miscalculated the effect of their heavy weapons. It is not a mistake we are ever going to repeat. My country is still neutral, but we have also followed the example of our French neighbours and renovated and enlarged all the old forts in this area.

'But we already know that will not be enough. This area is of vital strategic importance. To the north is the junction of the Meuse River with the Albert Canal, and three bridges that cross the canal. These two waterways are the biggest natural obstacle any German invasion would face here, and this fort dominates the whole area. We have plenty of armament. The main cupola, Cupola One Twenty, is equipped with two one hundred-and-twenty-millimetre cannons with a range of twenty kilometres – that's about twelve English miles – and they are integrated with the weapons installed at the other nearby forts. Then we have four reinforced concrete casemates, each armed with three seventy-five-millimetre cannons, with a range of five miles. Two are named Maastricht One and Two, and they cover the area to the north of the fort. The other two face south, towards Visé, and are called Visé One and Two. Then we have two further cupolas – Cupola Nord and Cupola Sud – each designed to be able to fire in all directions. They have two seventy-five-millimetre cannons each. Finally, just in case we need to engage the enemy at close range, we have two heavy-machine-gun positions, Mi-Nord and Mi-Sud, which cover the whole roof of the fort and the surrounding area. Believe me, we will cut any German advance to pieces long before Liège or

Antwerp are threatened,' Verbois finished triumphantly.

'Suppose this time that the Germans have got even bigger and better artillery than they had twenty-five years ago?'

'It would not matter. The tunnels that link the various sections of the fort are between twenty and thirty metres below the surface of the plateau in which we built the fort. The tunnels themselves are made of one-and-a-half-metre-thick reinforced concrete, as are all the other structures. The cupolas that house the weapons are protected by about thirty centimetres of steel, and can be retracted into the concrete surroundings. We have steel blast doors inside the fort that can seal off sections of it in event of an attack. Every strategic target within twenty kilometres has been plotted precisely, and can be accurately engaged by the weapons with no need for gun-layers to see their targets. At ground level the fort is protected by the Albert Canal itself, minefields and anti-tank ditches. All possible approaches are covered by observation posts and blockhouses equipped with machine-guns and sixty-millimetre anti-tank weapons. Finally, there is only a single entrance to the complex. So I say again – Fort Eben Emael is impregnable.'

Dawson had listened to the enthusiastic summary delivered by the young *capitaine* with keen interest, and now he nodded his head.

'You might even be right about that, sir.'

'You haven't mentioned anti-aircraft defences,' Sykes pointed out.

'We have never assessed that air raids will be a serious threat. Not even dive-bombers with heavy bombs can penetrate the huge thickness of earth and rock above the fort's main passageways. But we do have machine-guns.'

'Machine-guns?' Sykes echoed. 'No Vickers seventy-five millimetres, nothing like that?'

The Vickers-Armstrong model 1936/39 anti-aircraft gun was quite a successful weapon that could engage aircraft flying as high as 33,000 feet, and could fire twelve rounds of high-explosive a minute. Belgium was one of several European nations which had purchased the weapon.

Verbois shook his head. 'Our forces have Vickers guns, but they are deployed around softer targets than this fort. Major cities, for instance.'

'So how many machine-guns do you have?' Sykes asked. 'For anti-aircraft fire, I mean.'

'Four.'

Sykes glanced at Dawson, who just shrugged.

'It is not a problem, Major,' Verbois insisted. 'This fort is impregnable from a land assault, and any bombs would only shake hard the place, nothing more.'

Sykes nodded. 'One point of view, certainly. Personally, I'd stick an AA battery on each corner of the place and maybe a couple on the top as well, just in case, but not my decision, thank God. Anyway, could you give us a quick tour and then we'll get out of your way?'

In the late afternoon, just over three hours later, Sykes and Dawson emerged from the armoured steel door of Block One, the entrance to Fort Eben Emael, and took their leave of Capitaine Verbois.

'Interesting,' Dawson commented, as they walked away, heading for the staff car Sykes had been issued with, which he'd parked some distance from the fort itself. 'It's actually a pretty bloody impressive place. A full garrison of twelve hundred men – I know they've only got about six hundred there now – around five miles of tunnels, and those internal steel doors will stop pretty much any kind of explosive I know. It'd take days just to blast a hole in one of the blockhouses – that's if you can dodge the machine-gun bullets. And the interior is really well equipped as well, with its own generator for power and even a hospital. I think that young officer is probably right. This place is as impregnable as anywhere I've ever seen.'

Sykes didn't respond for a few moments, then he nodded. 'You're right. It *is* impregnable against a conventional attack, and that's what my report will say.'

'They don't seem the happiest of troops, sir. I can't talk to any of them, because I only know a few words of French, but it didn't look to me as if their morale is all that high.'

'They're probably just bored, running exercises all the time and doing drills. They might even welcome the chance to see a bit of action.'

Dawson shifted the sling of his Lee-Enfield .303 rifle slightly to avoid it chafing his shoulder and marched on without breaking his stride.

They made an odd couple. Dawson was tall, dark, solidly built and rugged, with features that seemed somehow rough-hewn. He towered over his companion. He'd been a mining engineer before the war, and was an expert with explosives of all kinds, which was why he'd been ordered to make up the other half of this unlikely team. He knew how to blow things up better than almost anyone else in the entire British army.

Sykes – a short, dapper major in a cavalry regiment – was the tactics expert, an experienced officer with a gift for strategic analysis and appreciation, both conventional and unconventional, of any given situation. He and Dawson had been tasked with assessing the static fortifications the French and Belgian armed forces were relying on to stop, or at the very least to slow down, the inevitable German invasion of Western Europe. They'd already investigated some of the Maginot Line forts in France, with mixed results, and the check they'd carried out at Eben Emael was their first job in Belgium. As soon as Sykes had written his report, they'd move on to inspect the fortifications at three of the other units in the area, at Diepenbeek, Barchon and Battice, the latter another newly built fort that was located a mere ten miles from the German border.

It took them only about fifteen minutes to drive the four miles to their temporary quarters in the village of Wonck. They were staying in a small guesthouse where Sykes – who spoke French like a native – had charmed the landlady into letting them stay in the two best rooms. That was a very non-standard arrangement, an officer and an NCO sharing the same billet, but it was a small village and there was no other available accommodation. And Sykes was a man who regarded rules as somewhat flexible.

After they'd eaten dinner together, Sykes retired to his room to work on his written report on Eben Emael. Dawson walked the couple of hundred yards to the nearest tavern to sample the local beer, but returned early. Half the fun of being in a bar was the conversation, and he spoke only very basic French, though ordering '*une bière, s'il vous plaît*' hadn't exactly taxed his linguistic ability. The beer, when it had arrived, hadn't been to his taste either. According to the label on the bottle, it was called 'Dubbel', and when he poured it out it was almost red in colour and both smelt and tasted of fruit rather than hops.

He walked back to the guesthouse through the dark-ened streets – blackout procedures were already in force – and was in bed by ten thirty. He fell asleep almost immediately.

CHAPTER 2

10 MAY 1940: WONCK, BELGIUM

The sudden roaring of an engine woke Dawson. For a moment or two he had no idea where he was or what he was doing. Then he glanced at the wall clock opposite him, its face faintly illuminated by the moonlight coming through the window. He climbed out of bed and walked across to the window, pulled back the curtain and looked down into the cobbled street below.

At first, he saw nothing. Then a small truck with an open back roared down the street, engine racing, and braked and bounced to a halt a few tens of yards away. Two men wearing Belgian army uniforms appeared from a building on the opposite side of the road, ran across to it and climbed into the loading area at the back. Then the vehicle drove on. Dawson could see there were perhaps a dozen or so soldiers sitting on bench seats in the back of the truck, some carrying weapons.

It could, he supposed, all be part of some military exercise. Somehow he didn't think so. He glanced again at the wall clock. A quarter past one in the morning. Outside, the new moon – the only illumination – was casting faint shadows across the cobbled street.

He stood beside the window for another few moments, then strode across to the chair where he'd placed his uniform and started to dress. He'd just pulled on his trousers when there was a brisk double knock on the door. Dawson slid back the bolt and Major Sykes stood on the threshold, in uniform but unshaven.

'Something's up,' he said, then noticed that Dawson was already half-dressed. 'Good man. I'll see you downstairs. Bring all your gear. We'll stow everything in the staff car until we can find out what's going on.'

By one thirty, Dawson and Sykes were in the Hillman and heading out of Wonck, back towards the fort at Eben Emael.

'Some flap at the fort, sir?' Dawson asked, driving through the now-silent streets.

'Maybe. If something *is* going on the staff at Eben Emael should know about it. Hopefully, we can get inside, talk to them and get some details.'

As they got closer to Eben Emael they encountered several trucks on the road, and saw numerous Belgian soldiers in battledress carrying rifles marching – some of them running – to and fro.

They reached the road near the fortress entrance a few minutes later, and Dawson drew the staff car to a halt on a level grassy area well clear of Block One. Then they both stared across at the huge underground structure.

'What the hell's going on?' Sykes muttered.

When they'd been at Eben Emael the previous afternoon, they'd noticed two wooden barrack buildings outside Block One, the entrance to the fort. Capitaine Verbois had explained they were used for administrative functions during the working day. That seemed perfectly reasonable, but what neither man understood was why now, in the middle of the night, the barracks were the scene of such frantic activity, lights blazing from the windows. Teams of men were busily engaged in emptying all the offices inside them. Others had apparently started tearing the buildings down.

'Funny time to be doing that,' Dawson remarked.

'Yes,' Sykes said shortly. 'I'll try and find an officer.'

He strode down the track towards Block One, Dawson a couple of paces behind him, having secured the car as best he could. They ignored the regular soldiers who passed by, carrying files, telephones and other office equipment. Finally the major spotted a junior officer – Dawson thought from his insignia that he was a lieutenant – marching briskly towards the fort entrance and stopped him with a shouted command.

The young Belgian officer stopped abruptly and peered towards Sykes. As soon as he spotted the major's rank badges he came to attention and saluted.

For a couple of minutes Sykes and the lieutenant held an animated conversation in French. The Belgian officer was clearly eager to get back to whatever he was supposed to be doing, but seemed to be answering every question Sykes asked him. Finally the major beckoned to Dawson, and the three men started walking together towards the Block One entrance.

'This is a bloody shambles,' Sykes said in English. 'Apparently the balloon went up at double-oh thirty, and the fort was put on full alert. The officer in charge is billeted in the village of Eben Emael itself, and he was summoned immediately. When he got here he contacted

Liège to confirm it wasn't just another exercise or a false alarm – apparently they've had quite a few of those – and he was told it was for real. I've no idea what intelligence the Belgians have received to prompt this action, but they seem to think the Germans might be heading this way.'

'But all that's what you'd expect the officer to do, isn't it?' Dawson asked, sounding puzzled.

'Yes. He did exactly what he should have done. That's not the problem. The reason these men are emptying these offices is that they're supposed to be demolished in time of war. Nobody seems to know why, but that's a part of the standing orders at Eben Emael. Nobody here seems to have noticed we've already declared war on Germany. It apparently didn't occur to anyone in the Belgian military that war was actually inevitable and to have demolished these buildings a lot earlier. So instead of manning the fort's defences and summoning the additional garrison, all the effort is going on this pointless activity.'

'Surely they must have gun crews manning the cupolas in the fort?' Dawson asked.

'The gun crews, Dawson, are the people trying to demolish those buildings over there. The point is they're not doing what they should be doing. That's why it's a shambles. And they're short-staffed as well. This place is supposed to be garrisoned by twelve hundred personnel. There are only about six hundred people actually in the building, and another couple of hundred billeted in the nearby villages. So even if all the available personnel were here, they'd still be about thirty per cent below complement. As it is, at the moment they're fifty per cent down.'

'So why haven't they summoned the extra staff living nearby?'

'I don't know,' Sykes muttered, 'but I'm going to try to find out.'

The three men arrived at the Block One main entrance, where they all had their identification checked before they were allowed inside.

Inside Fort Eben Emael were two levels of tunnels – the intermediate and lower. The intermediate tunnel system lay about sixty feet below the surface of the mound, and served the various gun emplacements that constituted the fort's principal armament. The lower level was about 120 feet below the plateau's surface, the same level as the ground outside the fortress, and housed the administrative areas, accommodation, mess-halls, galleys and shower rooms. It was along this level that the young Belgian lieutenant led Sykes and Dawson, stopping eventually outside a half-open door bearing a name and rank written in French. But Dawson didn't need to understand the language to recognize that it was the office of the commanding officer.

The Belgian army lieutenant rapped smartly on the door, then pushed it aside and stepped into the office.

'You wait out here, Dawson,' Sykes murmured, as the lieutenant gestured for him to enter. 'This won't take long.'

It didn't. Sykes emerged about two minutes later, his face flushed with anger or irritation.

'Let's go,' he snapped, and strode away down the corridor, Dawson following. The major didn't speak until they were once again outside the fort, then he turned and stared back at the massive structure.

'This is a bloody comedy show,' he said. 'God knows who drafted the standing orders for this place, but he's a fucking idiot. Those barracks are being demolished to avoid any documents and equipment falling into enemy hands in the event of an invasion. The OIC has pulled men off the gun crews to do the work, which means the guns are virtually unmanned. The man's following orders, but he's not really thinking. He doesn't seem to realize that, standing orders or no standing orders, it makes better sense to man the guns and forget about the barracks, if there really is an invasion threat.'

'And is there, sir?'

'I've still got no idea. Nor has the major who runs this place. He's talked to Liège, and the command there has confirmed the alert is real, without specifying what event or intelligence triggered it. But it's worse than that. If there *is* a German invasion, and enemy troops invade Belgium through Holland, the guns on this fort will stay silent. The orders forbid firing the weapons into Holland.'

'What – even if there are a couple of Panzer regiments heading this way?' Dawson asked.

'That's what the standing orders say,' Sykes confirmed. 'There are no circumstances in which the poor sod of an officer in charge can instruct his gunners to fire without a direct and specific order from one of the Belgian army units based in this area, and only then at targets nominated by them. So if that chain of communication breaks down, that's it. This place looks impressive, but as far as I can see it's going to be sod-all use in stopping a Jerry advance. Oh, the only other thing I gleaned from the officer was that a full country-wide alert was called at one thirty this morning, so all of Belgium's armed forces should now be at battle readiness. Which makes what's happening here all the more bloody ridiculous.'

Sykes and Dawson stood in silence for a few moments, leaning against the side of the staff car. Then Dawson returned to a point he'd raised earlier.

'And they still haven't called-in their extra staff, as far as I can see. Why not?'

'I asked. The reinforcement plan is for Cupola Nord – that's one of the two retractable steel firing points – to fire a sequence of twenty blank rounds. That cupola is fitted with twin seventy-five-millimetre cannons. Everybody for miles around will hear the sound of the shots. As well as a signal for all off-duty staff to return to the fort, it also alerts the Belgian army troops guarding the bridges near Liège that an attack is imminent, which allows them time to prepare to fire the charges and destroy the bridges. Part of the Belgian war plan is to blow up the three bridges over the Albert Canal as soon as they know an invasion is coming. That would stop an advancing German army from crossing the canal and the Meuse River, at least for a while.

'Actually,' Sykes said, considering, 'using the guns as an alarm system isn't that bad an idea, though twenty rounds seems a bit excessive. A volley of half a dozen would be enough. But the gunners who should be firing those blank shells are still down there' – Sykes pointed at the activity around the barrack buildings – 'walking about carrying typewriters and files and stuff. A comedy show.'

'Can't they send vehicles to alert the off-duty staff?' Dawson asked.

Sykes shook his head, then nodded. 'Probably,' he said, 'but the officer in command has decided not to. Instead, he's ordered the gun crew at the other cupola – that's Cupola Sud – to fire the rounds instead. That should happen any time now.'

Sykes pointed to his right, towards the top level of the fort, where a curved steel object, looking something like the top section of a huge buried steel ball, was just visible in the moonlight.

'That's Cupola Sud,' he said, 'so we should see movement any time now, when the crew prepare to fire it.'

'So what do we do, sir? Thin out or hang around and see what happens?'

Sykes looked again at the bustle of activity around them, at the teams of men working under the lights in and around the two barrack blocks.

'We'll stay in the area,' the major decided, 'at least until we find out what's really happening here. Make sure your rifle's loaded, in case the bloody Jerries really are heading this way.'

Sykes unsnapped his belt holster, pulled out his Webley & Scott Mark IV service revolver, opened it and checked that the chambers were loaded, then replaced the weapon in his holster.

'This could be a bloody long night,' he muttered, 'but let's hope they fire the alert signal very soon. At least that way they'll have all the available personnel on site, just in case this is for real.'

CHAPTER 3

10 MAY 1940: EBEN EMAEL, BELGIUM

But for well over an hour, Cupola Sud remained motionless. Like Cupola Nord, in action it was designed to rise some four feet clear of the surrounding armoured concrete structure. This would expose the holes in the side of the steel column through which the twin seventy-five-millimetre cannon would fire. There were actually three openings in the armoured steel – between the holes for the barrels of the weapons was the top of a periscope sight to allow the gunners to check the fall of shot.

At ten past three, Sykes lost patience, told Dawson to remain where he was and re-entered the fort. He was back in under ten minutes, shaking his head in disbelief.

'Un-bloody-believable,' he snapped. 'They aren't able to fire the cannon in Cupola Sud because during some previous exercise the firing pins were removed – presumably as a safety precaution – and they didn't put them back properly. They've had to find an armourer to refit the pins correctly. The OIC assures me the cannon are now ready to fire the alert signal. It's only three hours late, after all.'

At three twenty-five exactly Sykes and Dawson saw the cupola rise silently out of its concrete base and rotate slightly. Then the silence of the night was shattered by a thunderous explosion as the first blank round was fired from the seventy-five-millimetre cannon. A second round followed swiftly, then a third, but then the gun fell silent. Flames and smoke suddenly erupted from around the cupola.

'I think it's on fire,' Dawson muttered, staring upwards.

'It's made of armoured concrete and tempered steel. How the hell can it be on fire?' Sykes demanded, pulling a pair of binoculars from a door pocket on the staff car.

He focused the binoculars on the cupola, then lowered them.

'It's not the cupola that's burning – it's the camouflage netting around it. The muzzle flashes must have ignited it. I mean, didn't they even think about that, for God's sake? It looks as if the smoke's obscuring the view through the periscope sight, and that's why they've stopped firing. Can anything else possibly go wrong here?'

Even as Sykes fell silent, both men heard another sound. From high above them, somewhere in the dark sky to the south, came the sound of aeroplane engines. A lot of aeroplane engines. They stared upwards, trying to work out in which direction the aircraft were flying.

'I think they're heading west, sir,' Dawson suggested.

'I agree. That's not good. That could be a squadron of German bombers on their way to hit targets at home.' Sykes looked across at Dawson, his expression grim. 'I think this could be it, sapper. I think the show's about to start.'

Three-quarters of an hour later, klaxons sounded around the fort, and all the activity around the partially demolished barrack buildings ceased as the personnel streamed into the fort through the Block One entrance.

'They're manning the anti-aircraft machine-gun posts,' Sykes said, watching the activity through his binoculars. 'Time we moved away, I think.'

The two men climbed into the staff car. Dawson lifted the bonnet, replaced the rotor arm he'd removed as a basic anti-theft measure, then started the engine and sat in the driving seat.

'Leave the lights off,' Sykes instructed, 'just in case.'

'Where do you want to go, sir?'

'That small hill over there' – the major pointed to the south – 'looks as if it's the nearest high ground, and we can keep an eye on the fort from there. Park the car as close as you can, then we'll climb up to the summit on foot.'

Fifteen minutes later, the two men were lying prone behind a clump of scrubby bushes that provided the only cover on top of the small hillock and watching Fort Eben Emael carefully. Sykes was using his binoculars, slung on a cord round his neck. Dawson had his Lee-Enfield rifle beside him, fully loaded, but without a round in the chamber. He had four other loaded charger clips in his pouches, where he'd be able to grab them quickly if he needed to reload his weapon.

Dawson shifted his gaze from the fort, which looked deceptively quiet and peaceful, to cover the surrounding

24

countryside, which now seemed completely empty since all the personnel who'd previously been working outside had now vanished inside the fort. He glanced up at the sky as a sudden brief shadow obscured part of the new moon. But there appeared to be no clouds in the sky.

'What the fuck was that?' he muttered.

'What is it?' Sykes lowered the binoculars and glanced at his companion.

'I thought I saw something. An aircraft, maybe. Something crossed in front of the moon.'

Sykes listened carefully for a few seconds, then shook his head. 'You must be mistaken. I can't hear any engine noise.'

'I definitely saw something,' Dawson said stubbornly. 'Maybe it wasn't an aircraft. Perhaps it was somebody in a parachute?'

Sykes shook his head again. 'Same argument, Dawson. A parachutist has to have an aeroplane to jump out of. If there was an aircraft there we'd hear it. We heard those aircraft earlier, remember?'

'So what's that, then?'

Dawson pointed into the sky over to the south-east of the fort, where the unmistakable shape of an aircraft had just appeared, maybe a mile away, a darker grey against the grey sky. It was low down, apparently moving slowly, but clearly visible.

'Bloody hell, Dawson, you're right. Maybe the engine's failed and the pilot's trying for a forced landing.' Sykes raised the binoculars again and searched the sky for the aircraft, trying to get a better look at it.

'I think it's trying to land on top of the fort,' Dawson said. 'There's another one right behind it.'

At that moment, one of the anti-aircraft machine-guns protecting the fort opened up, a sudden assault on the night, and seconds later the other three anti-aircraft weapons also began firing. Streams of tracer rounds arced into the sky, a lethal fireworks display, seeking out the silent grey shapes that were now closing in on the fort.

'Bloody gliders,' Sykes muttered. 'Bloody great gliders. They have to be. The fucking Jerries are landing troops by glider to try to capture Eben Emael. Christ, that's clever.'

'Why?'

'The Belgians use sound-location arrays designed to pinpoint aircraft by the noise of their engines. No engines means no detection by the Belgian defenders. This is a real surprise attack. And Germany's full of glider pilots, so they'd have had no trouble finding men to fly them.'

Beside the major, Dawson brought his Lee-Enfield up to the aim and looked over the sights towards the fort, now alive with machine-gun fire from the four anti-aircraft emplacements. He estimated they were about half a mile from the fort, well outside the effective range of the .303 rifle, which was accurate to roughly 550 yards and, even if the range had been shorter, in the weak moonlight he'd have found it difficult to acquire a target. But if those were German soldiers landing on the grass-covered roof of the Eben Emael fort in front of them – and there wasn't much doubt about that – Dawson wanted to be ready for whatever lay ahead.

Sykes was still scanning the scene through his binoculars.

'There are troops pouring out of that first glider,' he said, 'and there's a second one just about to land. They're wearing combat smocks. I think they're Jerry paratroopers.' He shifted his view slightly. 'Yes, they're definitely German gliders. Now I can see tiny swastikas painted on their tail fins. It's no wonder the fort gun crews only opened fire at the last minute. They might have spotted the gliders approaching but couldn't see their markings until they were almost on the ground.'

'I can see more of them approaching,' Dawson said. 'At least three or four other gliders.'

Then the sound of machine-gun fire from the fort diminished abruptly. Sykes swung his binoculars to look at the anti-aircraft positions.

'Looks like at least one of the machine-guns has jammed,' he said. 'Not that they were doing a lot of good anyway.'

'But we've seen the defences that place has got,' Dawson said. 'What the hell can a few dozen German soldiers hope to do against that fort?'

Sykes didn't reply for a few seconds, concentrating on the view through his binoculars. Then he lowered them slowly and glanced over at Dawson. 'I don't know,' he said, 'but I don't think Adolf would have sent his troops here unless there was a reasonable chance of them succeeding in taking the fort. Despite the defences Eben Emael has got, because the Jerries are here, that means they must have a plan.'

Sykes turned his attention back to the view through his binoculars, then grunted, pulled the cord over his head and passed them to Dawson. 'More your field than mine,' he said. 'The only thing that makes sense is that they're intending to use explosive charges to destroy the cupolas and casemates, otherwise there's no point in them landing on the top. See if you can work out what they're doing.'

Dawson nodded his thanks, focused the binoculars and concentrated on the shadowy figures he could see running about on the vast grassed area on top of the fort.

'A group of them have just run over to one of the casemates,' he said. 'I think that's the one Verbois called Maastricht Two. At least two of them are carrying something between them.'

'What sort of thing?'

'I don't know. They're holding a pole, maybe a length of steel, and suspended from that is a round object, but I've no idea what it is.'

He concentrated, trying to keep the binoculars as still as possible so that he could watch what was happening on the distant fort. Even at that distance, the ground faintly illuminated by the white glow of the new moon, he could see the figures fairly clearly.

Several of them clambered up onto the top of the casemate and headed for the conical steel observation dome at one end of it. The two soldiers carrying the bar and the round object were in the lead. There, they placed the device on top of the dome, did something to the top of it and almost immediately scrambled into cover.

'They've put a charge of some sort on the top of the dome,' Dawson said, keeping up a commentary for Sykes, still lying beside him. 'But that steel's about a foot thick. It'll be a hell of a bang, but it'll just bounce off.'

About ten seconds later, the sound of a massive explosion ripped through the air. Dawson involuntarily flinched and closed his eyes. When he refocused the binoculars, he could see that a hole had been blown right through the top of the steel observation dome.

'Fucking hell,' he muttered. 'They've blown it. What the hell are they using?'

'What?'

Quickly Dawson explained to Sykes what he'd seen.

'You told me that explosives couldn't break through that thickness of steel,' the major pointed out.

'I know, but I've just seen the bloody Jerries do exactly that. They must have worked out some new technique or developed a new explosive – something like that.'

'This is important, Dawson. If the Germans have developed a new type of demolition charge, we need to know about it. It could affect everything we do – the thickness of warship armour, the design of tanks, how we build pill-boxes and bunkers, absolutely everything.'

Another explosion rocked the night. Dawson snapped the binoculars back to his eyes. Smoke was rising from the Maastricht Two casemate. Grey-clad figures were clambering over it, lobbing objects through the hole in the observation dome and through the gun ports.

'It looks like they're throwing grenades inside now,' he said. 'I don't see any return fire. Those first charges must have taken out most of the defenders.' He kept the binoculars to his eyes as he addressed Major Sykes. 'When you say it's "important", sir, what exactly do you mean?'

'I mean we – or rather you – need to find out how the Germans did it. And that means getting over there and onto the roof of that fort to take a good look at the damage.'

'Oh, fuck,' Dawson muttered quietly. 'I had a feeling you had something like that in mind.'

CHAPTER 4

10 MAY 1940: EBEN EMAEL, BELGIUM

'Now it looks like they're hitting the Maastricht One casemate,' Dawson said.

Seconds later, another huge explosion echoed from the roof of the fort as the Maastricht One observation dome was destroyed in a similar fashion to that on the other casemate. The breaching of the dome was followed by a rapid series of smaller explosions as the German troops lobbed hand grenades through the holes they'd blown in the structure. All this was clearly visible to Dawson as he stared through the binoculars, but he still had no idea how the Germans had managed to blast holes through the massive thickness of armoured steel fitted on the fort.

'It isn't that I'm not keen to investigate the way the Germans blew up that observation dome, sir, but there are now about a dozen of those bloody great gliders on the roof of that fort and at least seventy Jerries running around, armed to the teeth and shooting anything that moves.'

'I had noticed, Dawson,' Sykes said, taking back the binoculars to observe events at Eben Emael once more, 'and I'm working on it. We can't do anything yet, obviously. Either the Belgians will blow the Germans off the roof, or the Jerries will take out all the other casemates and cupolas and that'll be that. If I was a betting man, I'd put my money on the Germans. They seem to know exactly what they're doing.'

Sykes lowered the binoculars and looked across at Dawson. 'We'll wait for a while, until it's clear which side is winning, and then make our move. If the Belgians come out on top, it'll be easy. If it's the Germans, we'll need to think of something. Whatever it is, we'll go over there together, Dawson. I'm not in the habit of giving orders that I'm not prepared to follow myself.'

What they were looking at was now a full-scale battle. Smoke and fumes covered the top of Fort Eben Emael, and the noise of detonating grenades was almost constant, along with the distinctive sound of Schmeisser machine-pistols, the firing frequency mimicking the rate of a human heartbeat. Overlying that were the infrequent thumps as one of the fort's seventy-five-millimetre cannon fired at some distant target – they had to be distant because the heavy weapons were almost useless at close range.

What the Belgian defenders needed to engage the German troops were heavy machine-guns, which the fort had, but most of them were on the lower level, intended to engage enemy forces approaching the fort from the land surrounding the structure. The two casemates on top of Fort Eben Emael, Mi-Nord and Mi-Sud, fitted with heavy machine-guns, were the only protection the structure had against enemy troops actually on the roof. The architects of the fort had clearly assumed that the chances of this happening were extremely slight. They'd obviously never even considered the possibility of a glider-borne attack. And in any case, those machine-guns were silent.

'What's happening now, sir?' Dawson asked, as they heard another massive explosion blast out from the roof of the fort.

'Nothing good,' Sykes replied. 'Looks like Cupola Nord is getting the same treatment as the Maastricht casemates.' He shifted his field of focus slightly. 'I should have placed that bet,' he added. 'The crew of two of the anti-aircraft machine-guns have just surrendered to the Germans.'

Suddenly a sheet of flame erupted from a position close to the Mi-Nord casemate, and another explosion sounded.

'They're using flame-throwers against the machine-gun casemates,' Sykes said, 'and some kind of explosive charge. It looks like they've blown open the infantry exit door of Cupola Nord, because German troops seem to be entering the fort itself now, from the roof. What I don't understand is why the Belgians aren't firing at the Germans. They should be sitting targets for those heavy machine-guns.'

The roof area of Fort Eban Emael was now sheathed in smoke from the multiple explosions and bits of vegetation set on fire by the flame-throwers, but the noise of weapons firing and the detonation of explosive charges was now noticeably less. More ominously, many of the sounds of shots and the crack of grenades firing were muffled, which meant they were coming from *inside* Fort Eben Emael.

'I think it's pretty much all over now,' Sykes muttered. 'As far as I can see, the Germans have destroyed – or at least silenced – all the heavy weapons at the fort, and now they're obviously inside the building.' He glanced at his watch and smiled grimly. 'Any idea how long that attack took?'

'I didn't notice what time it started,' Dawson said.

'I did,' Sykes replied. 'The effective destruction of the impregnable fortress of Eben Emael took about sixty or seventy German soldiers just over twenty minutes. I hope to Christ that's not an indication of what's going to happen during the rest of this war, because if it is, the fucking Germans will be strutting around Piccadilly Circus in their jackboots by the end of the summer.'

'And you still want us to go over there to take a look at the damage?' Dawson asked.

Sykes nodded. 'Yes. It's vitally important. You could argue that Eben Emael fell through simple incompetence, and that's probably true. But if the defences were as impregnable as everybody told us yesterday, the Germans would still be wandering about on the roof of the place, trying to get inside. We have to find out how they breached the defences, and what this new kind of explosive they've developed really is.'

Dawson nodded, somewhat reluctantly. 'That makes sense, sir,' he conceded, 'though I don't know how much information I'll get from just looking at the hole the charge blew in a lump of steel.'

'Can't you work something out from seeing the dimensions of the hole, or looking at the debris?'

'That would tell me something, yes, but I already

know it must be some kind of a shaped charge. Nothing else could have done that damage.'

'A shaped charge is what?' Sykes enquired.

'A stick of dynamite just blasts out in all directions when it's fired, but a shaped charge focuses the detonation in a particular direction. It has to be a type of plastic explosive to do it, something like gelignite, which you can mould into a shape to attack a particular target in a certain direction – that's why it's called a "shaped charge". To bring down a steel bridge, for example, you'd shape the charges so that they cut horizontally through the supporting legs,' Dawson finished.

'Could a shaped charge have penetrated the thickness of steel over the cupolas and observation posts over there?' Sykes asked.

'Not in my opinion, no, because the metal is just too thick. Although the shaped charge focuses the blast, a lot of the explosive force will still bounce off the target, especially if the material it's trying to destroy is tough. And a foot of tempered steel is about as tough a target as you can find. However they did it, it definitely wasn't just a big shaped charge.'

'So,' Sykes said after a moment, 'just getting a look at the damage isn't going to be a hell of a lot of help. We need to get hold of one of the charges themselves.'

Dawson stared at him. He'd hoped to talk the major out of what was obviously a recipe for suicide, and somehow he'd just made the situation a hell of a lot worse.

'Frankly, sir,' he said quietly, 'it's going to be fucking difficult – at best – to get onto the roof of Eben Emael without getting our arses shot off. Finding one of those bloody charges and stealing it from the Jerries seems to pretty much guarantee we'll be carried away from here in a couple of wooden boxes.'

'Not necessarily, Dawson,' Sykes murmured, studying the fort through the binoculars. 'Think it through. Once the Germans have secured the building, their main task is going to be getting all the Belgian troops out of it and making sure they've permanently disabled all the fort's weapons. They'll probably leave a small garrison there to guard the fort, but I doubt they'll be mounting a guard over any of the explosive charges they haven't used. And now they're obviously inside the building, there might not even be any German soldiers left up on the roof.'

'They might have used all the charges in the attack, sir.'

'True, but if they're competent – and from what we've just seen they are *bloody* competent – they'd have had numerous extra weapons, in case some of them didn't detonate or got lost or damaged when they landed on the roof. Would you recognize one of the devices you saw those two German soldiers carrying, if you saw another one, I mean?'

'Probably, yes. It was quite a distinctive shape.'

'Good.' Sykes sounded pleased. 'Then that's what we'll do. We have to sort this out now, before daylight. We'll start working our way closer to the fort and see if we can spot one of those special charges. If we do, we'll nip in, get it and then head out of here.'

As a plan, Dawson thought, that definitely left something to be desired.

CHAPTER 5

10 MAY 1940: EBEN EMAEL, BELGIUM

Getting close to the fort wasn't the difficult bit. The German soldiers were fully focused on the structure as they tried to complete the destruction of all the heavy weapons mounted on the roof, and the Belgian soldiers inside it were literally fighting for their lives. And the noise of the battle had done what the aborted sequences of blank rounds fired from Cupola Sud had completely failed to do – it had finally attracted the attention of some of the off-duty troops stationed in the nearby villages, including Wonck. These men were now walking – individually or in small groups – down the roads towards the stricken fortress.

In the darkness, German, Belgian and British uniforms didn't look that dissimilar, and Sykes and Masters had no difficulty in blending in with the troops on foot. They walked down from the hillock and started following a group of about half a dozen Belgian troops along the road, keeping far enough behind them that their presence wouldn't be obvious, and well ahead of another three soldiers heading the same way.

When they reached the road that ran straight towards

the Block One entrance, but far enough away not to be spotted by any of the German soldiers running around on the roof of the fort, or to become targets for them, they stopped to consider their next move. The Belgian reinforcement troops were milling around aimlessly nearby, obviously unwilling to get too close to the huge fort while the battle was still raging – which was sensible.

'How the bloody hell are we going to climb up onto the roof?' Dawson asked.

'Good question,' Sykes said, rubbing his chin thoughtfully and looking across the grassy perimeter at the massive concrete walls of the fort, which rose almost vertically about twenty feet from the plain in front of them.

'We can't scale that, even if we had ladders or grappling hooks, not with the Jerries on top firing at anything that moves, and the Belgians inside the place doing the same. I reckon if we even walked over to the wall, one group or the other would shoot us down.'

Sykes nodded thoughtfully. 'You're right,' he said.

'Can we get out of here, then, sir?'

'Afraid not. If we can't get onto the roof from the outside, there's only one other option – we'll have to do it from the inside. Right, this is a direct order: cast away your weapon. Find somewhere here to hide your rifle – it's essential the Belgians don't think we're a threat. And hopefully the Germans will still have their hands full trying to destroy the last remaining casemates and they won't be interested in a couple of unarmed soldiers trying to surrender to the Belgians.'

Dawson stashed his Lee-Enfield in some undergrowth

near a couple of spindly trees behind a low hill, out of sight of the fort, a location he committed to memory, then walked back to where Sykes was waiting.

'Are you sure this is a good idea, sir?' Dawson was still far from convinced they wouldn't be shot down by the Belgian sentries as they made their approach to the Block One entrance.

'Actually, I'm not, but I don't see any other way. But we have to try, Dawson. You do see that, don't you? We have to at least get a sight of one of these new weapons.'

Another volley of shots rang out from the roof of Fort Eben Emael, the heavy thump of one of the cannon a counterpoint to the distinctive rattle of a couple of Schmeissers and the crack of rifle shots. A thick pall of smoke hung over the area, and they both heard and saw the sudden spurt of liquid fire from a flame-thrower close to one of the casemates on the roof.

'It sounds as if the Belgians haven't given up,' Dawson said. 'Or some of them haven't, anyway.'

The two men began working their way over towards the partly demolished barrack buildings outside the fort entrance. There was a perimeter area made from steel posts strung with wire which enclosed the two barracks and provided an outer layer of protection to the fort entrance, where in peacetime passes and other documents could be checked before personnel and visitors were allowed to approach Block One. But the guards who would normally be stationed at the gate were nowhere in sight – obviously they'd been withdrawn into the fort when the attack began.

'Right,' Sykes said, stopping close to some undergrowth that provided the final piece of cover before they stepped onto the open ground that led across to the perimeter fence and then on to Block One. 'We don't want the bloody Belgians to shoot us down, so we do this slowly and carefully. Get out your pay book and hold it in your hand.'

'They won't see it until we're right up close,' Dawson objected.

'I know that. But when we get to the entrance I don't want you fumbling around in your battledress looking for it. They'll think you're reaching for a weapon, and we definitely don't want that to happen.'

Dawson nodded, acknowledging the sense in what the major was saying. He reached into the left breast pocket of his battledress and took out a small reddish-brown booklet with rigid covers. At the top were the words 'Army Book 64', and in the centre of the front cover the legend 'Soldier's Service and Pay Book'.

Sykes took his own ID card out of his pocket, and also a large white handkerchief, which he unfolded and held in his right hand by one corner.

'When we get to the gate,' he ordered, 'raise both arms in the air and keep walking forward slowly.'

They could already see that the gate itself was half-open. The two men stepped forward, walking side by side, down the dusty track towards the gate in the perimeter fence.

Above and in front of them, the battle for Fort Eben Emael still raged, the night punctuated by explosions, the sound of shots, shouted orders and the occasional cry of pain as the German troops tried to eliminate the last pockets of resistance. And smoke still drifted over the roof of the fort, obscuring the action, though they could still see the occasional line of fire as one of the Germans triggered his flame-thrower. But the soldiers themselves were invisible in the murk.

'If we can't see them,' Sykes muttered, his words an uncanny match for Dawson's thought process, 'then hopefully they can't see us.'

'So we just have the Belgians to worry about.'

'Exactly.'

They walked through the gate, and Sykes held his white handkerchief as high as he could and waved it a couple of times, hoping to attract the attention of somebody inside the besieged building.

Dawson wasn't certain, but in the gloom it looked to him as if the barrel of the heavy machine-gun mounted in the Block One observation post had just swung towards them.

'They're aiming that fucking machine-gun right at us,' he said, his voice a hoarse and strained whisper.

'Keep walking,' Sykes said, flapping his handkerchief again, 'and keep your hands in the air.'

The last few yards to the armoured steel entrance door to Block One seemed an eternity. Dawson had been absolutely right – the barrel of the machine-gun *was* tracking them, and the two men knew that even a short burst of fire from that weapon would tear them both to pieces.

But they walked on, slowly and deliberately, both men with their hands held high, the universal sign of surrender, Sykes still waving his white handkerchief.

Finally, they reached the entrance, a massive concrete structure with wide steel double gates set in an archway on the right-hand side, the weapon ports on the left.

These were not the fort's principal gates, just an outer set, made from solid steel up to head-height and then barred above that. The main gates themselves were located within the reinforced concrete portico.

The right-hand side gate was open and, with the ominous black muzzle of the machine-gun still following their progress, they stepped through the gap and into the portico itself.

'Thank God for that,' Dawson muttered as they reached that temporary haven, beyond the arc the machine-gun could traverse.

A small slot slid open in the steel door to their left, a pair of hard brown eyes stared at them and an anonymous voice shouted something in French.

Sykes replied in the same language, and held up his ID card so that the Belgian soldier could see it. The major turned, grabbed Dawson's pay book and showed that to the man as well. Then he said something else in French, and a moment later the slot slammed closed again.

'We're in,' Sykes said, as the steel door swung open. 'Inside, quickly,' he snapped. The moment they were inside, the steel door shut behind them with a loud thud, a sound that was echoed seconds later by another muffled bang from somewhere high above them. The half dozen men in the guardhouse all glanced upwards, and one of them surreptitiously crossed himself.

'Why are you here, sir?' Capitaine Verbois, his uniform dishevelled and grubby, asked Sykes in English. Fear was in his eyes and he was clearly struggling to keep the panic at bay. 'There's nothing you can do to help us now.'

'I know that,' Sykes said. 'What's the situation here? How many men have you lost? And what's the damage so far?'

'We've no idea,' Verbois replied. 'Some of the casemates and cupolas are unmanned, so we don't know if they're destroyed or intact. Others aren't responding on the internal telephone system. We're fighting on, but . . .' His voice died away as he looked around at the strained faces of his fellow soldiers, and the realization that the so-called 'impregnable' fortress of Eben Emael was doomed to fall finally hit home.

'You're right,' Sykes said briskly, 'there's nothing we can do to help you, not now.'

'Then why are you here?' Verbois asked again.

'Because of what those Germans soldiers have done. I told you Dawson here was an explosives expert, and he has no idea how the Jerries managed to blow a hole through the steel top of that first armoured observation point.'

'Maastricht Two,' Verbois said, nodding. 'You saw it happen?'

Sykes nodded. 'We were watching from a hill some distance away. But we only saw the destruction of the observation dome. What happened after that?'

'I've talked to a couple of the soldiers who were in the casemate and managed to get out. The charge blew a hole into the observation dome and killed two of our men. Then the Germans placed a charge under the centre seventy-five-millimetre gun and detonated it. That blew the gun off its mountings and back into the casemate itself. The explosion killed two more soldiers and wounded several others. Then the Germans attacked with grenades. Nobody else was killed, but many more men suffered injuries. The surviving soldiers were forced to abandon the casemate and retreat to the intermediate corridor level.'

'And then they attacked Maastricht One?'

Verbois nodded. 'Yes. In a very similar manner, and unfortunately with exactly the same result. We lost both casemates within minutes of the gliders landing on the roof of Eben Emael.'

'We've seen and heard the weapons firing from some of the other casemates and cupolas, but not Cupola One Twenty. Is there a problem there?'

'Yes – the ammunition elevators aren't working and there's a problem with the guns. The cupola is manned, but we can't fire the cannon.'

Sykes nodded. That was news to him but, in view of everything else that had happened at the fort, it wasn't exactly surprising.

'And what about the machine-gun positions, Mi-Nord and Mi-Sud?'

'Unfortunately, they weren't manned. The personnel were still helping clear the barrack buildings outside Block One.' Verbois pointed vaguely to the south.

Again, no surprise. Sykes could almost have predicted that something of that sort must have happened. If the two machine-gun positions had been manned and working properly, they could have swept the Germans off the roof of the fort the moment the gliders landed. But it was far too late for that now.

'Right,' Sykes said. 'We're here for one reason only. Dawson needs to get a look at one of those charges the Germans used to blow holes through the steel domes.

It could be a new kind of weapon. How can we get up onto the roof?'

Verbois looked at the two of them as if they were mad. 'There are German soldiers all over the roof. How can you possibly hope to—'

'We're going to try,' Sykes said firmly. 'We won't involve any of your men. It'll just be the two of us. Now, how can we get up there?'

Verbois shook his head, then turned and led the way over to one side of the guardhouse, where a schematic diagram of the fort was screwed to the wall.

'We are here,' he said, pointing to the extreme left-hand side of the diagram, at the lowest level. 'This is Block One. The Albert Canal is over here on the right, the east side of the fortress. These two casemates' – he indicated a pair of square structures on the roof – 'are Maastricht One and Maastricht Two. We've sealed the doors to isolate both of them from the attackers, but we could open them to let you through. The Germans got into both the casemates from the roof, so they must have blown holes in them somewhere. You could get out the same way.'

Dawson looked distinctly unimpressed with this suggestion.

'Which one?' Sykes asked. 'Maastricht One or Maastricht Two?'

'It has to be Maastricht Two. The Germans who attacked Maastricht One dropped a bundle of hand grenades down the ammunition shaft, and that blew out the staircase.'

Sykes nodded slowly. 'Very well,' he said. 'That will have to do. Can you escort us up there, please, *Capitaine*?

45

And we'll need weapons as well. Can you supply us with a couple of rifles?'

'We have light machine-guns here.'

'What type?' Sykes asked.

'The FM 30,' Verbois replied. 'Our version of the Browning Automatic Rifle.'

'Show me.'

Verbois led the way to an armoury, the doors open wide and most of the weapons missing, presumably taken by members of the garrison. In one rack were half a dozen bulky weapons with box magazines attached.

Dawson picked one up to check its weight. 'It's quite hefty,' he said, 'even without a full magazine.'

'It's just under ten kilos unloaded,' Verbois confirmed.

'I think we'll just grab a couple of rifles,' Sykes said. 'The Browning's a good weapon, but it's bulky and there's a potential problem if we were to use it in automatic mode.'

'The rate of fire?' Dawson suggested.

'Exactly. The Schmeisser has a very distinctive and fairly slow firing rate. If we fired this up on the roof, it would sound so different to a Schmeisser that any German soldier would immediately know that enemy troops were up there with them, and that's the last thing we want. But a rifle shot is just a rifle shot, indistinguishable from any other.'

'Very well,' Verbois said. He selected two Mauser rifles – the Model 1898, virtually identical to the standard German infantry rifle – and handed them over. 'The ammunition is in the box on the floor there. Take as much as you want. Then we'll head up to the intermediate level.'

The Mauser magazine was charged from above, using five-round stripper clips, a thin length of steel that held the rimless cartridges by their base. The box contained layers of stripper clips, each already loaded with five 7.65-millimetre rounds. Dawson and Sykes grabbed half a dozen clips each. Dawson stowed his in the ammunition pouches he was wearing on his utility belt, but Sykes's uniform had no such containers.

'Just a moment,' Verbois said, opened another box and pulled out a black leather belt with a clasp in the form of a snake. Then he found a couple of sets of brown leather pouches, each comprising three containers, and designed to fit on the belt.

Sykes nodded his thanks, attached the containers and buckled the belt around his waist. He filled the leather containers with ammunition, and secured the lids, using the straps which he clipped to the base of each one, then picked up the Mauser rifle and loaded it with the first five rounds.

'We're ready,' he announced, with a sideways glance at Dawson. The big corporal didn't look happy, but he did look prepared for combat, which was more important. 'Lead the way.'

Verbois nodded agreement, issued orders to the men in the guardhouse, then ordered the internal steel door to be opened. Followed by Sykes and Dawson, the Mauser rifles at port arms, held in both hands diagonally in front of them and ready for immediate use, he led the way out of the guardhouse and down a long, straight passageway, heading deep into the heart of the fortress.

Groups of men sat or lay against the walls of the

corridor, weapons scattered about them. Some talked angrily with their colleagues; others just sat, apparently dazed. A faint blue miasma of tobacco smoke filled the corridor. As Verbois led the way past them, a few of the men glanced up, but most ignored the interruption.

A scream echoed down the passage, and the Belgian officer half-turned towards the two British soldiers.

'The hospital is on this level,' he explained, 'but we've had so many casualties the medical staff are barely able to cope. Some of our men have suffered the most terrible injuries.'

Sykes nodded. There didn't seem to be an appropriate response to that remark.

They climbed from the lower-level tunnel up to the intermediate level, to the maze of passageways and corridors that supplied and supported the casemates and cupolas. Other Belgian soldiers had taken refuge in these passages, some clearly suffering deep shock, others nursing minor injuries. Some were crying; whether from shock, pain, or simple anger and frustration wasn't clear. It was, by any standards, a piteous sight.

Verbois said nothing, just continued walking.

A few minutes later, they arrived at a pair of massive steel doors, each secured in place by thick steel bolts on all four sides of the door itself, driven into the surrounding steel frame by a large, centrally located handle and series of bars that mechanically linked all the bolts. Unsurprisingly, the bolts on both doors were in the locked position.

'We had calculated that these doors would be secure against all known types of explosive charge which could be manoeuvred into the casemate,' Verbois said, a little sadly. 'But that, of course, was before all this happened.'

'What's on the other side?' Dawson asked.

'There's a space that can be filled with sandbags as an extra layer of defence – we didn't have time to do that – and then another steel door identical to this one.'

Sykes looked thoughtfully at the steel door for a few seconds. 'Do you know if there are still any German soldiers in the casemate?' he asked.

Verbois shook his head. 'We've no idea. When our troops realized the position was lost, they grabbed the wounded men and retreated into the tunnel system, locking these doors behind them. We've no idea what the Germans did after that.'

'So there could be a squad of crack German troops sitting behind these doors, just waiting for somebody to be stupid enough to open one of them?'

'That's possible, yes,' Verbois agreed.

'Fucking wonderful,' Dawson said quietly, but still loud enough for both officers to hear.

Sykes glanced at him sharply. 'Well, we'll soon find out,' he said, looking back at Verbois. 'We'll open this door. Dawson and I will step through, and you close the door behind us. That will place us in the void. When this door is secure, we'll open the inner door. If the casemate is full of Germans, we'll try to close it again before they can overpower us. If we're captured, we'll be prisoners of war, which is our problem. But this door will still prevent the Jerries from breaking through here into the fort. And if there are no enemy troops inside the casemate, we'll proceed as planned.

'Now, we don't want to be up on the roof for any

longer than absolutely necessary, so I want to agree some signals with you before we go. If we need to get back here because there *are* German troops in possession of the casemate, and we get the other door shut, we'll bang on this door in a specific sequence. We'll bang three times, pause, then once, pause, and then twice more. Three, one, two. Got that?'

Verbois nodded.

'If you hear any other sequence of bangs, it's the Germans trying to get in and just ignore it. We'll push the other steel door closed, so it will look as if it's still locked. We don't know what we'll find through there, but if we can, we'll be back in the casemate in about thirty minutes, so make sure you or one of your men stays here. I don't want any mistakes, and I particularly don't want to find myself banging on that door with nobody on this side of it. Is all that clear, *Capitaine*?'

'Perfectly, Major. The sequence is three, one, two, and I myself will remain here until you return.'

Sykes nodded. 'If we're not back in two hours from now, that probably means we won't be coming back at all.'

'Comforting thought,' Dawson said, as he walked across to the steel door's central locking handle.

'Ready?' he asked, and Sykes nodded.

Dawson swung the handle, and the well-oiled bolts slid out of their sockets with a faint metallic grinding sound. He pulled on the door and it opened smoothly towards him. Dawson stopped the movement when the gap was a couple of feet wide, and peered inside. An empty space met his eyes, exactly as he'd expected. A few feet away, an identical steel door faced him.

Dawson and Sykes stepped forwards into the space between the doors, and waited while Capitaine Verbois closed and then locked the first door behind them.

Sykes motioned to Dawson to get ready beside the handle, and himself stood where the door would open, the Mauser in his hands. He flicked the safety catch all the way over to the left, readying the rifle for firing, then nodded for Dawson to turn the handle and unlock the inner steel door.

CHAPTER 6

10 MAY 1940: EBEN EMAEL, BELGIUM

As the steel door swung slowly open, moved by the impressive might of Dawson's powerful shoulder muscles, Sykes levelled his Mauser at the space beyond, part of the interior of the Maastricht Two casemate.

Lights were burning, though some of the bulbs had been smashed, presumably by the blasts of the grenades the Germans had used to clear the area, and the casemate reeked of cordite and explosives. Debris, abandoned equipment and empty shells cases were scattered across the floor and traces of smoke and dust particles hung in the air. But there was no sign of any life. Or even of any dead bodies.

Dawson carefully pushed the steel door closed behind him and stepped across to stand beside Sykes, his weapon at the ready.

'We'll keep it quiet, and take it slow,' Sykes whispered. He pointed to one side of the passageway they were standing in. 'Looks like the main part of the casemate is over there. Follow me.'

Moments later, they were standing behind the central seventy-five-millimetre cannon that had been installed in the Maastricht Two casemate, or what was left of it. That casemate was one of the two at Fort Eben Emael that were intended to fire on targets that lay to the north, towards Maastricht, hence the name. But it was abundantly clear that this particular cannon was never going to do that job again. Some huge explosive charge had obviously been placed under the barrel on the outside of the casemate and then detonated. The resulting explosion had not only bent the barrel of the weapon, it had also blown the entire gun clear of its mounting and back into the casemate itself.

Then the German troops had followed it up with a few bursts from a flame-thrower. The concrete was heavily blackened, and an unholy aroma filled the air. A mix of oil and petrol, and what smelt disgustingly almost like roast pork – burnt human flesh.

Two battered corpses lay close to the shattered weapon, a silent and gruesome testament to the power of the explosion that had done the work. Their skin was blackened from the effects of the flame-thrower, their hands bent into clutching claws.

'Did a special kind of explosive do this damage?' Sykes asked, gesturing towards the wrecked gun.

Dawson shook his head. 'No. Just a biggish lump of plastic explosive placed very close to the base of the barrel. The design of the casemate probably helped the Germans – the concrete under the barrel of the cannon would have funnelled the blast upwards, increasing its effectiveness. A twenty- or thirty-pound charge would probably have been enough to do this.'

Sykes glanced around them. They'd neither seen nor

heard any sign of any German troops since they'd stepped into the casemate.

'It looks like the Jerries blew their way in here and then left again once they were sure all the Belgian defenders had retreated,' he said. 'Now let's get outside and see how the land lies.'

Although they'd been speaking quietly together, there was probably no need. From outside the casemate they could hear the repeated sounds of rifle and sub-machine-gun fire, and the yells and shouts of the attacking German troops.

Sykes nodded his head towards the blackened hole where the seventy-five-millimetre cannon had been positioned. 'We'll go out that way,' he announced. 'With all that racket going on, they won't hear us.'

'What about the different colour of our uniforms?' Dawson said.

'That won't be a problem. Somebody once said, at night all cats look grey. I don't think there's enough light out there for them to spot the difference. And if one of them does challenge us, we shoot him down. This is no time for finesse, Dawson. One more rifle shot isn't going to be noticed. We need to move quickly, find what we're looking for, and get back here as soon as we can.'

'Where do we start looking?'

'Right outside this casemate, for a start. The Germans would have carried these new weapons to their principal targets, so maybe we'll be lucky and spot one right outside.'

'And if we don't, then what, sir?'

'They flew here in gliders, so any stores and supplies they haven't hauled out of the craft will still be inside them. Or maybe stacked up near them. That'll be our second option. OK?'

'I suppose so.'

'Right. You go first.'

Dawson strode across to the opening in the concrete wall, stepping gingerly over the remains of the cannon and the two dead Belgian soldiers, then slid his Mauser through and climbed up and wriggled out through the hole.

For a few seconds he just vanished from sight; then his face reappeared in the opening. 'It's all quiet out here, sir. Well, it's noisy, but there aren't any Germans nearby.'

Sykes nodded and followed the corporal out through the hole. Then he stood up and looked around.

The roof of the fort was absolutely immense, a grassy expanse that extended in all directions, though they could actually see very little of it because of the smoke and poor visibility, while a faint lightening of the sky showed that dawn was almost upon them. From over to the east, towards the Albert Canal, came the sound of gunfire and shouted orders, so he guessed that probably Cupola Nord or Cupola Sud, or maybe both of them, were under attack. That would be good news for them, because if the Germans were concentrating on hitting them, they wouldn't be looking out for a couple of British army soldiers running about the place, searching for explosive charges.

Lying on the ground in front of them was a length of worked wood, a pole about ten or twelve feet long, one end of it blackened and splintered. Dawson picked it up and looked carefully at the damaged end.

'What is it?' Sykes asked.

55

'I think this is how they put the charge under the barrel of the cannon. It's a bit risky standing right beside the muzzle, packing explosive in the gap. If the defenders realized what was happening, they could just fire the weapon, or move the barrel to dislodge the charge. I think the Jerries already had the charge attached to the end of this pole, with a ten-second fuse or something like that. They could ram the explosive right up beside the barrel with this, and not expose themselves. Then they could just pull the cord and scarper.'

'Clever,' Sykes muttered. 'This is a really well-planned raid. Right, let's look here first. Circle round the casemate that way. I'll meet you on the other side.'

A couple of minutes later, they were standing at the back of the casemate, neither having found any sign of the special explosive charges anywhere near the structure.

'The gliders approached from the south,' Sykes said, 'so they must have landed somewhere near the northern end of the fort. So we'll head that way. Keep your eyes open. I'll take point and left.'

In a hostile environment – and there was no doubt that description would apply to the roof of Fort Eben Emael at that moment – two soldiers would never walk side by side. Invariably, one would advance in front of the other, the leading man checking ahead and to one side, while the man behind covered their rear and the opposite side of their line of advance. As they started walking forward, Sykes moved slightly ahead, scanning the ground ahead and to their left, while Dawson followed a few paces behind, checking to the right and behind them.

For perhaps fifty yards, neither man saw anything to cause immediate concern. The sound of heavy firing and explosions still came from their right-hand side, over to the east, where the Nord and Sud cupolas were located, but there was no enemy activity directly in front of them.

Then Sykes froze, immediately raised his right arm to warn Dawson he was stopping, and sank to a crouch on the ground.

Dawson ducked down and moved closer to the major.

'Right, about two o'clock,' Sykes whispered, pointing ahead. 'I heard voices. German voices.'

'Cupola One Twenty is over that way,' Dawson whispered. 'Maybe the Jerries are taking out that one next.'

Sykes glanced at his watch. 'It's six forty-five now, so full light soon. Need to get a move on. We'll head over to the west, out-flank them and find these bloody gliders.'

He stood up again, then immediately ducked down, swinging the muzzle of his Mauser rifle over to the east.

Dawson moved a few paces backwards, and did exactly the same. There was no mistaking what they'd heard from over to their right – a shouted order, followed by the sound of running feet. Both men feared the same thing. Had they been spotted by some soldier? Was a squad of troops heading straight for them?

But no German troops appeared, and in seconds a brief silence fell.

Then a colossal explosion ripped across the roof of the fort, an echoing blast that seemed to suck the very air out of their lungs and, despite the fact that the explosion must have been dozens of yards away, clouds of dust and debris boiled around them.

'Fuck me,' Dawson muttered. 'That was a big bastard. You OK, sir?'

'Yes,' Sykes replied. 'We can assume Cupola One Twenty is now permanently out of action, even if the Belgians managed to get the ammunition elevators working again. Come on. Let's move while the Jerries are busy inspecting their handiwork.'

In a crouch, the two men angled their path slightly over to the west, away from the site of the explosion.

A couple of minutes later they saw a bulky, oblong object over to their left, the north-facing concrete front pierced by three holes, the rear covered with a grassy mound.

'I know exactly where we are now,' Sykes whispered. 'Maastricht One. According to Verbois, the Jerries have already knocked it out. We'll angle a bit more over to the east, to keep well clear of it.'

Less than four minutes later Sykes stopped again and peered into the gloom ahead of them.

'The tail-plane of a glider's right in front of us,' he said quietly. 'We'll split up and approach it from opposite sides, OK?'

Dawson nodded and moved away to his right, checking that the safety catch on his Mauser was off, just in case the Germans had left a guard – or even the pilot – with the glider.

As he got closer to the silent aircraft, Dawson was able to appreciate just how big it was. He was unfamiliar with aircraft – he'd never flown in one, or even stood beside one before – but the craft he was looking at seemed huge. It was at least forty feet long, with a wingspan nearly double that length. He marvelled that it could stay in the air without an engine.

It didn't seem to have an undercarriage, but there was a large skid that extended backwards from the nose and ran underneath the fuselage, and a deflated parachute was attached to the rear of the aircraft, presumably to slow it down more quickly on the limited roof area of the fort. There was a canopy in front of the wing, covering the cockpit where the pilot would have sat, but it was open and the cockpit itself clearly empty. Looking further towards the rear of the glider, Dawson could see a wide-open door on the right-hand side of the fuselage, and what looked like rows of empty fabric seats inside the craft. But what he didn't see was any sign of the troops who would have been inside the craft when it landed.

He approached the glider cautiously, crossed to the open door and glanced inside, looking in both directions, but the craft was empty. Dawson walked around the nose and saw Major Sykes checking the interior through an open door on the opposite side.

'Empty,' Sykes confirmed, as Dawson stepped up beside him.

'And no sign of any equipment,' Dawson said.

'No. Right, we'll move on to the next one.'

After taking a good look all round them, the two men started walking again, still heading north, towards the narrow apex of Fort Eben Emael.

The sky had now taken on the rosy tints of early dawn, and the visibility was improving quickly, which was both a blessing and a curse. They could see further, but it would also be easier for one of the German soldiers to spot them, to recognize the different style and colour of their British army uniforms and raise the alarm. Or maybe just shoot them.

The shape of another glider appeared in front of them, the nose section tangled in one of the barbed-wire fences that criss-crossed the roof of the fort. As with the first one, the canopy was open, and they could see the black oblong of the open door in the side of the fuselage as well.

'Same routine,' Sykes murmured. 'You go right, I'll go left.'

Dawson circled slightly, then approached the glider from the side. Again, there was no sign of life in or near the aircraft, and he reached it without incident. He looked inside the fuselage.

All the seats were empty, but close to the front of the fuselage, directly under the wing, was a large dark-grey object resting on the floor. It looked like the upper half of a globe, but with a rod or something projecting vertically from the top, and a circumferential joint about a third of the way up from the flat base. Dawson had never seen anything like it before, but he knew instinctively this was the weapon that had done such colossal damage to the fort's gun emplacements.

At that moment, Major Sykes stuck his head through the open door on the opposite side of the glider's fuselage and immediately saw what Dawson was looking at. He pointed at the dome-shaped object.

'Is that one of the charges they used?' he asked.

Dawson nodded. 'I think so. It looks like it's a two-piece device, probably with the explosive charge in the top section. It's even got carrying handles.'

He reached down, grabbed a heavy leather handle riveted to the side of the upper section of the globe, and lifted it.

'Bugger me, that's heavy,' he said.

While he was still bending forward, struggling to lift the object, Dawson heard a sound from behind him, and then a guttural voice shouted out something in German – an order or a question – he didn't know which. But he knew they were in trouble.

'Oh, shit,' Dawson muttered as he stood up, still facing into the glider's fuselage, his hands already reaching for the Mauser rifle slung over his right shoulder.

CHAPTER 7

10 MAY 1940: EBEN EMAEL, BELGIUM

As Dawson straightened up, he glanced inside the fuse-lage again, towards the open doorway on the opposite side of the glider. But Major Sykes had vanished.

He heard another shout in German from behind him. The soldier, whoever he was, was clearly getting impa-tient. Dawson knew he would have to turn and face him. When that happened, there was a good chance the man would simply shoot him out of hand, because in the growing daylight, Dawson's uniform and nationality would be obvious. If the soldier was competent – and everything he'd seen so far suggested that these Germans were *very* competent – he would already be covering Dawson with his own rifle or machine-pistol, so he knew his chances of bringing his own Mauser to bear were slim in the extreme.

But he had to take the chance.

Dawson started turning slowly to his left, which would hopefully hide what he was going to try and do from the German soldier. As he turned, he lifted the butt of the Mauser with his right hand, sliding the weapon's sling off his shoulder, bringing the butt up towards his face.

When he reckoned he'd moved the rifle far enough, to a vertical, but muzzle-down, position, he grasped the fore-end of the weapon with his left hand and slid his finger into the trigger guard, his thumb checking the position of the rifle's safety catch.

There was another shout from behind him, and then Dawson completed the move he planned from the moment he'd heard the German's challenge. The move that would make the difference between his life and death in the early dawn.

As he turned to face the German soldier, he dodged to his right and ducked down into a crouch. He swung the Mauser round to aim it from the waist – at that range he wouldn't need to use the sights. Dawson dragged the rifle's muzzle towards his target, desperately trying to aim the weapon. He fired the Mauser, but as he did so he knew his shot was going to miss the target. He'd pulled the trigger a split-second too soon. He grabbed for the bolt, but he knew he'd never get the chance for a second shot, because he could see the German soldier start to squeeze the trigger of his Schmeisser.

At that instant, a rifle shot rang out from somewhere over to Dawson's left, very close by, and the tunic of the German soldier's uniform suddenly flared red as he pitched backwards. The man's finger briefly squeezed the trigger of the machine-pistol and a short burst erupted from the barrel, but it was already harmlessly pointing up into the sky.

Sykes ran around from the nose of the glider and across to the fallen German soldier. Then he looked back at Dawson.

'You OK?' he asked.

Dawson nodded. 'Yes, thanks. Thought I was a goner then.'

Sykes grinned at him. 'You should have held your shot until you were sure of your aim. You had time, you know – just about. Now, let's get out of here before any other inquisitive Jerries come along.'

He and Dawson turned back to look at the grey two-part explosive charge sitting inside the glider.

'I still don't know how it works,' Dawson said. 'I'll need to take it apart, and find out what's in that lower section. That's the important bit, I think.'

'We'll take it with us,' Sykes said. 'It's got carrying handles, so it's obviously designed to be lifted by a man. We'll take one half of it each.'

Dawson shouldered his rifle again, bent down and seized the leather handle on the upper section of the weapon. It lifted smoothly off the lower part, which Sykes picked up.

'I'm guessing it weighs over a hundred pounds in total,' Dawson said, 'so it's a fucking serious weapon.'

'What's that rod sticking out of the top?' Sykes asked, pointing at the section Dawson was carrying.

'I think that's the fuse, and it probably runs for about five or ten seconds. You push it in or maybe pull it out, then run like fuck.'

Sykes looked at him. 'Then make sure you don't do either,' he snapped. 'But if you do, for Christ's sake tell me, then we'll both run like fuck. Right, let's get out of here.'

The two men looked all round them, but saw no enemy troops. There was still the sound of heavy firing from somewhere over to the east, but not very close to where they were standing. Interspersed in the rifle and machine-gun fire were the heavier explosions as one of Fort Eben Emael's remaining cannon fired at some unknown target.

'Sounds like there's still some fight left in the Belgians,' Sykes remarked, as two shots from a cannon sounded in quick succession. 'Right, back the way we came. Same routine. I'll take point and left. You follow me.'

'Understood.'

The sun was just starting to appear over the horizon, but visibility on the roof of the fort was still somewhat degraded because of the effects of the multiple explosions that had been triggered there. Dust swirled around them as they started walking.

The two components of the German demolition charge were both heavy and cumbersome to carry, and Dawson realized why the two soldiers he'd seen what seemed hours earlier had been carrying the device slung on a pole between them. He and Sykes didn't have that option – the only thing they could have used as a pole was one of the Mauser rifles, and they needed them to be immediately available. At least by each of them carrying one of the two sections of the weapon, they had the ability to drop them and use their weapons immediately if they encountered any enemy soldiers.

As the visibility started to improve, they could see both Cupola Nord and Cupola Sud. The northerly position was silent, and ominous tendrils of smoke were streaming out of the retractable steel dome and from a massive hole in the steel exit door at the back of the structure. The German troops had destroyed Cupola Nord's fighting capability.

But Cupola Sud still seemed to be operating. As Dawson watched, the steel dome rose to its maximum height of about four feet from the concrete surround, rotated slightly and then fired two rounds at some target down to the south.

'The fort's not quite finished,' Sykes said, watching the same spectacle, 'but it's only a matter of time.'

Dawson didn't reply. He was staring intently at the retractable dome itself.

'What is it?' Sykes asked.

'Might be good news. There's a black circle on the top of that dome, so the Jerries used one of their explosive charges on it, but the blast can't have penetrated the steel.'

Sykes stared across the grassy roof as well. 'You're right. Maybe the armour on that one's a bit thicker, or the charge was weaker. We'll never know. Now let's move.'

Dawson reckoned they'd only got about another three hundred yards to cover to get back to the Maastricht Two casemate, so if all went well they could be safely – a relative term in the circumstances – inside the fortress within about fifteen minutes.

But that forecast turned out to be extremely optimistic.

Sykes heard it first. He stopped in his tracks and stared upwards, scanning the sky.

'Stuka,' he snapped. 'Put that charge down and take cover.'

Dawson couldn't see the aircraft, but needed no encouragement. He'd heard enough about the German dive-bomber to be frankly terrified of it. As he hit the ground, getting as deep into a shallow depression as he could, he heard the unearthly and escalating wail of the siren fitted to the Stuka. This device was specifically intended to terrify anyone unfortunate enough to be a target, as if the prospect of being blown to pieces by the bomb carried by the aircraft wasn't enough. The troops called the siren the 'Jericho trumpet'. The howl increased in volume and intensity as the aircraft plummeted towards the ground in about a seventy-five-degree dive, and moments later Dawson saw it.

It was heading straight for the east side of the fort and, as he watched, he saw a bomb detach from the underside of the aircraft and spear straight down. Moments after the Stuka pulled up level at about 3,000 feet and then started to climb, the weapon exploded with a massive bang just to one side of Cupola Sud's armoured steel dome.

'That's a five-hundred-pounder,' Sykes called out. 'There's another one coming in. Stay down.'

'Why the fuck haven't we got any planes like these?' Dawson asked, looking up. 'They fucking terrify me.'

That attack was just the start. As soon as the first Stuka had climbed away from the fort, Dawson heard a second one starting its dive. But this one sounded as if it was further away, and moments later he saw the aircraft aiming for something down to the south of the fort. Its bomb exploded well away from Eben Emael, and for a moment Dawson cheered up.

'Do you think the Belgians have sent reinforcements, sir?' he asked. 'And the Jerries are bombing them?'

Sykes was in a better position to see where the bomb had landed, and as the smoke cleared he stood up and shook his head.

'You're half-right, Dawson,' he said. 'There *are* reinforcements on the road. The same soldiers we saw walking here from Wonck. But most of them are unarmed – a rifle would be no use against a dive-bomber anyway – so they're a nice soft target and the fucking Germans are blowing the hell out of them. There's virtually no cover down there.'

'Bastards,' Dawson muttered. He stood up and grabbed hold of the German explosive charge, being careful not to touch the fuse assembly, and followed the slight figure of Major Sykes as the officer resumed his erratic progress towards the Maastricht Two casemate.

Then all hell seemed to break out. There was a volley of rifle shots from directly ahead of them. And that was followed by a long burst of heavy-machine-gun fire from somewhere behind them, a hail of bullets that chewed up the ground about fifty yards over to their left.

Two separate groups of forces were firing towards them. And Sykes and Dawson were trapped right in the middle.

CHAPTER 8

10 MAY 1940: EBEN EMAEL, BELGIUM

Sykes and Dawson dropped flat to the ground, trying to make themselves as small as they possibly could.

'What the fuck's going on?' Dawson demanded. 'Have the Jerries spotted us, or what?'

'I don't know, but I doubt it. That machine-gun is a long way off – I think it's right up at the northern end of the fort, and at that distance I doubt if the gunner could tell that we aren't just a couple of German troops.'

'So what is it, then?'

For a few moments Sykes didn't reply, just lifted his head and stared in front of him, towards Maastricht Two, then ducked down again as the machine-gun fired again.

'I think,' he said, 'the Germans have spotted a Belgian counter-attack. It looks to me as if there are Belgian soldiers near the western south-facing casemate. I think that's Visé One. It looks as if they're firing towards the Germans who're down to the south, near Cupola Sud.'

'That's brilliant,' Dawson muttered. 'We could do with some help.'

'Not necessarily. A Belgian bullet will kill you just as certainly as a German one. Right now I think both sides are probably just shooting at anything that moves, and that would include you and me. The only good thing is the troops on either side aren't actually shooting at *us*. We just happen to be caught between them.'

'What do we do now?'

'Keep our heads down for the moment. I'm not bothered about the machine-gun: it's right up at the northern end of the roof. The Belgian troops *do* worry me. They've had a hell of a shock today, put the wind right up them, and they're probably out looking for blood.'

Dawson eased up slightly from his rudimentary cover and glanced over to the east, and then back over the ground they'd covered from the glider.

'That's not our only problem,' he said. 'I've just seen a couple of Jerries running over towards the glider. They're going to find the body of that soldier you shot.'

Sykes twisted round to stare in the direction Dawson was pointing. Perhaps 200 yards away, a couple of German soldiers, rifles slung over their shoulders, were running towards the distant grey shape of the Luftwaffe glider.

'The dead German isn't the problem,' Sykes said. 'They've probably been sent over there to pick up that demolition charge – the one we've got with us. When they don't find it, the Jerries will know that somebody else is up here with them. Then we'll really have problems.'

Dawson glanced at the major. 'You mean we don't have enough problems right now?' he asked.

Sykes grinned at him. 'More than enough,' he said, 'but this one we can do something about.'

He manoeuvred himself round so that he was facing

north, but still lying prone on the ground. He brought his Mauser up into the firing position and looked over the sights back towards the glider.

'If they're going somewhere else, just let them go, Dawson,' he ordered. 'But if they stop beside the glider, we shoot them. We can't risk them raising the alarm.'

Dawson slid a few feet away from the demolition charge he'd been carrying, found a hummock that would shield him from view to the north, and mirrored Sykes's actions, aiming his rifle towards the glider.

Then the two men lay in silence, almost side by side, watching the progress of the two distant figures.

The German soldiers slowed down to a trot as they neared the glider, and one of them almost immediately veered off to one side and bent down to examine something on the ground.

'They've seen the dead soldier,' Sykes muttered. 'Just wait and see what they do now.'

The second German trotted over to join his companion, and both crouched down. A few seconds later they stood again, and together walked across to the side door of the glider.

'Wait,' Sykes ordered. 'Wait until they step back.'

The two Germans remained beside the glider for what seemed like an age, though it could only have been about ten seconds, then moved away, talking together. One of them pointed back across the roof towards Cupola Sud.

'Right,' Sykes said. 'That's clear enough. They'll blow the whistle as soon as they get back. You take the one on the right.'

Dawson settled his breathing, keeping the right-hand target in the Mauser's iron sights. He took a deep breath, released about half of it and then held his breath, just as he'd been taught on the ranges back in Britain when he'd been training. He checked the sight picture one final time, then slowly squeezed the trigger.

The Mauser kicked back against his shoulder but, at the precise instant he fired, the German soldier turned to his left and started to run. The bullet probably passed within a couple of feet of the man.

Dawson worked the bolt rapidly and brought his rifle back to the aim.

Beside him, Sykes fired his weapon, and the other soldier's body jerked backwards and he tumbled, apparently lifeless, to the ground.

The remaining German soldier had ducked out of sight as his companion fell, no doubt looking for a target for his own rifle.

'He moved,' Dawson said, by way of explanation, and he stared northwards, looking for his target.

A shot rang out from in front of them, but the bullet came nowhere near Sykes or Dawson.

'He's shooting at the Belgians, I think,' Sykes said, glancing down to the south again.

An answering ragged volley of shots rang out from the Belgian soldiers clustered near Maastricht Two, and another one from the German soldier who'd taken cover near the glider.

'I still don't see him,' Dawson said.

'I do,' Sykes muttered. 'Or I think I do.'

The German soldier fired another round.

'Got him,' Sykes murmured. 'I just saw him fire.'

He concentrated on the spot where he'd seen the movement, and then fired his own weapon.

Dawson heard a yell of pain from the German, and then the soldier staggered to his feet, clutching his right arm and howling in agony.

Dawson slightly adjusted his aim, settled his breathing and squeezed the trigger.

This time the German lurched backwards a couple of steps, then collapsed and lay still.

'Teamwork,' Sykes said. 'Now let's see if we can get out of here.'

The Belgian troops were still firing over towards Cupola Sud, and the German soldiers there were shooting back at them. Then the man behind the machine-gun near the northern end of the fort roof opened up again, and Dawson saw two of the Belgian soldiers fall to the ground. That seemed to precipitate a retreat, and in a couple of minutes they'd all vanished from sight, presumably into the nearby casemate.

'Right,' Sykes said, easing up into a crouch, 'now they've buggered off, maybe we can make some progress.'

But before they could move, they heard the ominous howl of another Stuka dive-bomber somewhere above them, and both men dived into cover. Seconds later, the aircraft's bomb exploded somewhere near Cupola Sud, but without scoring a direct hit. Another Stuka followed it down. The second aircraft's target wasn't the pathetic stream of reinforcement troops heading towards Eben Emael, but a much closer target.

'Now they're hitting Block One,' Sykes said, as he saw an explosion right beside the fort's main entrance.

'So getting out of here is going to be fucking interesting,' Dawson said. 'Assuming we ever get back inside the bloody fort.'

'We'll cross that bridge when we come to it. Come on, let's move.'

Picking up the two sections of the demolition charge, Dawson and Sykes started heading south again, making their way slowly towards the Maastricht Two casemate.

CHAPTER 9

10 MAY 1940: EBEN EMAEL, BELGIUM

They'd covered barely seventy yards when another Stuka attack began, the atonal wail of the aircraft's siren sending shivers through Dawson's spine.

Yet again, they dived into cover, wrapping their arms around their heads as a feeble protection against both the metal fragments from the bomb and the terrific noise of the explosion. This attack, too, was directed against the Block One entrance to the fort, and Dawson saw the weapon score a direct hit, impacting against the massive reinforced concrete structure. When the smoke cleared, both men could clearly see that the upper surface of Block One was pitted and discoloured, but the fortification was still intact – the designers of Eben Emael had certainly got some things right.

'It'll take a lot more than a few bombs that size to blow a hole in this place,' Dawson said.

'You're right. But I think the Germans must realize that. They've probably just sent in the Stukas to make sure the Belgians keep their heads down.'

Before they moved again, Sykes stood up and scanned the whole area, trying to see where the German troops were operating. Most of the activity he could see seemed to be concentrated around Cupola Sud, which was still firing rounds from its twin seventy-five-millimetre cannon at targets down to the south of Eben Emael, presumably at other advancing German units.

'I think I can see their plan,' Sykes said, crouching down again. 'The first three targets the Germans hit were the Maastricht One and Two casemates and Cupola One Twenty. They held the main weapons the fort had that could fire at targets to the north. Once they knocked those out, they concentrated all their efforts on the other two weapon positions that can fire in any direction – Cupolas Nord and Sud. Cupola Sud is the only one left operating, and they're determined to silence it.'

Dawson nodded. 'So this is only a part of their plan,' he said. 'They must have troops heading for those three bridges over the Albert Canal, up to the north of here.'

'Exactly. And I'll bet you they probably used the same technique – sending in troops by glider so the defenders couldn't hear their approach. All those bridges were mined, and if the Belgians knew the Germans were approaching, they'd blow the charges. So the Jerries had to be stealthy about it. And that means this isn't just an isolated incident, not just the Germans trying to take out this fort to make way for their invasion attempt. This *is* the invasion of Belgium.'

'Oh, shit,' Dawson said.

'Beautifully put. Now let's move.'

The Maastricht Two casemate was now perhaps only 200 yards away – a half-minute sprint under normal circumstances. But the grassy and slightly undulating surface of the roof of Fort Eben Emael precluded very rapid movement, at least for two men each laden down with part of a heavy and lethal demolition charge. They made steady, but fairly slow, progress.

The two halves of the explosive charge each weighed about fifty pounds, and the single leather handle attached to each was obviously only intended to allow the weapon to be carried for short distances. Both men found they were having to stop frequently to change hands, to relieve the strain on their arms, and the objects swung awkwardly against their legs when they walked.

But they were getting closer to their objective, and for the moment, the Stukas seemed to be taking a break, though the aircraft were no doubt being rearmed and refuelled at some airfield on the other side of the German border.

'Nearly there,' Sykes murmured encouragingly, when they'd covered about half the distance to the casemate.

Then they heard a sound like an express train rushing through the air above them, and a massive column of earth suddenly erupted from the ground a couple of hundred yards over to their left. Again they both dived for cover.

'What the fuck was that?' Dawson demanded.

Before Sykes could reply, they heard another two identical sounds in quick succession – two loud screams – followed by another couple of explosions in the same area as the first.

'That's artillery fire,' Sykes said. 'We're being shelled.'

'You mean the bloody Germans have landed heavy weapons somewhere here as well?'

Another salvo of detonations made conversation

impossible for a few seconds, then Sykes lifted his head again and glanced around.

'It isn't the Germans,' he said.

'But if the Jerries have mounted a full-scale invasion—'

'They have, I'm certain, but why would they fire shells at this fort? No artillery shell could do the slightest bit of damage to it. No, I think it's the Belgians doing it, trying to shift the Germans from the roof.'

'Then let's hope they know where the Germans are, and that they're bloody good shots.'

'From what we've seen so far, I wouldn't put money on it,' Sykes said.

Another two shells screamed overhead and slammed into the ground ahead of them.

'Let's move,' Sykes said.

Dawson grabbed the demolition charge, stood up and headed off towards the casemate, Sykes a few feet behind him.

They'd only covered about ten yards before they heard the ominous noise of incoming rounds again, and threw themselves flat on the ground. As soon as the shells had landed – again some distance away, down in the southern section of the roof, near Cupola Sud – they climbed to their feet and carried on walking.

The pattern repeated itself, time after time. They'd stagger a few yards – both of them, even Dawson, who was by far the bigger and stronger man, were now feeling the strain of lugging a brutally heavy dead weight – then take cover as more shells screamed over them, the explosions getting ever closer as they approached the Maastricht Two casemate.

They ducked into cover about twenty yards from their objective as yet another salvo of artillery shells blasted earth and shrapnel in all directions, the impact point of the explosions less than seventy yards away from them, on the south side of the casemate.

Dawson eased up into a crouch, then tensed as Sykes raised a warning hand to stop him.

'What?'

'Voices,' Sykes hissed urgently. 'Voices right in front of us. German voices. They're inside the casemate.'

Their escape route was blocked.

CHAPTER 10

10 MAY 1940: EBEN EMAEL, BELGIUM

After a couple of seconds, Dawson heard the voices as well. Guttural accents. There was no doubting their origin. A group of German soldiers had obviously taken refuge in the fortification. Going through the casemate was the only way Sykes and Dawson had of getting off the roof of the fort – and staying on the roof was no longer feasible because of the increasing frequency of the barrage of artillery shells landing all around them.

'So what now?' Dawson's voice was tinged with fear. It wasn't the first time he'd faced death since the war had begun, but he really didn't like the odds they were facing – two of them against an unknown number of highly trained and well-armed German soldiers. And he particularly didn't like the idea of facing the enemy troops within the confines of the Maastricht Two casemate.

'Wait,' Sykes said. 'I'm thinking.'

The major looked ahead at the looming grey shape of the casemate, the three gun ports facing almost directly towards them, then glanced across at Dawson.

'We can't tackle those Jerries just with these two Mausers,' Sykes said. 'We need better weapons.'

'And grenades,' Dawson added.

Sykes nodded and glanced behind him. 'You wait here,' he ordered. 'Keep your eye on the casemate. I'll go back to the glider. One of the Germans we shot back there was carrying a Schmeisser, and maybe one or two of them had stick grenades as well. That'll improve the odds a little.'

'You want me to go?' Dawson asked.

Sykes shook his head. 'No. Just watch that casemate. There's nobody anywhere near the glider. I'll be back in a few minutes.'

The major slipped away, heading north across the roof of the fort, quickly vanishing from sight.

Dawson aimed his Mauser towards the casemate and settled down to wait. All he could hope was that Sykes would find some extra weapons, and would get back before any of the German troops decided to leave the casemate and walk in his direction, because he knew he was hopelessly outgunned.

Then he heard another roar as a further salvo of artillery shells howled overhead and exploded beyond and to the east of the casemate, and again lay flat, shielding his head and covering his ears.

Another half dozen salvos from one of the other Belgian forts in the area smashed into the roof all around him before Dawson heard a scuffling sound behind and glanced back, swinging the Mauser to cover the ground to the north, then relaxed slightly.

'It's me.'

Major Sykes ducked down beside Dawson, a Schmeisser machine-pistol in his hands, and another slung over his shoulder.

Dawson nodded, relief evident in his face. 'That'll even things up a bit, sir. Did you find any grenades?'

Sykes patted a canvas bag he had slung over his shoulder, next to the second Schmeisser machine-pistol.

'One of the soldiers had two. The others had one each, so we've got four of them between us. Here.' Sykes opened the bag and handed Dawson two of the weapons. The Model 24 *Stielhandgranate* – commonly known as a stick grenade, or more familiarly to British troops as the 'potato masher' – was a canister full of explosive mounted at the end of a wooden handle. The handle allowed it to be thrown up to three times further than the standard British Mills bomb, and relied on sheer blast for its destructive effect. Because of that, it was particularly lethal in confined spaces.

Like the interior of a reinforced concrete casemate on a Belgian fort, for example.

Dawson hefted one of the grenades in his hand and glanced thoughtfully across at the concrete casemate in front of them.

Sykes looked at him, and leaned closer. 'What we're going to do may not be very sporting, Dawson, but if we don't eliminate those German troops, and bloody fast, we're going to die up here, and that's the truth.'

Dawson switched his gaze to the major, and a slow grin started to work its way across his rugged features.

'I know that,' he muttered. 'I was just wondering if we could lob these potato mashers from here. No, I've got no problem using grenades against these bastards. They just dive-bombed a column of unarmed men. Let's give them a taste of their own medicine. The quicker we kill them the better, I reckon.'

'Right,' Sykes said. 'We've got four grenades. There are only the two of us, and we'll have just one chance to get this right. The first thing we do is throw one into the casemate where the gun's been blown inside the building – where we climbed out. That will kill any Germans hiding in that section. But there are a lot of rooms down there, so there might be other soldiers inside who'll only be dazed by the first explosion.

'After that we climb into the casemate immediately. With three grenades left, and these two machine-pistols, we should be able to kill any others before they regain their senses.'

It wasn't much of a plan, and both of them knew it. But Dawson hadn't any better ideas so he nodded agreement.

'You go left, and I'll go right,' Sykes said. 'We'll meet at the casemate itself, beside the blown-out cannon. OK?'

Dawson nodded again, left the Mauser rifle on the ground – he wouldn't need it any more – and checked the Schmeisser was cocked and loaded. He had handled the weapon before and was quite familiar with it. He picked up both grenades and stuck them in his belt, and then grabbed the demolition charge. He glanced across at Sykes, to make sure he was ready, and then both men started towards the casemate, their paths separating immediately.

They were reasonably certain they wouldn't be heard as they made their stealthy approach – the continuing artillery barrage would ensure that – but they were concerned they might be seen as they approached their objective. So they moved as slowly and as carefully as they could, keeping low and taking advantage of every scrap of cover they could find.

They reached the massive wall of the casemate without apparently being seen. Or, at least, nobody had fired at them. The outer two seventy-five-millimetre guns were still intact. Presumably the German troops hadn't yet got around to destroying them, or maybe they were even planning to use the weapons themselves, to support their invasion of Belgium, once they'd captured the entire fort. Only the centre cannon had been blown off its mountings during the initial attack, and that was the route they had used to get out of the fort, and it was also the only way back inside.

Dawson and Sykes crouched down directly below the opening and carefully lowered the two halves of the explosive charge to the ground.

'Leave the demolition charge out here,' Sykes whispered. 'You go in first when the grenade's exploded, and I'll follow you in immediately. We'll clear the casemate, then come back out here and get the charge.'

Dawson took one of the stick grenades from his belt, checked that Sykes was ready, then unscrewed the cap at the base of the wooden handle and pulled the ceramic ball, which started the detonation sequence. The grenade had a five-second fuse. The last thing he and Sykes needed was some quick-witted German grabbing the weapon and throwing it back out at them, so he counted a slow 'one, two, three'. Then he stood up and lobbed the grenade through the opening in the front wall of the casemate.

He heard a sudden yell from inside as he flattened himself against the ground, and almost immediately the stick grenade exploded inside the structure, the sound massively amplified by the enclosed space.

Dawson immediately stood up, took a quick glance inside the casemate, then levered himself up and wriggled through the opening. It was a tight fit, but eventually he managed to wriggle through. The moment the corporal's boots vanished from sight, Sykes followed him.

Dust hung everywhere, which made the place look as if it was full of fog, fog that was slowly clearing. Dawson stood up and looked around. He was staring at a scene that was straight from hell.

The bodies of the two Belgian soldiers, the men who'd been killed by the blast that had wrecked the cannon, were still lying on the floor, their limbs contorted by the new blast. Beyond them lay the bodies of four German soldiers, who had obviously taken shelter in the casemate against the artillery barrage. One of them must have been right next to the grenade when it exploded, because his torso was shredded, ribs and intestines blown out by the blast, a spreading pool of blood discolouring the floor around him. The three others had been a little further away from the epicentre, but were just as dead, the skin of their faces and hands ripped and torn, and no doubt with massive internal injuries. It would have been a quick death.

For a few seconds, Dawson just stared at the carnage, then a shout from the doorway snapped him out of it.

'Dawson!' Sykes yelled, the Schmeisser in one hand and a stick grenade clutched in the other. 'Check the space to your right, then follow me,' he ordered.

Dawson peered around the dividing wall, but there was no sign of life on the other side of it, just the intact but unmanned seventy-five-millimetre cannon on its mounting.

Sykes moved ahead, peering through the clouds of dust, Dawson right behind him. The major kicked open a door to his left, to check the room. As he did so, a figure lurched into view down the passage, a German soldier who'd survived the blast, his rifle hanging loosely over his shoulder, clearly dazed and confused.

But he was a threat, and Dawson reacted immediately, lifting the muzzle of his Schmeisser and firing three bullets straight into the German's chest. The man tumbled backwards and crashed to the ground, killed instantly.

Sykes spun round from his inspection of the sideroom – which was stacked with equipment but empty of people. He brought his own weapon to bear, took in the scene in a moment, then nodded to Dawson.

'Thanks,' he said.

For a few moments Dawson didn't move, just stared down at the body of the dead German soldier. Another man dead at his hands. He'd almost lost count of the number of men he'd killed since he'd been dragged into this conflict.

'Wake up, Dawson,' Sykes said sharply, pointing at the metal staircase ahead of them. 'The upper level's clear. Now we need to check down below.'

At the end of the short passageway was a railing and a metal staircase that linked the two levels inside the casemate.

The two men moved quickly towards the staircase, checking both sides of the passageway as they did so. They stopped at the railing and peered down into the darkness that cloaked the lower level. They saw no signs of any German soldiers, but there were faint noises, perhaps the sounds of people moving across the floor.

'Another grenade, I think,' Sykes said, pulling one out of his belt. 'Just in case.'

Dawson nodded, but before either of them could move there was a faint whistling sound, and a stick grenade suddenly flew up out of the darkness and landed on the ground a few feet behind them.

CHAPTER 11

10 MAY 1940: EBEN EMAEL, BELGIUM

Dawson reacted instantly.

He turned round, took two paces forward and kicked the canister end of the grenade as hard as he could. The weapon lifted into the air, spinning end over end, and clattered away down the passageway the two men had just walked along.

Then he dropped flat to the floor, his head and steel helmet pointing in the direction that he'd kicked the grenade, and rammed his hands over his ears. Beside him, Sykes did exactly the same thing.

Under a second later, the grenade exploded at the far end of the passageway with a blast that seemed to shake the very foundations of the casemate. A massive pressure wave slammed into the two soldiers, and dust and small bits of debris flew in all directions. The stick grenade wasn't a fragmentation weapon, relying solely on the blast effect. Fortunately, Dawson's massive kick had ensured they were outside the lethal radius of the weapon – just.

'Good job, Dawson,' Sykes muttered. 'You OK?'

'I think so, yeah.' Dawson shook himself like a dog, then climbed shakily to his feet.

'Right. Now we finish this.'

Sykes eased himself up into a crouch, armed the grenade he'd previously been preparing to throw, and dropped it over the edge of the steel railing.

When the explosion came, it sounded almost muted, but that was probably because their ears were still ringing from the blast of the grenade thrown at them.

'Come on.'

Sykes gripped his Schmeisser and led the way down the metal staircase, making no attempt to be silent, because speed was more important. They needed to get down to the base of the casemate before any other surviving German soldiers recovered their senses.

Their boots clattered on the pierced-steel treads as they ran down the staircase, their weapons held ready, both men trying to spot any threat before they were themselves attacked.

Nearing the lower level, Dawson spotted a shape off to one side and immediately stopped dead. He aimed the Schmeisser over the banister rail and fired a short burst, the sound of the sub-machine-gun echoing throughout the space. The first couple of rounds missed, smashing into the concrete floor and ricocheting away into the darkness, but the next one thudded into its target.

Quickly, Sykes and Dawson ran down the last few steps. While Dawson stood guard, his Schmeisser ready, the major bent to examine the body lying on the floor.

'He was dead already, Dawson. That grenade exploded quite close to him. But good shooting anyway.'

Quickly, they checked everywhere on the lower level, but there was no sign of any other enemy soldiers.

'Nothing?' Sykes asked.

'Nothing,' Dawson confirmed. 'Let me just check the door.'

He walked across to the pair of massive steel doors they'd originally used to get into the casemate. Both were firmly closed, but when he pulled the side of the one they'd come through, it opened slightly. Their escape route was still open.

'We'll grab that demolition charge and get out of here,' Sykes said, and led the way back towards the metal staircase.

Back on the upper level, they again looked in every room, but the space was still secure. They walked over to the central gun position, and Sykes stared out, checking for any enemy troops. The area appeared relatively quiet, though the artillery barrage continued from the adjacent Belgian forts.

'I'm smaller than you, Dawson. I'll get them,' Sykes said.

He leant his Schmeisser against the wall and clambered up and out of the casemate, slid easily through the opening and ducked down out of sight. In a few seconds he reappeared, holding the upper half of the demolition charge – the section that Dawson believed held the plastic explosive – in both hands. He passed it through the opening to the corporal, who took it from him and lowered it onto the floor behind him. Sykes disappeared again, to collect the other part of the charge.

Then a rifle shot rang out, and another, and Dawson clearly heard the impact of the bullets on the concrete walls of the casemate. Sykes suddenly yelled in pain and there was a thud from outside, as if a heavy weight – or a body – had fallen to the ground.

Dawson scrambled forward, thrust his Schmeisser through the opening in the casemate wall and looked around. Directly in front of him, he saw half a dozen indistinct shapes advancing cautiously through the swirling smoke towards the casemate. Below him, Major Sykes was writhing in agony, clutching his thigh, the left leg of his uniform soaked with blood. Beside him lay the lower – and probably the most important – part of the demolition charge.

Dawson barely took the time to aim, just levelled the Schmeisser at the approaching German troops and pulled the trigger in three short bursts. As far as he could see, he didn't hit anyone, but the unexpected machine-gun fire had the desired effect – the advancing soldiers scattered and dived for cover.

He pulled the trigger again, but the action clicked open after only a couple of rounds had been fired. He'd emptied the magazine. Dawson pressed the button to release it and slammed in a fresh one – Sykes had liberated four spare magazines as well as the weapons themselves from the dead soldiers – and fired another burst.

'Take the demolition charge,' Sykes gasped, the voice laced with pain. 'Leave me here, just get out. Save yourself.'

'No fucking way,' Dawson snapped, and then climbed out of the casemate, bent down and picked up Sykes bodily.

'I just gave you an order, Corporal,' Sykes said.

'Yeah? Well, I'm getting hard of hearing. Must be all

those fucking grenades going off all around me.'

With the major's body hanging over his shoulder, Dawson stood up and swung round to face the German soldiers. He'd looped the Schmeisser's sling over his shoulder, so he could fire it one-handed from the hip, and fired another short burst to make them keep their heads down. Then he manoeuvred himself until Sykes's head and shoulders were level with the opening in the casemate.

'Pull yourself inside,' he said.

A couple of the German soldiers fired their rifles as he said this, but both the bullets missed, hitting the casemate wall and throwing concrete splinters in all directions.

Dawson fired again, trying to keep the bursts short, because he doubted if he could reload the Schmeisser until Sykes had got off his shoulder and crawled inside the casemate.

'And get a fucking move on. Sir,' he added, as the major pulled his torso through the opening, his wounded leg dragging behind him.

Sykes screamed with pain as his left thigh hit some obstruction, but after a few seconds he managed to pull himself into the casemate.

Dawson emptied his magazine towards the Germans, snapped in the last full one he had, then bent down and picked up the demolition charge in one hand. Fear lent strength to his arm, and he thrust the charge straight through the hole and pushed it as far as he could. It tumbled away into the darkness to land heavily on the floor. That didn't worry him – as long as it had missed landing on Sykes, that was all that mattered. The explosive, he was sure, was in the other part of the weapon, so delicate handling wasn't needed.

Three more shots cracked out, the bullets much closer. Dawson emptied the magazine in short bursts, then dropped the weapon to the ground and dived straight into the opening in the casemate, desperately pulling himself inside and out of danger.

As the German soldiers saw what he was doing, they opened fire again. Two of the rifle bullets crashed into the stepped concrete of the gun position in the casemate, sending red-hot shards of copper searing into Dawson's right calf as he finally struggled clear.

'Bugger, that stings,' he muttered.

Sykes had hobbled a few feet away, and had dragged the top half of the demolition charge with him. He'd also rigged a rough tourniquet around the top of his left thigh, using his belt. Even in the relative darkness of the interior of the casemate, Dawson could see that his face was white and drawn.

'We'll talk later about your blatant insubordination, Dawson,' Sykes said. 'But in the meantime, thanks.'

'We're not out of the wood yet,' Dawson said. 'One of those Jerries is bound to lob a stick grenade inside here any minute, unless I can persuade them not to. Can you get yourself to the top of the staircase?'

Without waiting for a response, Dawson picked up the other Schmeisser, stuck the barrel out of the opening in the casemate wall and pulled the trigger, emptying the magazine in short bursts to avoid it jamming: the MP 38 was somewhat temperamental. Then he turned back, grabbed the spare magazines Sykes had left with the weapon and inserted a fresh one. He slung the sub-machine-gun around his neck, picked up both sections of the demolition charge and staggered down the passageway. He passed Sykes about halfway to the top of the staircase, but carried on. He lowered both sections of the charge to the ground by the railing, then went back, hoisted the major onto his shoulder again and jogged back to the staircase.

'You're a big, strong ugly bugger, Dawson,' Sykes muttered.

'And you're not – I couldn't carry you if you were.'

Dawson stopped by the railing, looked down into the darkness below, picked up the lower section of the charge and lifted it over the edge.

'Is that a good idea?' Sykes asked, panting with the exertion and probably blood loss as well.

'We'll find out in a couple of seconds,' Dawson replied, and dropped it.

There was a heavy thud as it hit somewhere on the floor below, but that was all.

'This is the tricky bit,' Dawson said, pointing to the top section. 'That's got the plastic explosive in it. I don't know how the fuse operates, and I don't have time to find out now. I'll have to carry it down and make sure the fuse assembly doesn't touch anything. If it's triggered, we're fucked.'

Sykes nodded. 'Colourfully put.'

'You'll have to hang round my neck while I carry the charge in one hand and hold onto the banister with the other. Just don't make me laugh.'

Dawson hoisted Sykes onto his back, made sure that the major was clinging on tightly, then grabbed the charge and walked backwards to the top of the staircase.

He seized the banister with his free hand and started stepping slowly and carefully backwards.

The strain on his arm was enormous because of the solid lump of the demolition charge, and he was having to concentrate hard on keeping it away from any object that could accidentally hit the fuse and trigger it. Added to that was the dead weight of Sykes on his back. Dawson was a very strong man, but even he found it difficult to handle the descent.

The steel staircase seemed endless. Dawson gritted his teeth and just concentrated on each step, every one of which was taking them nearer to safety. He tried to move as quickly as he could, but the combination of Sykes's weight and the demolition charge in his hand meant their progress was agonizingly slow. Finally, Dawson stepped off the staircase and onto the concrete floor of the lower level of the casemate, and lowered Sykes gratefully to the ground. The major leant against the wall, panting slightly.

At that moment, as Dawson thought they might actually be safe, he heard a metallic clatter from above them, from the passageway that led to the staircase, and moments later a deafening explosion blasted through the casemate. Obviously the Germans had reached the casemate wall and used a grenade to clear their way inside.

'Bugger,' Dawson said, his ears ringing from the noise of the blast – neither man had been able to protect his ears from the explosion. 'They're right behind us.'

At any moment one of the German soldiers could appear at the top of the staircase and lob a grenade down at them. And if that happened, they'd both die instantly.

He placed the demolition charge on the floor, ran over

to the pair of steel doors and started to pull the outer one open. It was heavy, he was exhausted, and it wasn't easy, but he managed to open it wide enough for Sykes to hobble through.

'Get in there and wait,' Dawson ordered. Sykes just nodded. He was in no fit state to react against the orders issued by a mere corporal. The descent of the staircase had taken it out of him, obviously.

As Major Sykes hopped and staggered towards the steel door, Dawson ran back across the room to the foot of the steel staircase, picked up the demolition charge and carried it carefully over to where Sykes was now waiting, in the space between the two steel doors. He bent down and lowered the charge to the ground, then turned to go back and collect the other part of the weapon. He hadn't seen where it had landed, but it was obviously out there somewhere.

But at that moment he heard a clattering noise and a thud just outside, and immediately guessed the Germans were inside the casemate and had just thrown a grenade down the stairs. They'd made it to the doors just in time.

Dawson seized the handle of the door and pulled it closed. As the edge slammed into the steel frame, the grenade detonated about ten feet away, on the other side of the door. But the steel on the door was so thick that the explosion was nothing more than a muffled 'crump', and they felt none of the blast.

'Wait here,' Dawson said, though it was obvious Sykes was going nowhere under his own steam. Dawson pulled the remaining stick grenade from his belt, then eased the door open just wide enough to allow him to get out. He unscrewed the cap from the end of the handle, pulled the cord to prime the weapon and then threw it with all his strength up the staircase and into the passageway above.

Then he ran back to the door and pulled it closed again. In seconds, the grenade exploded, the sound again muted by the steel of the door.

Dawson pushed the door and ran across the room once more, searching for the other section of the German demolition charge. All the lights in that section of the casemate had been blown out by the explosions of the grenades, and he had to search blindly in the dark.

His foot hit a hard object, and he thought that was it. He bent down and his hands felt the unmistakable shape of a German steel helmet, the deceased owner still wearing it. Dawson shuddered slightly as his fingers felt the dead man's features. He moved on.

He circled the passageway unsuccessfully and came back to the body of the dead German soldier.

A torch beam stabbed down in the darkness from the upper level of the casemate, and Dawson shrank back against the wall, directly underneath the metal staircase. He pulled the Schmeisser round and pointed the muzzle upwards, towards the source of the light.

As he did so, he saw the lower section of the demolition charge, lying on the floor no more than a few feet away from him, on top of the dead soldier. When he'd thrown it down from the upper level, it had landed squarely on the German's stomach. The soft landing had cushioned the impact, but the heavy weight had ruptured the body's abdomen, blowing out the intestines and soaking the floor in blood.

Dawson glanced up again. The soldier holding the torch was still quartering the area with the beam, looking for a target for a grenade or his rifle or Schmeisser. If the soldier decided to use a grenade, there'd be nothing Dawson could do in that confined space, unless he could get across to the steel door before it exploded.

He paused for a moment, weighing up his options, then made a decision. He reached forward, grabbed the handle of the demolition charge with his left hand and then moved, pointing his Schmeisser upwards and squeezing the trigger as he ran clumsily – the charge wasn't easy to carry – across the concrete floor.

Dawson heard a noise from above, movement, and then another Schmeisser joined in, the bullets kicking up the dust at his feet as he ran. Ricochets from the bullets were flying everywhere, bouncing off the solid concrete walls and metal fixtures, creating sparks and flashes of flame that vanished almost as soon as they appeared. In such a confined space, firing a high-velocity weapon was almost as dangerous to the firer as the person being aimed at.

Then another weapon joined the fray. Flat, separate cracks sounded, and Dawson looked ahead to see Sykes, his face twisted with pain, hanging on to the edge of the steel door and firing his Webley revolver up at the Germans on the landing.

A bullet tugged at Dawson's battledress jacket as he ran, and a couple of rounds smashed solidly into the demolition charge, the impact causing him to stumble. The steel door was only feet away, and with a last gasp he sprinted for the opening.

As he dodged behind it, he heard another noise

behind him. A soft thudding sound. Then another.

'Two grenades,' Sykes said hoarsely. 'Get inside.'

Dawson dropped the demolition charge on the floor, grabbed the handle of the door and pulled as hard as he could, Sykes trying to lend a hand as well.

But the door hadn't completely closed when the first of the two grenades exploded less than six feet away, followed a split-second later by the second one.

CHAPTER 12

10 MAY 1940: EBEN EMAEL, BELGIUM

The double explosion was deafening and, even though they were protected behind the massive steel door, the blast knocked both men down. But the pressure wave also slammed against the door, kicking it shut.

Dawson recovered first, ears ringing, and pulled the door completely closed, plunging the space into a silence deepened by the impenetrable darkness. Working by feel alone, he found the central lever and turned it, driving home the massive bolts that securely locked the door in place, and leant back against it. They were safe from the Germans – at least for the moment.

'Thank fuck for that,' he muttered, and felt his way across to where Major Sykes lay. The officer hadn't made a sound since they'd both been blown off their feet by the grenades.

'You OK, sir?' Dawson asked, bending over and searching for the recumbent figure.

A beam of light broke through the darkness as Sykes pulled a small torch from his pocket and switched it on.

The major looked up at him. 'Of course I'm not OK, Dawson,' he snapped, some of his old fire returning. 'I've been shot, had grenades thrown at me, been carried down a set of stairs like a helpless baby, and the man under my command persistently refuses to obey my direct orders. Now, if you don't want to find yourself on a charge, get that other door open so we can get the fuck out of here.'

'Very good, sir,' Dawson replied, a grin working its way across his face.

He crossed to the inner door, held the Schmeisser by the stock and lifted it to rap on the steel, to summon Verbois or whoever was the other side of it.

'You *do* remember the sequence, I hope?' Sykes asked.

'Yeah. Three, one, two,' Dawson said.

'Good. Get on with it.'

Dawson smashed the metal stock of the sub-machine-gun into the steel door three times, paused for a few seconds, then continued the sequence of the agreed signal. As the sound of the last bang died away, he stood back and waited.

Both men had expected the Belgian troops to open the door within seconds, but nothing happened.

'I hope they haven't buggered off,' Dawson muttered.

'So do I,' Sykes agreed grimly. 'Try it again.'

Dawson stepped forward and repeated the sequence, with the same result.

'Maybe they can't hear it,' he said. 'I mean, the stock of this Schmeisser is only a bit of bent metal. I really need something like a hammer.'

Dawson swung the torch beam around, looking for something more substantial to use. Sykes was still holding his Webley revolver, the weapon dangling from his right hand, the lanyard around his neck.

'That might do it, sir,' Dawson suggested, pointing at the pistol, and Sykes handed it over.

Dawson unloaded the cylinder and slipped the rounds into his pocket, then held the Webley by the barrel and slammed the butt onto the steel door, repeating the sequence they'd agreed with Verbois. The blows with the heavy pistol made a much louder noise than the Schmeisser had done.

'That should wake the buggers up,' Dawson said.

But still there was no response, no sign of the inner door opening.

'I'm getting a bad feeling about this,' Sykes said. 'The Belgians will have heard those grenades going off, and probably the noise of the fire-fight as well. I just hope they didn't retreat further into the fort.'

'When you say "retreat", what you really mean is they might have run away, don't you?'

Sykes nodded. 'Two expressions, two slightly different meanings,' he said.

'We're stuck here, then, at least for the moment. I'll knock on the door again in a minute. Let me just take a look at your leg, sir. Could you hold the torch, please?'

Sykes took it and aimed the beam at his left thigh.

Dawson still had his Lee-Enfield bayonet on his belt, in its scabbard, but that didn't seem the right tool to use, so he took out a pocket knife, snapped open the blade and sliced through the fabric of Sykes's trouser leg.

It wasn't a pretty sight. The high-velocity rifle bullet had torn through the side of his thigh, ripping apart the muscles. The entry wound was tiny, but where the bullet had come out was a hole a couple of inches across, ragged flesh protruding and blood still seeping out, despite the tourniquet. But there was no spurting, no sign of arterial blood.

'What's it look like?' Sykes asked, resolutely keeping his eyes averted.

Dawson glanced at the major. 'Well, there's good news and bad news, I suppose,' he said. 'The good news is that the bullet missed the bone and arteries and went straight through your leg.'

'And the bad news?'

'It's a hell of an exit wound, and you've lost a lot of blood. You need medical treatment – and quickly. You'll be limping for a while. Oh, and this pair of uniform trousers is ruined.'

Sykes smiled, despite the pain he was suffering.

Dawson dragged a field dressing out of one of his pouches, and placed it over the open wound. As gently as he could, he lifted Sykes's leg and tied the bandage around his thigh.

'Sorry about this,' he said, 'but I have to get this tight. It's going to hurt.'

'Just do it, man.'

Dawson pulled the ends of the bandage together, squeezing the dressing against the injury. He wrapped the bandage around Sykes's thigh, then knotted it tightly.

Sykes grunted with pain a couple of times, then lay back when Dawson finished his rudimentary medical treatment.

'Sorry,' Dawson said again, and took back the torch from the major. He picked up the revolver and stepped back to the inner steel door. Seizing the weapon by the barrel, he again slammed it into the steel, repeating the sequence of knocks.

Again there was no response.

'I'll kill that fucking Verbois if we ever get out of here,' Dawson muttered.

'And I'll give you a hand,' Sykes whispered.

Then they both heard a metallic clanging sound, and for the briefest of instants Dawson assumed it was the bolts on the inner door being withdrawn.

'At last,' he said, but Sykes shook his head.

'Wrong door,' he said, and Dawson spun round, aiming the torch at the officer.

Sykes pointed at the outer steel door, the one that gave access to the casemate itself. 'I think the Jerries have stuck a demolition charge on it.'

Dawson went white. 'Then we're fucked,' he said.

'A ten-second fuse, I think you said? It's been good knowing you, Dawson. We ought to—'

But whatever Major Sykes had been about to suggest was lost for ever as a massive explosion rocked the narrow space between the two steel doors.

CHAPTER 13

10 MAY 1940: EBEN EMAEL, BELGIUM

For a few seconds there was absolute silence, then Eddie Dawson opened his eyes.

'Bugger me,' he said, stating the obvious, 'we're alive.'

'They must have several sizes of demolition charges,' Sykes said, 'and that one was too small to penetrate the steel door.'

'Verbois said they were supposed to be proof against all conventional explosives. So at least that bit of Eben Emael has worked as advertised.'

'Yes, but now the Germans know they used the wrong type, so I'm sure they'll be bringing along one of those charges they used against the casemates. That'll have no trouble blowing a hole right through that door, and vaporizing us in the process. We've got to get out of here, Dawson.'

The corporal staggered over to the inner door and once again rapped out the sequence of knocks they'd agreed with Verbois, smashing the butt of the pistol as hard as he could onto the steel. He waited about half a minute, then repeated the process, the steel ringing with the impacts.

Four, five, six times he sounded the signal and finally, as the last blow with the now battered Webley revolver died away, they were rewarded. This time there was no mistaking the source of the sound – it was definitely the inner door – and it was a scraping sound as the bolts were pulled out of their housings.

'Thank God for that,' Sykes said, staggering clumsily to his feet.

The inner door swung open, and the two men found they were facing a reception committee. Beside Verbois was a group of Belgian soldiers, all holding rifles pointing straight at Dawson and Sykes.

'Lower those rifles,' Sykes snapped in French, staggering forwards into the corridor.

Verbois repeated the order and the soldiers obeyed.

As Dawson bent down to grab one section of the demolition charge, he heard an unmistakable clang from the outer door, and knew exactly what it was.

'Get clear,' he yelled, tossed the lower section of the charge out into the corridor, then turned back, grabbed the upper part and dragged it out. Pausing only to lower it to the ground, he spun round to close the inner door.

But Sykes had heard it too, and issued a brisk order in French.

As Dawson reached the door, three other soldiers appeared beside him and leant their considerable weight to the mechanism. Moments later the door slammed shut and Dawson turned the handle to slide the bolts home.

He stepped clear of the door, just as a massive explosion occurred in the casemate. The inner door seemed to shake, and bits of concrete and dust rose all around them, but the door itself remained intact.

'Bet the other bugger's got a bloody great hole blasted through it,' Dawson said, then turned to face Verbois.

'So where the fuck were you, matey? We bloody nearly got trapped in there. Those Jerries almost had us.'

If Capitaine Verbois objected to being shouted at by a mere corporal, he gave no sign of it. He simply shook his head and apologized.

'I'm truly sorry. The commanding officer summoned me and I've only just got back here.'

'Didn't you think of leaving somebody here to listen for us?' Sykes asked.

Verbois nodded. 'Of course I did. The problem was, there were so many bangs and noises from inside the casemate that the soldiers I'd left here weren't certain they'd heard the proper signal.'

Sykes and Dawson had to acknowledge that that, at least, was a valid argument.

'When he first heard the banging on the door, one of the men fetched me urgently. Then you banged much louder, and we were certain it was you two on the other side of the door.'

'Well, at least we got out of the casemate,' Sykes said.

'Your leg, Major,' Verbois said, clearly noticing Sykes's injury for the first time. 'What happened?'

'He took a bullet in the thigh,' Dawson said, 'and he needs medical treatment right away. Can we get him down to the hospital?'

'Of course.' Verbois issued orders to one of his men, who ran down the corridor and quickly returned with a stretcher. He opened it up, and Dawson helped Sykes lie down on it. The major looked even worse than before, much weaker and clearly in enormous pain.

As he lay back on the canvas stretcher, Sykes beckoned to Dawson, who bent closer to hear what he had to say.

'Get that demolition charge back to British lines, Dawson, and this time that really *is* an order. Get it to somebody in authority. If possible, find Lieutenant-Colonel Brace-Williams of the Royal Scots Greys, my regiment. My boss, in fact. Explain what we saw it do to the fort here.' Sykes gestured for Dawson to get closer still.

'But for fuck's sake don't give it to the bloody Belgians,' Sykes whispered. 'They'd just hand it straight back to Adolf's minions, or give it to the French, which would be just as bad. You must get it into senior British hands.'

Dawson nodded. 'Any idea how, sir?'

A ghost of a smile flitted across Sykes's face. 'As I said the very first time we met, Dawson, on the quay at Cherbourg last year, just use your initiative. You seem to be quite good at that.'

'I'll do my best,' Dawson said thickly, a lump forming in his throat as he looked down at the battered body of the man he'd shared the last few days with. Then he stood back as two of Verbois's men lifted the stretcher and headed off down the passageway.

'We need to get out of here,' Dawson said briskly, turning to Verbois. 'The Germans have probably blown a hole in the outer door, and the inner one won't hold them up for long, so we'd better scarper.'

'Scarper?' Verbois asked.

'Doesn't matter. We need to shift our arses. Allez bloody vite.'

Dawson glanced down the passageway and saw what looked like a metal box on wheels. 'What's that?' he asked.

Verbois looked where Dawson was pointing. 'An ammunition cart,' he said.

'That'll do nicely. Can you get one of your men to fetch it, please? This charge is heavy.'

Verbois detailed one of his men to bring the cart, then looked with interest at the object Sykes and Dawson had recovered. 'Is that what the Germans used to destroy our fortifications?' he asked.

'We think so, yes.'

'It doesn't look like much.'

'It's not what it looks like that's important – it's how it works. And this is a bloody complex bit of gear.'

The Belgian soldier appeared with the ammunition cart. Dawson picked up both sections of the demolition charge and placed them on the top of it, then started pushing the cart down the corridor.

'You're intending to take that back to your own lines?' Verbois asked.

'Yes.' Dawson didn't elaborate.

'We should retain it here,' Verbois said. 'It has been used against us, not against you British.'

'No chance, *Capitaine*. If I hand that over to you, I'll be disobeying a direct order from Major Sykes. And you know as well as I do that this place is doomed, so if it stays here, the bloody Jerries will just grab it back and use it to blow a fucking great hole in another one of your forts.'

Verbois looked at the big corporal for a moment, then shrugged. 'You could be right,' he said, his voice resigned. 'Getting back as far as Block One is not a problem, but the Germans are attacking with Stuka dive-bombers against it. I have no idea how you will get out of this fort, or anywhere else.'

'Right now, mate,' Dawson replied, 'nor have I.'

He saw more evidence of the damage caused to the fort as they made their way along the corridors to Block One. Many of the lights had been blown out, leaving long stretches of the passageways in darkness, and flakes of concrete and other debris littered the floor. Dawson wasn't prepared to use one of the various ammunition elevators to transport the two sections of the demolition charge down to the lower level, in case the power failed halfway between floors and left it stuck and inaccessible, so he insisted on carrying both sections down the staircase himself.

Eventually they reached Block One, where the damage inflicted on the structure by the German Stuka dive-bombers was very obvious. The entrance was one of the most exposed areas of the entire fort and, although none of the bombs had been able to penetrate the thick armoured concrete roof or walls of the building, every light bulb had been blown out and the repeated detonations had shaken most of the books, manuals and other objects off the shelves and onto the floor. None of the dazed and demoralized Belgian soldiers sitting or lying around in Block One and lining the corridors outside appeared to have the slightest interest in picking up anything. That fact alone made Dawson realize that the fort was doomed. That day, or the next day at the latest, somebody was going to walk outside waving a white flag and surrender the place to the Germans. It was a question of 'when', not 'if'.

That didn't help, obviously, but Dawson knew he'd have to be long gone – with the demolition charge – before that happened. What he still didn't know was how he was going to achieve it.

There were observation ports in Block One, and he strode across to one of them to inspect the scene outside. That wasn't encouraging either. The ground outside the blockhouse was pockmarked with craters and liberally covered in debris. Getting a vehicle anywhere near the main entrance to the fort would be difficult or impossible – not that Dawson had even considered it. However he managed to get out, he'd known all along it would have to be on foot, at least until he'd got away from the immediate vicinity of Fort Eben Emael. Then he'd be able to drive off in the Hillman staff car, assuming it hadn't been stolen or been hit by a bomb. The rotor arm for the distributor was in his pocket, and with any luck he'd be able to get away ahead of the German land forces, which must by now be approaching the Belgian border, if they weren't there already.

But first, somehow, he had to get out of Block One with the demolition charge.

Dawson stared through the observation port at the desolation outside for a couple of minutes, looking for inspiration. If he just walked out he'd be an immediate target for the enemy troops up on the roof and, until he was outside, he couldn't know if any of them were close enough to spot him. He also knew he couldn't run out, because he couldn't carry even one section of the demolition charge *and* a rifle at more than walking pace – it was just too heavy. And even then it would still leave the other part of it inside Fort Eben Emael, and he couldn't get back inside and pull the same trick again.

However he left the fort, it had to be with both sections of the demolition charge at the same time, with at least one other person to carry the other part. So he had to work out some way of getting two people out of the building without either of them getting shot. They had to become the kind of target that the Germans simply wouldn't fire at.

And there was only one way he could think of that might work. But first, he'd have to clear it with Sykes.

Dawson stepped away from the observation port and turned to Verbois. 'Can you take me to the hospital, please? There's something I need to talk about with Major Sykes.'

Just over thirty minutes later, two Belgian soldiers carried a stretcher towards Block One, Dawson walking just behind them. On the stretcher, Sykes lay flat, his slight frame covered by a sheet that was heavily bloodstained. It wasn't actually his blood, but that didn't matter.

The bullet wound in his thigh had been quickly treated by the Belgian medical team, and was now properly strapped up and padded to avoid any further blood loss. As the bullet had passed straight through the muscle, they'd checked that no threads from Sykes's uniform trousers, dirt or bullet fragments were stuck in the wound. Then they'd disinfected it, injected the area with antiseptic drugs, plugged the exit hole with a sterile dressing and strapped it up as tightly as possible.

They had no local anaesthetic, and all they'd been able to give Sykes was an opiate-based painkiller, and the major's face told its own grim story of the painful treatment he'd just endured. He was white, seemingly drained of blood, and his speech slightly slurred, as if he'd been drinking. This was a side-effect of the morphine. In his uniform pocket were three more glass phials of the drug, to be taken when the pain grew unbearable.

'This should be close enough,' Dawson said, when they reached a point in the corridor where the lights were still working, and where no Belgian soldiers had taken refuge. He didn't want to go into Block One itself until they were ready to go outside, because the Stukas were still making occasional attacks on the structure, though most of their efforts now seemed to be directed towards targets on the roof of the fort – the remaining gun emplacements.

'You're a devious bugger, Dawson,' Sykes muttered as the Belgian soldiers lowered his stretcher to the ground. 'Are you sure this is going to work?'

'Frankly, sir, no, but I can't see any other option. If we don't do it now, we'll still be inside here when the garrison surrenders. At best, we'd spend the rest of this war in a Jerry prison camp, and I don't think that's a great idea.'

'Nor do I, Dawson, so we'd best get on.'

Verbois looked troubled. 'There are – implications, shall we say – about what you're planning to do. The provisions of the Hague Convention might not—'

'The Hague Convention might also have something to say about Stuka dive-bombers attacking your unarmed reinforcement troops as they walked here from the villages where they were billeted,' Sykes interrupted, his voice slurring, but what he was saying perfectly clear and lucid. 'Adolf Hitler doesn't care about the Hague Convention or the laws of war or any other bits of paper. He's proved that often enough already. And if his troops can ignore what passes for the rules of combat, I can't think of any particularly good reason why we can't do the same.'

'And what we'll be doing won't affect the Germans or the outcome of this battle,' Dawson added. 'All we need are two volunteers and one of them has to be fairly strong.'

Verbois nodded, still unhappy but unable to marshal any arguments to counter Dawson.

'Very well,' he said. 'I'll leave you to make your preparations, and I'll find a couple of men prepared to assist you.'

As soon as Verbois had walked away down the corridor, followed by the two soldiers, Dawson turned his attention to the upper part of the demolition charge. He'd taken every precaution to ensure that the fuse assembly sticking out of the top hadn't been damaged. This was partly because he wanted to be able to examine it properly, but mainly because he knew that, if it was triggered, he wouldn't have been able to run far enough, or fast enough, to avoid being blown to bits when the charge exploded.

Now he looked at the charge closely. He had a great deal of respect for German engineering, and he was certain the fuse wasn't a permanent part of the weapon – it was too fragile and dangerous to incorporate it – so it had to be possible to remove it.

'Got it,' he said, after a few moments. He took a knife from his pocket and opened the spike instead of the blade, slid the point into a small hole drilled through the fuse, and gently tried to turn it. After a moment, the whole assembly began to rotate, and a few seconds later Dawson was able to lift the fuse away from the charge.

'Is that it?' Sykes asked from the stretcher.

'Yes. Simple enough. They transport the fuse separately and only insert it in the charge when they reach the battlefield.'

'So now we can lug it around the countryside without worrying about triggering it?'

'Assuming Verbois finds a couple of volunteers to help us, yes.'

While they waited for the Belgian officer to return, Dawson started on the rest of his preparations. Verbois had found him some stout cord, a length of rope and a wooden board about three feet long and eighteen inches wide. He'd also produced a small toolkit, which included a brace and several bits of various diameters.

Dawson held the bits up against the rope and selected the one that was very slightly larger in diameter than the rope. Then he propped the wooden board against the wall and started drilling a hole in one corner of it. Once the drill bit had gone right through, he passed the end of the rope through the hole and nodded in satisfaction – it was a good, tight fit. He didn't want there to be too much play.

Then he drilled three further holes, one at each corner of the wooden board, cut the rope into two halves and threaded one part through the two holes on the long side of the board, running the rope along the underside of the wood. He repeated the operation with the second length of rope, so that he was left with a wooden tray that could be picked up by two people using the ends of the lengths of rope.

'Will that be strong enough?' Sykes asked.

'It should be, yes.'

Then Dawson placed the two sections of the demolition charge on the board and set about securing them to the wood using the cord Verbois had found for him. The result wasn't pretty, but he had to be absolutely sure neither section could fall off, because that would ruin everything. He'd laced the cord through the leather carrying handles and run it around and over the two parts of the weapon. Finally, he found a piece of canvas and wrapped that around the board over the two sections of the charge, lashing it into place with cord as well. He made a final check of the knots, making sure that each was as tight as he could possibly get it, then stepped back to survey the result.

'That should do it,' he said, and turned to Sykes. 'The next bit would be easier if you weren't on the stretcher, sir. Any chance of you hopping off it for a couple of minutes?'

'"Hopping" is the right word, Dawson. Just give me a hand, will you?'

Dawson pulled the bloodstained sheet off the stretcher and put it to one side. He bent down and helped Sykes get to his feet, the officer ensuring he took all his weight on his right leg. There were no seats anywhere in that stretch of corridor, so Sykes just leant against the wall, his left hand clutching his thigh.

'I'll be as quick as I can, sir,' Dawson said, as he bent to start work.

He laid the now empty stretcher on top of the wooden

board and secured the end of each rope to one of the handles of the stretcher, pulling it as tight as he could. The result was that the stretcher now had a kind of undercarriage, a shelf underneath it, on which the two halves of the demolition charge were secured. And that 'extra' would, Dawson was sure, be completely invisible once Sykes was back on the stretcher with the sheet draped over his body.

It was the best, and in fact the only, idea he'd been able to come up with that he felt offered them any chance of getting themselves – and the demolition charge, of course – out of Fort Eben Emael.

Verbois walked back down the corridor, two Belgian soldiers following behind him. One of them was big – almost as big as Dawson – and both were unarmed and wearing white slip-on jackets emblazoned with large red crosses at the back and front. Verbois was carrying another Red Cross jacket, which he handed to Dawson.

'These men are prepared to assist you,' he said. 'In fact, they are happy to do so, because it will get them away from here. The commanding officer has agreed to let you leave the fort, if you can. You should not really have been in here anyway, and he thinks it will be less complicated if you are not here when we are forced to surrender to the Germans.'

Verbois handed Sykes a piece of paper containing a short message and with an impressed seal at the bottom. 'He has also given you this. It is a *passe-partout*, which authorizes you and your corporal to travel everywhere in Belgium, and pass through road-blocks and check-points. I know you will already have your own documentation, but this might help.'

'Thank you,' Sykes said, glancing at the paper. 'When will you surrender?' he asked.

'Probably today. We have to obtain permission from the command at Liège before we can do so, but the reality is that we have almost no defences left. We can do nothing to defeat our attackers. It is a complete disaster,' he finished.

'I know,' Sykes said, 'and I'm sorry about that.'

'We should get moving,' Dawson said, pulling on the jacket over his battledress, where it would also help to hide the different colour of his uniform, 'before the rest of the German army arrives to bugger up our chances of getting away with this.'

Dawson and the big Belgian soldier lifted the stretcher until the canvas just cleared the two parts of the demolition charge. Then Sykes clumsily climbed back onto it and lay down. Verbois draped the bloodstained sheet over him.

'Bloody uncomfortable, this,' he muttered, as his back pressed down on the canvas and met the top of the unyielding shape of the demolition charge underneath.

'I'm sorry about that, sir,' Dawson said, and turned to Verbois. 'Can you tell the bloke at the other end that this is going to be bloody heavy?'

The Belgian officer stepped forwards and said a couple of sentences to the big soldier in French. The man nodded his understanding and glanced back at Dawson.

'OK,' the corporal said, 'let's lift it now.'

It *was* heavy, not only with Sykes's weight, but also the hundred pounds or so of dead weight of the charge underneath the stretcher. But both men were strong, and lifted it smoothly off the ground. Hopefully they'd be able to walk fairly steadily as they carried it between them.

The small procession moved down the corridor to Block One. They hadn't heard any explosions from the entrance area for a while, which might mean the Stukas were busy elsewhere. Verbois strode on ahead to check the situation.

By the time Sykes arrived on the stretcher, Verbois was standing waiting by the main door. 'There is no sign of any German troops out there, so this is a good time to go. Good luck, Major,' he said, stepping forward to shake Sykes's hand, 'and you too, Corporal Dawson.'

He stepped back and stood at attention, clicking his heels together. He delivered a crisp salute, which Sykes returned as best he could from his recumbent position.

'Good luck, *Capitaine*,' the major said softly. 'I hope you and your men survive this.'

Verbois nodded. 'Whatever happens, Major, I intend to do my duty to the best of my ability.'

He saluted again, turned away and issued a series of orders in French.

In moments, the main door had swung open. The Belgian soldier wearing a Red Cross jacket went first, waving a piece of white fabric above his head, then Dawson and the other soldier stepped through the doorway, balancing the stretcher between them. The moment they'd done so, the door slammed shut behind them, heavy bolts sliding back into place.

They were outside the fort, unarmed apart from Sykes's battered Webley revolver in his belt holster, and about to walk into the full view of the dozens of heavily armed German troops on the roof of Fort Eben Emael.

The strain was already beginning to tell on Dawson's arms as they stepped forward, following the Belgian soldier who was still waving the white flag.

The moment they heard the steel door of Block One slam shut behind them, a new sound intruded – the unearthly scream of a Stuka beginning its dive, somewhere high above them.

Immediately, they all moved back, to stand right next to the reinforced concrete wall of Block One, just inside the archway. If the bomb exploded somewhere up on the roof of the fort, they should be safe, but if the German pilot was aiming for the main entrance itself, they all probably had less than thirty seconds to live. There was nothing they could do. There was no time to get back inside, and nowhere to run to, even if they dropped the stretcher.

Leaning against the wall, Dawson looked up, searching the skies for the aircraft. Suddenly he spotted the distinctive 'W' shape created by the Stuka's bent wings. Two seconds later he realized the aircraft's position in the sky hadn't changed, though it appeared much bigger, and that meant the dive-bomber was heading straight for them.

'Oh, fuck,' he said, 'it's aiming right at us.'

'Lower the stretcher,' Sykes ordered him, then repeated the instruction in French to the Belgian soldier.

'Cover your ears,' the major said, when the stretcher was on the ground, the two solid lumps of the demolition charge digging unbearably into his back and upper thighs.

'Fat lot of fucking good that'll do,' Dawson muttered, his eyes still fixed on the oncoming aircraft. But he rammed his palms over his ears anyway, as the scream from the Stuka's siren increased to a climax.

Then he saw a black object detach from the belly of the aircraft and plummet down towards them.

'Bomb's away,' he yelled, and they all – even Sykes, despite the constraints of the stretcher – shrank even closer to the wall, trying to make themselves as small as possible.

Dawson couldn't take his eyes off the approaching weapon, which now seemed to be moving more slowly – but maybe that was just wishful thinking, or perhaps his brain trying to stretch out the last few seconds of his life.

But then it seemed to accelerate, still heading directly towards them. At the last second the bomb seemed to dip slightly, but it was too late, far too late, to miss them.

Dawson closed his eyes and waited for death.

CHAPTER 14

10 MAY 1940: EBEN EMAEL, BELGIUM

There was a massive blast right beside them, earth-shaking and totally deafening, but against all the odds Dawson realized he was still alive.

He opened his eyes cautiously and glanced around. The others were alive as well. That didn't make sense. And there was no crater.

'It hit the other side, Dawson,' Sykes said, his voice unnaturally loud. 'It hit the other side of Block One. That's what saved us.'

He was right, Dawson realized immediately. The bomb *had* been heading directly towards them, but in the last few seconds gravity had pulled it slightly off course – he thought he'd seen it dip – and that was enough for it to smash into the northern side of Block One, instead of the top of the structure. The reinforced concrete of Block One had been between them and the explosion, and had shielded them completely from the blast. Their ears would take some time to fully recover, but they were otherwise completely unhurt.

'Right,' Sykes said. 'Let's get moving before another Jerry pilot decides to try his luck.'

It was now full daylight, a bright and sunny day, and visibility was no longer a problem. Dawson would have preferred a mist, or ideally a heavy fog, to obscure them from the view of the enemy soldiers. As it was, the moment they stepped away from Block One, he was immediately aware of a prickling sensation at the back of his neck, as his imagination conjured up images of German soldiers levelling their weapons at his unprotected back.

And then, despite the ringing in his ears, he heard shouts in German, the distinctive snicking sound as a rifle bolt was slid forward to chamber a round, from somewhere above and behind him. There was nothing he could do. He had to keep walking, and just hope that the sight of the red crosses they were all wearing, the soldier waving the white flag and the injured man on the stretcher would be enough to stop the Germans from shooting them down.

No shots came, and they continued to walk steadily and without haste – they couldn't have run with the weight they were carrying, obviously – away from the fort and towards the road that led to the village of Wonck.

Dawson had no doubt they'd been spotted by the enemy soldiers, but it looked as if their deception was working – or perhaps the Germans were so busy trying to eliminate the last of the fort's weapons that they weren't bothered about three men apparently trying to get an injured comrade to safety.

The scene outside Eben Emael was of almost total devastation. The bombs dropped by the Stukas had blown massive craters in the ground. The reinforced concrete of Block One was blackened and scarred by the searing heat of the explosions, and chipped and pock-marked by flying fragments from the bombs. The barbed wire entanglements and supporting frames that had protected the entrance had been blown aside into shapeless clumps. Discarded equipment and abandoned military materials were scattered everywhere. A couple of Belgian military vehicles had been the subject of individual attacks and had been tossed aside like toys, tyres ruptured and bodywork pulverized. And at least a dozen bodies lay unmoving on the ground.

'God help us,' Dawson muttered, more an expletive than a prayer, as they started finding a route across the shattered ground and away from the doomed fort.

They covered fifty yards, seventy, eighty, a hundred. Dawson started to breathe more easily. Their route took them behind a low hill that offered at least some measure of protection from the guns of the German soldiers on the fort. From behind them came the almost continuous sound of the bombardment of Eben Emael, the crump of high-explosive detonations of bombs and demolition charges drowning out the sound of rifle and machine-gun fire.

They started to see isolated groups of Belgian soldiers along the track, almost all of them unarmed and many of them looking shell-shocked – not entirely surprising if they'd been on the receiving end of a Stuka dive-bomb attack. Dawson and Sykes now knew exactly what that felt like. They had to pick their way carefully around the craters and debris and bodies – and even body parts – which littered the area. They passed close to several of the corpses, the bodies mangled and torn, their uniforms ripped and sodden with blood and flesh, some of them with limbs blown off, flies already gathering for the feast.

They walked on, the weight of the stretcher seeming to increase with every step, but every step was also taking them closer to safety. Safety of a temporary kind, no doubt, but at least they were getting closer to the limit of the range of the Germans' Mauser rifles.

When Dawson thought they were almost out of sight of the fort, he knew they had to take a break, and he knew exactly where. If they carried on walking, there was a real danger they'd drop the stretcher, and he couldn't allow that to happen.

'We've got to take a rest, sir,' he said. 'Can you tell this Belgie to stop? I'll have to put you on the ground for a few minutes or my fucking arms are going to drop off.'

Sykes nodded and spoke for a few moments in French. Immediately, the big Belgian soldier slowed his pace and then came to a stop.

Dawson gratefully lowered the stretcher far enough for Major Sykes to climb off it, with the assistance of the other soldier, then lowered it the rest of the way. As Sykes hobbled to one side and leant against a tree, Dawson stood up straight and stretched his aching back.

'Just a minute or two,' he said. 'That's all I need.'

Then he looked down at the major. 'Could you ask this Belgie to go and collect my rifle, sir? It's hidden near those two trees over there.'

Sykes glanced in the direction the corporal was pointing, nodded and then spoke to the Belgian soldier who'd preceded the stretcher party. The man nodded, tossed away the white cloth and then ran off towards a patch of undergrowth close to two spindly trees, and started rooting around there.

A minute or so later the Belgian soldier returned, holding a rifle in his hands.

Dawson nodded his thanks, took the weapon from him and checked it over. 'I feel happier having it back,' he said, 'with all these Jerries about.' Then he handed it to Sykes to stash under the sheet on the stretcher.

'You signed for it, just like you signed for everything else you've ever been issued in the army. You have no idea how many forms you'll have to fill in if you don't take it back with you. Now say "thank you" to the nice Belgian. That's *merci* in French.'

Coming out of Dawson's mouth, it sounded more like 'mercy', but the Belgian nodded and smiled at him.

Sykes said something else to the man in French, and he walked away to join a group of his comrades, who had watched the arrival of the short procession from the opposite side of the road.

'There's no point in him being with us now,' Sykes said. 'I think we're out of immediate danger. How far do you think we've covered?'

Dawson looked back along the track they'd been following. He could still see the northern, the most distant, section of the fort, but the southern part was now hidden from view.

'I don't know,' he said. 'Maybe six or seven hundred yards, something like that. But the Jerries can't see us now, I reckon, so that's good news.'

'We were lucky,' Sykes said. 'I looked back towards the fort, and a couple of the German soldiers spotted us almost as soon as we walked away from Block One. One of them even aimed his rifle at us, but another man – I think he was a corporal – ordered him to lower his weapon. If that NCO hadn't been there at that moment, we might all be dead right now.'

'You didn't say anything at the time,' Dawson said.

'Of course not. There was absolutely nothing you – or any of us – could have done. At that range we were sitting ducks. Anyway, just be thankful we got out without any problems. We've still got a hell of a long way to go. And if your arms have recovered, we should start now.'

Dawson nodded and bent down to seize the handles of the stretcher.

The big Belgian soldier, who hadn't spoken a word to them – in any language – since they'd left the fort, turned to Dawson and gave him a thumbs-up and a big grin, then grasped the other end of the stretcher and waited for Sykes to settle back onto it

They walked on for about another three or four hundred yards, then again moved over to the side of the road. Again, they lowered the stretcher and waited while Sykes clumsily climbed off it, then placed it on the ground.

'Right,' Sykes said, when the stretcher came to rest on the ground. 'Two things. First, we're well clear of Eben Emael now, so I think this is as far as we need to go with this stretcher. Second, Dawson, it's time the mountain came to Mohammed, rather than the other way around.'

'Sir?'

'The car, Dawson, the car. Instead of us walking to the car, why don't you walk to the car and bring it here? You've still got the rotor arm, I hope? And you do remember where we left it?'

Dawson grinned. 'That's why you're an officer, sir, and I'm not,' he said. 'You'll be OK here for a few minutes?'

Sykes nodded. 'I have my very battered Webley revolver to keep the German hordes at bay.'

'And you won't let the big Belgie slope off, just in case the car's been stolen or the Jerries have dropped a bomb on it or something, and we have to leg it?'

'Of course not. Take your Lee-Enfield, just in case you run into any trouble. Don't hang around, Dawson. We really do need to get out of here.'

Dawson removed the Red Cross vest – carrying a rifle while wearing that didn't seem to be a good idea – took the weapon and slung it on his shoulder. He paused for a few seconds, getting his bearings and trying to identify the hill from which they'd watched the German attack on the fort, what seemed like days, rather than just hours, ago. Then he set off confidently enough.

The hill was a fairly distinctive landmark in the generally level terrain, and was only about three hundred yards away. He covered the ground in a few minutes, and walked around the side of the hill to where Sykes had told him to park the staff car.

The good news was that the small car – it was a Hillman, painted in two shades of camouflage green – was exactly where they'd left it. The not so good news was that it was surrounded by about half a dozen Belgian soldiers. One of them was actually in the driver's seat, while another was poking about under the bonnet. They were trying to steal it, which Dawson didn't blame them for. But they weren't going to be successful. He would see to that.

He unslung the Lee-Enfield from his shoulder, checked it was loaded with the safety catch on, and walked towards the group of soldiers. None of them spotted him until he was about twenty yards away.

He stopped where he was, the rifle in his hands pointing slightly over to the left, not at any member of the group – the Belgians were, after all, supposed to be on the same side as the British – but close enough that he would be able to swing the muzzle around in an instant.

'My car,' Dawson said loudly, pointing at the staff car with his right hand and then making a kind of shooing gesture before gripping the stock of the rifle again. 'You go away, now.'

He had no idea whether any of the men in front of him spoke English, so he did what the British have always done when they've found themselves in foreign fields – he spoke simple sentences in a near-shout, as if the volume alone would somehow penetrate their non-English brains and allow them to grasp the meaning of his words.

The Belgian troops turned to face him, moving away from the car, but the man in the driver's seat stayed where he was. There were five soldiers, Dawson now realized, and two of them had Mauser rifles on their shoulders. The other three appeared to be unarmed.

'Go away. Hop it,' Dawson shouted, watching the two armed soldiers very carefully, but neither showed any inclination to unsling his rifle.

He very deliberately clicked the safety catch of his Lee-Enfield into the 'off' position, readying the weapon to fire, making sure the Belgians saw what he was doing.

That seemed almost to act as a catalyst, and the four soldiers standing outside the car began to walk slowly away.

Dawson watched them as they moved off, making sure the two Mausers stayed in view and on the shoulders of the soldiers carrying them, then walked forwards to the car when he was certain they were no threat.

The fifth soldier was still sitting in the driver's seat, one hand holding the steering wheel, watching Dawson as he approached.

'You. Out,' Dawson snapped, keeping his commands simple. He stopped beside the car door.

The Belgian grinned at him. 'This your car,' he said, in workable English, 'but now I think my car.' He produced a black semi-automatic pistol from his lap and pointed it straight at Dawson.

Dawson glanced to his right to see that the other four soldiers had stopped about fifty or sixty yards away and were watching expectantly.

In his past, Dawson had been involved in various brawls – he had worked in a tough industry as a quarry and mining engineer, and fights were not uncommon – and the one thing he'd learnt was that if you *were* going to fight, you didn't talk about it, you just got on with it.

'Right,' he said and, with a casual grace that belied his size, he changed his grip on the Lee-Enfield and swung it, butt-first, towards the Belgian soldier sitting in the car.

The man saw what was happening, but he couldn't duck because of the seat. He tried to twist away, but it did him no good. The steel plate on the butt of the rifle caught him on the side of the head and he flopped forwards onto the steering wheel, unconscious, the pistol tumbling from his grasp.

Dawson leant the rifle against the side of the car, opened the door and dragged out the unconscious man, dropping him on the ground a few feet away. He glanced over towards the other Belgian soldiers, but they had already drifted away.

He checked nothing had been tampered with in the engine compartment, and pulled the rotor arm out of one of his pouches. Military vehicles of the time didn't usually have keys, the ignition being turned on with a simple switch on the dashboard, and Dawson had removed the rotor arm from the distributor to prevent the vehicle being driven away. He'd also changed the order of the plug leads as a further precaution. He replaced the rotor arm, connected the leads correctly, then closed the bonnet and started the vehicle.

He drove away, his Lee-Enfield, the safety catch now back on, resting on the passenger seat beside him. The Belgian's pistol – according to the markings on the side it was a FN1910 – was tucked away inside his battle-dress. Having an extra weapon wasn't a bad idea, bearing in mind where they were and what was happening around them.

CHAPTER 15

10 MAY 1940: EASTERN BELGIUM

'You took your time,' Sykes complained, when Dawson finally drew the staff car to a stop beside the stretcher, switched off the engine and climbed out.

'It was a bit further away than I thought, and I had to explain the facts of life to a bunch of Belgians trying to nick it.'

'You didn't kill them, I hope.'

Dawson shook his head. 'No. One of them is probably still asleep. He'll have a blinder of a headache when he wakes up, but that's all.'

Assisted by the Belgian soldier, he helped Sykes stand up. Between them, they half-carried him to the passenger side of the staff car and settled him into the seat. The major would be sitting on his injured thigh, but there wasn't anything they could do about that. The staff car had seats for four people but only two doors, and getting onto the bench seat at the back was awkward for somebody fully mobile. Manoeuvring Sykes onto it would have been difficult, and getting him out worse, because of his injury, and the front seat seemed to both of them to be a far better option.

The major settled back in the seat with a sigh – it was a lot more comfortable in the car than the stretcher had been – and Dawson draped the sheet over his legs and closed the door. Sykes's trousers had been cut off him by the medical staff at Fort Eben Emael, and he was wearing a pair of Belgian officer's trousers that were a very poor fit, being much too big. Both of them had clothes in their kitbags locked in the boot of the staff car, but changing was a very low priority.

Sykes motioned for the Belgian soldier to approach him, and spoke to the man for a minute or so in French. The soldier shook his hand, and then Dawson's, removed the jacket with the red cross on it and walked away.

Meanwhile, Dawson had swiftly sliced through the knots in the ropes holding his makeshift shelf in place under the wood and canvas stretcher. He lifted up the stretcher, folded it and slid it onto the rear seat of the staff car, because there was a possibility they would need it again. He cut off the cords that had secured the demolition charge to the plank of wood and put both sections of the weapon in the boot of the car, along with the fuse assembly.

They were ready to go.

'Where to, sir?' Dawson asked.

'Anywhere away from here,' Sykes muttered. His face was white with strain and beads of sweat had appeared on his forehead. 'Just get moving. Head west, or south-west, obviously.'

Dawson guessed that the effects of the morphine were starting to wear off, and that Sykes was beginning to feel the pain from his leg. But there was nothing he could do about that, so he started the engine, slipped the car into gear and drove away, trying to pick the smoothest path he could find along the rutted and potholed track, putting some distance between themselves and Fort Eben Emael.

'One thing puzzles me about that fort,' Dawson said. 'The Jerry plan is clever, very clever, the way they attacked from an unexpected direction and these new demolition charges to take out the defences. But there is still a garrison of – well, I don't know exactly – but maybe six or seven hundred men inside Eben Emael, and there are only about sixty or seventy Germans in the attacking force. They're probably outnumbered about ten to one, and in a straight fight the Belgians should beat them. Adolf must know that, so where are their reinforcements?'

'Good point, Dawson,' Sykes said, with a weak smile. 'While we were wandering about on the roof I heard a few heavy explosions from both the north and south of the fort, and at least one of the Belgian heavy weapons kept on firing at some distant targets, not at the German attackers.'

'You think they have blown up some of the bridges, then?'

'Probably, yes. Even if the Jerries use the same technique – landing the attacking force by glider near their targets – there's a good chance the Belgians destroyed the bridges over the Albert Canal, either by triggering explosives wired to the bridges or with the barrage from the Eben Emeal guns. And if they have, that will have stopped – or at least severely delayed – the German land forces from getting here. Don't forget, Eben Emael isn't the only defensive fort in this area. It's the biggest and best-armed, but it's just one of a whole series, all designed to repel an invading army and to destroy various strategic objectives, like the bridges. I doubt if the Jerries have taken out all of the forts as easily as this one.'

'So you think the German reinforcements are quite close, just on the other side of the canal or the river?'

'Yes. And they probably expected some or all of the bridges to have been destroyed, so they'll have engineers and equipment with them to build pontoon bridges. They'll be all over this area some time today, Dawson, you mark my words.'

Sykes lapsed into silence, then produced a map of Belgium and began studying it, probably as much to take his mind off the pain in his thigh as for any other reason. Where they would be able to drive depended on which roads were open. And that, in turn, depended almost entirely on how fast the German land forces were able to advance across Belgium, once they'd managed to pass the barriers of the Meuse River and the Albert Canal.

'We need to link up with our own people as quickly as possible,' Sykes said, 'so the best direction to head is probably west, towards Brussels, and then turn south-west for the French border. Chances are the Germans have opened up a broad front, so everywhere from Liège to Maastricht is probably under attack by now. If we can get close to Brussels fairly quickly, we might be able to keep ahead of the Jerry advance. Once we're behind our own lines, we can cross into France and head for the Channel ports to find a boat to take this weapon back to England.'

The track turned into a narrow metalled road, a road

now choked by Belgian soldiers marching determinedly towards Fort Eben Emael. Dawson had to slow right down as he threaded his way through them. Sykes kept Dawson's Lee-Enfield clearly visible beside him, as a silent but potent threat against interference or delay. But the troops obviously recognized the staff car as an official army vehicle – not their army, but army nevertheless – carrying a senior officer and his driver, and parted easily enough to let them through. In fact, the uniform of a Belgian officer wasn't that dissimilar to the British version, so some of the soldiers probably didn't even realize that Sykes wasn't a Belgian officer.

A couple of times they had to stop and Sykes produced the *passe-partout* to show to Belgian officers, and in each case they were quickly waved through.

The troops they were seeing appeared to be of a very different calibre to the men they'd seen at and around the fort – they knew that many of the Belgian static defences were manned by second- or third-rate troops – but Sykes appeared unimpressed.

'They look tough enough to me, sir,' Dawson said.

'They probably are, but being tough isn't enough, because they just don't have the equipment to take on the Germans. Most of the Belgian air force is still flying around in obsolete biplanes, useless against the modern Messerschmitts and Stukas the Jerries have. And their armour is just pathetic. Last I heard, they only had ten tanks altogether – the Germans probably have almost a thousand, so they're outnumbered about a hundred to one.'

'They've only got ten tanks?' Dawson was incredulous.

136

'Something like that, yes. A political decision. Apparently the Belgian government believes a tank is an offensive weapon, and as Belgium is always neutral, they decided having tanks would send the wrong message to their neighbours. A typically idiotic decision made by some politician who has absolutely no idea what he's talking about. Anyway, in a straight fight, the Jerries will walk all over them. The only chance is if the Belgians can hold the Germans at a strong defensive line. If the Eben Emael fiasco is anything to go by, that's a pretty vain hope.'

'Do they have another line, then?'

Sykes nodded. 'Yes. Their primary defensive line was the one we've just left, along the Albert Canal and Meuse River, but that was never intended to actually stop a German advance, only slow it down for long enough for British and French forces to advance as far as a line running between Antwerp and Namur, and then on down to Givet in France. That's why we're trying to head west, so hopefully we can meet up with the advancing British troops.

'The idea is that the Belgians should hold that eastern line for at least three days, to allow Allied troops to get into position. Then the Belgians will withdraw ahead of the Germans and stop their advance. It's called the Dyle Plan, but it doesn't look to me as if there's much chance of it working now. Don't get me wrong – there's nothing wrong with the Belgians as fighting men. They're tough and brave fighters, but they just don't have anything like the level of equipment they need to tackle Adolf's hordes. I'm not even sure we have, either.'

'You don't think either the British or French forces

will be in position by the time we get to Brussels, if we make it that far?'

'Hopefully we'll be a bit further south than that, much closer to Namur. But you're right, Dawson. I don't think any of our troops will have reached that area by the time we get there.'

It took them almost twenty minutes to reach the village of Eben Emael itself, just because of the numbers of soldiers on the road. Dawson swung the car left at the T-junction in the centre, turning south, and pulled the car to a stop beside the road. To continue heading west, they would have had to leave the better road they were now on and take to an unmade track again, and after consulting the map for a few moments Sykes vetoed that idea.

'I know it's really going the wrong way,' he said, 'but I think we should stay on this road and go south, to Wonck. The road swings over to the south-west before it reaches the village, and then heads west for quite some way. When we reach Boirs we can reassess the situation. There's a main road there, and a crossroads, so we can either head south on the main road or continue to the west if that looks like it's still the safer option.'

Dawson obediently pulled the car back onto the road and continued through the village, towards Wonck.

There were fewer soldiers on the road. Most of the people they passed were civilians who were heading in the same direction as the staff car – away from the fighting. They all carried bags; some pushed bicycles so festooned with bags and boxes that riding them was clearly impossible, others pulled wooden hand-carts piled high with their possessions. These were the people who really suffer in any armed conflict – the innocent civilians who lose everything, including their lives, as armies battle for supremacy around them.

'Obviously news of what's happened at Eben Emael has spread,' Sykes commented, as they drove past one long line of civilian refugees, their faces reflecting both fear and resignation. 'The trouble is, once the German troops get across the river and the canal, they'll probably launch another of their *Blitzkrieg* attacks, and leap-frog their way across Belgium, and these poor sods will find themselves behind enemy lines. They'll have nowhere to run or hide.'

It was early afternoon as Dawson drove through the village of Wonck. He swung the staff car right at the T-junction, retracing the route he himself had followed when he'd first arrived in the area. The road turned almost due north, but in a few yards bent sharply to the left, to the west. About a mile and a half in front of them was the village of Boirs, where they'd have to make a decision about the next part of their route.

And there was something else they needed to do, as well.

'We're pretty low on petrol, sir,' Dawson said, tapping the fuel gauge on the dashboard in front of him. 'We're down to under half a tank, and the two cans in the boot are empty.'

He hadn't seen any fuel pumps in either Eben Emael or Wonck, and Boirs was a lot smaller place than either of them.

'Can we make it as far as Brussels?' Sykes asked. 'It's about fifty miles or so.'

Dawson shook his head. 'I doubt it,' he said.

Sykes turned his attention back to the map, then glanced across at Dawson.

'Right,' he said, 'I don't like it because we don't know what the tactical situation is, but we'll have to drive down to the south, to Liège, and see if we can find a petrol pump somewhere there.'

'Or maybe an abandoned car,' Dawson suggested. 'I've got a length of hose I can use.'

'At a pinch, yes,' Sykes agreed.

At Boirs there was no need for any further discussion. Dawson turned the car left, and they started driving south, towards Liège.

Ahead of them, the signs were ominous. Clouds of smoke were rising from several different locations in the city, though it wasn't clear whether these were the result of bombing or artillery attacks by the Germans, or ground assault by armour or infantry. The latter would have been bad news, because it could mean that there were already enemy troops on the streets of Liège. That was the last thing they wanted.

And equally disturbing was the stream of refugees heading straight for them, intent on getting out of the city. That slowed their progress enormously, because the refugees blocked almost the entire width of the road with bicycles and carts and anything else that could be pressed into service to carry their most precious possessions. And it wasn't just civilians. Various groups of soldiers were also walking westwards away from Liège.

'Are they all deserting?' Dawson asked.

'No. The Dyle Plan recognizes that the Belgians won't be able to hold on in this area, and there's supposed to be a controlled withdrawal to the next defensive line, so that's probably what's happening.'

On the outskirts of Liège, Sykes spotted two soldiers walking along the road among the crowds of civilians, and ordered Dawson to stop the car beside them.

Recognizing Sykes as an officer, both men gave shaky salutes, and responded somewhat hesitantly to the major's stream of questions, in French. After a couple of minutes, Sykes waved for them to continue on their way, Dawson slipped the car back into gear and moved off again.

'It's not good news,' the major announced, 'but perhaps not as bad as it could be. The German troops have reached the east side of the city, which is what I'd expected. The Belgian soldiers have been ordered to pull back to the west. But some of the bridges across the river in Liège have been destroyed, so the Germans are making slow progress in getting across to this side. The other bit of bad news is that there's a major evacuation going on – according to those two soldiers most of the population of Liège is heading this way – so I doubt if we'll be able to find a working petrol pump anywhere. So you probably *will* have to steal some fuel from a car. I don't like doing that, but we haven't got any option.'

They entered the outskirts of Liège, which seemed strangely empty. They saw a few civilians heading away from the centre, towards the west, but the streets weren't as crowded as they'd expected. Tram lines ran down the main roads, and a couple of times Dawson had to swerve the staff car around abandoned tramcars, just left in the street.

'Maybe they left them because the power was cut,' Sykes suggested.

They also saw a few carts and a handful of dead horses, but no sign of a petrol station or a car they could get some fuel from. Before they'd got too close to the centre of the city, Dawson left the main road and started working his way slowly through the back streets.

'That might do us,' he said, pointing ahead down a deserted street at a small car that had obviously crashed into a wall and was parked drunkenly, half on and half off, the pavement.

'Good. Stop where we've got good visibility,' Sykes said, checking the Lee-Enfield rifle. 'I'll keep watch.'

Dawson stopped the staff car a few feet from the wreck, walked across to it and unscrewed the petrol filler cap. Then he took the two petrol cans and a short length of hose out of the boot of the staff car, and knelt down beside the other vehicle. He thrust the hose into the fuel tank, blew down it as he listened for the sound of bubbling, which confirmed that there was fuel in the tank, then started sucking. He got a mouthful of petrol as he wasn't quick enough getting the end of the hose into one of the cans, but spat it out and started filling the can.

'Wouldn't have a cigarette for a while, Dawson,' Sykes called, a smile on his face.

'Lucky I don't smoke,' Dawson said, spitting again.

In about five minutes he'd filled both the cans, and lifted up the hose to stop the siphon effect. He emptied the contents of both cans into the staff car's fuel tank, then returned and sucked the tank dry, which gave him another couple of gallons in reserve.

'Good work, Dawson,' Sykes said, as the corporal

resumed his place behind the wheel of the car. 'That'll get us up to Brussels, no problem. Time we had a bit of luck.'

Then they heard a yell from behind them, a challenge shouted in German, and both swung round to look.

Less than a hundred yards or so behind them, a three-man German patrol – an NCO and a couple of soldiers – had just walked around the corner from the main road. The two soldiers were aiming their rifles straight at the staff car.

Sykes's remark about 'a bit of luck' had been somewhat premature.

CHAPTER 16

10 MAY 1940: LIÈGE, BELGIUM

Dawson rammed the gear lever into first and twisted the steering wheel to the left as he did so. The car lurched away from the kerb, bucking as the rear tyres scrabbled for grip, the engine roaring as it laboured to get the vehicle moving.

There was a bang from behind them, and one corner of the windscreen suddenly cracked as a bullet speared through it.

A second shot echoed, and then another. The sudden movement of the vehicle ensured both the German soldiers' bullets missed their targets, smashing into the wall of the house right beside the staff car. But Dawson and Sykes knew they'd be reloading and aiming immediately.

Sykes still had the Lee-Enfield rifle lying across his lap, but the injury to his leg meant he couldn't easily twist around in his seat and aim the weapon properly. So he did the next best thing. He slipped off the safety catch, pointed the rifle back over his shoulder and squeezed the trigger. The recoil kicked the weapon backwards in his hands. He had no idea where the shot ended up, and he didn't care. Firing the rifle just showed the

Germans their target was capable of fighting back, that was all. Getting them away from the patrol wasn't about fighting their way out – they had to make a run for it, and that was down to Dawson.

'Quickly, man,' Sykes ordered, working the bolt to reload the Lee-Enfield. The spent cartridge case spun out of the breech and flew through the air to land with a clatter on the floor beside his feet.

Dawson didn't reply, just concentrated on getting the staff car moving as fast as he could. The road had no turnings for about another 200 yards, but there was a large and very battered lorry parked some seventy yards ahead, on the left-hand side of the road. If he could just get their vehicle on to the far side of that, Dawson knew it would offer them some protection. At the very least, the German soldiers would have to cross to the opposite side of the road to continue firing at them.

Another well-aimed bullet smashed through the windscreen, right between the two men, and another hit somewhere at the back of the staff car, the thud of its impact clearly audible.

Dawson immediately swerved to the right to try to make the car as difficult a target as he could, then dodged back to the left again.

'Get us behind that lorry,' Sykes ordered, pointing ahead at the parked vehicle.

'I'm trying to,' Dawson snapped, wrestling with the steering wheel and changing up a gear.

He swung the car right again, weaving from side to side as much as the fairly narrow street allowed. Then he reached the parked lorry and immediately steered the car behind it, then braked hard.

145

'What the hell are you doing?' Sykes demanded. 'Get us out of here.'

'If we carry on down this street, we'll never make it. Those Jerries are too good shots. Give me the rifle.'

'You'd better know what you're doing,' Sykes muttered, handing over the weapon.

Dawson grabbed the Lee-Enfield and ran back towards the parked lorry, then dropped flat on the road so that he could see underneath the vehicle. He wound the sling of the rifle around his left arm, positioned his elbows in the familiar tripod position to hold the weapon as steady as possible, then looked at the approaching soldiers.

At the far end of the street, the three German soldiers were moving, running up the pavement directly towards him. Two of them were carrying Mauser rifles, and the NCO – he looked like a sergeant – had a Schmeisser MP 38 in his hands. The machine-gun didn't worry Dawson, because it was a very short-range weapon even in expert hands, but the Mausers did.

He checked his Lee-Enfield to ensure Sykes had chambered another round and that the safety catch was off, then took careful aim, settling his breathing. The leading soldier was heading straight at him, jogging in a straight line with barely any sideways motion at all – an easy target.

Dawson held his breath, looked over the sights at the German soldier, alert for any deviation in his approach, adjusted his point of aim for the centre of the man's torso, and squeezed the trigger.

The German seemed to stumble, his momentum carrying him forwards, but Dawson already knew his shot had been good. The rifle fell from the man's hands, and then he pitched onto his face and lay still.

Not for the first time Dawson wondered about the casual ease with which he seemed able to take another man's life. Aim the weapon, pull the trigger, and another life ended. The first time he'd killed another human being, back in the Warndt Forest, he'd been hopelessly outgunned, fighting for his life with whatever weapons he could find. Since then, he genuinely couldn't remember the number of times he'd seen an enemy soldier tumble to the ground in front of him, knowing he was the man's executioner.

And he was still fighting for his life, fully aware that if he didn't kill these enemy soldiers, they would most assuredly kill him, without a second thought. Dawson concentrated, forcing his attention back to the task in hand. One man was down, but there were still two to go. He worked the bolt, chambered another round and settled down to aim again.

The second soldier stopped, looked towards his fallen comrade for a bare second, then he himself dodged to the side, flattening himself against one of the houses, where an alleyway or door offered some protection. The NCO ran across to the opposite side of the street and did the same.

Dawson knew they'd be trying to work out where the shot had come from, but he also knew it wouldn't take them long to realize where he had to be.

He checked his sight picture again. The soldier carrying the Mauser was still visible, or at least a part of him was. Dawson could see the man's right shoulder and arm, and a part of his face, but with only the iron sights on the Lee-Enfield he wasn't certain he could hit him. Then he saw the soldier bring the Mauser up to the aim, and immediately rolled sideways, over to his right, into the gutter, a move that brought him directly behind one of the wheels of the parked lorry.

Before he'd even stopped moving, the soldier fired. The round from the Mauser blasted splinters of stone off one of the cobbles where Dawson had been lying just a second before. At almost the same moment, the German NCO opened up with the Schmeisser, the bullets thudding into the bodywork of the parked lorry, some ricocheting off the road beneath it.

They obviously knew exactly where he was.

Dawson flattened himself as much as he could, turning his face towards the road so that the top of his steel helmet pointed in the direction of the bullets. That wouldn't stop a direct hit from blowing his head apart, but it made him feel better.

The rattle of the Schmeisser stopped abruptly. Maybe the NCO was out of ammunition, or perhaps the weapon had jammed – the MP 38 wasn't the most reliable of sub-machine-guns.

Dawson moved forward a couple of feet, and even further over to the right, pointing his Lee-Enfield around the wheel of the parked lorry, searching for a target.

The German soldier was working the bolt of his Mauser again – presumably he'd fired another round but Dawson hadn't heard the sound of the shot over the noise of the Schmeisser's bursts of fire. Before the soldier could bring his rifle back to the aim, Dawson snapped off a shot that missed its target, but only just. He saw chips of stone scatter from just in front of the

German's face as the bullet ploughed into the bricks of the house. The man flinched and ducked back.

Dawson reloaded, eased back slightly and swung his rifle round to aim it at the alleyway on the opposite side of the road where the NCO had taken refuge, but the sergeant was completely invisible. There was no point wasting a round, and the enemy soldier he was most worried about was the man with the Mauser – the rifle was far more dangerous to them than the machine-gun – so Dawson turned back to target the remaining soldier again.

As he did so, another burst of fire echoed off the surrounding houses as the NCO fired his MP 38 again. One of the nine-millimetre bullets ripped through the back tyre on the offside of the lorry, and it blew with a bang that was surprisingly loud. The vehicle crashed down onto the rim of the wheel.

Dawson cursed, the sudden lurch of the lorry startling him more than the firing of the enemy soldiers, then aimed his rifle again. The German soldier had crouched down, the better to fire his weapon under the lorry, and in doing so he'd moved slightly out of the doorway. That gave Dawson the chance he needed. He adjusted his aim and squeezed the trigger, at the same instant as the German fired at him.

The bullet from the Mauser tore into the tyre directly in front of Dawson's face. The carcase ruptured with a massive bang, lumps of tread scattering in all directions, a couple of pieces hitting Dawson in the face, one opening up a cut on his left cheek. But the tyre and wheel had stopped the bullet.

Further up the street, the German soldier screamed

in pain and tumbled backwards, dropping his Mauser and clutching at his right shoulder.

Dawson scrambled to his feet and ran back down the road. He reached the staff car, handed his Lee-Enfield to Major Sykes and dropped into the driver's seat.

About a hundred yards behind them, the German NCO stepped out of cover and opened up with his Schmeisser MP 38. But the range was too great for accurate fire from the machine-gun – it was essentially a very short-range weapon, intended for close combat.

'You missed one,' Sykes muttered, as nine-millimetre bullets screamed past them.

'Bastard,' Dawson snapped, got out of the car, grabbed back the rifle and aimed it down the road.

The NCO was now clearly visible, his dark uniform silhouetting him against the lighter-coloured brickwork of the houses behind him. Dawson aimed his rifle and squeezed the trigger. But at the moment he fired, the German stepped back into cover, and Dawson's bullet smashed harmlessly into the wall of the adjacent house.

Dawson passed the rifle back to Sykes and sat down again. The engine of the staff car was still running, so he rammed the gear lever into first and pulled away from the kerb. Before they'd covered fifty yards, the NCO fired another short burst from his Schmeisser, but none of the bullets even came close to them.

At the first junction, Dawson swung the wheel to the right and accelerated. Then he immediately hit the brakes.

There was another German patrol right in front of them.

CHAPTER 17

10 MAY 1940: LIÈGE, BELGIUM

'Shit,' Dawson muttered.

Perhaps 200 yards in front, about half a dozen German soldiers were walking towards them, spread across the entire width of the road, weapons held ready.

'Get back, get back,' Sykes ordered, raising the Lee-Enfield in readiness. 'We can't tangle with them. They'll cut us to pieces before we got anywhere near them.'

'You got that right,' Dawson said, swinging the car across the road to turn it round. The road was too narrow to allow him to achieve this in a single manoeuvre, and as the front wheels hit the opposite kerb he engaged reverse and backed the car.

But the German soldiers had obviously seen what he was doing, and had also realized the car was an enemy vehicle. As Dawson again put the gearbox into first, an opening salvo of rifle shots echoed from behind them.

'Get down!' he shouted.

Sykes slid forward in his seat, ducking his head below the level of the sides of the staff car, though how much protection the thin metal of the vehicle would offer him was a matter of opinion.

Two rounds hit somewhere at the back of the car, and another ploughed explosively through the right-hand side headlamp, deforming the metal and shattering the glass.

Dawson weaved the car from side to side, keeping the movement as erratic as he could within the confines of the fairly narrow street. More shots sounded, almost a volley, and, despite his evasive action, Dawson both heard and felt two or three more bullets hit the staff car.

'I think that fucking demolition charge might be acting like a bullet-proof shield,' he said.

Sykes stared at him. 'Could they make it explode?' he demanded.

Dawson swerved the car again, then shook his head. 'Nope. Dynamite and gelignite are really stable, until they're fused. You can hit them with a hammer and noth-ing'll happen. Nitro's a different matter.'

'Yes, but what about the other bit – the lower section. Maybe that contains some kind of new explosive?'

They reached the end of the road and Dawson cut the corner, driving the car over to the right, away from the remaining member of the first German patrol they'd encountered. No shots followed them as he accelerated away. He glanced in the rear-view mirror, and then grinned at Sykes.

'I hadn't thought of that,' he admitted. 'If it *is* filled with something unstable and one of those bullets cooks it off, we'll be the first to know about it. My guess is it doesn't contain any kind of explosive. I still think the upper section is a shaped charge, and the lower part is something completely different, something to concen-trate and direct the explosion. And that's the clever bit.'

'And that's why we *have* to get out of here, Dawson. We must get that weapon back to our own lines.'

'I'm doing my best.'

They were rapidly approaching the T-junction at the end of the road.

'Left or right?' Dawson asked.

'Go right,' Sykes instructed. 'That should take us either west or north-west.'

Dawson stopped the car at the junction and checked both ways. There were several groups of civilians on the road, mostly heading away from the centre of the city, but he couldn't see any German army patrols in either direction. He swung the wheel to the right and started weaving his way through the pedestrians.

'I reckon we might be clear now,' he said, staring ahead.

'You're optimistic, Dawson,' Sykes replied, looking around the next bend.

Just coming into view was a long queue of refugees and, right at the far end, perhaps a couple of hundred yards ahead, they could now see a group of soldiers wearing grey uniforms.

'A German road-block,' Sykes said. 'We've no chance of getting through that. Take the next turning.'

'Left or right?'

'It doesn't matter. Just get us off this road before they spot us.'

There was a turning a short distance ahead, on the right-hand side of the main road. Dawson waited for a gap in the stream of dull-eyed refugees plodding along beside them, and swung the staff car down the side-street, picking up speed quickly. They were still stuck in the outskirts of Liège and, Dawson guessed, more and more enemy soldiers would be deployed there as the hours passed. They needed to get out, to get ahead of the advancing Germans.

'We still need to get out of here,' Sykes said, his words echoing Dawson's thoughts. 'Start heading west as soon as you can.'

The street appeared to be deserted, the doors of most of the houses standing wide open, presumably abandoned by their owners as the German attack on the city started, and all the Belgians they'd seen had been on the roads heading away from Liège.

There was a crossroads a few dozen yards in front of them, but Dawson didn't drive the car around the corner, just in case there was a road-block on it. Instead, he braked to a halt about thirty yards back, hopped out and ran to the last house on that side of the street. He peered cautiously up the road, to the west, then drew back and returned to the staff car.

'More Jerries,' he said shortly. 'They've blocked the road about seventy yards ahead.' He pointed at the crossroads. 'We'll have to go straight over and try our luck further on.'

He slipped the car into gear and accelerated straight over the junction.

The staff car took only a few seconds to cross the road, but that was long enough for one of the German soldiers at the road-block to shout something, and for two of them to aim and fire their rifles, taking snap-shots at the vehicle.

Neither bullet hit the car, but the fact the Germans had opened fire immediately told its own story.

'These aren't just routine road-blocks, are they?' Dawson asked. 'Those buggers are looking for us.'

'You could be right,' Sykes agreed. 'We did a lot of damage to that Jerry patrol, and we were spotted by those other soldiers. They don't know who we are, obviously, but they're looking for two enemy soldiers in a British staff car. They're not interested in taking us prisoner or asking us questions – they're just shooting.'

'Is it worth trying another road out of the city?'

'I don't think so. The Germans have blocked the last two roads we tried. They'll have positioned patrols on every route out of the city. I think we're stuck inside the perimeter. It looks like we were very lucky – or rather unlucky – to get into Liège in the first place.'

Dawson eased off on the accelerator pedal and the vehicle started to slow down. 'If you're right, sir, then we've got to go to ground somewhere until the search winds down.'

'Only one problem, Dawson. We're dealing with Germans here, and one thing I do know about the Teutonic mind is that they're very thorough. Once they start something, they carry right on to the end. The search won't wind down, as you put it, until either they've found us or a counter-attack has driven them back across the border. I don't think that's likely.'

'So what can we do?'

'We have no choice. We'll ditch the car and get out of here some other way.'

'How?' Dawson asked simply.

'I'm working on it,' Sykes replied, 'but we'll have to get rid of our uniforms and weapons as well as the car. Somehow, we have to become Belgian civilians to get past those road-blocks. Maybe we can find a cart or something I can ride in.'

Dawson glanced at the officer unhappily, and shook his head. 'What about the rules of combat—' he began.

'I know what you're going to say, Dawson,' Sykes interrupted, 'but we've got no choice in this case. We *have* to get that demolition charge into Allied hands, and the only way we can do that is to become civilians. It's a fine line anyway – if a soldier is engaged in combat he is required to wear a uniform or something that identifies him as a soldier. We'll be unarmed and, obviously, we won't be engaging in combat. The other side of the coin is that the Germans might regard us as spies, because we'll be carrying a piece of secret equipment and trying to get it into British hands.'

'That makes it better, does it? I thought they shot spies?'

'They do,' Sykes said with a weary smile, 'so we'll just have to blend in with the rest of the refugees and hope for the best. We'll only be passing through a road-block or, at least, I hope we will.'

Dawson still didn't look happy, but he didn't see that they had any options.

'So how do we do it, sir?'

But before Sykes could reply, a shot sounded from behind them.

Dawson pressed down on the accelerator pedal, swung the steering wheel over to the left, and looked in the rear-view mirror.

Another German soldier, apparently by himself, had just appeared from a narrow alleyway. He was standing beside a house, his rifle raised and pointing at the staff car, and preparing to fire again.

'Bloody place is full of fucking Jerries,' Dawson muttered, then powered the vehicle round the next corner, just as the soldier pulled the trigger.

It was a good shot, bearing in mind the target was moving. The bullet slammed into the left-hand side of the staff car directly behind the door, went right through the metal and buried itself deep in the rear seat.

'Bloody good job I was in the front,' Sykes said, glancing behind him at the rip in the upholstery.

Dawson spotted another side-street over to their right – the area seemed to be a virtual maze of narrow roads, some little more than alleys – and swung the car down it.

'Find somewhere to dump this car,' Sykes ordered. 'Sooner or later we're going to run into a patrol that we can't fight our way through or run away from.'

The street Dawson was driving down was even narrower than the one they'd just left. Deserted terraced houses lined the right-hand side of the road, while on the left was a worryingly open expanse of waste ground. If a German patrol was in that area, the staff car would immediately be visible. Dawson kept turning his head to the left, but saw nobody.

'We really need to dump this car and make the Jerries think they've got rid of us at the same time,' he said. 'This car is far too conspicuous.'

'How?' Sykes asked, sounding interested.

Dawson pointed ahead, towards the end of the street, where a bomb or perhaps a salvo of artillery shells had virtually demolished two of the houses. Three dark shapes lay unmoving on the road near the wreckage.

'It's a bit fucking ghoulish, I know, but I think those are dead bodies down there – civilians killed in the German attack. We could put a couple of them in this car, and then torch it. When the Jerries come along to investigate they'll find what's left of a British staff car with two bodies inside it. They'll think we crashed the car or something, and then the fuel tank exploded. But whatever they think happened, when they find the car they'll probably call off their search for us.'

'I don't like the idea, Dawson,' Sykes said slowly, 'but you're right. If we can make it look convincing enough, we might just get away with it. Two dead Belgians aren't going to complain. They might even get military burials, which is better than being left to rot or getting eaten by rats. Let's do it.'

Dawson drove on down the road, still watching out for any sign of enemy patrols.

The houses at the end had been ripped apart by high explosive, their walls blown down, shards of broken glass, lengths of wood, curtaining, electric cables, pipes and lumps of plaster lying around in tangled heaps. And over it all lay a pathetic detritus of bits of broken household goods and equipment, the ruined remains of some anonymous family's shattered life.

But neither man was interested in the demolished properties. What grabbed their attention, as Dawson pulled the staff car to a halt, were the three bodies lying just outside the collapsed front wall of the left-hand house. Somebody had covered each of them with an old blanket – a neighbour or a passer-by, who knew? – and weighed down the fabric with stones they'd pulled from the rubble.

'Poor sods,' Sykes murmured. 'Probably never knew what hit them.'

Dawson nodded and climbed out of the staff car. He walked over to the nearest corpse and gently lifted up the ragged and bloodstained blanket to reveal the body lying beneath.

The corpse was that of an old man, maybe seventy or so years old and slightly built. His clothes were ripped and sodden with blood, and his dull eyes stared sightlessly upwards. The open wounds on his face were the temporary abode of a number of flies, which buzzed angrily into the air as Dawson flapped his hand over the body. The trails of blood that had run from his nose and ears suggested he'd probably been killed by a blast – Dawson had seen enough bodies in his civilian career to spot the signs.

'Male or female?' Sykes asked.

'Male. An old man. I'll check the others.'

Dawson looked at the second body for only a brief moment, then dropped the blanket back into place.

'No good?' Sykes asked.

'A little girl, maybe ten or twelve,' Dawson said, a catch in his voice. 'Blonde and pretty.'

He strode across to the third still and silent blanket-covered mound, lifted the corner of the fabric, looked down and then shook his head.

'This one's no good,' he said. 'It's a woman – a middle-aged woman.'

'That might not matter,' Sykes called out from the passenger seat of the staff car. 'We're going to have to burn the car. By the time we've finished one charred corpse is going to look pretty much like any other charred corpse.'

Dawson just stared at him. 'You're serious about this?'

'Definitely. This is no time to be squeamish. The woman's dead, Dawson, and that's a fact. There's nothing you or anyone else can do to help her now, but maybe, just maybe, she can help us. Getting back to our own lines with that demolition charge is crucial. Right now we're almost out of options.'

Sykes undid the door and struggled to get out of the car. 'Give me a hand,' he said. 'I can barely move this bloody leg.'

Dawson jogged back to the staff car and grabbed Sykes around the shoulders, lifting the officer out of the vehicle.

'Can you stand?' he asked.

Perspiration stood out on the major's forehead as he gingerly tried to put some of his weight onto his injured leg. Despite the bandages and strapping, the leg of his trousers was red with blood that had leaked from the wound. He shook his head. 'No. I'll have to sit or lie down. It fucking hurts, Dawson. I'm sorry, I can't help you with this.'

The corporal nodded sympathetically, and helped Sykes stumble across the rubble to where a mattress had been blown out of one of the houses. It was covered in debris and several lengths of timber, but it was the only thing he could see that gave the major a place to lie without exacerbating the pain of his wound.

Part of a wall still stood a few feet from the mattress, and Dawson helped Sykes over to it.

'Just lean against this for a few seconds, sir,' he said. He made sure the officer was able to support himself on his good leg, then strode across to the mattress. He grabbed one side of it and picked it up bodily, flicking all the rubble and other debris off it, and carried it over to the remains of the wall. He put it on the ground close to where Sykes was standing, and helped the major to hobble across and lie down on it.

'Thanks, Dawson,' Sykes said, gritting his teeth against the pain. 'Now, you know what you have to do?'

'Yes. Get that demolition charge out of the car, put these two bodies in the front seats and light it up.'

Sykes nodded. 'Put plenty of petrol over the corpses. They have to be completely unrecognizable.' The officer looked at the expression on Dawson's face. 'I know,' he said. 'No soldier should have to do this sort of thing, but we have no choice. If I could do it myself, I would. You know that.'

Dawson nodded in his turn, then spun round, checked the street was still deserted, and walked back towards the staff car.

Before he'd taken more than a couple of steps the sound of an engine echoed between the houses. He immediately ducked down amongst the rubble, staring towards the other end of the road.

'What is it?' Sykes hissed. 'A truck?'

Dawson glanced across at the major and shook his head. 'Good news is it isn't a lorry full of Jerry soldiers. Bad news is a motorcycle combination has just driven around the corner of the street, and the passenger has a machine-gun mounted in front of him. And the even worse news is that my Lee-Enfield is still over there in the staff car.'

CHAPTER 18

10 MAY 1940: LIÈGE, BELGIUM

The sound of the motorcycle engine got louder as the combination approached slowly. The two German soldiers had obviously seen the empty staff car and were being cautious, possibly fearing a trap.

'Maybe they'll see the car's empty and guess we've abandoned it and run off on foot,' Dawson suggested.

'They might,' Sykes said, 'but only after they've stopped and searched the area.'

He unsnapped his holster, pulled out his Webley revolver and checked it was fully loaded. 'I should have remembered to bring the rifle,' he said. 'I'm sorry, Dawson. That's my fault. You're unarmed. I don't think I'll be able to take them both with this revolver.'

'Actually, I'm not quite unarmed,' Dawson said, and pulled out the automatic pistol he'd taken off the Belgian soldier back at Eben Emael.

Sykes grinned weakly at him. 'So now it's two pistols against a machine-gun and whatever the motorcycle rider is armed with. Not the best odds.'

Dawson didn't reply. He checked the position of the approaching motorcycle combination and crept back into the ruined house, out of sight of the road, and crossed over to a position slightly closer to the staff car. He knew Sykes couldn't be seen unless one of the Germans walked into the demolished house itself – the position of the mattress behind the wall ensured that. The only hope they had was if both the enemy soldiers walked into the ruined property and he and Sykes could engage them at close range almost simultaneously.

But what the two Germans did next showed just how forlorn a hope that was. The rider swung the combination around so that it faced back the way it had come, ready for a quick getaway. The rider remained in the saddle, with the engine running. Obviously only the passenger was going to investigate the empty car and the ruined houses beside it. The moment Dawson or Sykes shot at him, the rider would be off, fleeing the scene and raising the alarm.

At that moment Dawson realized they would probably both be dead within minutes.

The passenger stood up in the sidecar and stared at the staff car for a few seconds, then stepped out of the vehicle. He took the Schmeisser sub-machine-gun that the rider offered him, checked it and then stepped forwards.

He walked across to the staff car, the weapon held ready, and peered inside it. As soon as he'd verified that it was empty, he called out something to the rider and turned to face the demolished houses. He took a couple of steps forward and then stopped abruptly as a moan sounded from somewhere in front of him.

Dawson guessed the major was trying to entice the soldier into the building so that either he or Dawson could get a clear shot at him. But that wouldn't stop the motorcycle rider from powering away from the scene and returning with a dozen heavily armed German soldiers.

The German shouted something over his shoulder to his companion, then took another couple of steps forward.

Dawson eased back to a vantage point from which he could see Major Sykes. But what he saw shocked him. The Webley had fallen from Sykes's grasp, and lay on the ground beside the mattress. The major appeared to be unconscious, his eyes closed and his body limp. It looked as if the pain from his wound had finally been too much to bear.

The German soldier moved forward more quickly now, swinging his Schmeisser from side to side. Then he saw the major's body. He stopped moving and aimed the machine-pistol at the recumbent form, his finger resting on the trigger. He took another couple of strides and, before Dawson could do anything, he kicked out – a short, savage blow that drove the toe of his boot hard into Sykes's wounded thigh. The major screamed with the pain, his whole back arching as his hands sought to close around the wound, to do something – anything – to ease his agony.

The German soldier smiled, and lifted his right leg to repeat the kick.

Then Dawson shot him.

The Browning pistol bucked twice in his hands as he squeezed the trigger. At that range – he was only about fifteen feet from his target – both rounds hit home, smashing into the right-hand side of the German's chest.

164

The soldier lurched sideways, the Schmeisser falling from his grasp, and he tumbled lifelessly to the ground.

Dawson didn't wait to see the results of his attack. Somehow, he had to stop the motorcycle rider. He turned and sprinted out of the ruined house, aiming the pistol as best he could. But even as he lined up the sights, he knew he was too late. The target was too far out of range. The rider was already gunning the engine, dust flying from the back wheel as he accelerated away.

He fired a couple of rounds at the fleeing vehicle, but neither hit the rider. Dawson ran straight over to the staff car, reached inside and grabbed the Lee-Enfield. The target was too far away for accurate shooting with a pistol, but he was well within range of a rifle shot. He leant against the side of the vehicle, steadying his breathing and aiming down the street.

The German soldier had traded evasive action for speed, simply getting away from the scene as fast as he could, riding the motorcycle combination straight down the middle of the street. Perhaps his partner hadn't spotted the rifle in the staff car, or at least hadn't mentioned it.

Dawson concentrated hard, aiming for the middle of the German's back, then pulled the trigger, the rifle kicking against his shoulder.

The sound of the motorcycle engine abruptly died away as the German soldier slumped forward over the handlebars, losing his grip on the throttle, and then toppled sideways off the machine. The motorcycle combination veered over to the left, slowed down enormously and then began moving at little more than

165

walking speed. Finally it ran into the wall of one of the houses which lined that side of the road and stopped, the engine stalled.

Dawson stared down the street for a few seconds, to make sure his shot had killed, or at least mortally wounded, the German soldier. The man lay motionless near the centre of the road, showing no signs of life. Dawson guessed his single bullet had done its deadly work. If he'd only wounded the man, the German would probably have been able to hold on to the handlebars of the motorcycle. His sudden tumble off the machine suggested he'd died instantly.

A soft call from inside the ruined house made up Dawson's mind for him. He turned and ran back to where he'd left Sykes.

The major still lay on the stained and torn mattress, both his hands pressed against the wound on his thigh, but he was fully conscious.

'You OK, sir?' Dawson asked, glancing first at the German soldier he'd shot and then down at the injured British officer.

'Not really, Dawson, no, if I'm honest. I never thought that bastard would kick me. I was just trying to attract his attention so you'd have a clear shot at him. Now my leg feels as if it's on fire.'

'I'm sorry. He moved so quickly that—'

'It doesn't matter. What's done is done. He won't be kicking anyone else. Did you get the rider as well?'

Dawson nodded. 'Yes. And now we've got two male bodies to put in the staff car.'

From somewhere, Sykes conjured up a smile. 'Good. That's better than disturbing the Belgian corpses. I'd rather burn the Boche any day of the week. Forget the laws of war.'

'What?'

'There are rules about the disposal of bodies, Dawson. You're not supposed to just set fire to them.'

'Doesn't bother me,' Dawson said. 'I'll sort that out right now.' He bent over the body of the soldier lying near Sykes. Swiftly, he pulled off the man's helmet, the goggles still wrapped around it, removed the leather belt that held his shin-length coat closed and pulled off the outer garment.

Dawson picked up the limp body, hoisted it onto his shoulder and strode away, back to the staff car. He dumped the dead soldier in the passenger seat, then started the engine and got behind the wheel himself. For the burnt-out car to convince anybody, it had to have crashed, so he drove the vehicle forwards, the front wheels bouncing over rubble, and smashed the nose of the car into the low wall at the end of the street. It wasn't an ideal scenario, because even a halfway competent driver would surely have realized he was driving down a dead-end, but it was the best he could do in the circumstances. He just hoped the German soldiers who would eventually find the wreckage wouldn't wonder too much about how the crash had happened.

Then he ran off down the road to where the body of the second enemy soldier still lay face-down and motionless in the middle of the street.

Dawson checked the man was dead, dragged him across to the motorcycle combination and lay the body across the top of the sidecar. He pulled the vehicle away from the wall of the house where it had stopped and turned it round, then sat astride the motorcycle and tried to kick the engine into life. But he'd never ridden a motorcycle before, though he'd seen them often enough, and his first attempts failed because it was still in gear.

Eventually, Dawson guessed what was happening and fiddled about with the gear lever mounted on the petrol tank, and then got the engine started. The vehicle lurched and hopped as he wrestled with the unfamiliar controls, but he managed to get the combination moving and rode it back down the road to where the staff car was parked.

He lifted the body of the second soldier off the sidecar and again stripped off the helmet, goggles and coat before placing the corpse behind the wheel of the staff car. Now he had two male bodies to use in their deception plan. They were even wearing military uniforms – the wrong uniforms, granted, but after the fire he doubted if anyone would be able to tell the difference. He put his own British helmet on the floor of the vehicle just in front of the driver as a final touch.

Dawson opened the boot of the staff car and removed the two sections of the demolition charge. One at a time, he carried them over to the motorcycle combination and placed them on the floor of the sidecar, but still left enough room for Sykes to sit in the vehicle. Getting away from the area using the German combination seemed the obvious thing to do now.

He looked down at their personal gear still stowed in the boot of the car, then he shook his head. There was simply no room in the sidecar to take that as well, so he closed the boot and walked back into the ruins.

Dawson bent down beside the major. 'We need to get moving, sir,' he said. 'Can you stand up?'

'Give me a hand.'

Grimacing with the pain, Sykes struggled to his feet, Dawson almost lifting him bodily. The major leant back against the remains of the wall, white and sweating with the effort.

'Just hold on there for a second,' Dawson said, and picked up the motorcycle coat he'd removed from the dead soldier. The inside was soaked with blood in one patch, but that couldn't be helped, and at least there was little sign of blood on the outside. Sykes eased forwards from the wall and, with the corporal's help, slid his arms into the sleeves. The coat was far too big for him, but that didn't matter – the important thing was that it covered both his tattered British uniform and the wound on his leg.

'What now?' Sykes asked, as the two men made their way slowly out of the ruins and back to the street.

'A change of plan, sir,' Dawson said. 'We've just joined the Wehrmacht's motorcycle corps, or whatever they call it. That should get us away from here without the bloody Germans shooting at us again.'

Sykes nodded. 'It should let us reach one of the roadblocks, yes, but getting through it might prove to be a bit more difficult.'

'We'll cross that bridge when we come to it. First, we need to get away from here, before some other Germans pitch up and start nosing around.'

Dawson helped Sykes get into the sidecar, and handed him one of the helmets he'd taken off the German soldiers. Then he manually swung the combination around so that it – and more importantly the heavy machine-gun mounted on the sidecar – faced down the street, and the direction from which any enemy troops were likely to appear.

'I'll be as quick as I can,' he said, then strode back into the ruined house.

Sykes nodded, then cracked the top off one of the phials of morphine. The drug would help dull the agony of his mutilated thigh.

On one side of the house a wooden wardrobe lay on its back, one of the doors blown off and the sides shattered, presumably having fallen from the upper floor of the house, which simply no longer existed. Inside it, Dawson found an assortment of clothes, both male and female. He picked out a couple of pairs of trousers and two jackets, the biggest he could see, and carried them back to the sidecar. He passed the garments to Sykes, who placed them over the demolition charge lying under his legs.

'Good idea, Dawson. We might need to become civilians pretty soon. In the meantime they'll help hide this device.'

The corporal nodded and walked back into the ruined building, emerging with the German soldier's Schmeisser MP 38 machine-pistol slung around his neck. He strode over to the staff car and removed all the spare magazines the soldier had been carrying, then went through his pouches to recover every round of ammunition the man had on him. He repeated the process with the other soldier.

Finally, he opened the boot of the staff car and took out the box of compo rations they'd been living on when no other food was available. The box was too big to fit in the sidecar, so he just put the few bits that were left down by Sykes's feet and replaced the box in the boot of the car.

Then Dawson pulled the can of petrol out of the boot and poured the contents over the two bodies in the seats, and over the rear of the vehicle. He took out his bayonet, bent down at the back of the staff car and drove the tip of the weapon straight into the side of the fuel tank. That started a small drip, so he repeated the operation half a dozen times more, until there was a reasonable flow.

Dawson found a tattered newspaper just inside the building, screwed it into a ball and walked back to the car, lit the paper and tossed it under the rear of the vehicle. At first nothing happened, then the spilt petrol caught with a 'whump' sound, and in an instant the rear of the car was engulfed in flames.

He checked to make sure that the two bodies inside it were also burning, then ran across to the motorcycle combination and pulled on the other long coat, also bloodstained. He tried to put on the German helmet, but it was too small for his head, so he tore out the lining and tried again. That was better, but it was still tight around his temples. He started the engine and looked back at the flames licking around the car.

'Hopefully burning out the staff car will muddy the waters a bit. It'll take the Jerries a while to get close enough to the car to investigate it.'

Sykes turned round in his seat to stare at the conflagration, and nodded in satisfaction. 'That's a pretty good job, Dawson,' he muttered. 'Now get us out of here.'

CHAPTER 19

10 MAY 1940: LIÈGE, BELGIUM

Eddie Dawson was getting the hang of the BMW motorcycle. It had a large horizontally opposed engine of a type he'd never seen before, but he'd quickly mastered the controls. The machine seemed tough and well built, and the heavy machine-gun mounted on the front of the sidecar was a bonus. Major Sykes had inspected it and told him it was a Mauser MG 34, a powerful weapon with a high rate of fire. That meant they might be able to shoot their way out of trouble, though both men hoped they wouldn't need to. Sykes had checked the weapon, which had a full fifty-round drum magazine attached, and had declared himself happy with the way it operated.

As they'd driven through the largely empty streets of the western part of Liège, they'd seen only a few more refugees – they assumed most of them were sticking to the main roads that led out of the city – but they'd spotted numerous German patrols and a handful of vehicles, including several other motorcycle combinations. None of the enemy troops had taken the slightest notice of them – the German vehicle Dawson was driving

172

and their 'borrowed' uniforms allowed them to blend in seamlessly.

But they still had to get out of Liège. Dawson pulled the motorcycle to a halt in another side-road, a short distance from a T-junction where a stream of refugees was moving slowly past. Then he walked to the end of the road, looked out to the west and then strode back to where Sykes sat in the sidecar, waiting.

As Dawson reached the combination, both men looked up as a squadron of German aircraft flew over the city. They'd seen several aircraft above the city during the day, some heading east but most of them flying west. The sound of distant explosions as the bombers dropped their loads had become almost constant, like thunder heard a long way off. But these aircraft were lower than most of the others they'd seen. Dawson and Sykes watched until the last aircraft vanished from sight behind a building.

'So what did you see?' Sykes asked.

'There's a road-block about a hundred yards away,' Dawson said. 'Four soldiers armed with rifles, but there are no vehicles there. If we can find a way past them, we should be able to get clear.'

'I don't suppose you speak German, do you?' Sykes asked hopefully.

Dawson shook his head. 'Only a couple of words,' he admitted. 'We definitely won't be able to talk our way through that road-block. Is it worth pulling on those civvy clothes and trying to blend in with the refugees? Trying to slip through that way?'

'Not an option for me, I'm afraid, Dawson,' Sykes said. 'I can barely stand upright, and I certainly can't walk. We need to find a cart or something like that for me to ride on. It would probably mean taking one off some Belgians, and I really don't want to do that. We're also running out of time. With every minute that passes, the Germans will be tightening their grip on Liège, so the longer we wait, the less chance we'll have of getting out of here.'

'Right, then,' Dawson said, and climbed back onto the motorcycle. 'I'm going to be as noisy and conspicuous as I can. Lights on, horn sounding, scattering the refugees out of our way. That way we might just convince the soldiers at the road-block that we're on an important mission and hopefully they'll just move the barrier and let us through.'

'Hope's a wonderful thing,' Sykes said. He leant forward in his seat and again checked the magazine of the machine-gun, ensuring it was ready to fire. 'I think we're more likely to have to shoot our way through.'

Dawson nodded but didn't reply, just started the engine of the motorcycle. He pulled the goggles down over his eyes, which had the effect of hiding more of his face, conveying a more anonymous image.

Beside him, Sykes did the same, then nodded his readiness.

Dawson switched on the bike's headlamp, engaged first gear, released the clutch and started accelerating towards the junction in front of them, towards the slowly moving line of refugees. When he got to about twenty yards away, he thumbed the horn button repeatedly, and waved his left arm at the civilians walking across in front of them.

Men and women slowed down, opening up a narrow

gap in the seemingly unending stream of humanity clogging the road.

Dawson dropped the speed as he approached the junction, weaving his way around and through the mass of slow-moving people, then accelerated again as he swung the motorcycle into the main road and turned towards the road-block that they could both see clearly. They were now heading in the same direction as the refugees, so getting through the crowds of people was slightly easier. But he was still having to weave and dodge around them, despite his almost constant use of the bike's horn.

Ahead of them, Dawson could see two of the German soldiers looking in their direction, probably wondering what a Wehrmacht motorcycle team was doing, travelling so quickly towards them.

The road-block was a simple structure, just a wooden barrier that blocked about half of the width of the road, forcing the refugees to pass through the remaining gap, which allowed the German soldiers to check their documentation before letting them proceed.

Dawson kept sounding the bike's horn. Both he and Sykes waved to try to get the Belgian refugees out of their way, and to convey to the watching sentries they were in a hurry and needed to be allowed through the road-block as quickly as possible.

'I don't think this is going to work,' Dawson shouted, over the roaring of the engine of the motorcycle and the thumping of the tyres on the cobbled road surface. 'They're just watching us, not shifting the barrier.'

'Keep on going,' Sykes replied. 'We're committed now.'

They reached about twenty yards from the road-block before any of the soldiers guarding it reacted. One of the German troops stepped forward and made a repeated downward motion with his left arm, apparently indicating that they should slow down, while two other soldiers positioned themselves at either end of the barrier.

Dawson knew they had only one chance, so he sounded the horn yet again, and waved his left arm violently from side to side, a universal gesture meaning 'get out of the way'. He kept the speed up, kept the motorcycle travelling as quickly as he could.

'It's now or never,' he said. 'If they don't shift the barrier right now, you'll have to use that machine-gun and shoot them all down before one of them can use his rifle against us.'

Sykes nodded grimly and seized the pistol grip of the MG 34 with his right hand.

'In fact, fire a few rounds over their heads,' Dawson said, as the German soldiers still showed no sign of moving the barrier.

Sykes glanced at the big corporal, then ahead at the road-block.

'We've got nothing to lose now,' the major said, and depressed the pistol grip of the machine-gun to raise the muzzle of the weapon. He squeezed the trigger for just a moment, sending a burst of about half a dozen bullets screaming high over the heads of the German sentries.

The results were immediate. Some of the Belgian refugees screamed and shouted in terror, and scattered. The soldier in front of them ran off to the side of the road, while the two men manning the wooden barrier dragged it a short distance across the road. That didn't completely clear their path, but it opened up a big enough gap for Dawson to steer the motorcycle combination around the barrier.

As he accelerated past the German sentries, Dawson glanced at them. Two were looking at him in shock – being fired on by enemy soldiers was one thing, but being shot at by your own side was different – but another one was staring fixedly at the speeding machine, his attention apparently drawn to something low down on the motorcycle. More worryingly, he was also unslinging his rifle.

As he passed the man, Dawson glanced down, and in an instant realized what the man had seen, and why his suspicions had been raised.

'My uniform,' he yelled at Sykes. 'Must have spotted my uniform trousers under this coat. They're the wrong colour.'

Dawson risked a quick glance over his shoulder. The German soldier had stepped away from the barrier and was bringing his rifle up to his shoulder.

The road ahead was crowded with Belgian civilians. The machine-gun fire had frightened and alarmed them. Most of them had stopped walking and stood around in small groups, looking either back towards the road-block or at the speeding motorcycle combination.

Dawson had to try to throw off the soldier's aim, so he steered the vehicle directly towards one group of refugees, gambling that the German wouldn't fire if there was a chance his bullet would miss its intended target and hit one of the Belgian civilians.

That proved to be a vain hope as the German's

Mauser cracked. The bullet actually passed through the gap between the motorcycle and the sidecar, hitting the end of the cylinder head of the engine as it did so and snapping off a couple of the cooling fins. Then it smashed into the cobbled surface of the road and ricocheted off into the distance, fortunately missing the civilians in front of the motorcycle, who scattered in all directions.

'Fuck, that was close,' Dawson said, and weaved the machine from side to side, steering around the civilians and trying to put as much distance as he could between the two of them and the German soldiers behind. But he knew they were still well within range of the man with the Mauser.

Sykes yelled out something incomprehensible to Dawson, a couple of words in French, then shouted it again. As they heard the order, most of the nearby Belgian civilians dropped whatever they were carrying or pulling behind them and flattened themselves on the ground. Obviously Sykes had told them to drop flat.

Sykes was leaning forward, and as Dawson glanced down he saw what the major was doing. He had released the clip that held the Mauser MG 34 machine-gun onto the mount on the front of the cockpit of the sidecar.

Grimacing with the effort, his face contorted with the pain from his injured leg, Sykes swung the Mauser around to point behind them. He twisted awkwardly in his seat, turning around as far as he could in the very confined space of the sidecar. He held the weapon by the perforated tube that covered the barrel with his left hand, and grasped the pistol grip with his right.

As the German soldier brought his rifle back to the aim, Sykes pointed the Mauser machine-gun towards the barrier, keeping the barrel low, and pulled the trigger. He wasn't aiming directly at the soldier – with the weapon removed from its mount, accurate shot placement would be impossible – but just trying to disrupt his aim.

As Sykes fired, the muzzle of the weapon lifted with the recoil, and the Mauser made a ripping sound: the weapon fired about 800 rounds a minute. The successor weapon to the MG 34, the Mauser MG 42, later became known as 'Hitler's buzzsaw' or, less politely, as 'Hitler's zipper', because of the sound it made when it fired.

The brief burst was probably less than a dozen rounds. The first couple struck the road surface well in front of the barrier, but at least one of the following bullets must have hit the German soldier in the leg. He staggered backwards and dropped his rifle, then tumbled sideways to the ground, his hands reaching towards his leg.

Dawson glanced back as the shots rang out, and realized that Sykes had effectively eliminated the immediate danger from the German sentries. He stopped weaving to throw off the aim of any enemy soldiers behind them, and concentrated on avoiding the Belgian civilians clogging the road, and on putting as much distance as possible behind them.

'Keep going,' Sykes said, swinging the heavy machine-gun around to point forward again. He reattached the weapon to the mount at the front of the cockpit of the sidecar, checked that it was secure, then leant back in the seat, looking drained and grey. Dawson knew his actions would have robbed him of most of the little strength he had left.

They were through the road-block and heading into the countryside to the west of Liège, but both men knew they were a long way from being safe. And they still had tens of miles to go before they could possibly reach the relative safety afforded by any Allied forces that might have reached the area.

CHAPTER 20

10 MAY 1940: EASTERN BELGIUM

Dawson stayed on the main road for about twenty minutes, but slowed down as soon as he was well clear of the road-block at the edge of the city, which probably represented the western limit – the front line – of the German advance. Then he pulled off it to the right and drove down a narrow country road towards a village called Verlaine. Dusk was fast approaching, and he found he now needed the motorcycle's headlight to see where he was going.

'We daren't stay on that road,' Dawson said, the noise level diminishing considerably as he slowed down the motorcycle to little more than walking pace, about as fast as he could safely travel on the twisting and narrow road. 'By now, the Jerries will know that we've busted out of Liège. They'll probably be sending troops after us. We didn't have enough of a lead to outrun them. There's another reason as well.'

'What?' Sykes asked. His voice was weak but the major sounded fully alert.

'I've just checked the fuel level, and the tank's nearly empty. I should have looked at it before I soaked the car with petrol. The last thing we need is to run out of fuel on the main road, with nowhere to run or hide.'

Sykes nodded. 'But we still need to keep moving,' he said.

'I know. We'll have to dump this bike and find a cart or something like that, some sort of vehicle we can use to keep heading west, while we pretend to be a couple of Belgian peasants.'

Dawson braked the combination to a stop by the side of the road when they reached the edge of the small village, and both men peered down the main street.

'There doesn't seem to be anybody about,' Dawson said. With Sykes holding the heavy machine-gun ready for any trouble, he put the motorcycle back into gear and they rode on slowly.

Verlaine appeared to be an old village, some of the ancient stone buildings looking as if they might even be medieval in origin. It boasted a large church with a prominent spire, positioned on a low hill. It also appeared to be deserted, which was a good thing, because the distinctive rumble of the BMW's engine echoing off the buildings would have advertised their presence very obviously.

'We need three things,' Sykes said. 'Somewhere to sleep, some food – because my stomach thinks my throat's been cut – and something to drink.'

'And what about the combination?' Dawson asked. 'Should we just hide it in a barn or dump it out in the sticks?'

'It's not good to leave it close to the village. When the Germans find it they'll take reprisals against the inhabitants – if any of them are left, that is. More pressing is that I can't walk, so driving it out of the village, dumping it and then walking back isn't an option.'

'I could leave you somewhere here, get rid of the bike myself and then come back,' Dawson suggested, but Sykes shook his head.

'We need to stick together – at least for my sake. You'll need to lift me out of this sidecar. I've no idea if I'll even be able to stand up when you do. Plus we still have to guard the two bits of this demolition charge that have been bouncing around between my legs ever since we left Liège. We'll have to risk leaving the motorcycle combination here in the village tonight. Once we've found a cart or something tomorrow, you can dump the bike. I want to be sure we have a way of getting out of here before we do, though.'

'OK, then,' Dawson said, and swung the motorcycle combination around in a tight circle to head back the way they'd come. 'I spotted a small farm at the other end of the village. With a bit of luck I can stash this in one of the barns or outbuildings, and we can probably sleep somewhere there as well. Once I've got you settled, I'll try and scavenge some nosh.'

It wasn't much of a farm, just a small two-storey house that appeared to be deserted – or, at least, there were no lights showing in any of the windows that were visible from the road as they approached the property – and beyond it they could see three somewhat dilapidated buildings.

Dawson pulled the motorcycle to a stop beside the closed gate that barred the way into the farm from the road.

'No sign of life,' he said, and climbed off the motor-cycle to open the gate. When he reached it, he examined it and then turned back to Sykes. 'It's locked. There's a padlock and chain around it, so I guess the occupants have fled.'

'Can you break it?' Sykes asked.

'Just give me a second.' Dawson pulled out his bay-onet, stuck the blade into the hasp of the padlock and levered. For a second or two nothing happened, then the lock gave with a crack and the broken padlock fell to the ground. He unwrapped the chain from around the post and opened the gate wide.

Then he walked back to the motorcycle combination, put it into gear and drove it through the gateway. As soon as he was well inside the property, he climbed off again, walked back and closed the gate, looping the chain around the post as he'd found it. He secured the ends with the broken padlock, so that from the road it would appear the same as it had previously.

Dawson drove around to the back of the small house, checking to see that there were no lights visible at the back of the property either, and crossed a small and muddy yard towards the closest, and largest, of the three outbuildings.

It was a barn, of sorts, the front open to the elements, and with loose hay stacked up against the back wall, away from the entrance. Dawson drove the motorcycle inside, right to the rear of the structure, then turned it round to face the open end of the barn. He switched off the engine, and pushed the combination backwards until the rear bumper was almost against the hay. That way, the machine-gun faced the direction of any possible threat, and if they had to make a getaway on the bike, he wouldn't need to manoeuvre it first.

For a moment, he just sat there, listening, but the only sound he could hear was the slow metallic ticking as the motorcycle's engine started to cool down. Then he climbed off and walked round to the sidecar, where Sykes was trying to lever himself up with his arms.

'Don't worry, sir, I'll lift you out of there,' he said, and bent down. He grabbed the major under his arms, and slid his other hand under Sykes's knees, being as gentle as he could. As Dawson straightened up and lifted him out of the sidecar, Sykes cried out with pain, but there was nothing Dawson could do about that.

He carried the officer over to the hay and laid him down as gently as he could on a level section. The hay was less comfortable than it looked, protruding stalks jabbing into Sykes's flesh even through the material of the heavy motorcycle coat he was wearing, but it was still marginally more comfortable for him than lying on the floor. And Dawson was sure he could find a blanket or something that he could use as padding.

With the major lying flat on his back, and as comfortable as he could be in the circumstances, Dawson took a look around their overnight accommodation. It was obviously a building on a working farm – there were implements of various sorts and different types of farming equipment ranged along the walls and on the floor – and the mud in the yard outside showed the marks of both animal hooves and cart wheels. There was a pile of old sacks, which had possibly originally contained grain of some sort, beside a workbench.

Dawson picked up half a dozen and carried them back to where Sykes lay, at the rear of the barn.

He arranged the sacks on the hay close to the major, then helped Sykes move over until he was lying on them, and was slightly more comfortable.

Sykes felt in his uniform pocket and pulled out another one of the phials of morphine, cracked the top and swallowed the liquid inside. It would take a while to work, but the pain from his injured thigh was worse because of the rough treatment he'd endured during the day.

'I'm going to check out the house,' Dawson said softly, handing the officer the Schmeisser machine-pistol. 'I'll be back in a few minutes.'

The major lifted his arm in acknowledgement, but didn't reply.

Dawson checked he still had the Browning pistol in his pocket, then took the Lee-Enfield rifle out of the motorcycle sidecar, ensured it was loaded and slung it over his shoulder. He strode across to the open entrance, stopped there and looked in both directions. The only sound he could hear in the quiet of mid-evening was birdsong and, faintly, from somewhere in the distance, the lowing of cattle.

He crossed over to the rear of the small farmhouse and peered in through the windows, but could see almost nothing inside the building, because all the curtains were drawn and there were only tiny gaps between them. Dawson stepped across to the back door and tried the handle, but it was locked – which was hardly a surprise.

He retraced his steps and crossed the yard to the other two outbuildings to inspect them, but both were virtual clones of the first one they'd entered – open spaces filled with various types of farming equipment and supplies. There were some fuel cans stacked along one side of the third barn he looked into. He lifted each one, but they were all empty apart from the final one he tried, which stood a little apart from the others. That one felt about half-full, and Dawson uncapped it so he could sniff the contents. The sharp, unmistakable aroma of petrol filled his nose, and he knew that, if all else failed, he could top-up the tank of the motorcycle combination and keep it running for a few more miles yet.

But, as Dawson's rumbling stomach seemed to emphasize to him, neither structure contained any form of food or drink. Or, at least, none that he could see.

He'd spotted a pump in the yard, so getting some water wouldn't be a problem, but both he and Sykes desperately needed something to eat, and there was only one place he was likely to find any food. If there was nothing in the farmhouse, they'd have to rely on the remains of the compo ration pack they'd been issued with before arriving at Eben Emael, and there was hardly anything left of that. In fact, Dawson had already checked it – it had been labelled 'Composite Ration Pack Type E' – and all that was now left of it was a packet of biscuits, three partially empty tins of milk powder, sugar and tea, a bar of soap and a few sheets of latrine paper. Plus a solid-fuel stove. Not exactly the makings of a gourmet dinner, though they would at least be able to have a hot drink.

Dawson walked back to the farmhouse and stepped across to the rear door. Without hesitation, he rammed the butt of the Lee-Enfield into the small window just above the door handle. The glass shattered instantly, and he broke out the remaining shards from around the edge of the window, then reached through the gap and felt for the lock, hoping to find a key on the inside. But his probing fingers found nothing. Obviously the owners or occupants had locked the rear door from the outside when they left – Dawson had hoped they might have left the building by the other door, leaving the key to the rear door in the lock.

He'd just have to do it the hard way. He stepped back and kicked out, the sole of his size-twelve army boot striking the door right beside the lock. There was a cracking sound and the door swung open. The force of the blow ripped the striker plate completely off the frame, the lump of metal clattering down onto the tiled floor of the small rear hall of the house.

Dawson strode forward into the hall, his rifle held ready, just in case there was somebody still in the building. He stood and listened for a moment, but heard nothing to alarm him. He left the door wide open behind him so that the faint moonlight provided some illumination inside the house. Three doors opened off it, one on either side of him, and the third directly in front, behind a wooden ladder up to the floor above.

He chose the one on his right, but that led only into a small sitting room, so he backed out and opened the one opposite.

That opened up to reveal a tiny kitchen. Dawson walked across to the window and pulled back the curtains, then looked around him. Pots and pans were hanging from hooks on the wall above a scarred and scratched working surface, dimly visible in the gloom.

On one side of the working surface was a metal jug, half-full of water, and an empty round steel bowl. Opposite that was a black-painted free-standing stove with an open chimney above it. The stove was covered in blue tiles, the steel top obviously used for cooking. On the front was a towel rail and two doors, and Dawson opened both of them to look inside. One was the oven – empty – and the other the fire box, in which a pile of grey-brown ash was visible. He held his hand directly above the ash. There was just the faintest trace of residual heat left in the embers, so he guessed the house had been empty for at least twelve hours. That, perhaps, was good news, because it could mean that the occupants might have left some edible food in the place.

To one side of the old cooking range was another door. Dawson pulled it open and found himself looking into a pantry, tins and jars and packets stacked neatly on the shelves. Any one of them might have contained something they could eat, but would probably need cooking. Better than compo rations, but not much.

But as he looked around the kitchen again Dawson realized he and Sykes would be able to eat well without opening any of the containers. Hanging above the stove, suspended from a hook in the open chimney where the smoke would preserve it and keep the flies away, was the remains of a large ham, presumably left there because there wasn't too much meat still on it. Dawson had seen similar hams in a couple of places since he'd arrived in France the previous year, and knew they were made from an entire leg of pork, air-dried with the bone still in place. And the meat was simply delicious.

'Fucking brilliant,' he muttered, slung his Lee-Enfield

from his shoulder and stepped forwards to lift down the ham. He backed out of the chimney carrying his prize, grabbed a couple of tin mugs, a carving knife, and the jug of water with his free hand, then walked out of the house. He crossed the yard back to the open-fronted barn and walked straight to the back of the structure.

It didn't look as if Sykes had moved since Dawson had left him, but as the corporal approached he noticed that the major was holding the Schmeisser, the weapon resting on his chest, the barrel pointing straight at him.

'Easy, sir,' Dawson said. 'It's me.'

'Good,' Sykes muttered, and lowered the machine-pistol to his side. 'Any luck?'

'Definitely, as long as you're a carnivore.'

'Right now, Dawson,' Sykes muttered, his voice again slurring as the morphine took hold, 'I'd turn cannibal if it would get me a decent meal. What have you found?'

'What's left of a ham, but no wine – we'll have to make do with tea and some water, I'm afraid.'

'Oh, bugger. I hate tea. But good news about the ham. Give me a hand to sit up, will you?'

Dawson carefully balanced the ham on the rim of the metal jug to keep it clear of the ground, then helped Sykes manoeuvre himself into a sitting position.

'You should have something to drink first, sir, I think,' he said, lifting up the ham, and poured some water into the mugs.

Both men drained the liquid, and Dawson refilled the two mugs. Then he produced the carving knife, cut a piece of ham – more a chunk than a slice – and passed it to the major. He repeated the operation, carving a lump of the meat for himself, and for a minute or so the only sound in the barn was their contented chewing.

'Bugger me, Dawson, that tastes good,' Sykes said. 'Any chance of a second helping?'

'Absolutely.' The corporal carved another couple of pieces off the ham.

'No sign of the occupants of the farmhouse, I suppose?' Sykes asked.

Dawson shook his head. 'The building was locked up and deserted, but there was ash from a fire in the kitchen stove that was still just barely warm. My guess is the family left here no later than early this morning, perhaps when the German attack started on Liège.'

'Probably joined the stream of refugees heading west. Did you find a cart or something we can use to get out of here?'

Dawson shook his head as he cut more slices of meat from the ham. 'No, nothing. There are a couple of ploughs in one of the other barns, but no sign of horses to pull them. But I did find some petrol in a can in the smallest barn, so we can keep going on the combination for a bit longer, if we can't find anything better.'

'We might have to. I can't walk anywhere – that's for sure – and we need to transport the demolition charge. The machine-gun on the sidecar can be a persuasive argument if we encounter any enemy soldiers.' Sykes chewed thoughtfully on the last piece of ham Dawson had given him. 'Better bring that can of petrol in here and fill the tank, just in case we have to get out in a hurry.'

Dawson nodded. 'Was going to,' he said, 'soon as I've finished this. Then I'll take a look at your wound, to make sure it's still clean. Then you need to have some rest to get your strength back.'

When they finished eating, Dawson went out and returned with a petrol can and poured the fuel into the motorcycle fuel tank. Then he took out the tins of tea, sugar and milk powder and found a piece of hard and level ground on which to stand the Tommy's cooker. This was a circular cooking ring that sat on a tin of solid fuel. Not very efficient, but it was all they had. Dawson set a can of water on it.

While he waited for it to boil, he checked the bullet wound in Sykes's thigh – which seemed fine, apart from the heavy bruising left by the German soldier when he'd kicked the major – and settled the officer as comfortably as he could on his bed of hay.

Sykes drank his tea black and with plenty of sugar, declaring it was barely palatable even then. Dawson added several spoonfuls of milk powder to his mug.

'I'll take the first watch,' Dawson said, when he'd finished his drink, 'but I'll have to get my head down later or I'll fall over. I'll give you a shake at about three, if that's OK, sir.'

Sykes nodded, checked that his Webley revolver was right beside him, then lay back and closed his eyes.

'Right,' Dawson said, taking out his gun oil and pull-through and picking up the Lee-Enfield. 'I'll give the rifle a clean, then I'll go and walk the perimeter, just make sure it's still all quiet out there.'

CHAPTER 21

11 MAY 1940: EASTERN BELGIUM

Eddie Dawson had half-expected the farm to be assaulted by German troops during the night, such was the apparent speed and competence of the enemy advance and the demonstrable impotence of the Belgian defences. But, as the hours dragged by, he neither saw nor heard anything to alarm him. The village of Verlaine still seemed to be completely deserted.

But thinking about it – and the one thing he had plenty of that night was time to think about things – he realized the Germans couldn't possibly have any idea where they were, and might not even be chasing them any more.

Looking back on what had happened in Liège, their first contact with the foot patrol would have alerted the Germans to the presence of two British soldiers in the city, but their staff car was now a burnt-out wreck with two bodies in it. There was a pretty good chance the Germans would believe the deception. Even if they didn't, so what? The German forces were occupying an entire country, just one of the first steps in Hitler's plan to conquer the whole of Europe, so why would they bother about two British soldiers wandering around near the front line?

When they'd driven through the road-block on the way out of the city they'd exchanged fire with the sentries. It was still possible that the incident would be written off as a case of mistaken identity. Two soldiers on a motorcycle on an urgent mission that meant they didn't have time to stop. And it was a German vehicle and they had been wearing German riding coats and helmets. The sentry might have seen the colour of Dawson's uniform trousers, but would any officer believe him? But, again, even if the Germans guessed, so what? In the overall scheme of the enemy's plan, they were nothing – totally insignificant. A temporary irritation, nothing more.

But he couldn't just assume that they'd escaped detection and were no longer in any danger. And it certainly didn't mean he could get his head down. So he continued with his patrols – over to the gate where they'd entered the property, around the outside of all three barns, and along the edge of the small field that bordered the muddy yard. He did that about twice every hour, varying the timings and the route he walked, because a predictable sentry was probably worse than no sentry at all.

The night stayed silent and innocent in the pale moonlight.

At three-twenty, by Dawson's watch, he knew he'd have to get some sleep or he'd drop off anyway. He walked back into the barn, crossed over to where Sykes lay on his back on his bed of hay, snoring gently, and shook the officer gently by the shoulder.

'Nearly half past three, sir,' he said quietly.

Sykes opened his eyes and instinctively started to stretch, an action he stopped abruptly as his wounded leg protested.

'Help me to sit up, will you?' he asked. 'If I keep lying down here I'll probably doze off again.'

Dawson lifted the major's shoulders and settled him into as comfortable a position as he could, leaning his back against the hay behind him.

'Anything to report?'

Dawson shook his head. 'Nothing. It's quiet as the grave out there, sir. I've been around the farm, but there's been no noise, no lights, and no sign of enemy troops or even any of the Belgies from the village. I think they've all buggered off.'

'I hope you're right. I've still got the Schmeisser here, but give me the rifle as well. Then you get your head down. I'm not walking anywhere, obviously, but if I hear anything I'll give you a shake.'

Dawson handed over the Lee-Enfield with a certain relief. 'The magazine's fully charged, sir,' he said, 'and there's one up the spout. The safety catch is on.'

A few minutes later, the sound of snoring echoed through the barn. Dawson lay on his back, his mouth open. Sykes prodded him with the butt of the rifle. The corporal turned onto his side, the noise diminishing immediately

A little over four hours later, Sykes prodded Dawson again, but not to stop him snoring. This time he wanted him to wake up.

Dawson grunted a couple of times, then his eyes

snapped open. He glanced at Sykes, then towards the open end of the barn, where the first rays of sunlight were illuminating the upper branches of the trees in the adjacent field.

'Morning, sir,' he said, and sat up. 'All quiet, was it?'

'All quiet,' Sykes confirmed. 'It's just after seven. Time we got started.'

Dawson nodded agreement, stood up and stretched. 'I'll check outside and get us some more water,' he said. 'I can probably hack another three or four bits of meat off that ham for breakfast.'

'Excellent,' Sykes said. 'Not quite what I'm used to in the regimental officers' mess, but good enough in the circumstances. There's no chance of any toast, I suppose?'

'Not unless you know how to make bread, sir, no. Everything else in that pantry is in tins and packets. I don't really think we've got time to start cooking anything.'

'Relax, Dawson. Only joking. Ham and water – or even another mug of that bloody awful tea – isn't a bad start to the day.'

Dawson picked up the Lee-Enfield, checked it was loaded, with the safety catch on, then slung the rifle over his shoulder.

'I'll just take a quick look-see, then I'll get the water,' he said.

Dawson was back in under five minutes, the metal water jug in his hands.

'Still no movement, and no sound,' he reported. 'It's like a bloody ghost town out there. Which is good for us,' he added.

He carved a couple of chunks of meat off the ham bone, passed one to Sykes and then ate the other.

'Now we have to make a decision,' Sykes said, when they'd finished their scratch breakfast.

'I don't think we've got a lot of choice, sir. You can't walk any distance and there's no cart or anything here. So why don't we just use what we've got?' Dawson asked. 'That's the simplest way out of here. Let's pull on the German coats and helmets, climb back on the bike, fire it up and head west. If the uniforms don't get us a clear passage, the machine-gun will.'

'I'm not disputing that. The problem is, we've no idea what's been going on since we shot our way out of Liège. We've no intelligence at all. No way of finding out the situation until we actually get back on the main road – if we decide to go that way.'

'You mean we won't know if it's the Germans who are in control, or the Belgians, or nobody?'

'Exactly,' Sykes nodded. 'We know that yesterday afternoon the Germans had arrived in Liège and were taking control of the city. But according to those Belgian soldiers we spoke to, most of the enemy forces were still on the east side of the river, because some of the bridges had been blown up. Overnight, one of three things could have happened. The German forces might have advanced all the way to the Belgian fall-back position, a line running from Antwerp down to Namur, and then on to Givet in France. Or the Belgian forces might have launched a counter-attack and taken back the territory they'd lost.'

'With what we've seen so far, that seems pretty bloody unlikely,' Dawson commented.

'I agree.'

'And the third possibility?'

'Some variant of the first two, with the area between Liège and Namur becoming a battle-ground as the two sides face each other.'

'So when we drive back onto the main road, we'll have no idea if it's held by German or Belgian troops, or if we'll be stepping into the middle of a full-scale battle?'

'I think we'd probably hear it if the fighting was that close, Dawson, but yes – that's right. And whatever colour uniforms we see when we reach the road, wearing German coats and driving a German BMW motorcycle combination won't necessarily be a good thing. Whoever has control up on that road will certainly be surprised to see us. What we won't know is whether that surprise will be translated into a volley of rifle shots from some Belgian soldiers or a bunch of orders shouted at us in German. That's the problem.'

Dawson grinned at him. 'So why don't we avoid going on the road altogether? Keep heading west but stay on the country roads? Or even go cross-country? I think that motorbike would be pretty good on the rough stuff.'

'It would, Dawson. I had thought about that. Two problems: we don't have a detailed map of the area – the one I've got only shows the main roads, not all the little tracks and country lanes – and I don't know how much punishment my leg can take if the going gets really rough.' Sykes paused for a moment. 'But on balance, that might still be our best option. We can navigate by the sun if all else fails. We'll just have to make sure we ditch the German uniforms and helmets well before we reach the Belgian lines. It would be really ironic to be shot to death by Allied soldiers as we tried to cross over to our own side of the line.'

Ten minutes later, Dawson helped Sykes to stand up and then settled him in the sidecar as best he could. He passed the major the Lee-Enfield, which Sykes tucked down beside his legs. The machine-gun clipped to the sidecar made the rifle somewhat redundant as either a defensive or offensive weapon. Sykes settled the German helmet on his head and nodded to show that he was ready to go.

Dawson pulled on the other heavy motorcycle coat, jammed on his helmet and started the bike's engine. He nosed the machine out of the barn and rode it slowly around the side of the farmhouse. He stopped, removed the chain from the gatepost, swung the gate wide and drove out onto the narrow and unmade road.

Then he stopped, closed the gate and looped the chain around the post. He glanced at the sun, noting its position in the sky, then checked his watch.

'That's about north,' he said, pointing towards the main part of the village they'd driven through the previous evening. 'So we need to head over in that direction.' Dawson swung his arm through about ninety degrees, towards a couple of fields.

'And there are no tracks anywhere over there as far as I can see,' Sykes said. 'At least to start with, let's try and stick to some kind of prepared surface. We can go cross-country – through the fields – later, when we might not have any choice.'

Dawson looked along the poorly surfaced road down which they'd approached the village. 'We didn't pass any roads heading that way when we drove here last night,' he said thoughtfully. 'Or, at least, I don't remember seeing any.'

'Nor do I. So I suggest you turn right and head north. That'll take us away from the main road, which is probably a good thing. We might even see a signpost somewhere that will help.'

Sykes took out the map he'd used the previous day, unfolded it and placed it on his lap. For a few moments he looked down at it, then glanced across at Dawson.

'As I said, this isn't going to be much use. It doesn't even show Verlaine, nor this road we're on right now, so it certainly won't have any of the even more minor roads on it. But if we *do* see a signpost somewhere, and the place-name is on the map, I'll be able to work out approximately where we're heading. Right, let's get going.'

Dawson nodded agreement and pulled the motor-cycle goggles down over his eyes. Then he engaged first gear and released the clutch, and steered the combination back towards the centre of the village, retracing their route of the previous evening.

Again, the village of Verlaine – it would probably have been more accurate to call it a hamlet – appeared utterly deserted. No people, no farm animals. They didn't even see a dog or a cat.

Dawson drove the motorcycle slowly through the village and out the other side, the exhaust note of the big twin-cylinder engine echoing off the deserted houses. The condition of the road deteriorated quite quickly as they left the last couple of houses behind them, and what had been a fairly wide but unmade street through the village soon became just as narrow and twisting as the road to the south of Verlaine had been. The surface went from mud with occasional cobbles to just hard-packed mud, rutted with cart tracks and potholes. Trees grew on both sides. Within a fairly short distance they realized the track was taking them through the outskirts of a wood.

They rode on for what Dawson estimated was about a mile before they encountered a junction – in reality little more than another track branching off the one they were following – and that was to the right, and would have taken them back towards Liège, which was the last thing they wanted. So Dawson forged on, continuing to the north, or north-west.

About three or four miles from Verlaine, he suddenly braked the combination to a stop and switched off the engine.

'What is it?' Sykes asked.

'I think that's a road dead ahead of us. Looks like a T-junction. I'm going to check it before we try to drive across it.'

Dawson took the Lee-Enfield from Sykes and walked cautiously up the track, which started widening slightly and also began sloping gently uphill. The wood was much thicker all around them, trees crowding them on all sides. Before he stepped onto what he could now see was a rough cobbled road, Dawson paused and listened intently. But apart from birdsong, he could detect nothing.

He moved to the left-hand side of the track and stepped forward another couple of paces, still concealed by the undergrowth. He snatched two quick glances – left and right – but the road, such as it was, appeared to be empty. Dawson strode out into the centre of the cobbles, where he would have a completely unobstructed view to confirm it. Nothing moved in either direction. He glanced over to the opposite side of the road, where the track they'd been following continued into the forest.

Then he walked back to where Sykes was waiting.

'All clear,' he said, starting the motorcycle again. 'It's a cobbled road, not very wide. No sign of any vehicles or people on it.'

'Good,' Sykes said.

Dawson accelerated the combination to the edge of the road, looked left and right again, just to make sure it was still all clear, then powered the motorcycle over the road and back into the forest. As the combination's wheels ran over the cobbles, the whole machine shook and rattled.

'Why do the Belgies put cobbles everywhere, sir?' Dawson asked. 'Haven't they ever heard of tarmac?'

'They call it *pavé*,' Sykes said, 'and they don't put it everywhere, but you're right – they certainly do use it quite a lot.'

The track ran straight for about 200 yards, then bent sharply around to the left, to the west, and straightened out again, for no reason that seemed to make sense.

'I've no idea,' Sykes said, in answer to Dawson's unspoken question. 'But it's going the right way, so just keep following it. Maybe there's another village in front of us.'

Sykes's guess was right. Within about ten minutes they entered the eastern end of another small settlement, which appeared to be just as deserted as Verlaine had been.

Dawson spotted a small shop on the right-hand side of the main street and pulled the BMW combination to a stop just outside it.

'What are you doing?' Sykes asked.

'Trying to find out where we are, sir,' Dawson replied. He climbed off the motorbike, walked across to the shop front and peered inside the window beside the door. A few moments later he returned.

'Might be called Dreye,' he said. 'Seen a couple of signs inside that mention that name.'

Sykes looked closely at his map, then nodded. 'Could be,' he said, 'could be. There is a village marked on the map named Dreye. If that's where we are, we're definitely heading in the right direction.' He checked the map again, measuring distances by eye. 'If we *are* at Dreye – and I can't see anywhere else with a name anything like that – then we've covered nearly half the distance between Liège and Namur.'

'And that's where the Belgian troops should be massing to stop the Jerries?' Dawson asked.

'That's their fallback position, yes. So I think we're probably close enough now to lose these blasted coalscuttles we've got on our heads and ditch the coats as well. We definitely don't want to reach the Belgian lines dressed like German soldiers.'

Sykes reached up, seized the steel helmet he'd been wearing since they left Liège and tossed it away. Then he unbuttoned the coat and, with Dawson's help, managed to take it off. The major sat back in the sidecar, his face again grey with pain.

'In fact, sir,' Dawson said, after a moment, 'I think we might be better hanging on to these coats. They're really warm. If I hack off all the insignia they shouldn't even look that military.'

Sykes nodded his agreement, and Dawson took out his pocket knife, sliced through the stitching holding the rank and regiment badges in place and tossed away the insignia. Then he wrapped the coat around Sykes's legs to keep him warm. He repeated the operation on his own coat, but shrugged it back on – riding the bike was a little chilly if he was driving at over about ten miles an hour, and in the saddle he was totally exposed to the elements. But, like Sykes, he lobbed the coal-scuttle helmet well away from the motorcycle combination. He'd left his own British army issue steel helmet back in the staff car with the bodies of the two German soldiers he'd incinerated, so he'd have to ride bareheaded, but at least the goggles would keep the wind out of his eyes.

He started the bike again, and they drove slowly through the silent village and out the other side, and neither saw nor heard anyone.

At the far end of the village, Dawson found a track that seemed to be heading broadly west, again straight into a wood, and turned the motorcycle combination onto it. The surface was rutted and uneven, a mixture of stones and hard-packed earth. He had to keep the speed down as much as he could to avoid jolting Major Sykes more than necessary. That meant they were only travelling at about walking pace for most of the time.

Sykes had abandoned the map, simply because none of the tracks they'd seen were marked on it. They were navigating primarily by the position of the sun, using their watches to work out directions because neither man had a compass. Dawson had never been issued with one, and Sykes's marching compass was somewhere in the medical centre back at Eben Emael, removed from his belt when his wound had been dressed. But as the morning wore on, and the sun climbed higher, they were both satisfied they were going in more or less the right direction, broadly speaking west, and heading towards a point somewhere to the north of Namur.

'A bit bloody spooky, this,' Dawson said, as the woodland opened out to one side of them and they could see perhaps half a dozen small farm cottages over to their left, dotted around the fields. None showing any signs of life whatsoever. 'This reminds me of when I got stuck behind German lines with old Watson, near the Warndt Forest. The Jerries had evacuated everyone from their homes, just in case the Frogs got a sudden injection of courage and tried to invade. And they'd taken everything – horses, cows, sheep, the lot – just like here.'

'And for pretty much the same reason,' Sykes commented, 'except that here, the Belgian civilians know for certain that the German army will be overrunning the area. The only thing they don't know is when – whether it'll be today, tomorrow or the day after. But they do know the Jerries are on their way. That's why they've all legged it. The main roads are probably jammed solid with refugees by now. That's not going to help us get our troops into position.'

'Might slow down the German advance, though,' Dawson said.

Sykes shook his head. 'Based on their performance up to now, I don't think the German troops have quite the same scruples as we have. We'd manoeuvre around groups of civilians. I think the Germans would simply aim straight for them, expecting them to jump out of the way. If they didn't, too bad.'

The track they were following was getting slightly wider, the surface generally smoother and less rutted, but Dawson still kept the speed down because they literally didn't know what was around the next corner.

If he *had* known what was around the corner, he might have wished he'd been going faster, because moments later the motorcycle combination drove into a small clearing, and virtually into the middle of a group of German soldiers relaxing around a half-track.

A half-track that was parked squarely across the track Dawson and Sykes had been following.

CHAPTER 22

11 MAY 1940: EASTERN BELGIUM

For an instant, time stood still as Dawson took in the unexpected – and massively unwelcome – sight. He'd hoped they'd left the enemy troops a long way behind, consolidating their hold over Liège. Or, if they'd already started to advance west, he and Sykes presumed they'd only use the main roads. What the hell was a squad of soldiers doing so deep in the woods?

With their route ahead completely blocked, Dawson did the only thing he could. He twisted the throttle and steered the motorcycle combination over to the left side of the clearing, where he could see a break in the under-growth.

'Hang on!' he yelled, though his instruction was probably superfluous.

Sykes was already hunkering down in the sidecar, making himself a smaller target and at the same time jamming the knee of his good leg under the metal of the covering to wedge himself in. And he hadn't forgotten the machine-gun.

As Dawson accelerated the vehicle across the clearing, Sykes swung the Mauser MG 34 towards the German troops and squeezed the trigger. The bucking and twisting of the sidecar made accurate shooting impossible, but the Mauser spat a hail of fire towards the enemy soldiers. They ducked and dived into cover, reaching for their weapons.

'The half-track!' Dawson shouted. 'Go for the tyres. And the radio.'

The half-track was a reconnaissance vehicle, fitted with a large aerial and a radio set.

Sykes nodded, released the trigger and shifted his point of aim towards the parked vehicle. He concentrated on the radio first, then switched his aim to the front end of the half-track, the machine-gun bouncing up and down with the violent movement of the motorcycle combination.

Bullets smashed into the radiator and headlamps. Sykes tried to lower the barrel slightly, but it was all he could do to just keep the weapon pointing in the general direction of his target. A couple of rounds bounced off the steel of one of the front wheels of the half-track. He kept firing, more in hope than expectation, pouring an almost continuous stream of bullets towards the vehicle.

Then two things happened almost simultaneously. The Mauser's bolt slammed open – the fifty-round magazine was empty – and there was a sudden loud bang as one of the front tyres of the half-track exploded.

But by then one of the German soldiers had his weapon and returned fire. There was a crack and a rifle bullet screamed past Dawson, slamming into the trunk of a tree on one side of the clearing.

The gap in the undergrowth Dawson was aiming for

looked vanishingly small as he accelerated towards it. But they had nowhere else to go. No other options at all. With the Mauser machine-gun now out of ammunition, the only other effective close-quarter weapon they possessed was the Schmeisser machine-pistol he had slung around his neck. But Dawson knew that trying to take on half a dozen German front-line troops armed only with that would be nothing short of suicidal.

The combination bounced across the ground, the tyres scrabbling for grip, the engine roaring. Two more shots rang out behind them, but then the motorcycle smashed through a couple of low bushes that marked the edge of the clearing and plunged into the undergrowth beyond.

A six-foot-tall sapling rose up in front of them. There was no chance for Dawson to avoid it. The sapling stood no chance either. The front of the sidecar hit it at about twenty-five miles an hour and completely flattened it. Beyond it, trees loomed. Dawson knew if they hit one of them it would be all over. If they survived the impact, the German soldiers would be on them in seconds.

But they were hidden from the view of the soldiers in the clearing – at least for a few seconds. Another couple of shots were fired in their general direction, the bullets whistling menacingly through the undergrowth, but, like the earlier ones, they both missed.

Dawson slowed the motorcycle a fraction and looked round, trying to pick the best way out. He swung right, back towards the track through the wood, because that was their only hope. Trees blocked them in every direction. They had to pray the track beyond the clearing wasn't full of German troops.

He accelerated again, aiming the motorcycle combination towards a clump of bushes beyond which he could see the sun-dappled space where the track had to be.

'Hang on!' he shouted again. 'This could get bumpy.'

The bushes vanished under the wheel and body of the sidecar, and then the whole vehicle bounced violently up into the air as the front wheel of the motorcycle hit a mound of earth, before crashing back down again.

Sykes yelped with pain as the impact jarred his wounded leg.

They burst through the undergrowth and out onto the track. Dawson steered to the left, away from the clearing. The track in front of them was empty, so he twisted the accelerator as far as it would go. The BMW responded instantly, the distinctive exhaust note filling the wood. The combination accelerated rapidly, powering them away from danger.

But even over the noise of the motorcycle's engine, Dawson could hear the angry yells and shouts from the German soldiers behind them. He knew they had seconds at the most before the enemy soldiers appeared on the track behind them and started shooting.

The same thought had obviously occurred to Sykes as well. 'Give me the Schmeisser,' he ordered.

Dawson took his left hand off the handlebars, lifted the machine-pistol over his head and handed it to the major. Sykes cocked the weapon and swung around as far as he could in the sidecar.

'Start weaving,' he said. 'I'll make them keep their heads down.'

Dawson swung left, then right, increasing speed as

quickly as he could. He drove as unpredictably as he could across the whole width of the track.

Beside him, Sykes aimed the Schmeisser towards the clearing, watching for the first sign of German troops. A soldier appeared, stepped forwards and lifted his rifle to his shoulder. The major immediately fired a short burst towards him. The range was far too great for the Schmeisser to be accurate – the combination was probably over a hundred yards from the clearing already – but Sykes was counting on the psychological effect of being fired at by a machine-gun to ruin the man's aim.

It seemed to work, because almost as soon as Sykes started firing, the soldier scrambled back into cover.

But the Germans didn't need to expose themselves to fire their rifles – they only needed to see their target – and that fact was immediately apparent when they heard three shots in quick succession from behind them. Despite Dawson's evasive manoeuvring, two of the bullets hit somewhere at the back of the sidecar, but both missed Sykes.

The major fired another couple of bursts towards the clearing as Dawson tried to make the movements of the motorcycle combination even more erratic than before. Despite Sykes's attempts to frighten off the Germans, more shots sounded. But now the vehicle was kicking up a cloud of dust as well, and that was obviously unsighting the German soldiers, because every shot missed them.

They drove around a bend, the shooting behind them stopped and they could breathe more easily again.

'What the hell were those Jerries doing there?'

Dawson demanded. 'I thought we were miles from the nearest road.'

'Reconnaissance,' Sykes replied shortly. 'You saw it was fitted with a radio set. They're probably checking all the tracks in the area.'

'What do you want to do, sir? Stay on this track or another route? If we can find one, that is,' he added, under his breath.

'Keep going. At least until we get out of this wood. Right now I've no idea where we are. We're still heading roughly west, but without a detailed map we're virtually lost. But we have to keep moving. It won't take those soldiers long to change the wheel on the half-track and come after us. And if their radio is still working they'll be calling for reinforcements.'

'Did you hit the radio?' Dawson asked.

'I think so, but I can't be sure,' Sykes said.

Almost as soon as Sykes spoke, the trees started thinning out. Within seconds the track moved clear of the edge of the wood. Fields opened up on both sides of them, allowing an unrestricted view of their surroundings.

Conscious that if they carried on along the track they would become visible to any enemy soldiers there might be in the vicinity, Dawson drew the combination to a stop in the middle of the track, but left the engine running.

'Time for a look-see,' he said, and climbed up onto the saddle of the motorcycle, bracing himself by placing one foot on the top of the sidecar. Shading his eyes with his hand, he looked over to the north. There, the fields were empty of both human and animal life, but as he moved his field of view towards the west, he froze suddenly, then quickly climbed down again.

'What is it?' Sykes asked.

'I know why that Jerry patrol was lurking down that track in the woods,' Dawson said grimly. 'That field over there' – he pointed – 'is full of fucking German soldiers. We've got a pissed-off Jerry patrol right behind us and half the German army in front of us. We're buggered.'

CHAPTER 23

11 MAY 1940: EASTERN BELGIUM

'We're not dead yet, Dawson,' Sykes muttered. 'We just have to find a way to get out of this.'

'There's something else,' Dawson said. 'Just beyond that field where I saw all those Jerry soldiers, there's a major road and a railway line. I think we've come a lot further south than we expected. That could be the main road between Liège and Namur, the one we drove off last night.'

At that moment the sound of aeroplane engines – multiple aeroplane engines – suddenly intruded on their senses, and they stared up into the sky.

About a dozen multi-engined aircraft – they couldn't tell if they had two engines or three, with the third one mounted in the nose of the fuselage – were flying above them, heading south-west, and quite high. And at almost the same moment as they heard the aircraft, they also heard a distant volley of shots, and then another.

'Sounds like ack-ack – anti-aircraft – guns,' Sykes said.

As he spoke, a number of small and harmless-looking puffs of grey and black smoke suddenly appeared close to the leading aircraft in the formation.

'They're targeting the German bombers. We must be close to the Belgian positions. They must have set up ack-ack batteries there.'

A few moments later, tiny black objects began falling from the enemy aircraft as the German bombardiers selected their targets and released their weapons.

'They're dropping their bombs,' Dawson pointed out, just in case Sykes hadn't noticed.

'I know, but from the position of the aircraft I reckon we must be at least a mile away from the target, so we're in no danger.'

Dawson knew Sykes was probably right, but even so the detonation of the first bomb was shockingly loud. It felt as if the very ground shook with the impact. That was followed less than a second afterwards by a whole series of explosions, a discordant volley of high-explosive blasts that seemed to rip the very air apart. And the ground *was* shaking, Dawson was certain of it.

The anti-aircraft barrage continued unabated as the bombs dropped. Then a new and unpleasantly familiar sound intruded.

'Hear that?' Dawson asked. 'That's a bloody Stuka. They're sending in dive-bombers as well.'

For a few seconds they couldn't see the Stukas, but then Dawson spotted about half a dozen of the canted-winged aircraft following each other down in a steep dive, the unearthly scream of their sirens clearly audible even over the noise of the exploding bombs and the continuous firing of the Belgian anti-aircraft guns.

'They're getting a bloody pasting over there, that's for sure,' Dawson said gloomily, as a second wave of Stukas formed up and then began their attack dive in sequence.

215

'Yes,' Sykes agreed, 'but the good news is we must now be really close to the Belgian lines. Once we're the other side of them we'll be safe. Or safer, anyway.'

'I know. The trick's going to be getting through. With all the stick those Belgies are getting, I think they'll shoot at anything that moves. Including us, if we're still riding around in this Jerry motorcycle combination.'

Sykes nodded. 'Yes. We're going to have to work out how and when to try our luck. We can't do anything until the bombing stops, obviously, so we'd better find somewhere we can hide out for a while. You said that field to the north was empty?'

'Yes.'

'Right. We can't stay here in case those Germans have managed to fix the half-track and are already heading towards us. Let's go cross-country.'

Dawson climbed back onto the motorcycle, put it into gear and moved off, looking for a gap in the undergrowth wide enough to accommodate the combination. There were various spaces that would do, but Dawson was looking for something else as well. Eventually he made his decision, and swung the motorcycle over to the right-hand side of the track, which puzzled Sykes.

'Where are you going?' he asked.

'Just hold on, sir,' Dawson replied. 'It's time to muddy the waters a bit.'

He accelerated across to the southern edge of the track and smashed the bike through the undergrowth, driving a hole clean through it and uprooting a shrub. Then he drove the bike hard across the field, spinning the rear wheel for about twenty yards.

Then Dawson almost shut the throttle and motored

the combination in a wide, gentle turn, taking care not to leave any marks on the rough grass tussocks until he was right back at the hole he'd driven through the side of the track. With the combination moving at barely walking pace, he eased the machine through the gap and, proceeding just as carefully, rode it right across the track and through the other gap he'd spotted a few yards down on the opposite side.

Keeping the speed down, he continued across the field, hugging the edge of the woodland, until they were well out of sight of the track. Then Dawson eased the combination into the wood itself, picking an area where there were no substantial trees but plenty of shrubs and bushes that would allow them to get the machine out of sight. He swung it round so that it pointed out of the wood, slipped the gear lever into neutral and turned off the engine.

The thunderous explosions of the German bombing, interspersed by the sound of repeated volleys from the rapid-fire anti-aircraft guns of the Belgian defenders, was still deafening.

Dawson climbed off the motorcycle and walked around to the sidecar.

'Do you want me to give you a hand to get out of there, sir, or are you going to stay put?'

'I'd rather stay put, but I can't. I need to have a pee. Quite urgently, actually.'

'Understood, sir.'

Dawson bent down and lifted Sykes bodily out of the sidecar and helped him stagger across to a tree he could use for support while he urinated. When Sykes had finished, Dawson helped him back over to the combination.

The major actually seemed able to put a little weight on his wounded leg.

'You're using your left leg a bit more now, sir,' Dawson said.

Sykes nodded. 'I'm trying to. It still hurts like hell, but I've got used to that now. I know the bone's intact, so there's no reason why I can't start trying to stand up on it.'

'So what do we do now?'

Sykes leant against the motorcycle saddle and got himself as comfortable as he could before he replied. 'We get across the Belgian lines. That's the short answer. The difficult bit is how we do it. The only two things I'm certain of are that we'll have to use this motorcycle combination or another vehicle, because, although I'm trying to stand on this blasted leg, there's no way I'm going to be able to walk or run on it for a long time yet.'

'And the second thing?' Dawson prompted.

'We have to do it in daylight. If we try it at night, you're quite right – the Belgians will shoot first and ask questions later. Other than that, right now I don't have too many ideas. Any suggestions?'

Dawson shook his head. 'Not really, no. The first thing we – or rather I – ought to do is try and find out where the Jerries are positioned. The last thing we want to do is try and break through the German lines where they've got the highest concentration of troops stationed.'

'Good thinking. If we *did* try and break through at that point, it probably *would* be the last thing we ever did. So what's your plan?'

Dawson thought for a few seconds. 'I reckon the first thing is to get you settled somewhere, sir. You can't lean against that motorcycle all afternoon. Then I need to check that pannier thing on the back of the sidecar, just in case there's another magazine in it for the Mauser machine-gun. If there isn't, we might as well ditch the weapon. It'll be useless to us. Then I'll grab the Lee-Enfield or the Schmeisser and walk over to the west with your binoculars and a pencil and paper. I'll keep out of sight and do a bit of spying. I should be able to get at least some idea of their strength and dispositions. When I get back, we can decide what to do and when to do it.'

Sykes nodded. 'You're the boss, Corporal,' he said, his face creasing into a smile. 'You know what I mean,' he added.

Ten minutes later, Sykes was propped up against a tree a short distance away from the motorcycle combination, as well hidden from view as Dawson could manage, but the major still had a reasonable view of the immediate area. Beside him was one of their two canteens that Dawson had filled with water at the farm on the outskirts of Verlaine – the other one was attached to Dawson's webbing – and lying across his lap was the Lee-Enfield rifle, loaded and ready to fire, and with two full loading clips to hand.

When Dawson checked the pannier at the back of the sidecar, he found it didn't contain a replacement magazine for the Mauser MG 34: it had three of them, all fully loaded. But Dawson and Sykes decided it made better sense not to reload the Mauser, at least, not for the moment. If the combination was discovered by a German patrol, and the weapon was unloaded, it might imply that the vehicle had been abandoned. A reloaded machine-gun could suggest an intention to return, and the Germans might leave a couple of sentries to guard the vehicle, which would scupper their plan good and proper. The last thing Dawson did was to pull out the two halves of the demolition charge and conceal them in the undergrowth nearby.

Dawson picked up the Schmeisser machine-pistol – it was a much better close-quarter weapon than his trusty Lee-Enfield, and would be more effective in making any German troops he encountered keep their heads down – gave it a quick but thorough clean, loaded it and slung it over his shoulder, then walked to the edge of the wood and peered out. The fields in front of him were still deserted. He could see no sign of movement from the direction of the track they'd been driving along, so presumably either the German soldiers were still working on their vehicle or they'd followed the tracks he'd made in the field lying over to the south. Or, the thought suddenly occurred to him with an unpleasant rush, they might have driven straight down to the main German force to summon reinforcements to carry out a full search of the area. Then he dismissed the idea. The German forces were massing to break through the main Belgian line of defence. They'd hardly waste their time and energy mounting an exhaustive search for two lost enemy soldiers. At least, that was what he hoped.

Dawson took a last look back into the wood. The motorcycle combination was far from obvious but, because he knew exactly where it was, he could still see it. But Major Sykes was completely invisible. Dawson gave an encouraging thumbs-up in the direction he thought the officer was hidden, then turned round and stepped forward, keeping to the outskirts of the wood, and hopefully out of sight.

CHAPTER 24

11 MAY 1940: EASTERN BELGIUM

The edge of the wood angled more or less north-west, as far as Dawson could estimate, based on the time of day and the position of the sun. That wasn't really the direction he wanted to go, but it would have to do. He certainly wasn't going to wander across the open field, exposed to view from all sides.

He was able to move fairly quickly, just because he was within the tree-line and so effectively invisible to anyone outside the wood itself. But he'd only covered about a hundred yards before he realized that the wood was coming to an end. And, in fact, to a point. He kept getting glimpses of the open sky from over to his right. It was soon obvious that there was another field on that side, only a few yards away.

Dawson cut across to his right to check the lie of the land. That edge of the wood was fairly straight, like the side of it he'd been following, but both sides were narrowing towards an apex about thirty yards ahead. On the north wide of the wood lay another field, about the same size as the one to the south, and that, too, appeared to be completely empty.

He continued to the last handful of trees and stopped, still hidden by the undergrowth. Dawson checked in all directions, looking for trouble, while he decided where to go next. The German soldiers, he was fairly sure, were in the next field down to the south, or possibly the one beyond that – the gently undulating landscape meant that he couldn't see them from his present position. This also meant, obviously, they couldn't see him.

In front of him, an uneven line of undergrowth – not really thick enough to be called a hedge – ran along the dividing line between the two fields. It didn't look to him as if the fields were big enough to justify being separated, but maybe they belonged to different farms. The undergrowth petered out after about fifty yards, where another line of stumpy bushes crossed it at right angles before it, too, straggled to an untidy halt. Beyond that, all the way to the next patch of woodland, which was where Dawson needed to get to, was open ground with not a shred of cover.

He looked around, but there were no other routes he could take to reach his objective, just as he'd guessed when he first checked the terrain before leaving Sykes and the motorcycle.

Dawson unslung the Schmeisser from his shoulder and grasped it in his hands. He needed to be ready for any eventuality now he was about to leave the cover afforded by the wood. He took a final glance all around him, making sure no German troops had appeared since the last time he'd checked, then stepped forward cautiously on to the right-hand – the northern – side of the line of growth.

The undergrowth wasn't tall enough to conceal him

if he walked, so he ducked down into a crouch, making sure no part of his body projected above the level of the bushes. He was aware that he would be in view of anyone in the field to the north, but hoped he'd be difficult to spot with the line of tangled undergrowth immediately behind him.

He made his way slowly and steadily to the point where the undergrowth was intersected by the other line of bushes, checking both in front and behind him every few seconds. But he neither saw nor heard anybody. Of course, hearing anything wasn't easy, because, although the high-level bombers were giving the Belgians a rest – presumably they'd returned to their base in Germany to rearm and refuel – the Stukas were still pounding the Belgian lines in waves. But the Belgians were still putting up a furious defence, their anti-aircraft guns hurling their defiance into the air in the face of the plummeting bombers, an almost constant hammering of explosions that peppered the sky with lethal black clouds of shrapnel.

As Dawson watched, one of the mid-air bursts detonated right in front of the wing of one of the Stukas. The explosion ripped a section of the skin of the wing off, and a blazing fire started instantly in the wing root. The pilot jinked in the opposite direction and tried to pull out of the dive. But it was too late. The aircraft's nose lifted slightly, then it rolled to the right and plunged to the ground, crashing in a ball of fire, the top of which was visible to Dawson even over the tops of the trees ahead of him.

'Got the bastard,' he muttered to himself, but then realized the Belgian anti-aircraft gunners might have actually made the situation on that part of the front line even worse. Instead of just coping with bombs, they were now probably also contending with burning aviation fuel, not to mention the devastating impact of the aircraft itself. But the fact that they'd hit one of the Stukas might make the pilots of the others a bit more cautious. At least, that's what he hoped.

Before he moved, he checked all around again, but the fields still appeared to be as empty as before. Dawson looked at the seventy yards or so of open ground in front of him. He was fairly sure nobody could see him, but ambling across the field as if he was out for a Sunday afternoon stroll didn't seem the most sensible way to cover the ground. So he took a deep breath, then erupted from the undergrowth and started to run.

He jigged from side to side as well, presenting as difficult a target as possible, just in case he'd been wrong, and there were enemy troops watching his progress.

But no shots rang out, and he heard no cries of alarm. He ran headlong into the wood on the opposite side of the open field and stopped the instant he was inside the tree-line. For a few seconds he stood there, catching his breath and checking his immediate vicinity, his rifle held ready. Dawson was fit, but no army uniform is designed for sprinting, and he hadn't had much to eat for the last couple of days, one way and the other.

When he'd got his breath back, he checked the Schmeisser again, an essential reflex action, once more inspected the field he'd just crossed, then set off through the trees towards the field where he'd seen the German soldiers.

As before, he kept just inside the wood, the trees affording him adequate cover. But now he moved much more slowly, because he knew he had to be getting closer to the German lines. Every few feet he stopped dead and scanned all round, looking for anything out of place, for any sign of the presence of the enemy troops.

But it wasn't until he'd almost reached the edge of that small section of woodland that he finally saw them. A large number of German soldiers milling around in the field to the left of him, all fully armed and clearly ready for combat. A babble of voices reached him – orders and instructions, and conversations between soldiers who were bored, worried or frankly terrified as they waited for something to happen. There were sentries posted around the edge of the field, but none close to his observation point. Or, none that he could see, anyway.

Drawn up in lines, and also obviously just waiting for the order to advance, was a motley collection of commercial trucks, a few civilian cars and several carts, the horses that would be used to pull them tethered on the far side of the field. And there were half-tracks, many with artillery pieces hitched behind them, motorcycle combinations and, more ominously, at least a dozen tanks.

Before Dawson had left Britain the previous year, by which time war with Germany was an inevitability, he'd attended a number of briefings, including several concerned with the recognition of enemy vehicles and weapons. He shaded his eyes and stared at the tanks, recognizing the closest one as a Panzer IV, and the one parked next to it as a Panzer III. The others were only partially visible, but he guessed they were probably models of the same two types. He could see a *lot* of tanks drawn up in rows. In fact, now he was able to get a proper look at the enemy forces, he realized they didn't look as if they were preparing for immediate combat. It seemed more like a forward holding position, where the troops and armour would wait for additional reinforcements before assembling in battle formation to advance on the enemy. And now he could smell cooking as well, and saw several groups of German soldiers carrying mess tins and obviously eating meals.

Dawson made sure he was still unobserved, rested the machine-pistol against a tree trunk, then took out a pencil and paper, licked the end of the pencil and made swift notes about the disposition of the German vehicles he could see, counting the vehicles and trying to get a rough estimate of the numbers of soldiers. Many of these were clad in the black 'boiler suits' used by Panzer crews. When he'd finished, he glanced at what he'd written. It seemed a depressingly large and well-balanced force to throw at whatever defences the Belgians had been able to muster. If Sykes had been right about the number of tanks the Belgian army possessed – Dawson thought the major had said they only had about ten of them in total – then the Germans should have no trouble punching a hole straight through the Belgian lines.

And the other thing Dawson knew was he was probably only looking at one small part of the German forces in the area.

He put away his notes, grabbed the Schmeisser and started working his way through the wood to the north-west, towards the next open area, the other part of the same field which ran to the south-west of the woodland, where the Germans might also have been massing their forces. When he got there and peered out cautiously, he found it was almost a repeat of what he'd seen in the first part of the field – a mix of soldiers and vehicles, all clearly just waiting for orders, and for the dive-bombers to finish their deadly work.

Again, Dawson made notes. When they – or rather *if* they – made it through the lines, the information he'd gleaned would be invaluable to the commander of the defending forces. At least he'd know exactly what he would be facing when the German advance finally started, and knowing the enemy's strength and disposition was always invaluable, even if it proved to be somewhat depressing knowledge.

The patch of woodland Dawson was sheltering in had German forces on both sides of it, that much he now knew. But he wasn't any further forward in finding some route that he and Sykes could use to get past them. Going down to the south didn't seem to be a viable option, because Dawson was almost certain it was the main road between Liège and Namur down there. The Germans would probably be massing their troops on that road when they were ready to continue the invasion. He presumed they were using the open fields either side of the road as additional parking and holding areas for their forces, as he'd just observed in the two fields close to him.

So the only possible way through, he figured, was to go further north, deeper into the wooded countryside and away from that main road, and hope to find a track they could use somewhere up there. Dawson picked up the machine-pistol again and stealthily began to retrace his steps.

At the eastern end of the wood he paused for a few seconds to both check his surroundings and get his bearings. Yet again he wished he had a compass to be sure of the direction he should be heading, but without one he would just have to rely on the sun, which in fact he couldn't see from where he was standing. But what he could see were shadows, and that was almost as good. He hoped.

Dawson glanced at his watch, then looked at the angle of the shadows cast by the trees on the edge of the wood across the open field in front of him. They suggested that he was looking almost due east, so he needed to turn left ninety degrees and head that way. That didn't look too bad, as the wood extended for perhaps a hundred yards in that direction. He stepped away from the edge of the undergrowth and started walking.

None of the woods he'd walked through were particularly overgrown, but the narrow gaps between the trees mean that they wouldn't be able to ride the motorcycle combination through any of them. What he needed to find was another track, something like the one they'd been following earlier in the day. And he'd only covered about seventy yards, he guessed, when he found one.

It wasn't quite as wide as the previous one, but it was more than adequate to cope with the combination. What Dawson now had to do was find out where it went – which hopefully wasn't directly into some other field being used as an encampment for German soldiers. He kept in the wood to one side of the track, about twenty feet away, which he hoped would be far enough if there were German sentries posted anywhere along it, and started walking. He checked the sun's position again, from the direction of the shadows he could see, and he estimated he was now heading north-west. Not exactly where he was hoping to go, but close enough.

The wood got thicker the further he penetrated, the trees bigger and closer together, and the undergrowth denser, which he assumed meant that the wood was older than the others he'd explored. He was making more noise as he walked through it, breaking branches and crushing undergrowth, but making a noise still wasn't a problem because of the continuing bombing nearby.

And then, through a gap in the trees over to his left, to the west, he saw more German uniforms, and even the sound of big petrol engines running. He froze in mid-step, then made his way carefully over to that side of the wood, chose a vantage point and looked out.

After a few moments, Dawson guessed he was probably looking at the far end of the northern part of the field he'd checked before, the second holding area for the German forces. There was the same mix of vehicles and men, and the only obvious difference was that these tanks and trucks were pointing to the south, which was presumably the direction from which they'd arrived. And more vehicles seemed to be arriving all the time, mainly trucks and horse-drawn carts, and a number of half-tracks, many of them towing artillery pieces. He guessed the German plan was to send the invasion force towards Namur using the roads as much as possible, simply because the terrain didn't favour a cross-country advance: there were too many woods and ditches to make that a viable option. Even the tanks would find getting through the woods difficult or even impossible. Trees made really effective natural anti-tank defences – that was one of the reasons why the French apparently believed the German invasion of their country would come from the Belgian plains, not through the Ardennes Forest.

And that was a bit of good news. Dawson looked back towards the track. Between the field and the track was quite a substantial stand of timber which would provide a natural, and almost impregnable, barricade against any German attack on them, as long as they stayed on the track. He checked up and down the track, then crossed to the other side. But the forest there was just as thick, and appeared to extend at least fifty yards to the north-east – another natural defence for anyone using the track.

Just one more question needed to be answered: where did the track go?

Still keeping away from the track itself, just in case, Dawson plodded onwards, getting deeper and deeper into the forest. Then, as the track curved gently around to the left and then straightened up again, he saw a flash of grey in the distance, and stopped immediately. He moved slightly to one side so he could see better, and brought the binoculars up to his eyes.

He should have expected it. The Germans were nothing if not thorough, and there was no way they'd not place a guard of some sort on any roads or tracks leading to their next objective. He was looking at a simple road-block. He could see two German soldiers, one armed with a rifle and the other carrying a Schmeisser machine-pistol, and in front of them a wooden trestle that blocked over half the width of the road. It wouldn't prove a serious barrier to a car or truck, but it was certainly enough to stop a motorcycle combination.

The barrier would have to be moved. Unless, Dawson thought, looking more carefully, he could simply ride around it. It really all depended on what the ground was like at the side of the track. But it was a possible escape route, the best way out – in fact it was the only way out – he'd found so far.

And there was another factor. He glanced up. The sun was high in the sky, rays of light lancing through the tops of the trees and turning the woodland gold and green. It was now early afternoon. He and Sykes had already decided they had to attempt their crossing in daylight, so the Belgian soldiers would be able to see their uniforms and the white flag Sykes would be holding up. Trying to cross the border in the evening – or even worse at night – especially after the pounding the Belgians had been suffering, would simply be too dangerous, almost suicidal.

Dawson made his decision. They'd have to use the track, and sort out the road-block, one way or the other, when they reached it. He took a last look up the track, fixing the position of the road-block in his mind, then set off back the way he'd come.

As on his outward journey, he saw nobody and heard nothing apart from the continuing noise of the bombardment of the Belgian defences. That situation continued until he'd almost reached the spot where he'd parked the motorcycle combination. He was probably about a hundred yards away when, even over the noise of the bombs and the rapid-fire guns, he heard a vehicle engine, quite close by.

Instantly, Dawson froze, looking round to identify the source of the noise. Then he saw it. A German half-track, its nose scarred by numerous bullet holes, was creeping steadily along the edge of the wood towards him. It didn't take a genius to realize it was the same vehicle Sykes had riddled with machine-gun fire back in the clearing, and that probably meant the Jerries had seen through his spur-of-the-moment deception back on the track. Or maybe they'd investigated the field opposite and found nothing, so now they were checking this one as well.

Whatever had happened, it didn't matter. All that was important was that they were here now, right in front of him, clearly still searching. But then Dawson realized something else. The half-track was between him and the motorcycle combination, and they must have missed seeing it. So as long as he could stay under cover until it had gone past – and that wouldn't be difficult – he could get back to Sykes, and hopefully they'd be able to make their escape as soon as the German vehicle had left the area.

Dawson eased down into a crouch and then lay full-length behind a bush as the half-track drew closer. He could clearly see the driver and passenger, both staring into the wood as they drove along the periphery, and another couple of soldiers sitting in the flat-bed section of the half-track, and doing exactly the same, their weapons held ready.

None of the four men spotted Dawson. He waited until the vehicle had driven at least seventy yards behind him before he moved. Then he stood up, and started walking quickly towards his objective.

But then something struck him. He suddenly remembered there had been six soldiers with the vehicle

233

previously, not four. He didn't think Sykes had killed any when they'd blasted past it – he'd been concentrating on disabling the half-track. So where the hell were the other two Jerry soldiers?

CHAPTER 25

11 MAY 1940: EASTERN BELGIUM

It was a question that was answered almost immediately. Not in a way Dawson would have hoped.

He heard a yell from somewhere in front of him and saw a man in a grey uniform standing just at the edge of the wood, maybe fifty or sixty yards away. Dawson instinctively dodged into cover, a split-second before a rifle bullet ploughed through the undergrowth right beside him. A couple of seconds later, another shot rang out and the bullet thudded into the trunk of a tree a few yards away.

The German tactic was now obvious. They'd sent the half-track on ahead to make the enemy soldiers keep their heads down, then had a couple of soldiers following it about a hundred yards behind, very quietly, so that when the idiot Englishman – that was Dawson, in this case – popped up out of cover and started strolling around, they could shoot him down. The only mistake the Jerry had made was in shouting – presumably for his companion – before he pulled the trigger of his Mauser. If he hadn't done that, Dawson knew he'd now very probably be lying dead in a pool of blood.

That could still happen. He had the Schmeisser MP 38 machine-pistol, certainly, but it was a fairly unreliable weapon. At least one, maybe both, of the German soldiers was armed with a Mauser Karabiner 98K rifle, a proper combat rifle that was accurate up to about 800 yards. For the first time he regretted not having taken the Lee-Enfield when he set off on his reconnaissance mission.

Dawson weighed these facts in his mind, his brain spinning as he figured the angles. If he ran through the wood, sooner or later they'd catch sight of him and, the moment they did so, they'd kill him. The wood wasn't thick enough for him to get away like that. His only chance, he realized, was to stay hidden and get them closer – a lot closer – to where he'd taken cover, to bring them within range of the Schmeisser.

He'd only seen one of the soldiers in front of him: the man who'd fired at him and called out. But he knew there were two of them because of the second shot, the one that had hit the tree behind him. Dawson was already caught in the crossfire, and he had no idea where the second soldier was located. In fact, he didn't even have that much idea where the first one was either, because he'd also ducked down after he fired.

He had another problem as well. Despite the noise of the bombing and anti-aircraft gunfire, and the sound of the engine of the half-track, Dawson was quite sure the noise of the rifle shots would have been clearly audible to the German soldiers in the vehicle. So he could expect them to join the party any time.

Dawson waited, the Schmeisser with its bolt back, ready to fire. There was no rate-of-fire selector: the MP

38 was an open-bolt, blowback-operated weapon that only worked in fully automatic mode, but its comparatively slow rate of fire meant short bursts or even single shots were possible if the trigger was only pulled very briefly.

He scanned the wood ahead of him, desperate to catch any glimpse of either of the enemy soldiers. Dawson drew in a breath and held it, so that not even the sound of his own breathing could spoil his absolute concentration. He swivelled his head from side to side, straining for the slightest sign of movement.

Somewhere nearby a twig snapped, the sound bizarrely audible even over the continued bombing only two or three miles away, but Dawson couldn't pinpoint the location. Maybe he could try a little distraction of his own. Keeping hold of the Schmeisser with his right hand, he felt about in the undergrowth beside him for a stone or a length of wood or something. His questing fingers closed around a section of branch about a foot long. He rolled over slightly onto his right side, and lobbed the branch backwards, over his shoulder.

It landed a couple of dozen feet behind him, and tumbled away into the undergrowth, the noise very audible. But absolutely nothing happened. Obviously the Germans knew that old trick just as well as Dawson. He needed to try something else. He couldn't afford to wait until they flanked him.

There was another patch of undergrowth about ten feet to Dawson's right. Running through it was the substantial trunk of a fallen tree, which might provide a measure of protection against bullets fired from directly in front, which is where Dawson still thought at least one of the soldiers was concealed. He remembered the

Browning. If the Jerries thought he only had a pistol they might be tempted to be a bit less cautious. He could only have been in the sight of the German soldiers for a bare second or two, and perhaps neither man had seen the Schmeisser.

It was worth a try. Dawson took out the Browning, pulled back the slide to load it and aimed it roughly at the spot where he'd seen the German soldier dive for cover. He had no hope of hitting anything. Then he squeezed the trigger, fired a single shot, and immediately leapt to his feet and dived over to his right, flattening himself behind the illusory safety of the fallen log – which, he noticed the moment he could see the wood clearly, was obviously fairly rotten.

No shots came, but from somewhere over to his left Dawson heard a mocking laugh, followed by a couple of sentences shouted in German. Maybe they'd decided he really did only have a pistol, and was terrified and cornered, firing at random, shooting at shadows. If so, that suited Dawson. He placed the Browning on the ground within easy reach and aimed the Schmeisser to his front.

Then he saw a grey shape a few yards to one side of where the soldier had ducked down, and a dark object which he knew in an instant was the barrel of a rifle. Dawson tensed, but there was no time to fire. If he tried to bring the Schmeisser to bear he'd never get the first shot off before the German soldier fired his weapon. And the distance was about forty yards – point-blank range for a Mauser carbine, approaching the limit of accuracy for the MP 38. Better to let the other man shoot first.

Dawson rolled to one side and tried to make himself as small a target as possible, down behind the fallen tree trunk. Almost immediately, the German fired, the shot driving splinters of wood off the top of the log within a foot of Dawson's head. There was no disputing the soldier knew where he was hiding.

But now Dawson had his chance. It would take the man with the Mauser at least a second or two to reload the weapon. For that brief period of time he was essentially unarmed.

Dawson raised his head just high enough to sight towards the patch of undergrowth where he'd seen the German soldier, took careful aim with the Schmeisser and squeezed the trigger. Two short bursts, maybe two or three rounds each time.

He had no idea if he'd hit the soldier or not. No sounds came from that location, but a rifle cracked from somewhere over to his left, and another bullet smacked into the log in front of him. Dawson ducked down again. Rotten wood or not, that old tree trunk was keeping him safe.

Then another shot sounded. A single round from a rifle, but some distance away. And that was followed by a scream of pain, again from over to the left. And then another shot from directly in front of Dawson, but apparently not aimed at him.

It didn't make sense. If the Germans weren't shooting at him, who were they firing at? Then he realized. He must be closer to the motorcycle combination than he'd thought. Sykes was armed with the Lee-Enfield rifle. It wasn't just Dawson who was caught in a crossfire, it was the two Germans as well.

Dawson aimed the Schmeisser again and fired another short burst towards the position of the first enemy soldier. Clearly his first couple of bursts had missed. Then he ducked again, as another bullet slammed into the log. And, moments later, the German fired another shot towards Sykes.

But this time Dawson saw exactly where he was. He'd have to take a chance, and hope that Sykes had taken out the soldier over to his left. He rose into a crouch, aimed the MP 38 as accurately as he could, and squeezed the trigger. The barrel started to lift after the first short burst. He paused, adjusted his aim and fired again, moving the muzzle slightly left and right so the spread of the bullets covered a wider area. And he kept on firing until the bolt stopped moving and the magazine was empty. He dropped the empty mag to the ground, slotted in a new one and cocked the weapon again. Then he just looked and listened.

For a few seconds there was no sound in the wood, just the constant background thunder of the bombing and the blasting of the anti-aircraft guns.

Cautiously, Dawson stared to his left, and straight ahead. Nobody moved. There was only one way to find out what had happened, and that was to go and take a look. He tucked the Browning back into his pocket and eased up into a crouch, the Schmeisser aimed at the spot he'd been firing at. Still no movement. He stood up and ran over to his right, keeping his distance and using the trees for cover, aiming to circle around behind the German soldier.

He was halfway there when another shot sounded. Dawson dropped flat to the ground, but had no idea where the bullet had gone. As far as he could tell, it had passed nowhere near him.

After a few seconds, he got back to his feet and resumed his cautious progress.

He finally saw the German soldier about fifty yards to his left. The man was lying on his back, his grey uniform puddled with dark-red circles of blood, the Mauser rifle held across his body. Dawson thought he was dead, but as he watched, the German slowly and painfully worked the bolt of his rifle, trying to load another round into the chamber.

Dawson jumped to his feet and ran across to him, just as the man completed the operation and started to swing the muzzle of the rifle towards him. He sprinted the last few feet, then dived off to his right as the German soldier's finger started to tighten on the trigger.

The shot went wild, well above Dawson's head, and then it was over. He got up, stepped forwards and wrenched the Mauser out of the man's hands. It looked as if about half a dozen of the rounds from the Schmeisser had hit the German, badly wounding him. But obviously they'd missed one of the vital organs – his heart or lungs – and there was no doubting the man's courage. Even as his blood pumped out onto the ground around him, he was still trying to fight on.

The German looked up at Dawson with pain-racked eyes, and the big corporal felt a surge of pity. There was nothing he could do for him, no medical treatment he could offer. And the man was his enemy.

Dawson bent forward and pulled out the Mauser bayonet from the scabbard on the wounded soldier's belt. The man watched him with haunted eyes.

Dawson snapped the bayonet onto the clip at the end

of the muzzle and looked down at the German, hefting the rifle in his hands.

Then he shook his head. 'I'm not going to kill you, Fritz,' he said softly. 'I admire somebody who won't give up. I just hope some of your mates come along and find you before you peg out. But I've got problems of my own. And I've got to go.'

Dawson turned, walked a few paces clear of the wounded German, reversed his grip on the Mauser carbine and rammed the bayonet deep into the ground. The upright rifle would act as an unmistakable marker for the wounded man's position if any other German soldiers came along. Then Dawson lifted a hand in silent acknowledgement to the man and strode on.

The lack of any shots from the second German soldier told its own story. When Dawson found him, about seventy yards deeper in the wood, flies were already swarming around the dead man's torso. Sykes's bullet – and it had to have been fired by the major, because nothing else made sense – had taken him in the centre of his chest. Death would have come in seconds.

Dawson barely glanced at the dead man, just picked up the German's Mauser and the ammunition he'd been carrying, then walked on.

About fifty yards later he spotted the motorcycle combination, still parked exactly where he'd left it. And a few yards behind the vehicle, Major Sykes was standing, leaning against a tree, blood streaming down his face. The moment he spotted the officer, Dawson jogged over to him.

'You OK, sir?' he asked, his eyes searching Sykes's face.

Sykes nodded. 'It looks worse than it is,' he said, 'and I was *really* lucky. A blasted wood splinter ripped a cut in my forehead.'

'A wood splinter?' Dawson didn't understand. 'How'd you get a wood splinter there?'

But before Sykes could reply, both men heard the heavy rumbling of an engine somewhere behind them. The enemy soldiers in the half-track had taken their time, but now they were getting closer.

Dawson glanced behind him and tensed. 'It's that bloody half-track,' he said.

About fifty or sixty yards away, he could make out the shape of the German vehicle as it moved slowly along the edge of the wood.

'They're probably looking for the two foot soldiers,' Sykes suggested. 'They must have heard the shots but won't know where they came from. This time when they search, they'll find us. We need to get out of here – right now.'

Dawson grunted agreement, ran across to the bushes where he'd hidden the two sections of the demolition charge, picked up one in each hand and staggered back to the combination with them. He loaded them both into the sidecar, then wrapped his arm around the major's shoulders, hustled him over to the sidecar and settled him inside it. Then he opened the rear pannier and pulled out all three spare magazines for the Mauser MG 34 mounted on the sidecar. He snapped one into place, cocked and checked the weapon, and then tucked the others onto the floor of the sidecar, where Sykes would be able to reach them easily.

It looked as if the major was right. The men in the

half-track must have heard the shots – there couldn't be any doubt about that – but they were having to search the whole of the wood to try to locate the source, and find the two soldiers they'd had on foot patrol. That was why the vehicle was moving so slowly.

'There are four of them in that half-track,' Dawson said, 'so we're outnumbered two to one, but we're not outgunned, thanks to that Mauser.'

'The odds are a bit better than that,' Sykes muttered, grasping the handle of the Mauser machine-gun, ready to fire. 'One of them is driving, so he won't be able to shoot at us, or not very quickly, anyway, so that's three against two. And we have the element of surprise on our side. And if you can drive out of here behind that half-track, that might help unsight the soldier in the front seat as well.'

'Good plan,' Dawson muttered, swinging his leg over the saddle of the motorcycle and preparing to start the engine.

Then they heard a yell from the direction of the German vehicle, and a shot rang out, narrowly missing the front of the sidecar.

'Let's go,' Dawson said, starting the engine and putting the motorcycle into gear. 'Hit the front tyres again,' he yelled, over the noise of the BMW's engine. 'Try and get them both this time. That'll stop those bastards.'

Sykes didn't respond, just squeezed the trigger of the Mauser MG 34 as the motorcycle combination leapt forward. He sent a long burst ripping through the undergrowth towards the German vehicle, which now seemed to have stopped about fifty yards away.

Rifle fire rattled out in response, but the Germans were essentially firing blind, shooting into the wood, and trying to hit a rapidly-moving target they could barely see.

Dawson steered the motorcycle combination out of the undergrowth, engine snarling and the back wheel struggling for grip on the loose surface. He swung the vehicle in a wide arc around the half-track, trying to give Sykes the best possible opportunity to engage the enemy soldiers with the machine-gun.

The Germans were shooting back, but the Mauser kept up its deadly assault on the enemy truck, forcing them to keep their heads down.

'Magazine's empty,' Sykes snapped, after a few seconds. He unclipped the empty mag and fumbled around beneath his legs to find one of the two remaining full ones.

Dawson glanced down at the major, and made a decision. They'd now turned away from the half-track. Even if Sykes managed to get another magazine loaded, the Mauser was pointing away from the target. It was time they cut and ran.

Dawson accelerated as hard as he could towards the far corner of the field, where he knew he could drive the combination onto the track he'd found. He weaved the vehicle from side to side, throwing the German soldiers off their aim. He lost count of the number of shots fired at them, and he knew at least two or three had hit the combination somewhere, but he just kept going.

He glanced behind, and saw the half-track had now started moving again, and was turning to follow them across the field. The one thing they couldn't risk was getting caught on the track with a road-block in front of them and the half-track coming up from behind.

There was only one thing he could do.

CHAPTER 26

11 MAY 1940: EASTERN BELGIUM

On the far side of the field, Dawson drove the combination behind the first clump of undergrowth he saw that would completely conceal it, shifted the gear lever into neutral and jumped off the motorcycle.

He grabbed the Mauser 98K carbine he'd taken off the dead German soldier and ran back to the edge of the undergrowth. He slipped off the safety catch, steadied his breathing and looked across the field.

The half-track was heading straight for him, picking up speed. He could see the four soldiers still in the vehicle – obviously Sykes hadn't hit any of them or done any damage to the half-track. Well, that was something he could rectify.

The Mauser's sights rested for a moment on the driver, but Dawson knew that killing or wounding him wouldn't necessarily stop the vehicle. What he needed to do was stop it mechanically, by blowing another of the front tyres. Obviously the Germans had replaced the one Sykes had shot out in the clearing, but the half-track only carried two spares. If he could shoot out one of them, that would stop the vehicle for a while. If he could destroy them both, the Germans would have to wait until another vehicle could bring them an extra wheel and tyre. And by the time that happened, he and Sykes should be long gone.

He lowered the muzzle of the Mauser and concentrated his aim on the left-hand front wheel, which was pitching and bouncing on the uneven surface. Gently, he squeezed the trigger.

The Mauser kicked against his shoulder, but Dawson knew immediately that he'd missed. The half-track had moved very slightly to one side at the crucial moment, and that had been enough for him to miss his target.

He cursed, worked the bolt to load another round and again focused all his attention on the sight picture. Again he fired, and again the bullet missed. The third time, he held the aim for longer, although he was very conscious that whatever safety margin he had was rapidly eroding – the half-track was now only about seventy yards away.

This time, the Mauser's bullet slammed straight into the tyre. Dawson heard the dull bang as it exploded, and the vehicle immediately lurched to one side, the steel wheel digging deep into the soft ground of the field.

The next shot was easy, because the target was no longer moving. Dawson drilled the fourth round neatly through the right-hand front tyre. Whatever the Germans did now, the half-track would be out of commission for at least an hour.

Heedless of the rattle of rifle shots from behind – the enemy soldiers had to be firing blind, towards the direction from which they thought he'd been shooting – he ran over to the combination, slid the Mauser into Sykes's waiting hands and climbed back onto the motorcycle.

'Done?' Sykes asked.

'It's done,' Dawson confirmed. 'I've shot out both front tyres. That truck's going nowhere fast.'

He accelerated down the track, concentrating on putting distance between them and the German soldiers, just in case they decided to follow them on foot. In about a quarter of a mile, with the track clear behind them, Dawson pulled the combination to a stop in an open area just to one side.

'Right, sir,' he said. 'Let me just take a look at your head.'

He walked around to the sidecar, quickly pulled open one of the pouches on his webbing, extracted his medical kit and started cleaning the wound on Sykes's forehead. The cut wasn't deep, just long and ragged.

'So what happened to you?' Dawson asked.

'I heard those two German soldiers walking through the wood back there,' the major said. 'How they missed the motorcycle I don't know. One was right at the edge of the wood and the other quite a long way inside, so maybe neither of them looked in the right direction. I don't know. Anyway, then I heard those two shots, one after the other. I guessed they'd spotted you. So I crawled along until I could see one of the soldiers, and I took a shot at him.'

'A good one too, sir,' Dawson interrupted. 'You drilled him right through the chest.'

'I was in an awkward position with the rifle, just because of the ground I was lying on. I had to lift up the muzzle of the Lee-Enfield, raise it up in the air, to reload it. Then the second German shot at me. The bullet smashed into the fore-end of the rifle and blew it apart, then ricocheted off the metal and ended up somewhere behind me. That's when the splinter of wood speared into my forehead. But if I hadn't had the rifle at that odd angle, the bullet would probably have gone right through my head. The Lee-Enfield's a write-off. I left it there.'

'Fuck the rifle, sir. The important thing is that you're OK.'

Dawson finished cleaning the cut, pulled out a wound dressing and held it firmly over the injury on Sykes's forehead while he tied the attached bandage around the major's head to hold the dressing in place.

'Don't forget you signed for that Lee-Enfield, Dawson,' Sykes said, with a faint smile.

'And you signed for that staff car, sir, and that went up in flames in Liège, so I think losing a rifle is probably the least of our worries.'

Sykes smiled slightly. 'So did you find a way out of here?'

'Sort of,' Dawson said, nodding. 'We're on it. This track seems to head almost straight for the Belgian lines.'

'Sounds to me like there might be a "but" at the end of that sentence,' Sykes observed.

'Yes.' Dawson grinned shortly. 'This track runs right past a whole bunch of German troops and armour, but they're all the other side of a stand of trees. There's a road-block a bit further down it. I think we'll probably have to shoot our way past it.'

'Right.' Sykes put a wealth of meaning into that single syllable. 'A big road-block?' he asked.

'No. Just a couple of Jerry soldiers and a kind of wooden trestle thing. It only blocks about half of the width of the track. If we can take out the sentries we might even be able to drive around it.' Dawson stepped back and looked down at his handiwork. 'Is that OK, sir?' he asked. 'The bandage isn't too tight?'

'No. That's fine. Let's get going.'

Dawson snapped another full magazine into place on the Mauser MG 34 machine-gun and cocked the weapon ready for Sykes. Then he started the BMW's engine again and eased the combination back onto the track, heading west towards the Belgian lines.

They'd covered only a couple of hundred yards when Dawson saw a sudden flicker of movement in the motor-cycle's rear-view mirror. He slowed down very slightly and straightened up the combination while he stared in the mirror, trying to make out what had attracted his attention. But the mirror, which was mounted on a length of steel, was vibrating so much he couldn't be sure of what he'd seen – or even if he'd seen anything at all.

'What is it?' Sykes asked, noticing Dawson had slowed down the vehicle slightly.

'I don't know. Thought I saw something behind us. I'm not sure now.'

'Keep going,' Sykes instructed. 'I'll watch behind.'

As Dawson speeded up again, the major swung round in the seat in the sidecar as much as he could and stared back down the track.

They'd driven through a series of gentle bends on the track, and large sections of it were invisible behind the foliage that lined the hardened surface. But occasionally the curves lined up and Sykes was able to see some distance back.

'Will this thing go any faster?' he asked.

'Maybe, sir. Why?'

'Because you're right. There is something back there. Two motorcycle combinations, just like this one, as far as I can tell. I think they're gaining on us.'

'Oh, shit,' Dawson muttered.

'Beautifully put. Now get us out of here.'

CHAPTER 27

11 MAY 1940: EASTERN BELGIUM

Seconds later, they heard the first crackle of machine-gun fire from behind them, and a short burst of fire crashed through the undergrowth over to the right of the track.

Dawson cranked the throttle open as wide as he could, because, no matter what happened, they had to keep ahead of the pursuing vehicles. He knew the advantage lay with the soldiers behind them. All Dawson could do was try to keep in front of them, out of range of their weapons.

They rounded the next bend and there, right in front of them, was the road-block.

With imminent death approaching from behind, it was no time for finesse. Sykes aimed the Mauser at the road-block and pulled the trigger, sending a short burst of fire slamming into the centre of the wooden trestle. The two soldiers standing guard stared at the approaching motorcycle combination, froze for an instant and dived sideways, in opposite directions.

Sykes fired again, two very short bursts either side of the trestle, to persuade the two German soldiers to keep out of the way.

'Can you get through that gap?' he demanded, looking at the narrow space between the edge of the track and the left-hand side of the trestle. The opening on the right-hand side was even more constricted – they obviously had to go to the left of the obstruction.

'I bloody hope so,' Dawson replied. 'We'll find out in a few seconds.'

Another burst of machine-gun fire crashed out from behind them. Again the bullets went wide. Dawson glanced in his mirror. The leading German motorcycle combination was noticeably closer to them now, but he ignored it. There was nothing else he could do.

He started weaving from side to side as he concentrated on the gap ahead. As Sykes said, it *was* very narrow. The combination was going to be a tight fit, but there was nowhere else they could go.

Another volley of shots echoed from behind them, this time raking the wood and undergrowth to the left of the track. Even over the noise of the motorcycle's engine, both Sykes and Dawson heard a scream. One of the German soldiers at the road-block suddenly reappeared on the track, staggering backwards, his hands clutching his chest. He fell down in an untidy heap.

'Now they're killing their own men,' Sykes observed drily.

'Just hang on.' Dawson instructed.

He stopped weaving and concentrated on the gap. He braked hard and swung left, aiming the combination squarely at the space.

Then the other German soldier stepped back into view, on the right-hand side of the track, his weapon slung over his shoulder.

'Watch him!' Dawson yelled, pointing to his right. 'Maybe he's got a grenade.'

But the German didn't raise his arm to throw anything at them. Instead, he lurched towards the trestle. It was quite obvious what he intended to do. If he pushed the trestle even a couple of feet to the left, he would block their escape. In fact, he'd probably kill them, because they were travelling far too fast to stop in the remaining distance.

'Stop him,' Dawson said urgently.

The German soldier ducked down behind the wooden trestle. Dawson could see him bracing his legs against the ground, his back to the wooden structure, as he tried to force the barrier across the track in front of them.

Sykes had already traversed the Mauser machine-gun to the right on its mount and, as Dawson finally lined up the combination to aim at the diminishing gap, the major opened fire.

It was almost point-blank range. The salvo of bullets smashed into the German soldier's side and threw him bodily backwards into the undergrowth, away from the end of the trestle.

But the damage was already done. He had managed to shift the wooden structure by at least a foot or so.

Dawson's left boot was already scraping along the line of shrubs and bushes at the edge of the track, the branches tugging and pulling at his foot and leg and clattering against the steel of the motorcycle. He dropped the speed even further, because he daren't risk getting stuck. If he did, the pursuing Germans would be on them in seconds.

Then the right-hand side of the sidecar crashed into

the end of the trestle. The sidecar mudguard jammed into the wood and acted as a pivot, swinging the vehicle around to the right and bringing it to a noisy, juddering and violent halt.

Dawson jammed the gear lever into neutral and leapt off the motorcycle. He passed the Schmeisser to Sykes as he ran around the back of the sidecar.

'Cover me,' he yelled.

The moment Dawson moved clear of the major's line of fire, Sykes aimed the machine-pistol back down the track towards the two approaching motorcycle combinations and squeezed the trigger. He fired three short bursts, with no particular hope of hitting anything. He just intended to keep the German soldiers at a distance while Dawson tried to extricate the combination from the wooden trestle.

But even as Sykes opened fire, so did the gunner in the leading combination. Bullets ripped into the trestle, sending splinters of wood flying in all directions. A bullet ripped into the tyre on the sidecar, blowing it to pieces and buckling the wheel itself, and another smashed into one of the steel tubes at the rear of the motorcycle, catching it a glancing blow. The ricochet slammed into Dawson as he bent forward over the wheel of the sidecar.

He grunted with the sudden impact and fell backwards, clutching his stomach.

Sykes looked down, and saw an ominous dark stain spreading across the corporal's groin and thigh as he rolled onto his back.

At that moment, with the combination crippled by the blown tyre and Dawson obviously badly injured, the major assumed they were both seconds away from death.

CHAPTER 28

11 MAY 1940: EASTERN BELGIUM

'Dawson!' Sykes yelled, firing another desperate burst at their pursuers. 'You're hit!'

For a moment, Dawson just lay there, flat on his back. But then the big corporal rolled over, and sat up.

'No,' he said, his voice strained. 'I'm OK. Just winded me a bit.'

'But you're bleeding.'

Dawson reached down and touched his discoloured uniform, then shook his head.

'I'm not,' he said. 'That bullet just punctured my water bottle, that's all. I'm wet, not bleeding.'

'Then for Christ's sake get us out of here. Those fucking Germans are almost on us.'

Dawson nodded, rose to his feet and grabbed the twisted mudguard with both hands. He braced his foot against the buckled wheel of the sidecar and pulled as hard as he could. There was a metallic ripping sound and the mudguard came away in his hand, wrenched free from its remaining mounting point on the sidecar. He tossed it away and glanced behind him, back down the track, figuring the distances.

As he did so, the gunner in the leading motorcycle combination fired again. But the bullets went wide because the sidecar was bouncing violently up and down, a hopelessly unstable platform for shooting any weapon.

'Don't stand there admiring the bloody view, Dawson,' Sykes snapped, returning fire again. 'Get us out of here.'

Then the Schmeisser fell silent as the magazine emptied. Sykes pressed the button to release it and reached for another one.

The closest German combination was then about seventy yards behind them, the second one perhaps a further hundred yards back.

Dawson made his decision. He reached down to the sidecar, unclipped the Mauser MG 34 machine-gun and carried it around behind the trestle. He placed it on top of the wood, jammed it into place as firmly as he could, sighted down the barrel and squeezed the trigger.

The first burst went wide, slightly over to the left of the approaching combination. Dawson corrected his aim and 'walked' the bullets directly across the track to his target. Sparks flew as the heavy machine-gun bullets smashed into the front of the vehicle, then the front tyre blew and the combination lurched sideways. An instant later, another of his bullets speared through the motorcycle's petrol tank and the vehicle exploded in a ball of flame, two marionette figures jumping aside, trailing flames and smoke as they rolled desperately over and over on the ground beside the wreckage.

'Right. That'll slow them down a bit,' Dawson muttered, 'and maybe there's something else I can do as well.'

In the distance, he could see the second combination slowing down as it approached the burning wreckage of the first vehicle, but he didn't have a clear shot at it through the flames and smoke. They had a bare few seconds in hand.

Dawson replaced the Mauser in its mount on the sidecar, then jumped back on board the motorcycle and drove the combination beyond the gap between the edge of the track and the trestle. Then he stopped it again and got off.

'What are you doing?' Sykes demanded.

Dawson didn't reply, just ran back to the trestle. It was a heavy, crudely built piece of carpentry, but undeniably effective for all that. Just as the German soldier had done minutes earlier, he braced himself against the end of it, and forced the whole structure about two feet across the road, closing the gap even more.

Then he got back on the motorcycle, put it into gear and drove away.

'Those Jerries will have to stop and shift that trestle,' he said. 'It might buy us a few more seconds.'

The moment the combination was back on the track itself, Dawson accelerated, but the blown tyre on the sidecar meant he could only go fairly slowly. The ruined wheel kept digging into the dirt of the track, pulling the whole vehicle over to the right, and he knew if he tried to go fast there was a real risk of losing control and crashing it.

Now their safety depended on how fast the pursuing Germans could get through the same gap. The position of the wooden trestle, blocking the centre of the track, meant Dawson and Sykes were safe from machine-gun fire, at least for the moment, because it was hiding them from the view of the enemy soldiers.

Sykes swung round in his seat, trying to make out what was happening, but the bulk of the trestle prevented him from seeing very much.

'I can see wheels below the trestle,' he said at last. 'The second motorcycle combination must have just reached it. Yes. Two German soldiers have just appeared beside it. They're trying to move it out of the way.'

Then the combination swept around a bend in the track, and the previous section was lost to view.

Sykes turned back to face the way they were going. 'It'll only take them a few seconds to move the trestle,' he said, 'so I reckon we've got maybe a two-minute start on them. And they've got all three wheels, so they're going to catch up pretty quickly.'

Dawson didn't reply. He was too busy trying to keep the combination moving as quickly as possible in a straight line.

'I wish I knew how far we were from the Belgian lines,' Sykes said.

'So do I,' Dawson replied.

The combination twitched wildly to the right as the sidecar wheel slammed into a pothole in the track, then bounced upwards, and Dawson had to fight to keep the vehicle heading in the right direction. Their speed was down to probably about ten miles per hour, and both men knew that the Germans pursuing them could travel at least three times faster than that.

'They'll catch us any time now, I reckon,' Sykes said. He checked the Schmeisser and started to turn back in his seat again.

At that moment, they both heard the hammering of a machine-gun from somewhere behind them, and bullets flew all around the combination.

'Oh, shit,' Sykes muttered, and opened up with the Schmeisser, an almost completely ineffective weapon at the distance he was aiming. He could tell that the pursuing motorcycle combination was at least a hundred yards behind them.

'I know what they'll do,' Dawson said. 'They'll close up to about fifty yards, then stop to give the gunner a stable platform, and blast us to kingdom come.' He thought for a couple of seconds. 'Shout out when they're about seventy yards away,' he added.

Sykes nodded. 'They're catching us very quickly,' he said. 'They're only about seventy yards away now.'

'Right. Hang on.'

Dawson steered the combination over to the left, then hit the brakes and swung it into a tight right-hand turn that brought them to a stop facing the way they'd come.

'Now hit them,' Dawson ordered.

Sykes needed no encouragement. He aimed the Mauser straight at the German vehicle and fired a long burst.

But the Germans did something neither he nor Dawson had expected. As the first bullets from the Mauser machine-gun blasted into the surface of the track a few yards in front of the German combination, the rider steered it off the hard surface and over to one side. In a couple of seconds it was completely hidden from view.

'Cunning,' Sykes muttered.

There was no point in staying where they were. The

enemy soldiers could stay hidden in the undergrowth for as long as they wanted. And if the German gunner unhitched his Mauser and carried it to the edge of the track, Dawson and Sykes would be sitting ducks.

'Let's go,' Dawson said, and swung the combination round on the track to head west again.

Sykes kept on looking behind, and a few seconds after Dawson had started to accelerate away, the German motorcycle combination again appeared in his rear-view mirror.

'They're behind us again.'

Dawson increased speed as much as he dared. The only advantage he had, as far as he could see, was that the section of the track they were driving along had a number of bends in it, which meant they would be hidden from the view of their pursuers for quite a lot of the time.

They couldn't see the German vehicle, but both men knew it was getting closer all the time.

Then the twisty part of the track ended, just as suddenly as it had begun, and a long straight section opened up in front of them.

Dawson looked at it and cursed. 'We've two choices, as I see it,' he said. 'Either we keep running and just hope we can keep ahead of those bloody Jerries until we get to the next section, or we stop somewhere along here and try to ambush them, and I don't see anywhere we could do that.'

'I still don't see them,' Sykes said, looking back down the track. 'They must still be at least a hundred yards behind us. Let's keep going.'

'OK.'

Dawson accelerated gently, trying to pick the smoothest possible course for the damaged wheel of the sidecar to follow, avoiding all the rocks and potholes in the track. Even so, their speed was still agonizingly slow.

They'd covered about eighty yards down the track before Sykes spoke again.

'Here they come,' he said tightly.

Dawson dragged his eyes away from the track for the brief second it took to check the rear-view mirror. The motorcycle combination was just emerging from the twisty section of the track.

Dawson looked back at the track, and concentrated on dragging every bit of speed he could from the combination. Then he glanced further ahead, towards the trees into which the track vanished. For an instant, he thought he saw something there, some object or movement. He couldn't be sure.

Then he saw a man walk across the track, from one side to the other. He glanced at Sykes.

'We need something white,' he said, 'something to wave, I mean. I just saw a Belgian soldier in the wood about two hundred yards in front of us. After all this, I'd hate to die with a Belgie bullet in my guts.'

'Got it,' Sykes muttered. He pulled a large and slightly grubby white handkerchief from his pocket and swiftly and securely tied it around the muzzle of the Mauser MG 34. He lifted the muzzle of the machine-gun so that it pointed into the air, turning his handkerchief into a makeshift flag. Then he turned back towards the pursuing Germans and fired another burst from the Schmeisser.

But still the enemy soldiers came on, gaining on their crippled vehicle all the time, the gunner in the sidecar firing occasional bursts towards them.

And suddenly they couldn't outrun them, couldn't even try to escape. A long burst from the German machine-gun pounded the surface of the track all around them, several rounds hitting the back of the combination. Then there was a sudden bang and the rear of the motorcycle lurched upwards, then crashed down.

One glance told Dawson everything he needed to know. One or more bullets had hit the back tyre, blowing it to pieces, tattered bits of rubber barely clinging to the rim. Within a few yards, despite all Dawson's efforts, the combination shuddered to a halt.

They were caught like rats in a trap. Their only option was to stand and fight.

CHAPTER 29

11 MAY 1940: EASTERN BELGIUM

Sykes aimed the Schmeisser and fired a couple of bursts. Dawson seized the Mauser machine-gun and hunkered down beside the motorcycle, trying to find a stable position from which he could fire. But before he was able to pull the trigger, a volley of shots rang out from the wood to the west of them.

And, as Dawson watched, both the pursuing Germans – the motorcycle rider and the gunner – tumbled backwards, the rider falling off the machine, the gunner slumping back in the sidecar. The combination continued forward for a few yards, out of control, then veered off to one side and ploughed into the undergrowth, coming to a sudden stop.

'The Belgian lines,' Sykes muttered. 'We're at the Belgian lines. Thank God for that. When you get up, Dawson, just make bloody sure you're waving that white flag.'

Dawson rolled over on the ground and glanced to the west. About half a dozen Belgian soldiers were advancing cautiously towards them, their rifles held ready, clearly expecting trouble.

'Slowly, Dawson,' Sykes cautioned. 'Make sure you move really slowly.'

The corporal nodded and eased himself carefully to his feet. He lifted up the Mauser machine-gun in his right hand and pointed it up in the air. The weapon was heavy, but Dawson was a very strong man. He moved the Mauser from side to side, making the handkerchief flap slightly, a rudimentary signal of surrender. Then he tossed the machine-gun to one side and just stood there motionless, both arms raised high above his head.

Beside him, in the sidecar, Sykes had lowered the Schmeisser onto his lap and had also lifted both his arms in the air.

The two Britons watched the Belgians approach. Two of the soldiers were walking straight towards them down the centre of the track, but the others had spread out, covering both sides, obviously alert for any tricks.

Once they got to within about thirty yards, Sykes shouted out something in French.

'Just told them we're British soldiers,' he murmured to Dawson.

There was no response from the approaching Belgians, who still had their rifles raised. But when they got to about fifteen yards away, Dawson could see the tension starting to ease. The uniforms he and Sykes were wearing under the heavy motorcycle coats were un-mistakably British, not German, and quite clearly the Belgian soldiers recognized that.

Four of the Belgian troops continued down the track, towards the two German soldiers. The other two stopped in front of Sykes and Dawson.

The major said something else in French, and the leading soldier – his insignia suggested to Dawson that he was probably the equivalent of a sergeant – replied in the same language, then held out his hand.

Sykes dug around in his pockets, then turned to Dawson. 'He wants to see your pay book. And the *passe-partout*.'

'Right,' Dawson replied, and after a moment produced the document and handed it over.

The Belgian soldier inspected both sets of documentation and the pass while his companion stood watchfully beside him, his rifle raised and ready. Then the soldier nodded, passed back the documents and gave Sykes a casual salute.

'Welcome to Belgium,' he said, in thickly accented English. 'Why do you ride in a German motorcycle?'

'It's a long story,' Sykes replied, 'and this isn't the time to explain. Thanks for stopping those Germans – if you hadn't opened fire when you did, we'd probably already be dead. Now, we need to see the most senior officer here, and we need a car or some other vehicle to get to your lines.'

The soldier shook his head. 'You can walk there. It is two hundred metres only.'

'No, he can't,' Dawson said. 'The major's been shot through the leg. He can barely stand.'

The Belgian soldier shook his head. 'I'm sorry, I did not see,' he said, peering down into the sidecar and glancing at Skyes's bloodied thigh. 'But we have nothing here we can use. We have heavy truck, but is far too big for this track.'

'Not a problem,' Dawson said briskly. 'The motorcycle combination that was chasing us will do. If you hang on here, I'll go and get it.'

The Belgian soldier nodded. 'Good idea, but you wait here,' he said. 'My men bring it.' He switched to French and shouted an order to the four men who'd gone down the track to inspect the German vehicle.

A couple of minutes later, Dawson heard the motorcycle engine starting up, and shortly after that the combination drew to a stop beside them. Between them, Dawson and the Belgian soldier lifted Sykes out of the sidecar and got him upright. The major leant against the side of the vehicle, catching his breath after the exertion, and clearly still in considerable pain.

'What are those?' the Belgian asked, pointing at the two rounded grey lumps that comprised the German demolition charge.

'Those,' Sykes said, 'are the reason we need to see your most senior officer. That's a new kind of explosive charge the Germans used to destroy Fort Eben Emael.'

The Belgian's face fell. 'We heard about that, but none of us believe it was true. Eben Emael is impregnable.'

Sykes shook his head. 'It isn't, I'm afraid.'

'The Germans captured it? We heard they used gas.'

'We saw no evidence of that. When we got away, Eben Emael was still in Belgian hands. The German troops used charges like these to destroy most of the fort's weapons, so the garrison was almost helpless and was being held prisoner inside the building. I don't know if they've surrendered yet or not, but it's really only a matter of time.'

'Sir,' Dawson said urgently, 'we need to move. We're stuck out here in no man's land, and the Jerries could send another patrol out after us any time.'

'You're right,' Sykes said. 'Let's get going.'

268

Dawson plucked out the two parts of the demolition charge from the battered sidecar of the combination they'd ridden all the way from Liège, and carefully placed them on the floor of the other sidecar. Then he helped Sykes get inside that vehicle and settled him as comfortably as he could.

With the Belgian sergeant and his companion walking in front of them, and the other four soldiers bringing up the rear to cover their back, Dawson started the motorcycle's engine. He rode the combination slowly towards the far end of the track, where, in the shadows cast by the trees, he could now clearly see other Belgian troops watching and waiting.

When they passed beneath the canopy, Dawson saw that there were about a couple of dozen Belgian troops positioned there, presumably to guard that end of the track, and all armed with Mauser carbines.

'Where is your officer?' Sykes asked.

'He is not here,' the sergeant replied. 'I am in charge of these men. We are to stop any German approach along this track' – that confirmed Dawson's guess – 'but our main forces are behind us, closer to the main road between Liège and Namur. That is where we expect the main German attack. There you will find our officers.'

'My corporal here made a note of those German forces we could see. That could be valuable intelligence for the defence of this line.'

'One of my men will go with you,' the sergeant said, 'to make sure you have no trouble with our sentries or patrols.'

He issued an order, and one of his men stepped forward and climbed onto the motorcycle behind Dawson.

'Go straight up this track,' the sergeant said, pointing west, 'for half a kilometre, then go left at the fork. The main camp is a few hundred metres beyond that.'

'Thanks for that,' Dawson said, and opened the throttle, easing the combination into motion.

They passed nobody until they reached the fork in the track, where a handful of troops were standing. The Belgian soldier sitting behind Dawson gestured for him to slow down and stop while he explained what they were doing. Then they rode on, and in a couple of minutes reached a large open area, where trucks of various sorts were parked, and men were milling about. There was an immediate sense of urgency, and of fear.

The German bombing had stopped, at least for the moment, but the effects of the prolonged attack were visible everywhere. The ground was studded with craters, and several of the vehicles had clearly been hit by bombs and were now smouldering wrecks. Two medical tents had been set up, with prominent red crosses displayed on their roofs, and from one of them came the sound of prolonged and agonized screaming. There had obviously been human casualties of the bombing as well.

The ground beyond was fairly level, and in the distance Dawson could see a handful of small artillery pieces, their muzzles pointing east, towards the German lines, their gun crews standing by, presumably just waiting for the order to fire. For a moment, he wondered why they weren't firing already, but then guessed that they still had no idea where the German forces were located. The attacks on the Belgian positions had been from the air, using bombers, not tanks or field guns. Well, hopefully the information he had in his pocket would help with that, though from what he could see the Belgian forces were totally outnumbered and out-gunned by the massed German troops waiting only a couple of miles away.

The Belgian soldier tapped Dawson on the shoulder and gestured to an open-fronted tent a short distance ahead of them. A number of Belgian officers were visible, some standing inside it, and several others talking together close to the tent.

Dawson pulled the combination to a stop and switched off the engine. He shook hands with the Belgian soldier, who nodded at him and then wandered off. Dawson climbed off the motorcycle combination and walked over to the tent.

The officers standing outside it had stopped talking and were staring at him, presumably wondering exactly what a British army corporal, wearing a filthy, tattered and bloodstained uniform, was doing in the middle of their camp. For a fleeting second, Dawson wondered that as well.

Then he stepped up to the closest group of officers, threw up a sketchy salute and asked a simple question.

'Do any of you officers speak English?'

Three or four of the men nodded, and one stepped forward.

'I speak English, yes. Who are you, and why are you driving a German motorcycle combination?'

That was the second time they'd been asked that question, and Dawson was in no mood to explain right then.

'My name's Dawson,' he said, 'and I'm a corporal in the British army's Royal Engineers. I need to speak to the most senior officer here.'

The Belgian smiled slightly, then shook his head. 'With all that's going on here, I doubt very much if our commanding officer will be interested in talking to you. What did you want to say to him?'

Behind the Belgian, Dawson could see smiles forming on the faces of the other officers, who were standing there listening.

'Two things,' Dawson said crisply. 'First, we've worked our way through the German lines all the way from Liège. I've made a note of the disposition of the enemy forces that are facing you on the ground over there.' He pointed over towards the east.

The smiles had vanished from the faces of the other officers.

'Have you indeed?' the officer in front of Dawson said, his manner now completely different. 'In that case, I think our commanding officer might well be interested in talking to you. And what was the second thing?'

Dawson pointed backwards, towards the sidecar. 'The major has a favour to ask, but I'll let him explain it himself. He's been shot through the leg, by the way, and he can't walk, so you'll need to get your CO out here to speak to him.'

The officer nodded. 'Just wait here,' he instructed, and vanished into the tent behind him.

He was back less than a minute later, followed by an older man with grey hair and very different rank badges on his epaulettes. Dawson was unfamiliar with the Belgian insignia, but guessed the officer was probably at least a colonel. The senior officer nodded to Dawson, who gestured towards the motorcycle combination and led the way over to the vehicle.

When they reached it, Sykes saluted as best he could, which was awkward from a sitting position, and introduced himself to the senior officer in French.

The Belgian officer returned the major's salute, but replied to him in English.

'English is easier for us all, I think,' he said. 'I'm Colonel Lefèvre, and this officer is Major Herbellin. We're both officers in the Belgian First Chasseurs Ardennais.' Then he turned to Dawson. 'I gather you have a note of the German force dispositions in this area?' he asked.

'Yes, sir.' Dawson reached into his battledress pocket and pulled out the pages of notes he'd made. Like Dawson himself, the bits of paper were grubby and torn, but the information he'd recorded was clear enough.

For the next few minutes, Dawson explained where he'd walked when he'd been looking for a way to cross the Belgian lines, and exactly where he'd seen the German forces. Major Herbellin stood right beside him, making copious notes as the corporal described what he'd seen.

'You're sure about this?' Lefèvre asked, his face troubled. 'We weren't expecting this level of German armour to have reached here so quickly. We had mined all the bridges over the Albert Canal and the Meuse River, and stationed troops there to trigger the explosions as soon as we knew the Germans were definitely launching an invasion. That was intended to delay the movement of German heavy vehicles. We know that at least some of the bridges were destroyed. Unfortunately, we also know that in some cases the attacks were so sudden that our troops were overwhelmed before they could execute their orders.'

He turned back to Dawson. 'You didn't count any of them twice, nothing like that?' he asked.

The corporal shook his head firmly. 'Definitely not, sir. Those are the vehicles and approximate troop numbers that I saw.'

Colonel Lefèvre shook his head. 'This is not good news,' he said. 'One of our main lines of defence followed the natural barrier of the Meuse River through Liège to Maastricht, but the speed and power of the German advance took us by surprise and we had to abandon those positions much sooner than we had anticipated. As part of our retreat from Liège and the Albert Canal area we blocked and mined most of the main roads. It sounds as if the German engineers must have repaired the damage much more quickly than we expected. Our air force has been trying to destroy some of the bridges we were forced to abandon, but I can only assume those operations weren't that successful either. If what you say is correct, Corporal Dawson, and I'm not doubting what you saw, then I doubt if we can hold them off here for very long. But we'll do what we can.' He turned to Major Herbellin. 'Fetch a map,' he ordered.

For the next few minutes, Herbellin and Dawson attempted to work out exactly where the corporal had been, the tracks he'd followed and the fields he'd surveyed when he'd been looking for a route across towards Namur. Then they plotted the German positions on the map, to the best of Dawson's recollection.

'You're certain about this, Corporal?' Lefèvre asked again.

'About the numbers and disposition, sir, yes. I'm a bit woolly about some of the locations, because I didn't have a map with me at the time, but I'm reasonably sure I've got most of them pretty much right.'

'Good enough,' Lefèvre said. 'Herbellin, work out the coordinates for all these positions and pass the information on to the gun crews. Then order them to fire at will. Let's see if we can slow down the German advance, or at least give them a taste of their own medicine.'

Major Herbellin saluted, took the map and walked away briskly.

'Have any of the French and British reinforcements arrived yet?' Sykes asked.

Colonel Lefèvre nodded. 'The Twelfth French Infantry Division has already arrived at Namur to reinforce our troops – that's the Sixth Corps' Fifth Infantry Division and the Second Chasseurs Ardennais – in that part of the KW Line, what you British call the Dyle Line. We're much further to the east, and the French Prioux Cavalry Corps is already in position here. They've formed a screening line between Hannut to the north and Huy, down to the south. That line brackets the Liège to Namur main road, which we expect the German forces will most probably use for their advance westwards. The intention is for the French armour – the Prioux Corps is a tank regiment, and it's equipped with Hotchkiss, Renault and Panhard tanks and armoured cars – to delay the enemy advance until further reinforcements are able to arrive in the area. Personally, I'm still not convinced that force disposition is right, though the figures your corporal supplied about the enemy forces do worry me.'

'What do you mean, sir?'

'The French planners still seem to believe that the Ardennes Forest and their Maginot Line will be enough to prevent any enemy invasion into that part of northern France, so they're leaving the Ardennes virtually undefended and moving most of their troops all the way up to Zeeland, on the Dutch coast. So the only forces covering the Ardennes are the reservists of the French Second and Ninth Armies. I'm not sure that's a good decision. In view of what's happened already, I don't think the Maginot Line will stop the Germans. And while the Ardennes Forest might be a problem for tanks to get through, their infantry forces could traverse it very quickly. But my guess is that the main thrust of the attack will in the area between here and the north of Namur, through the central part of the country, and our defences are fairly thin there. The French First Army is due to arrive at Hannut sometime tomorrow to protect the Gembloux Gap.'

'So some of the French have arrived already, and others are on their way here. What about the British forces?' Sykes asked.

'We understand that your Third Infantry Division will reach Leuven no later than tonight.'

'Leuven?'

Colonel Lefèvre gestured to another officer, who quickly brought out a map of Belgium and the surrounding countries. 'We're just here, to the south-west of Dreye,' the colonel said, pointing at the map, 'Hannut is here, to the north-west and Leuven is about fifty kilometres – that's roughly thirty miles – to the north-west of Hannut, and just east of Brussels. That line' – his finger traced a path from Antwerp in the north all the way down through Namur to Givet, south of the French border – 'is our second line of defence against the Germans. The northern part, down to Wavre here, is the KW Line, and from there we've built a continuous anti-tank barrier, all the way south across the Gembloux Gap to the PFN, the *Position Fortifiée de Namur*. Our first line of defence was our eastern border, and we had hoped to hold the Germans there, at least for a while, because of the heavy fortifications we'd built since the last war.'

'You mean Eben Emael and the other forts?' Sykes said.

'Exactly. Did you hear that the garrison of Fort Eben Emael has surrendered?' the colonel asked.

Sykes nodded. 'I didn't know they'd surrendered, but we knew the Germans had beaten the fort's defences. We were there,' he added. 'We actually watched the assault.'

The major explained what he and Dawson had seen after the first glider landed on the roof of the fort in the early hours of the previous morning.

'And that, Colonel,' Sykes finished, 'is the real reason we're here, and why we need your help.' He pointed down, between his legs, into the sidecar. 'This is one of the demolition charges the Germans used to destroy the cupolas at Fort Eben Emael. Dawson and I managed to steal it from the roof of the fort. It appears to be a completely new kind of explosive, and we believe it's essential to have it examined by experts back in Britain to find out how it works.'

Colonel Lefèvre peered at the two solid grey lumps with interest. 'That's probably a good idea,' he said, 'but I'm not sure how I can help you do that.'

'We had a staff car,' Sykes explained, 'but we were cornered by the Germans back in Liège and we had to abandon it there. Since then, we've been using one of these motorcycle combinations to get around. This is the second one we've borrowed from the Germans, actually. The trouble is, I'm not very mobile because of this bullet wound in my thigh and I can't get comfortable in this thing, especially because I'm sharing it with the two parts of this demolition charge. Is there any chance we could take one of your staff cars or even a small truck to get us and this weapon to the British lines? I'm not happy at the idea of driving around behind the front line in a German vehicle, just in case some soldier thinks we're part of the enemy forces and shoots us down.'

The Belgian officer nodded. 'I'll see what I can do,' he said. 'The trouble is that most of the vehicles we have here are heavy lorries, and the transport situation is so critical – we might be ordered to pull back at any moment or move to a different location as the situation changes – that I can't afford to let you have one of those. That's simply because we'll need all of them to carry our troops and equipment. Give me a few minutes and I'll check exactly what we have available.'

'Thank you, sir.'

'In the meantime, get your wounds dressed and treated over there.' The colonel pointed towards the nearest of the two dressing stations.

Dawson helped Sykes out of the sidecar and half-carried him across to the tent. Fifteen minutes later, the major had new dressings on both his head and leg wounds, and the two men made the same journey in reverse, back to the motorcycle combination.

'And at least now we can relax a bit,' Dawson said, as Sykes settled himself back in the sidecar: it was as comfortable a place for him to sit as anywhere else. 'We're finally on the right side of the lines, and that means we should be able to get some decent food and drink inside us and get our heads down for a few hours.'

'I hope so, Dawson, because I'm hurting, knackered, hungry and thirsty.'

'Let me see what I can do.'

Dawson stood up and walked over to the open-fronted tent. One of the junior officers swung round to look at him as he approached.

'Can I help you?' he asked, in English.

'Just a question, sir. We've been on the road all day with nothing to eat or drink. Any chance of a bevvy or some scoff?'

The officer looked uncomprehendingly at him. Dawson belatedly realized that although many Belgians spoke English, army slang would be incomprehensible to them.

'Sorry, sir,' he said, and quickly amended his previous question. 'I mean, could we get some food and drink somewhere?'

'Yes, of course.' The officer pointed to a tent about fifty yards away from which a thin spiral of smoke was rising. 'That is what you would call a mess hall, I think? They will serve you hot food and drink there.'

'Thanks, sir,' Dawson said, gave Sykes a thumbs-up and walked across to the tent the officer had indicated.

Inside, he joined a short queue of soldiers waiting in line at the field kitchen, and grabbed a tray, plates, utensils and mugs. Five minutes later he was sitting on the saddle of the motorcycle tucking into a thick stew, a steaming mug of black coffee on the ground beside his feet.

Next to him, Sykes sat in the sidecar, his tray precariously balanced on his knees, eating with undisguised relish.

'Tell you what, sir,' Dawson muttered between mouthfuls, 'this Belgie scoff is a hell of a lot better than we get at home. This stew is bloody delicious. Just a shame they didn't have any tea.'

'I can't argue about the stew,' Sykes replied, 'because it really is excellent. But I think you already know my views on British army tea. I'd rather have a decent cup of coffee any day.'

A couple of minutes later Dawson belched loudly and put the fork down on his plate. 'You fancy another helping?' he asked, glancing at Sykes's empty plate.

'If they'll give you one, Dawson, I'm definitely up for it. And then you could see if there's any chance of finding a couple of beds somewhere here. I can't sleep in this bloody tin can.'

Colonel Lefèvre returned a few minutes later. He walked across to the sidecar and leant down to speak to Major Sykes.

'All I can offer you is a small civilian car that we commandeered as a utility vehicle,' he said. 'It's not a staff car, but it does have two seats and a luggage area at the rear where you can store the German explosive device. And it will be a lot more comfortable than that sidecar for you. Will that do?'

Sykes nodded. 'That would be excellent, sir. Thank you very much.'

'I'll get it fuelled and have one of my staff officers write out an authorization for you to use it, just in case you're stopped by a patrol anywhere on the road. And another *passe-partout* as well.'

'Thank you, sir. I was going to ask if there's anywhere here we can sleep tonight,' Sykes asked.

Colonel Lefèvre looked doubtful. 'In view of what's happened so far today, and what we now know about the strength of the enemy forces facing us, I don't think that's a very good idea. I think the Germans will attack without warning, and we don't have the strength in depth to resist them for long. I would suggest, Major, that a far better option for you two would be to get moving as soon as possible, and find somewhere to sleep when you've put a good few kilometres between yourselves and the front line.' The Belgian officer paused for a moment. 'With all you've gone through to obtain that new German weapon, it would be a tragedy if the first wave of enemy soldiers broke through here and killed or captured you, and then managed to recover it.'

'That does make sense, sir,' Sykes said, pleasant thoughts of a decent night's sleep vanishing instantly from his mind. 'We'd better get moving, then, while we've still got some of the afternoon in front of us.'

'I'll have the vehicle brought over here.'

As the colonel turned away, the first of the Belgian artillery pieces fired, the boom a deafening assault on the ears. The first round was quickly followed by a salvo from the other heavy weapons. The Belgian bombardment of the German positions had started.

CHAPTER 30

A little over thirty minutes later, Dawson helped Sykes lower himself gratefully into the front passenger seat of a very small car, painted in Belgian army colours and with military registration plates.

'This is a funny little job,' Dawson muttered. 'I've never seen a car like this before.'

'You wouldn't, in Britain,' Sykes said. 'It's an Italian Fiat Five Hundred. I've seen a few of them on the roads on the Continent, and most people call it a *Topolino*, which is Italian for "little mouse".'

'I can see why,' Dawson said drily, staring at the vehicle. Then he shut the passenger side door and walked around to the other open door.

The tiny car had two seats and two doors which were hinged at rear and fitted with sliding windows. Moving the seats forward revealed a limited amount of luggage space, and a spare wheel was bolted to the rear panel, at the back of the car.

In the luggage area behind the seats Dawson had placed the two sections of the German demolition charge, two canteens of water and a couple of packs of dry rations, a solid-fuel stove, pots, plates and utensils, plus two sleeping bags the Belgian officers had found somewhere. On top of the sleeping bags were two Mauser Karabiner 98K rifles and ample spare ammunition, and Sykes had the Schmeisser machine-pistol slung around his neck, all the magazines fully loaded and a spare box of nine-millimetre ammunition beside him. The Schmeisser was such a useful close-quarter weapon that they'd decided to hang on to it, not knowing what the next few hours or days might bring. Dawson had even remembered to reload the Browning pistol he'd acquired.

All in all, the two men were now better prepared and equipped than they'd been at any time since they'd left Eben Emael. What they now had to decide was where to go, and that was far from an easy choice, though they knew they had to move fairly quickly.

'This won't be a ball of fire to drive,' Sykes said. 'The engine's under half a litre in size, and it'll only do about fifty miles an hour. And the acceleration will be very slow.'

'Still better than that blasted motorcycle combination,' Dawson insisted.

'You're right there.'

The major's leg wound had been examined in the dressing station by one of the doctors, the man's heavily bloodstained white coat a mute testimony to the injuries suffered by the Belgian soldiers during the German bombardment. The good news was that Sykes's wound was clean and had even started healing, despite the punishment that had been inflicted on his leg during the last few hours. The bad news was that it still ached appallingly, and he had no more morphine phials left to take the edge off it.

The Belgian bombardment was still continuing, the salvoes of shells from howitzers blasting apart the evening sky, followed by the distant crump of the projectiles exploding over to the east.

And then the German troops started firing back, answering fire with fire, the first shells landing well short of the main Belgian line.

'That's our cue to get out of here right now, Dawson,' Sykes said, 'before those Jerry bastards sort out the range and start turning this place into hell on earth.'

The corporal started the engine, slid the gear lever into first and accelerated away down another forest track, heading for the road that they'd been told led west, the main road that would take them to Namur itself and then on, following the south bank of the river Meuse, to the town of Charleroi. Colonel Lefèvre hoped the German advance wouldn't reach there for at least a day or two, but they both knew he was only guessing. Nobody, not the Belgians and probably not even the Germans, knew exactly what was actually going to happen next.

Sykes had the map open in front of him, but it was fairly useless until they actually reached a road – none of the tracks that wound through the woods were marked on it. They hadn't been able to take one of the Belgian army maps because they were classified documents which showed the positions of important assets such as fortified facilities and ammunition dumps, but Colonel Lefèvre had allowed Dawson to make a rough drawing of the network of tracks that led from the camp to the main road. Sykes had that in his hand as well.

'Not a terribly good map, this,' Sykes said, turning the piece of paper in his hand to try to work out some of Dawson's annotations.

'I'm a sapper, sir, not a cartigropher or whatever they're called.'

'Cartographer,' Sykes supplied.

'Exactly. My speciality is blowing things up. I've never been much good at stuff like drawing. But that Herbellin bloke reckoned it was only about a mile or two to the road, so as long as we keep heading more or less west, we should be fine.'

Behind them, the two sets of field guns, the heavy artillery of the Belgian and German armies, traded shot after shot as the colours of the late afternoon sky in front of them started to show the first signs of the reds and violets of evening.

Herbellin had been right. In spite of, rather than because of, Dawson's map, about fifteen minutes after they'd driven out of the Belgian camp the corporal swung the car right onto a proper road. It was cobbled, but wide enough for two vehicles to pass side-by-side, and lined with trees.

There was also a road-block on it, but obviously Sykes and Dawson wouldn't have to shoot their way past this one. They pulled up behind a couple of Belgian army trucks, and when they reached the barrier the major simply showed the guards their British army identification documents and the *passe-partout* Colonel Lefèvre had prepared for them. Almost immediately the barrier was lifted and they drove on.

'Makes a nice change,' Dawson remarked, as he accelerated slowly – he had no choice in that regard – away from the road-block. 'So how far do you want to go, sir? Before we try and find somewhere to stop, I mean?'

'Let's try and get to the other side of Namur, at least,' Sykes said. 'That'll put us to the west of the main Belgian defensive line in this area. If anything's going to slow the Jerries down, that will.'

After a few minutes they reached the main road that ran east–west between Liège and Namur, passed through another checkpoint and started heading west. The situation on the road was remarkably similar to what they had found when they'd driven out of Liège, except that the German troops hadn't yet got anywhere near the town. But the road was still clogged with refugees pushing carts or staggering along, bowed down under the weight of huge and unwieldy bundles of personal possessions. Predictably enough, all the refugees were heading west. There were occasional road-blocks too, all of which Dawson and Sykes passed through without difficulty, thanks to the authorization they held, although the inevitable queuing to get past the checkpoints slowed them down considerably. The road-blocks got more frequent as they approached the eastern edge of Namur.

Evening was drawing in as they neared the outskirts of the city. Sykes checked the map and made a decision.

'We won't go into Namur,' he said. 'The main road from Liège to Charleroi loops around to the north of the city. I think we'll stay on that. It'll probably have more road-blocks, but hopefully we might be able to go a bit faster than we would through Namur itself.' Sykes glanced at the groups of plodding refugees who were still all around them, and still heading west into an uncertain future. 'And maybe some of these poor sods might decide to spend the night in Namur, so perhaps the main road might be a bit clearer.'

The road was wider, but there were also more refugees on it, so their speed of advance was still quite slow. But at least they were going in the right direction. The distance from Namur to Charleroi was only about fifteen miles, and they were approaching the outskirts when the numbers of refugees started to increase dramatically, almost as if there was some kind of hold-up, another road-block or something, ahead of them.

And then, as the little Fiat rounded a bend in the road, they saw the reason for the problem. There *was* a hold-up in front, but it was one that brought a smile to Sykes's face. The Belgian troops had closed the road they were on to allow a column of soldiers – a long column of soldiers – to cross it from left to right, heading north. And despite the steadily fading light, both Dawson and Sykes could see from the shape of the steel helmets and the colour of the uniforms that they were British.

'Bloody good, eh?' Dawson said, stopping the car and getting out to take a better look.

'Colonel Lefèvre said the Third Infantry Division was heading up towards Leuven, so that's who we're looking at.'

'Is it worth trying to join up with them?'

Sykes shook his head. 'No. They're going the wrong way. If we tagged along behind them, we'd end up back at the front line again, just at a different part of it. Our first priority has to be to deliver this weapon, and that means heading in the opposite direction.'

Sykes glanced at his watch and then back at the column of marching men and their accompanying vehicles.

'We're not going to be able to get into Charleroi for ages, not with this number of refugees in front of us, and especially not with those troops moving north. Let's get off this road and find somewhere nearby to rest up overnight.'

Dawson nodded agreement, got back into the driver's seat and slammed the door closed.

'We passed a junction about a quarter of a mile back. I'll pull off the road there.'

He turned the car around and headed slowly back the way they'd come, moving against the tide of humanity that rolled inexorably towards them. The turn-off at the junction, when they reached it, proved to be a very minor road, quite narrow, but still with a reasonable paved surface.

Dawson drove slowly down it, looking out for somewhere suitable for them to rest. Ideally, they needed another farm – Sykes wasn't prepared to order Dawson to break into a Belgian house – with an outbuilding big enough for them to both sleep in and conceal their vehicle.

Deserted houses, it soon became apparent, were the norm. After a few minutes they rolled through a tiny hamlet, and every building appeared to be shuttered and barred, the inhabitants long since fled. Just beyond the hamlet – they couldn't even see a name anywhere, and it didn't seem to be marked on Sykes's map – they spotted a collection of farm buildings, although there was no sign of the farmhouse itself.

Dawson climbed out to inspect them, then walked back over to the little Fiat.

'These should do us nicely, I think,' he said. 'They

look like sheds or barns for the farm. None of them are locked, and that one' – he pointed at the building furthest from the road – 'has a big open space in the middle, easily able to take this car.'

Minutes later, he'd backed the car into the barn and switched off the engine. They took the two Mausers and the Schmeisser to keep them to hand, just in case. Sykes lay beside the stove, watching a can of water come to the boil on the Belgian solid-fuel stove, while Dawson arranged the sleeping bags on a collection of old sacks that would provide some insulation underneath them during the night. Then the corporal picked up the Schmeisser and took a walk around the exterior of the buildings and the surrounding area, just as a precaution.

'Anything?' Sykes asked, when Dawson walked back inside and sat down.

Dawson shook his head. 'Nothing moving. No lights anywhere and no sounds, apart from the noise of artillery and bombing, but they're a long way off, way over to the east. In fact, it all seems remarkably quiet out there, bearing in mind what we've seen.'

'Probably just the lull before the storm. No doubt the Boche are regrouping ready for a major push towards the Channel ports.'

They ate a scratch meal from their rations. Dawson warmed up a kind of beef stew that was, like their previous experience of Belgian army food, surprisingly tasty, and they followed that with a couple of dried biscuits each. They drank mugs of hot black coffee – the Belgian packs hadn't included tea – and then both men turned in. Dawson had seen nothing on his patrol, and they had driven well to the west of the Belgian lines, so for one of them to remain awake and on watch seemed pointless. They were hidden inside a deserted barn in a field on a deserted farm at the edge of a deserted hamlet that would be of no possible interest to the advancing German troops even if – or, more realistically, when – they broke through the lines. For the moment, they were probably as safe there as they would be anywhere else in Belgium.

And both of them desperately needed to get some sleep, so they took the risk.

CHAPTER 31

12 MAY 1940: EASTERN BELGIUM

When Dawson opened his eyes the following morning, Major Sykes was already wide awake and studying his map.

'Good morning, sir,' Dawson said, automatically checking that his Schmeisser was beside him and within easy reach. He sat up and stretched. 'Have you heard anything?' he asked. 'Any noises outside, I mean?'

Sykes shook his head. 'Distant artillery, and I've heard a few aeroplane engines, but nothing close to us.'

'Good. I'll take a look round anyway.'

Dawson picked up the machine-pistol, checked it and walked to the open door of the barn. He peered cautiously in both directions, nodded reassuringly to Sykes and then stepped outside, vanishing from sight.

Dawson was back in under five minutes. 'Quiet as the grave, sir. Not even a cow or a sheep out there.'

He walked across to the back of the Fiat *Topolino*, took out the solid fuel stove and lit it for a breakfast brew, then glanced at the map Sykes was still studying.

'Are we lost, sir?'

The major smiled at him. 'Not any more than we were

yesterday. No, I've been looking at where we need to get to and, more importantly, how we're going to get there. And to work that out depends on where exactly the Germans might decide to punch their way through the Belgian lines.'

'And where's that, sir?' Dawson asked.

'Immediately to the north of where we were yesterday, if I'm any judge. Between Wavre, up here to the north, and Namur, which is more or less where we crossed the Belgian lines, there's a flat plain known as the Gembloux Gap. According to that Belgian army colonel, all there is to stop the Jerry tanks rolling right over it is a single line of anti-tank defences. I didn't ask Lefèvre what sort they were – ditches, ramparts or barriers, or maybe a combination of those – but we both know that *any* anti-tank obstacle can be defeated. You fill in the ditch with rubble, flatten the ramparts or blow up the barriers, and that can be done very quickly if there's no opposition. And once the tanks are over them, there's nothing much else to stop a German advance between here and the coast.'

'Apart from the French army positioned north of Namur,' Dawson pointed out, 'if I understood what that colonel said. But we're not going to get involved in any of this, are we? We'll be heading west or south-west to hand over the weapon to our people. We're already well behind the Belgian front line, I mean, so we should be clear of this area quite soon.'

'Quite right, Dawson, we should be. But I was also wondering about our own troops. Colonel Lefèvre said the Third Infantry Division was heading up towards Leuven, and we actually saw them last night, heading north. What worries me is that, if the Jerries do break through in force between here and Wavre, that division could be cut off and surrounded.'

'But there's nothing we can do about that, is there, sir? And if you've worked out that there could be a problem, surely the Third's CO will do the same.'

'I think that's Monty – General Montgomery – but he'll have to follow orders, even if he disagrees with them. The problem with the Allies' strategy is that it's static rather than fluid. The idea is to hold a fortified line, then order a controlled retreat to another fortified line and so on. That's essentially a Great War tactic. The problem is that the Germans have already shown that they're not prepared to follow the same plan. Using their *Blitzkrieg* tactics, they don't have to fight their way through a series of defences. Instead, their plan seems to be to go around or over obstacles like a defensive line, which allows them to isolate the enemy forces into pockets and then destroy them. They even have a name for that tactic. They call it a *Kesselschlacht*, which means an encirclement battle, but its literal meaning is rather more apt: *Kesselschlacht* actually translates as a "cauldron slaughter". And we know that Adolf and his generals have produced some even more radical ideas, like taking out Eben Emael by landing gliders on the roof.'

'But it's not our problem, sir,' Dawson insisted. 'We're just tiny cogs in a huge machine – well, you're a bigger cog than me, obviously, but you know what I mean.'

Sykes nodded. 'You're quite right. I was just thinking aloud. We have a different job to do. Right, is that coffee ready yet?'

Dawson handed him a steaming tin mug, then rooted

around in the ration packs to find something for them to eat.

Forty-five minutes later they were ready to move out. They'd both washed, using water from the pump in the yard, and had even managed to shave for the first time since leavening Eben-Emael, so they looked and felt better. The rest had done Sykes good, and he was able to walk the few steps to the passenger side of the car without assistance, though Dawson hovered anxiously beside him all the way, just in case his leg gave out.

The corporal started the little Fiat and drove it out of the barn and onto the street that ran through the hamlet. He turned left, to the south, and headed back towards the main road they'd been driving down the previous evening.

'We go west, I suppose?' he asked, as they neared the junction.

'Yes. We'll see how the main road looks and then make a decision.'

If anything, there were even more refugees on the road than there had been the previous day, and Dawson had to slow to a crawl to try to ease his way around them.

After about twenty minutes, during which Dawson reckoned they'd covered no more than a mile, Sykes shook his head in frustration.

'This is ridiculous,' he said. 'We'll never get anywhere at this rate. There's a side road just ahead, over there on the right. Take that, and we'll try and use the minor roads. That will take us north of Charleroi when we really need to be south of the town, but it'll probably still be faster than staying on this road.'

Even the side road was quite busy, but most of the

Belgians walking along it, pushing carts or just carrying stuff, seemed to be making for Charleroi, and Dawson found it much easier, and a lot faster, to drive against the flow of pedestrians.

Within half an hour they'd reached a village named Brunehault, which, according to Sykes's map, was almost due north of the centre of Charleroi. As they drove through the streets, Dawson spotted soldiers wearing French uniforms manning checkpoints, and the little Italian car was stopped by a patrol near the centre of the village.

'I suppose these guys are from the Twelfth French Infantry Division,' Dawson said, braking the *Topolino* to a halt beside a handful of French soldiers.

'No doubt,' Sykes replied, then launched into high-speed French as one of the armed soldiers stepped forward to the car to demand identification papers. Obediently, the two men produced their documents.

The soldier inspected them but appeared unimpressed, and pointed at the car and then at Sykes and Dawson.

'Giving trouble, is he?' Dawson asked, taking back his pay book.

'He doesn't like the fact that we're two British soldiers driving a civilian vehicle painted in Belgian army colours,' Sykes replied quietly. 'He also doesn't see why we're trying to head west when all the fighting is over to the east of here. He hasn't said it in so many words, but I suspect he thinks we're deserters.'

'Deserters?' Dawson muttered, his voice dangerous and low. 'I'll give him fucking deserters, after all we've been through.'

'Quiet,' Sykes ordered, 'and just keep calm. I'll sort this out.'

The major produced the *passe-partout* signed by Colonel Lefèvre and waved it under the French soldier's nose, pointing at the signature, but the man batted it away angrily, knocking the sheet of paper out of Sykes's hand.

Dawson climbed out of the driver's side of the Fiat and walked slowly around the rear of the car, the French soldier watching him suspiciously. He bent down, picked up the authorization and handed it back to Sykes.

'Here you are, sir,' he said, then turned to stare at the Frenchman.

'Careful, Dawson,' Sykes muttered from behind him.

Before anyone could react – Sykes or any of the other French soldiers manning the checkpoint – Dawson raised a fist like a side of beef and drove it straight into the soldier's forehead, under the steel brim of his helmet. The man tumbled backwards, instantly knocked unconscious, and before he'd hit the ground Dawson had the Schmeisser in his hand, covering the other French soldiers.

'That's just a lesson in manners, you ignorant fucking Frog,' he said crisply.

Then he opened the passenger door and passed the Schmeisser to Sykes. 'If you'd like to take this, sir,' he said.

The major held his door open and trained the weapon on the French troops.

Dawson walked around the back of the *Topolino*, to keep well out of Sykes's line of fire, and got back behind the wheel. He engaged first gear and simply drove on, ignoring the hostile looks of the other French soldiers, who had been rendered temporarily impotent by the machine-pistol the major was holding, their rifles still slung over their shoulders.

'That wasn't perhaps the most tactful way to settle an argument,' Sykes said, lowering the Schmeisser and pulling his door closed once they'd driven out of sight of the checkpoint, 'but it was undeniably effective.'

'It worked,' Dawson agreed.

'Did you ever box? Before you joined the army, I mean?'

'A bit, sir, yes. Strictly amateur stuff, like, but I wasn't too bad at it. And that Frog'll have no ill effects afterwards, apart from a blinding headache that'll remind him to be a bit more polite next time. If I'd hit his jaw, he'd be spitting blood and teeth for the rest of the day.'

'I don't doubt that. You have a killer right arm there, Dawson. Remind me not to argue with you.'

They passed through the next checkpoint without incident, and then drove to the centre of Brunehault. There they stopped at a T-junction with a major road which ran from north to south through the village itself. If there'd been the slightest doubt that a major conflict was imminent, the sheer number of troops they were seeing on that road, all heading north towards Leuven, was proof enough. Most of them were British, and Sykes and Dawson wearing their British uniforms, but sitting in a car with Belgian army registration plates, attracted some curious glances.

It was perfectly obvious that they wouldn't be able to turn left, against the traffic flow, because the northbound vehicles were using both sides of the road. North was the one direction they definitely didn't want to go, but they simply didn't have a choice.

'Bugger,' Sykes muttered. 'You'll have to turn right, and then look out for a turning to the left to get us off this road. Any road heading west will do. If you see a signpost, I'm trying to get us to a village called Azebois, which should take us in the right direction.'

Dawson waited for a break in the stream of trucks and other vehicles, and then swung the Fiat across the road. As he did so, the drivers of the approaching vehicles began swerving across the road, heading for the houses that lined the sides of the street.

'What the hell are they doing?' Dawson muttered.

Sykes swung round in his seat and stuck his head out of the side window. 'Aircraft!' he yelled. 'Enemy aircraft. Get us out of here.'

CHAPTER 32

12 MAY 1940: EASTERN BELGIUM

Above the rumbling noise of the big engines in the trucks, Dawson could hear a higher-pitched roar, the sound of a high-performance aircraft engine. And then the lethal hammering of a cannon echoed off the buildings, and shells began tearing up the surface of the road and smashing into the military vehicles, which were sitting targets.

The noise was deafening, the onslaught terrifying. Bullet fragments, shards of steel and slivers of stone from the road surface flew everywhere under the impact of the rapid-fire cannon's shells. A British truck directly in front of the Fiat took several direct hits and slewed to a stop, steam pouring from the engine compartment. The vehicle behind was also hit, and its cargo – probably fuel – exploded with a roar into a massive fireball. Fortunately for Dawson and Sykes, the stationary truck acted as a barrier in front of them.

Rifle shots and machine-gun fire sounded as the Allied soldiers started to return fire, but small-arms were essentially useless against aircraft, especially low-flying fighters, because the targets were simply moving too fast.

It would be a miracle if any of the bullets hit the air-craft, and an even bigger one if rifle fire did any damage to them.

Dawson glanced in his rear-view mirror, but could see nothing – the field of view was too restricted. All he could see was the road behind him, through the Fiat's small rear window. He looked over his shoulder, through the side window, and then the ominous sight of two enemy fighters, low down and travelling fast, heading directly towards them and following the line of the road, was only too apparent.

He turned the wheel to the right, desperately looking for any cover, anywhere they could get off the street.

There were gaps between the houses, but most of them were far too narrow to accommodate any vehicle, even one as small as the car Dawson was driving. Then he saw a wooden fence maybe ten feet wide. He had no idea what was behind it, and at that moment he didn't care. He just aimed the car straight towards it and floored the accelerator pedal.

'Hold on,' he shouted, as the car quickly gathered speed.

The fence splintered under the onslaught of maybe half a ton of metal moving at about twenty miles an hour, and the little *Topolino* crashed through it.

Sykes crossed both his arms in front of his face as the vehicle hit.

Dawson still had to steer, so he just pulled off his steel helmet and held that in front of him with one hand. The moment they were through the fence, Dawson hit the brakes as hard as he could, and the car slid sideways a few feet before coming to a stop, its front end just a matter of inches from a low stone wall – an immovable barrier that would have wrecked the vehicle if they'd smashed into it.

'Thank Christ you stopped before we hit that,' Sykes said.

Dawson nodded but didn't reply. He jumped out, grabbed one of the Mauser 98K rifles from the rear compartment of the car and ran back to the main road.

He was greeted with a scene of chaos. Vehicles were stopped on the street, and some were on fire, others moving slowly as their drivers looked for anywhere they could find shelter from the air assault. The bodies of soldiers lay scattered across the cobbles, some moving weakly, others ominously still and many lying in seemingly vast pools of blood. Right beside Dawson one corpse had been blasted apart by rounds from the cannon on the fighters, his head virtually cut from his body and his torso ripped apart, blood and ruptured internal organs splattered everywhere, grey coils of intestine gleaming wetly in the sunshine.

Dawson gave the body a single appalled glance, then looked up into the sky. The two German aircraft had vanished from sight, but if they still had ammunition for their weapons he had no doubt they'd be back for another strafing run any time.

Even as that thought crossed his mind, he heard the aero engines again, from somewhere over to his right – the opposite direction from the way they'd attacked before, presumably hoping to catch the soldiers by surprise and looking the wrong way. Dawson loaded a round into the breech of the Mauser, clicked off the safety catch and waited for a target.

The noise of the engines increased, and then he saw them approaching, again at low level, and fast, their yellow nose-cones glinting in the sun. He steadied the rifle against the wall of the building, giving himself a stable rest, sighted carefully, allowing a little leeway ahead to account for the aircraft's speed, and pulled the trigger.

The Mauser kicked into his shoulder. He thought he must have hit the aircraft, purely because he'd taken his time and it was flying almost directly towards him, but as far as he could see the enemy fighter was undamaged. He worked the bolt to reload the rifle.

The aircraft was now much closer, and again Dawson thought he'd hit it – the Mauser was a very accurate rifle – but without any obvious result.

Then the pilot opened up, sending a solid stream of bullets lancing down into the mêlée of vehicles and men. Shells carved furrows in the wall of the building Dawson had taken shelter behind, and he ducked backwards, moving away from the road. He'd done his best with the Mauser, but what he needed to take on an aircraft was a heavy machine-gun, like the .303 Vickers, and preferably a proper quick-firing anti-aircraft weapon.

Then a more lethal weapon joined the fray. Dawson heard the distinctive rat-tat-tat of a machine-gun firing nearby and peered across the road. A British soldier was standing directly in front of one of the stationary lorries and had rested the bipod of his Bren gun on the bonnet. The weapon, Dawson noted, was fitted with the flat 100-round pancake magazine rather than the smaller but distinctive top-mounted curved box magazine.

The soldier was firing the weapon continuously,

tracking the aircraft as it screamed towards him, heedless of the cannon fire erupting all over the street. But as Dawson watched, willing the soldier to bring down the fighter, the shells fired by the attacking aircraft smashed into the lorry in front of the man. Something blew under the bonnet, and the explosion tossed the soldier and his weapon carelessly backwards. The man tumbled to the ground and lay still, unconscious or dead.

Dawson took a quick glance upwards. The aircraft was nearly on them. He lowered the Mauser to the ground and ran across the road. He scooped up the Bren, leant against the side of the damaged lorry, aimed at the dark shadow streaking directly overhead and pulled the trigger.

The German fighter was so low that Dawson could actually see the heads of the rivets holding its panels together. And he could also see the first rounds from the machine-gun chewing their way through the thin aluminium skin as he kept the trigger pulled. But again, despite taking at least a dozen hits from the .303 bullets the weapon fired, the aircraft seemed unaffected.

'Bugger,' he muttered, as the aircraft flew out of range and he lowered the Bren. But then the German aircraft seemed to almost shudder in flight. The left wing dipped and moments later it cartwheeled into the ground perhaps a mile away, exploding in a massive fireball. The second German aircraft, following for its own attacking run, pitched sharply nose-up. It climbed away and was quickly lost to sight.

A couple of British squaddies ran up to Dawson and clapped him on the back, but he shook them off and strode across to the soldier who'd first opened fire with the Bren. He bent down beside him and quickly checked for a pulse, because he seemed to be uninjured. As he did so, the soldier opened his eyes, grimaced and lifted his hand to the side of his head.

'My fucking bonce,' he muttered. 'Feels like I've been kicked by a bloody mule.'

Dawson grinned at him, then helped the man to his feet. 'But we got the bastard,' he said, pointing ahead at the distant flames still licking around the wreckage of the aircraft, above which a heavy plume of dark smoke was rising into the clear blue sky.

'Fucking good-oh. Where's his mate?'

'He buggered off,' one of the other men said.

'Here.' Dawson handed the soldier the Bren gun he was still holding. 'I think this belongs to you.'

'Ta, mate,' he said, looking for the first time at Dawson's uniform and insignia. 'You're a sapper, aren't you? So where did you spring from?'

Dawson nodded. 'I am, and it's a long story. And right now I've got to go. Hope it all goes well for you.'

'With Monty in charge of this picnic? No fucking chance.'

Dawson grinned again, then ran back over the road, collected the Mauser and walked over to the Fiat *Topolino*.

'I heard a hell of a bang,' Sykes said. 'Did you get one of them?'

Dawson nodded. 'It was a joint effort – me and a bloke with a Bren. I don't know which of us did the most damage, but I know I hit the aircraft because I saw the bullets stitching a pattern down the fuselage. Anyway, it's time we went, before some other Jerry aviators decide they want to join this party.'

He checked the front of the car for obvious damage. One of the mounting points for the bumper had been ripped off, and both front wings were badly dented. Dawson pulled the bumper upwards and out. Metal groaned and tore, but the other mount remained obstinately attached to the front of the chassis. He repeated the treatment and the third time he heaved at the bumper the mounting point tore free. He tossed the steel to one side, then kicked and tugged at the wings until he'd pulled the metal clear of the front wheels and tyres.

Then he started the car and reversed cautiously out of the open space and over the wooden fence he'd demolished. He got the Fiat back onto the street, gave a wave to the soldiers he'd talked to, then headed off, this time to the south, still looking for a road they could take that would allow them to track over to the west.

After a few minutes, he spotted a battered wooden signpost leaning drunkenly against a hedge on the right-hand side of the road. Most of the writing on it was illegible, but Dawson could just make out one of the words carved into its horizontal arm: the name was 'Azebois'.

'That'll do us. Turn right here, Dawson,' Sykes ordered, and the corporal dutifully steered the Fiat down the narrow lane.

The lane wound on, the surface alternating between hard-packed earth and stones, and poor-quality Belgian pavé. But it was almost deserted, so at least they didn't have to contend with either crowds of refugees or soldiers and military vehicles.

After about fifteen minutes they rolled into another village, which Sykes guessed was probably Azebois, though there was a total lack of any road signs or anything else to confirm his suspicion. Perhaps because they were now some miles from the front line, and actually to the west of Charleroi itself, there was more activity in the village. A few people were standing outside their houses, and looked with expectant curiosity at the battered little Fiat as it bumped and rattled its way down the main street.

'This lot haven't evacuated yet,' Dawson observed. 'Maybe they think they're still safe here.'

'Well, they're not safe, here or anywhere else in Belgium, but they aren't our problem,' Sykes replied. 'Just keep on going – keep heading south. You probably won't see any other road signs, but we're looking for Motte or Roux, or even Charleroi itself, at a pinch.'

Dawson steered the Fiat through the village and out of the southern end of the small settlement. And Sykes had been right. He didn't see any road signs, but from the position of the sun in the sky – it was another beautiful day – he knew they were still heading in roughly the right direction. And there were no turnings or junctions on the road anyway, so they really had no choice.

For some distance the road followed the path of a railway line which was also running north–south, but they saw no sign of any trains on it. In fact, apart from the curious civilian spectators they'd seen in Azebois, or whatever the village had been called, there seemed little activity of any sort in the area, which was slightly surprising.

They didn't pass through either Motte or Roux, as

far as Dawson could tell, but within a short time they entered the north-western outskirts of Charleroi, which was the scene of far more activity, both military and civilian. Again, there were hundreds, or more probably thousands, of refugees streaming west through the city's streets, the sheer mass of slow-moving humanity making progress towards the east virtually impossible – not that Dawson and Sykes wanted to go that way. They wanted to head south-west but that, too, proved to be something they couldn't do. Troops, both sitting in the backs of trucks and as loose columns of marching men, were blocking the roads as they made their way towards the front line. Dawson tried to take two or three roads that Sykes believed were heading in the right direction, but each time they were turned back by Belgian police officers and army patrols charged with keeping the main thoroughfares clear for the essential troop movements.

'This is hopeless,' Sykes said, as they again found themselves forced back towards the south.

'We can't argue with them, though, sir,' Dawson said. 'What they're doing is more important than us getting this demolition charge back to Blighty. Getting reinforcements up to the front is vital. If they can't stop the Jerry advance, whether or not we know how that device works probably won't matter. We'll all be wearing jackboots and shouting "Heil Hitler" within the year.'

As if to reinforce Dawson's statement, at that moment they both heard the sound of either bombing or artillery fire somewhere in the distance, over to the east.

Sykes nodded, but didn't look up from his map. 'I know, and I think we're wasting our time even trying to find a road that's open. OK, change of plan. Just keep going straight. It looks like there's a decent road running almost due south out of Charleroi that'll take us down to the French border.'

'How far's that, sir?'

Sykes used his fingers and the scale at the side of the map to estimate the distance involved. 'It's about thirty miles,' he replied, 'maybe thirty-five. But not far. That'll bring us into France not far from Charleville-Mézières in the Champagne-Ardenne region. Once we're across the border, we can head west over to the Channel ports or track a bit further south towards Amiens and Abbeville. One of the big Allied command centres was still there, the last I heard.'

'That should work, as long as the Jerries haven't beaten us to it,' Dawson said. 'That Belgie colonel reckoned Adolf's troops might try to hack their way through the Ardennes Forest, didn't he?'

Sykes nodded. 'Yes, but unless the Germans can also get their tanks through there – which I think is doubtful, simply because of the terrain – then even the French should be able to hold them.'

'Well, let's hope so.'

Dawson switched his attention back to the road, because even going due south through Charleroi wasn't easy. Most of the junctions were clogged with people – either refugees or troops – and frequently they had to wait several minutes before a small gap opened up and Dawson could steer the *Topolino* over the junction and continue heading south. Although the distance from one side of the city to the other was small, perhaps only about a mile or so, it was still over an hour before they finally cleared the southern outskirts of Charleroi and Dawson was able to get the little Fiat out of first gear and actually make some real, albeit still fairly slow, progress. Even this road was busy, but it was nothing like as congested as the city itself had been, and in a few minutes they were approaching another village, this one almost straddling the main road. Sykes thought this one was probably a place called Tarcienne.

After that, the traffic, both vehicular and pedestrian, diminished considerably, and they didn't drive through any other villages or towns for some time. About an hour after leaving Tarcienne, they crossed a railway line and then a river in quick succession, and then drove through the village of Frasnes, where there was another spur of the railway.

'That's good,' Sykes said, as they cleared the edge of the built-up area, which had been about as quiet as all the other small settlements they'd passed through. 'We're approaching the border area now. It's probably only about ten miles away.'

The road was still heading more or less south as they drove into Couvin, a slightly bigger village.

'According to the map, this is about the last place of any size that we'll go through before we reach the border,' Sykes said.

The terrain had changed as well. The area around Charleroi had been mainly level and open, but for the last few miles they'd been driving through countryside that was becoming more hilly the further south they went and increasingly heavily forested.

'I suppose this is the Ardennes Forest we're coming up to,' Dawson suggested, gesturing to the land that lay in front of them as they reached the southern end of

Couvin. Already the road was starting to slope upwards, and he had to change down a gear to keep the little Fiat moving up the hill.

Sykes nodded. 'Yes. Well, a part of it, anyway.' He pointed ahead of them, through the Fiat's windscreen. 'You can see that the land is rising in front of us. If this map is right, we'll reach the French border before we get to the top of those hills, and then keep climbing for another mile or so to reach the highest point. Then it'll be downhill all the way. We won't have much choice over which road we take because there aren't many there, but once we've driven down out of the hills on the French side it'll be a lot easier.'

'Not a lot of activity here, is there?' Dawson asked. 'We've not seen any Belgian troops for a few miles, or any civilians.'

'That's not surprising because we're a long way from the threat area. I imagine most of the civilians will already have left here for the west of the country, and the Belgian forces will be massing behind the Dyle Line, preparing to face the German attacks that they know will be coming from the east. There'd be no point in stationing Belgian troops anywhere down here, this far south, but once we cross the border we'll probably meet some French soldiers. If Colonel Lefèvre was right, they'll probably only be reservists from the Second Army, hoping to stop any German troops who make it through the Ardennes Forest.'

'Well,' Dawson said, a smile on his face, 'as long as we don't get shot by any of the Frogs once we cross the border, at least we'll be safe from the Germans.'

Then he suddenly cursed under his breath and

slammed on the brakes. The Fiat came to a rapid stop as both gravity and the rudimentary brakes worked in tandem to slow down the little car.

'What is it?' Sykes demanded.

Dawson pointed to the front, then swung the Fiat around in a tight circle to point back down the hill, back the way they'd come. 'Troops,' he said. 'There's a bunch of soldiers up there in the trees, maybe eighty yards ahead of us. And from the shape of their helmets they're fucking Jerries.'

Dawson steered the *Topolino* down the hill, the speed picking up quickly. But as he rounded another bend in the road he hit the brakes hard again. The car slewed sideways, skidding to a halt with the rear wheels right at the edge of the road.

Just appearing from a forest track on their right-hand side, perhaps a hundred yards in front of them, was the unmistakable shape of a Panzer IV, the turret with its stubby, short-barrelled cannon already swinging around to point towards the Fiat.

CHAPTER 33

12 MAY 1940: EASTERN BELGIUM

Dawson again swung the Fiat's wheel hard over to the left, slammed the gear lever into first and floored the accelerator pedal. The little car lurched into motion and started heading slowly back up the hill again.

Somehow, they'd driven right into the path of the enemy forces. They were trapped between two groups of Germans. But the immediate danger was the tank.

There was an echoing crack behind them, and a shell from the Panzer IV screamed past them and exploded against the trunk of a big tree about fifty yards away, the seventy-five-millimetre high-explosive armour-piercing round blasting a hole in the side of the trunk, red-hot shards of metal flying everywhere.

'What's the reload time for that bastard?' Dawson asked, wrenching the Fiat's gear lever into second.

'Fucked if I know. It's got a forward-mounted machine-gun as well. So just keep moving. Get us around that corner and out of sight.'

Sykes turned round in his seat to stare out of the car's back window. The Panzer had turned up the hill and was starting to follow them. He could hear the rattling and clattering of the steel caterpillar tracks on the hard surface of the road. Then the muzzle of the cannon moved again as the German gunner prepared to fire a second round.

'Swerve!' the major ordered.

Dawson wrenched the steering wheel – to the right this time – forcing the Fiat close to the side of the road, aiming for the apex of the corner, which would get them out of sight of the crew of the Panzer as quickly as possible.

Again the German weapon fired, just as the *Topolino* rounded the bend.

There was a thump from the back of the Fiat, and the car lurched sideways. Immediately afterwards the shell exploded in the trees on the other side of the road.

'What the hell happened?' Dawson demanded.

'I've no idea. Is the car still driveable?'

Dawson checked the steering, touched the brakes and then pressed down hard on the accelerator pedal again.

'Everything seems to be working,' he said.

'Good,' Sykes said briskly. 'Those troops you saw were on the left-hand side of the road, weren't they?'

Dawson nodded. 'Yes.'

'That Panzer came out of the woods to the east as well. Maybe we've run into the advance guard of a German armoured patrol. We have to get off this road, so take any track you can see on the right.'

'And if we've run into the middle of a patrol and they're all over this hillside?'

'Then we're buggered, Dawson.'

There seemed to be no sensible answer to that.

A gap in the trees appeared on their right. Dawson

braked sharply, swung the wheel to aim the car straight at it and accelerated. Undergrowth brushed and scraped down both sides of the car as he weaved his way between the thick trunks of the trees.

'At least that bloody Panzer won't be able to follow us through this lot.'

'Don't talk, Dawson. Just drive,' Sykes said, still looking behind them.

'More troops,' Dawson said, pointing to their left.

Sykes turned back immediately. About 100 yards away, through the trees, a handful of grey-clad shapes moved indistinctly.

'Keep going,' the major said, unnecessarily. 'They'll never get a clear shot at us through these trees.'

As if to reinforce what he was saying, several dozen yards behind them, at the edge of the forest, the front end of the Panzer appeared, and moments later the crew fired another round towards them. But the shell exploded against a tree well behind the Fiat.

Dawson weaved the Fiat around the trunks of the trees, and for the first time since they'd been given the car by the Belgian colonel, he was grateful it was so small. A normal-sized staff car wouldn't have been able to get through the forest, and they'd probably both be dead by now. Even so, the lack of power was a problem on the loose surface, and Dawson was having to keep going down the slope, just to keep the vehicle moving.

A ragged volley of rifle shots sounded from over to their left, up the hill, as the German infantry soldiers opened fire on them. Most of the bullets missed – by how much, the two British soldiers had no idea – but one smashed into the rear of the Fiat somewhere. Whatever part of the vehicle had been hit, the car was still moving, and that was all they cared about.

Sitting in the passenger seat of the bouncing and lurching vehicle, Sykes was switching his attention between watching out for other German soldiers and trying to see where the nearest road was that they could use to make their escape. As they'd already found out, the map wasn't very detailed.

'Just keep going,' the major said. 'As far as I can see, the only road anywhere near here is the one we were on.'

'I don't know how long I can manage to do that,' Dawson said, his voice shaking as the Fiat was bounced around. 'Sooner or later we're going to find ourselves hemmed in by trees growing too close together for us to drive between, or down in a valley somewhere.'

'We'll tackle that when we come to it,' Sykes said.

Another handful of shots rang out from their left, but none of the bullets came anywhere near them. They were now too far away and were probably barely even visible through the trees, which acted as a natural barrier between them and the enemy troops. No more rounds were fired at them by the Panzer, so they were obviously out of sight of the tank crew, or at least not in a direct line of sight for the gunner. With the thickening forest behind them, firing the main gun again would have been a waste of ammunition.

After another couple of minutes, Dawson pulled the Fiat to a halt and turned off the engine. Over to their right, the slope dropped away gently, but the trees were much closer together and he worried they wouldn't be able to get the car between them if they went that way.

315

In front of them, the trees were widely separated, but the ground was mainly level and in some parts there was even a slight slope upwards.

He glanced at Sykes, but as he did so the major shook his head.

'I'm sorry, Dawson. I really am lost. This map is completely useless once you leave the main roads. It's not even very good when you're actually on the road. I do know we're near the French border, but probably still in Belgium. I think we're heading more or less west, but I wouldn't even want to put any money on that.'

Dawson nodded, opened the door of the *Topolino* and climbed out.

'Where are you going?' Sykes asked.

'To check for any damage to the car, and see if there are any Jerries in sight.'

He was back in less than a minute, and leant down beside the car to talk to the major. 'We were bloody lucky with that Jerry Panzer, because that second shell they fired did hit us. It was another armour-piercing job. It caught the top of the spare wheel and must have gone straight through the tyre because there's a fucking great hole in it. If it had hit the metal of the wheel, the high explosive would probably have cooked off, and we'd just be a big red stain on the road back there.'

Sykes grunted. 'What about that rifle round?'

'That's not a problem. The bullet hit the car about two feet behind our seats and went straight through and out the other side. I've looked around, but I can't see any sign of the Jerries. We know there's at least one tank somewhere behind us. It's still on the road because I can hear its tracks clattering on the hard surface. But we've driven far enough into the forest to get well away from the German soldiers.'

'They're probably going to stay on the road, or near it, so the tanks and supply trucks – I know we didn't see any of them, but they'll definitely be out there some-where – will have a decent surface to drive along,' Sykes mused. 'So Colonel Lefèvre was right. We know the French have only lightly defended the area to the south of the Ardennes Forest, because they're relying on this terrain to keep the Germans out. So that's where Adolf has decided to try to push his way through into France itself.'

'So we're stuck in the middle, between the Jerries behind us and the Frogs somewhere in front.'

'Exactly. Apart from the Germans themselves, the only people who know what they're planning to do are the two of us. We have to get through the French lines as soon as possible and sound the alarm. Let's hope we're not too late.'

'That's easier said than done, Major,' Dawson said. 'There's just us two and this "little mouse". It wouldn't surprise me if this car shook itself to pieces long before we got anywhere near the border. It's just not built for this kind of driving. Unless we can find another road, and quickly, I reckon we're screwed.'

Dawson took another look around them, then walked back to the driver's side of the *Topolino*. He started the engine again, then a thought struck him and he looked across at Major Sykes.

'I've just remembered something,' he said. 'When we started climbing up the slope out of that last village – I forget what it was called.'

'Couvin,' Sykes supplied.

'Yeah, Couvin. Anyway, there was a road junction off to the right. Not a road, really, it looked more like a track, and I guess it wasn't marked on that map you've got.'

Sykes looked down at the map on his lap and shook his head. 'No. In fact, there's bugger-all marked on it in this area, apart from that road we were following.'

'Well, ever since we took to the woods, we've been heading more or less west, I guess, so maybe we've sort of driven along two sides of a triangle. And if we have, and if that track runs more or less straight, it might be down there, somewhere in front of us.' Dawson pointed ahead of the Fiat.

Sykes nodded slowly. 'I've no idea if you're right or not, but I haven't got any better ideas at the moment. Let's just keep going.'

Dawson slipped the *Topolino* into gear and the car moved off slowly across the soft surface of the forest floor, the wheels slipping slightly as the tyres struggled for grip. He tried to keep to the high ground as much as possible, where the timber growth was thinner. But the low power of the Fiat's engine meant that inevitably they were slowly losing more and more height the further they went through the forest, simply because Dawson kept having to steer the car downhill just to keep it moving forward. Trying to stay at the same level or even climb slightly invariably resulted in the Fiat's wheels spinning fruitlessly on the soft ground.

His big fear was that they'd end up with the vehicle trapped on a downhill slope and unable to move forward because of the trees and undergrowth. Although Major

Sykes was now able to stand and even manage to stagger a few steps on his injured leg, walking out of the forest and across the Franco-Belgian border simply wasn't an option for them. Sykes definitely wouldn't be able to make it, and they'd have to dump the German demolition charge. Neither Dawson nor Sykes was prepared to even consider doing that, unless there genuinely was no other option. Dawson *had* to keep the car moving forwards. The little *Topolino* – their tiny Italian mouse – was their only way out of the Ardennes Forest.

Then Dawson spotted something in front of them, some distance further down the slope.

'There's a gap in that line of trees,' he said, pointing. 'You reckon that could be a track?'

'God knows,' Sykes replied. 'But don't drive down there until you're sure.'

Dawson stopped the Fiat, grabbed the Schmeisser and climbed out of the car. He checked all around him, but the only noise he could hear in the woods was the engine of the car. He strode down the slope until he could see the land better, then nodded and climbed back up to where Sykes sat waiting patiently in the car, one of the Mauser carbines held loosely across his lap.

'It *is* a track,' Dawson said shortly, 'and from the position of the sun I reckon it's heading south or maybe south-west. But wherever it goes, it's a better bet than staying up here in the trees. There's no sign of movement on it in either direction, so it looks as if we're still ahead of the Jerries.'

He engaged first gear and let the Fiat *Topolino* roll gently down the slope towards a gap in the trees that lined the side of the track. There was a slight rise from the forest floor up to the track's surface, and he accelerated as soon as he saw it – Dawson knew instantly that if he didn't get the car moving faster there wouldn't be enough momentum to get the vehicle up that slope.

'Hang on,' he said, concentrating on getting the Fiat cleanly through the gap.

In fact, he was probably going a bit too quickly when he hit the rise, because both the front wheels left the ground and the car bounced out of the cover of the trees and crashed down onto the track. Dawson braked to a stop, the Fiat sliding and skidding sideways across the loose and rutted surface. Once again he got out of the car, this time to check that the violent manoeuvre hadn't caused any damage to the vehicle.

'It all seems to be OK,' he said, resuming his seat behind the wheel, 'so let's get moving.'

Dawson put the car back into gear and headed off down the track. It ran straight in front of them for perhaps 100 yards, then bent slightly to the left. There was no traffic on it, which wasn't exactly a surprise. No sign of any German troops either.

Sykes was constantly checking back the way they'd come, just to ensure they weren't being followed, and that the enemy soldiers hadn't somehow managed to get behind them. They both knew that the thin metal of the little Fiat would offer virtually no protection against rifle bullets.

Dawson kept his attention focused ahead of them, and on the forest that extended on both sides of the track, preternaturally alert for any sign of danger.

As he approached a bend, he slowed right down, reducing his speed to little more than walking pace, just in case a problem was lurking just around the corner. But beyond the bend, the track ran straight down to the south, and was completely deserted. And at the far end, it actually appeared to leave the forest, because in the distance Dawson could see that the trees thinned out considerably, to be replaced by largely open fields.

'Could that be the French border?' he asked.

Sykes glanced at his map and shook his head. 'I don't think so. Unless we came a lot further through the forest than I thought, we're still not that far from Couvin, which means we're still well inside Belgium. So keep your eyes open for those bloody Germans, because they're still out there somewhere.'

Dawson nodded, and accelerated down the track, the Fiat bouncing and lurching over the uneven ground. As he neared the edge of the tree-line, he slowed down again, because the more open ground meant they could be seen from a distance, and if the Germans had already established a presence on the farmland the Fiat would be an easy target as it emerged from the edge of the forest.

But as Dawson slowed the car and the two men scanned the terrain over to their right, they saw no signs of enemy activity.

'Maybe we're still ahead of them,' Sykes said. 'They'll be coming this way. This open ground will be far easier for them to negotiate than the forest, especially with their trucks and tanks. But for the moment it looks like we've got clear of them. Now let's just crack on for the border. Keep heading on down this track.'

Dawson could see the straight section ended about seventy or eighty yards in front of them, but the rough track clearly continued, swinging quite sharply over to the right, to the south-west, which was still taking them in the correct direction. He slowed for the corner, then accelerated again,

On the left-hand side, one last triangular stand of trees marked the edge of the forest in that area, and beyond it, over to the south and east, more cultivated fields appeared. And as Dawson straightened up the Fiat just past the point of the triangle of trees, the car drove out of the forest completely.

They'd made about 200 yards down the new section of the track when the first shell landed a few yards over to their left and slightly behind the Fiat. The noise of the explosion was instant and shockingly loud. A plume of earth and smoke rose into the air, scattering stones and clods over the rear of the car, which thudded ominously into the thin steel of the bodywork.

Dawson looked in his mirror. The last time he'd checked, the view behind had been empty of any activity, just fields, trees and the hills behind. Now, in a hideous reprise of what they'd seen just minutes earlier on the road up to the border, another tank had emerged from the shelter of the trees behind them and was now clearly visible, trundling slowly towards the narrow track.

CHAPTER 34

12 MAY 1940: FRANCO-BELGIAN BORDER REGION

Sykes span round in his seat as Dawson flattened the accelerator pedal to the floor and started sawing away at the steering wheel, weaving the car from side to side to try to throw the tank's gunner off his aim.

'It's got a long-barrelled main gun,' the major said, his voice high with tension. 'It's a Panzer Three. They're only fitted with machine-guns and a thirty-seven-millimetre cannon – that's about one and a half inches. That's smaller than the seventy-five millimetre weapon on the Panzer Four.'

'Like that's going to make any fucking difference,' Dawson muttered.

'Small mercies, Dawson, small mercies. Won't this thing go any faster?'

'Nope. If I press any harder, my foot'll go straight through the floor of this tin can.'

There was another crack from behind them, and a second shell screamed past the little Fiat. It detonated a short distance ahead of them and to their right, and Dawson instinctively steered over to the left-hand side of the track.

'Keep weaving,' Sykes ordered, 'and look out for cover – somewhere we can hide.'

'Hiding isn't going to work,' Dawson said, 'because there'll be Jerry troops following it. We can't outrun it either. If you're right and that bugger *is* a Panzer Three, it'll do about twelve miles an hour cross-country and over twenty on a decent surface.'

'Thanks for the reminder, Dawson,' Sykes said, still watching the tank, which was trundling over the ground in pursuit of the small car.

There was a slight kink in the track ahead – it wasn't a big enough change of direction to be called a bend – and on the right was a reasonably thick hedge. Dawson swung the Fiat over to that side to take advantage of the tiny scrap of cover. The hedge obviously wouldn't stop a shell from the Panzer's main gun, but if the gunner couldn't see his target, he'd be firing blind. The bad news was that the tank was also fitted with twin coaxially-mounted 7.92-millimetre MG 34 machine-guns. If Dawson had been the tank commander, he'd have told his gunner to use it to spray the hedge the moment the car vanished from view.

Unfortunately, the tank commander obviously thought the same way, and seconds afterwards a volley of machine-gun fire shredded the vegetation on their right. The only good thing was that the gunner had clearly overestimated their speed, because all the bullets ploughed through the hedge several feet in front of them.

Dawson braked to give them a small margin of safety, but both men knew that, if the gunner reversed his direction of fire, they'd probably be dead in seconds.

Then the machine-gun abruptly fell silent. Maybe the

gunner was waiting to see the results of his first salvo, because the Panzer was still just out of sight. In seconds, though, it would move forward far enough to allow him to see down the length of the track. Or maybe the weapon had jammed. Or perhaps he was just changing magazines.

Whatever the reason, Dawson took a chance and floored the accelerator again. The little Fiat staggered forwards, slowly picking up speed once more as the corporal drove it along the side of the track, hugging the hedge.

Unlike the earlier sections of the track, this part was both narrower and more twisty, with frequent changes of direction, and was bounded by thick hedges on both sides. There was a possibility Dawson could keep the *Topolino* out of sight of the pursuing German troops for at least some of the time, but they were stuck on the track – there were no exits either man could see, at least not on the section they were traversing. But getting off the track and trying to drive across the adjacent fields wasn't an option anyway, because the Fiat would probably have got bogged down in a matter of seconds on the ploughed fields, most of which were devoid of crops. So their only option was to keep going along the track. And to keep hoping for the best.

'Where's that fucking tank?' Dawson demanded, switching his attention between the narrow and twisting track ahead and the very restricted view available in the Fiat's rear-view mirror.

'Can't see it,' Sykes replied, sliding open his side window and sticking his head out of the car to check the view behind.

'We must be about five or six hundred yards clear of it now.'

'We're still within range of that bloody cannon, though,' Sykes pointed out. 'Once he gets a clear shot at us, he'll fire again.'

Then the track straightened out again, and almost immediately Sykes called out a warning. 'I see the Panzer,' he said. 'Maybe six hundred yards back, with a clear line of sight. You'd better start weaving, otherwise we'll be blown to buggery as soon as the gunner sorts out the range.'

'We can't move much. The bloody track's only about ten feet wide.'

But Dawson did what he could, slaloming the *Topolino* left and right, from one side of the track to the other, trying to be as erratic as possible.

And it worked. The Panzer gunner fired just as Dawson swung the wheel to the right, and the shell passed a couple of feet to the left of the car, to explode some hundred yards ahead of them.

'There's a bend in front of us,' Dawson said. 'If we can just get round that we'll be safe.'

'For how long?' Sykes asked rhetorically.

Dawson swung the wheel left, then right, and then accelerated as hard as he could towards the slight left-hand bend in the track. In the instant before the Fiat reached it, the main gun on the Panzer fired again.

And this time the German gunner got everything right.

The shell slammed into the left side of the car, right at the back. Both the side windows of the Fiat blew out and the *Topolino* lurched across the track, over to the right, the side of the car crashing into the hedge. The blast was enormous, a colossal bang that deafened Dawson, followed instantly by an even bigger explosion from somewhere outside the vehicle.

For a moment, the corporal thought that was it, that he was dead.

Then he realized he wasn't, he was still in one piece, still sitting in the driver's seat of the Fiat. The little car was still running, limping slowly along the track. Working by instinct, without conscious thought, he steered the car away from the hedge and carried on around the bend, out of sight of the tank.

'What the fuck?' he muttered, and glanced at Sykes.

The major looked as shocked as Dawson felt, and was staring behind him at the back of the car.

'Fucking hell,' Dawson mouthed. 'What the fuck?' he repeated.

But Sykes didn't seem to hear him, and Dawson realized that both of them had been deafened – temporarily, he hoped – by the explosion.

'It didn't go off,' Sykes shouted, looking straight at Dawson, who heard his words faintly.

'What?'

'Thank Christ we were driving something like this,' Sykes said, still shouting. 'The steel on this car is so thin it didn't trigger the explosive charge. The shell went right through the car, just behind the seats. In one side and out the other. Thank God it was above the demolition charge. If it had been a foot lower it would have hit it and then we'd have been blown to kingdom come. A foot further to the left, and we'd both have lost our heads.'

Dawson took his eyes off the view through the *Topolino*'s windscreen, at the track he was still following, and glanced quickly behind him. Directly behind Sykes's head was a fist-sized hole in the side of the car. Dawson swivelled his head around and looked behind his own seat, where he saw a similar hole, this one showing where the shell had hit the vehicle. Torn and ripped and blackened metal was bent inwards.

But the 1.5-inch high-explosive round hadn't exploded. Or, at least, not in the car. Instead, the round had obviously carried on, through the right-hand side of the Fiat, then burst through the hedge and finally detonated some dozen yards beyond when it hit the ground. That had been the second explosion the two men had heard a moment after the car had been hit.

'We've been bloody lucky,' Dawson agreed, shaking his head to try to clear the ringing in his ears.

About a quarter of a mile further on the track came to an end, simply petering out, and the Fiat moved clear of the hedgerows into a wide open area of grass and occasional shrubs. Dawson kept the accelerator flat on the floor, the engine of the little Fiat screaming as he did his best to cover the ground as quickly as possible. The open terrain meant that the tank crew would be able to spot them as soon as the Panzer came into view, and their only hope was to put as much distance as they could between themselves and the Germans.

The land rose gently, a slope that slowed the Fiat, but not too drastically, and in a couple of minutes they reached the crest of the hill and started to descend the land on the far side.

Dawson looked ahead, eased off the accelerator and muttered a curse. 'I think our luck's about to run out,' he said.

'What?' Sykes asked, staring through the windscreen and following Dawson's glance.

'There,' Dawson said, pointing. 'That's a fucking great ditch in front of us. It runs all the way over the field.'

'You're right. And I know what it is.'

'What? Irrigation or something?'

'Nothing so mundane. Unless I'm mistaken, we must have already crossed the border. We're in France now, and that has to be one of the defences the French have put in place. They obviously haven't just relied on the barrier of the Ardennes Forest. That's an anti-tank ditch, and it's big enough to stop that Panzer.'

Dawson looked in both directions at the open ditch which extended all the way across the ground in front of them.

'Yeah,' he agreed, 'it's big enough to stop that Panzer. The trouble is, it'll stop us just the same. We're buggered. We're trapped on the wrong side.'

CHAPTER 35

12 MAY 1940: FRANCO-BELGIAN BORDER REGION

Dawson braked the Fiat to a halt and looked around. The anti-tank ditch was a straight, uncompromising line that stretched across the whole width of the open field. Some sections of it were edged with steel posts and laced with coils of barbed wire on the French side, work that had clearly not been completed before hostilities commenced, because the area directly in front of them hadn't been wired. Grey coils of wire lay piled in heaps on the far side of the ditch, ready to be installed.

'There's no fucking way round that bastard, that's for sure,' Dawson said.

Sykes looked back the way they'd come, but the Panzer was out of sight on the opposite side of the hill, and hopefully now at least a mile or so behind them. But both men knew the tank was coming. Once it crested the brow of the hill, they would have nowhere to run, and certainly nowhere to hide.

'Look, Dawson,' Sykes said, his voice oddly muted. 'We've had a bloody good run. Been lucky to get this far, but there's no way out of this. I can't run anywhere, but you've got time to cross that ditch and get away. Just help me out of the car so I can stand up and surrender, then go. If you can take one half of that demolition charge, that would be a bonus. But right here is where it ends for us.'

Dawson glanced at him pensively for a moment, then shook his head firmly.

'No fucking chance. We're in this together, win or lose.'

'I can make it an order, Dawson.'

'And you know where you can stuff your bloody orders, too, Major. We're not dead yet.'

Dawson looked around, hoping for inspiration.

Apart from the anti-tank ditch, the only structure anywhere near them was a wooden agricultural building, something like a large shed, that had probably been used for storing farm machinery, ploughs and the like, or equipment.

Dawson slid the gear lever into first and swung the wheel towards the building. One end of it was open, and it appeared to be completely empty.

'That'll do,' he said.

Sykes looked at him as if he was mad. 'What do you mean, "That'll do"?' he demanded. 'We can't hide in there. The moment the German troops appear it'll be the first place they look.'

'Hiding wasn't what I had in mind,' Dawson said, 'now just hang on.'

He steered the Fiat towards the end of the building and accelerated. The battered front end of the little car struck the wooden corner pillar a glancing blow and ripped it completely out of the ground, carrying it forwards about a dozen yards. The wooden planks making up the side and back walls of the shed tumbled to the ground behind the car.

Dawson climbed out, walked around to the front of the vehicle to inspect the damage. Coolant was dripping steadily from a puncture in the radiator, but otherwise the *Topolino* seemed undamaged mechanically, just very battered.

He nodded in satisfaction and ran back to the remains of the shed. Dawson picked up one of the wooden planks and staggered across to the edge of the anti-tank ditch, carrying it in both hands.

He knew a bit about the design of anti-tank structures – he'd done a course early in his time in the Royal Engineers. Basically, they comprised ditches, ramps and steel barriers and, of the three types, ditches were the easiest and cheapest to build, which was probably why the French had created this one. The trick was to make the ditch wide enough that a tank's treads couldn't reach the far side before it toppled into it, but still so narrow that no tank could drive down one side of it, across the base and then up the other side, which meant the sides had to be as near vertical as possible, and it had to be quite deep.

Dawson paused on the edge of the anti-tank ditch and looked down. The French engineers hadn't done too bad a job of it. The ditch was about six feet deep, scattered pools of water dotting the base, and with sheer sides, but still quite narrow. That was what Dawson had hoped.

He placed the plank vertically in front of him, rested the base firmly on the ground and then let it topple forwards, his heart in his mouth. If the other end fell straight down into the ditch, they were screwed. But it didn't. The far end of the plank hit the edge of the ditch, bounced up a couple of times, then settled, straight and level, bridging the gap from one side to the other.

'Bloody brilliant,' Dawson muttered, and ran back to the ruined farm building.

'I can't walk across that,' Sykes called out, as the corporal passed the Fiat

'Don't worry. You won't have to.'

Dawson picked up another plank, carried it over to the ditch and manoeuvred it into position directly alongside the first. Then he took a look at the front of the Fiat, grabbed a third plank of wood and hauled that over to the ditch as well.

But he didn't lower that one across the top of the ditch. Instead, he ran back to the Fiat and drove it to the edge of the ditch, lining up the left front wheel with the first two planks he'd positioned there. Then he dropped the other plank across the ditch in line with the right front wheel of the car.

'You have *got* to be bloody joking,' Sykes said, as he realized what Dawson was intending to do. 'There's no possible way those planks will take the weight of this car.'

Dawson paused for an instant and looked at him. 'It's a light car,' he said. 'You said that yourself. I think it's worth a try. I'll get you, and the demolition charge, out of the car before I drive it across. Then I'm the one taking the risk. And if I crash, you can still surrender.'

Before Sykes could reply, Dawson ran back, grabbed a fourth plank and positioned that across the ditch beside the third one he'd laid.

He opened the driver's door of the Fiat, and hauled out one of the two halves of the German demolition charge, grunting with the effort. He placed it carefully on the ground, right at the edge of the ditch to one side of the two runs of planks, then pulled out the second half as well and placed it beside the first. Removing those would significantly reduce the laden weight of the Fiat.

'Right, sir,' he said, running around the car to the passenger side and opening the door.

But Sykes shook his head decisively. 'You said it, Dawson. We're in this together. Succeed or fail, I'm staying right here.'

For an instant, Dawson just stared at the major, then nodded. 'Your choice,' he muttered, and got back into the driver's seat.

He started the car and backed it away from the edge of the ditch. He checked that he was lined up precisely with the rudimentary bridge he'd constructed, then engaged first gear and pressed down on the accelerator pedal. The Fiat trundled forwards, Dawson ensuring he kept the car heading directly towards the planks.

The front wheels hit the edges of the wooden boards, pressing them down into the earth, and an instant later the Fiat was supported only by the planks. They dipped alarmingly as the full weight of the car settled onto them, bending deeply, the ends moving across the edge of the ditch. But they held as Dawson kept up the pressure on the accelerator, and kept the car moving.

They'd almost reached the far side of the ditch when there was a loud crack. The back of the car lurched sideways, and then the Fiat crashed down onto its chassis. The rear wheels span uselessly, suspended over empty space. They'd almost made it, but now they were stuck fast.

CHAPTER 36

12 MAY 1940: FRANCO-BELGIAN BORDER REGION

'Fuck,' Dawson said. He slipped the gear lever into neutral, opened his door – the *Topolino*'s doors were hinged at the rear – and stepped out to see what had happened.

One of the planks had broken, and when the rear wheel of the Fiat broke through the wood, the opposite wheel had obviously slipped off the opposite planks, forcing them sideways and sending them tumbling down to the bottom of the ditch. The rear wheels of the car were only a matter of inches from the southern edge of the ditch.

Dawson clocked that in an instant, and then looked back across to the other side, towards Belgian territory. Well over to his right, in the far distance, perhaps three-quarters of a mile away, he could see the first of the German soldiers starting to emerge from the woods. Very soon, he and Sykes would be within range of their Mauser carbines. The Panzer was still hidden from view, on the other side of the hill, but he knew it could appear at any second. And then they'd be a sitting target.

He looked back at the car, its engine still running, and made a decision. He wrenched open the passenger door and looked down at Sykes.

'You have to get behind the wheel,' he said. 'You drive and I'll push it from the back. We might just get it out.'

Sykes nodded and levered himself clumsily out of his seat. 'I can manage,' he said. 'You do your stuff.'

Dawson ran back to the rear of the Fiat and looked at it. There was only one way this was going to work. He jumped down into the ditch, his boots splashing in one of the puddles, and turned back towards the car.

'Put it in gear,' he yelled.

'I'm doing it now,' Sykes responded.

In the anti-tank ditch, Dawson waited until the rear wheels started turning, then stepped underneath the back of the trapped car and reached up to grab the back axle. He braced himself and pushed upwards with all his strength. The car barely moved. Light car it may have been, but the weight was brutal.

He simply wasn't strong enough to lift it. He needed some kind of a lever, and a fulcrum, otherwise it was never going to work.

He grabbed one of the planks, stepped back under the rear of the car and rammed the end of it under the axle, near the central differential, and moved to the end of the plank. When he lifted this time, the plank moved upwards and the rear of the car also moved up. The rear wheels were now almost touching the wall of the ditch, still spinning as Sykes kept his foot resting on the accelerator pedal.

Dawson repositioned the plank, and again stepped back to repeat the process. The spinning rear wheels grazed the edge of the ditch, driving a spray of earth and mud downwards. He lifted the plank still higher. One wheel gripped the earth and stopped rotating. The other wheel was still spinning uselessly. Dawson's arms were now fully extended, but it still wasn't enough. He lowered the plank, took a couple of steps forwards and lifted again. He'd lost some leverage, but if he could fully extend his arms, that might just be enough.

Grunting with the incredible strain, Dawson pushed upwards, watching the wheels of the Fiat, willing the little car's tyres to grip the soil and move the *Topolino* forward. Again, one wheel gripped while the other span. Dawson took a deep breath and pushed upwards with every bit of strength he possessed. The plank bent with the strain, but the car moved an inch or two further forward. And then, with a sudden lurch, both the Fiat's rear tyres gripped the ground and, with a suddenness that was almost shocking, it vanished from Dawson's view.

He dropped the plank, grabbed the edge of the ditch and pulled himself up so he could see what had happened. He had no idea whether or not Major Sykes could actually drive. If the vehicle careered out of sight and out of control, he didn't know what he'd do.

But he needn't have worried – about that, at any rate. The Fiat had stopped a few yards away. As Dawson looked, Sykes clambered out of the driver's seat and made his way around to the other side of the vehicle. When he and Sykes had first met, the major had told him about motoring holidays he'd enjoyed on the Continent. Obviously he could drive.

'Bloody good,' Dawson muttered, then stepped across to the northern side of the ditch, reached up and seized one part of the demolition charge. As he lifted it down, he heard a distant shot and guessed the German soldiers had now approached within rifle-range. That shot was followed by a volley of others. They had to get going as quickly as possible.

He carried the charge across to the other side, then repeated the operation with the second part. From above him, he heard half a dozen shots from the Fiat as Sykes started returning fire with one of their Mausers.

Getting out of the ditch didn't prove that difficult. Dawson simply leant one of the planks against the side and walked up it, then immediately dropped to the ground as he came into view of the approaching Germans.

He grabbed one part of the charge and ran over to the car, dodging and weaving from side to side, then ran back to collect the other half, heedless of the bullets now whizzing all around him. Several rounds hit the rear of the Fiat, either driving straight through the little car or ricocheting if they hit anything solid, like the spare wheel, but none hit either man or anything vital on the car. Others ploughed into the ground close beside the vehicle.

Dawson stowed the demolition charge in the back of the battered little Fiat. Sykes was now leaning out of the passenger-side window – he'd obviously changed seats – and was twisted into an uncomfortable position so he could fire the Mauser back towards the enemy. He couldn't aim very accurately because he had nothing to lean the weapon on to provide a stable platform, but he kept up a decent rate of fire towards the Jerries.

Dawson jumped into the driver's seat, slammed the gear lever into first and lifted the clutch. The car shot forward, aided by the slight down-slope, and began to increase speed. Two other bullets hit the car at that moment, both passing directly between the two men and spearing through the windscreen, crazing the glass.

'Fuck,' Dawson muttered. 'They're getting too bloody close for my liking.'

'Yes, but we're moving now, and we're pretty much at the Mauser's maximum range already.'

The firing continued from the German infantry, but the Fiat was moving further and further out of range, and was also now a moving target, and no more shots came anywhere near them.

'Tank!' Sykes yelled suddenly, as the Fiat bounced over a patch of uneven ground.

The Panzer III had just reappeared over the brow of the hill about 500 yards behind them, the massive steel hull an ominous black shape on the horizon. The barrel of its main gun swung to the left as the gunner started searching for a target.

Dawson immediately turned the Fiat's steering wheel to the left, already starting to take evasive action, waiting for the first shot from the 1.5-inch cannon, then switched direction to the right. The only problem was that weaving around meant he had to go a lot more slowly than if he was driving in a straight line. There was a stand of trees a couple of hundred yards in front of them, over reasonably hard and level ground that had a slight down-slope. If they could just reach those, they'd be safe, at least for a while.

There was nothing Sykes could do to help him. Everything depended on how good the German gunner was at guessing Dawson's next change of direction.

'He's fired!' Sykes yelled, seeing the unmistakable puff of smoke from the barrel of the cannon. The Panzer was now perhaps 600 yards away, but they were still well within the effective range of its cannon.

An instant later, the shell landed about seventy yards away from the Fiat, and over to their right. A cloud of earth exploded into the air as the high-explosive charge in the shell detonated.

'He'll be reloading,' Sykes said. 'Now go straight, as fast as you can. I'll tell you when to turn.'

Dawson straightened up and pressed down hard on the accelerator pedal, then eased up slightly. The rough ground didn't really allow him to go flat out, or he risked losing control of the car. But he went as fast as he could, the Fiat bouncing and lurching from side to side as he powered it across the field.

'Now start weaving,' Sykes ordered, after a few more seconds.

Dawson braked to slow down the car slightly, then turned right, before jinking left. Then right again, his movements erratic and, he hoped, completely unpredictable.

Sykes saw another puff of smoke from the tank's cannon, and again shouted a warning.

Dawson immediately reversed the turn he was taking and sent the car skittering in the opposite direction. The shell ploughed into the ground behind them, less than twenty yards away. Shrapnel, stones and earth flew from the crater and rattled against the back of the *Topolino*. The German gunner had their range.

CHAPTER 37

12 MAY 1940: FRANCO-BELGIAN BORDER REGION

'He's getting bloody close,' Dawson said, as he again aimed the car straight down the slope towards the woods in front.

'Yes, but we haven't got far to go.'

They were now so close to the line of trees Dawson was able to pick a spot wide enough for him to drive the car under cover, but he'd have to slow right down to do so, simply because he had no idea what was waiting for them inside the wood. Tree trunks didn't bend or give, and the last thing he wanted to do was drive the Fiat into some massive oak or some other solid tree that would write off both them and the car. That would be a really stupid way to die.

'Start weaving!' Sykes yelled again.

Once more Dawson slowed the car and then turned the wheel, to the left this time, flipping a mental coin as he did so.

'He hasn't fired yet, as far as I can see, but he must have reloaded by now,' Sykes said.

Dawson swung the car over to the right. A cannon shell ripped past the door of the Fiat and punched a hole through the thin metal of the right front wing, before smashing into a tree at the edge of the wood.

'Fuck this,' Dawson said. 'That German's too bloody good at this.' He swung the wheel to aim for the gap he'd already selected between a couple of trees, and drove straight at it.

In a few seconds, he jammed on the brakes and stopped the Fiat just inside the wood. He waited a moment for his eyes to adapt to the gloom under the canopy of leaves, then weaved the tiny car around the trees, driving deep into the wood, the trunks of the trees creating a natural barrier between the fragile car and the German tank.

Just seconds later, a cannon shell smashed into a tree close to where they had entered the wood, but they were protected from the German weapon because they were no longer visible. The trees would stop any shells fired at random towards them.

'I'll go and see what the Jerries are up to,' Dawson said, once they were deep enough in the wood to be effectively invisible and invulnerable, except to the ground troops who he was sure were coming. 'Then we can work out what the hell to do next.'

He took one of the Mausers and some spare ammunition, and made his way to the edge of the wood, to a position well away from the point where they'd left the open field. The first thing he looked for was the Panzer, which was clearly visible, and now a lot closer. In fact, it seemed to be almost at the anti-tank ditch.

As Dawson watched, a hatch opened in the top of the turret, and the black-uniformed tank commander appeared, wearing earphones and with a chest mike, and bringing up a pair of binoculars to his face, obviously looking through them to try to spot the tank's quarry.

That was too good a target to miss. Dawson cranked a round into the Mauser's breech, rested the fore-end of the carbine on a thick horizontal branch right in front of him, and took careful aim. The Panzer was now within about 250 yards of Dawson's position, and heading almost straight for him. It wasn't a difficult shot.

Dawson settled the sights on the upper part of the German soldier's chest, controlled his breathing and gently squeezed the trigger. The Mauser kicked against his shoulder, but he barely even noticed. He was too busy checking the result of his shot.

The German jerked as if he'd been punched, slamming limply backwards into the metal of the turret, then slumped sideways, before sliding slowly out of sight, back down into the Panzer.

'Got you,' Dawson murmured, and immediately reloaded the Mauser, though there were no other visible targets anywhere in sight.

But still the Panzer came on, heading directly towards the anti-tank ditch, now only a matter of a few yards in front of it. And suddenly Dawson knew why it hadn't stopped. The officer he'd shot hadn't yet given the order to the driver to do so. Through the thin armoured slit in front of the driver, which was all he had to see through, the anti-tank ditch would be far from visible. Dawson guessed the collapse of the tank commander would have shocked the five-man crew, and nobody had given the driver any other orders.

The tank drew closer and closer to the ditch, then suddenly slowed. Someone had belatedly realized the danger. The tank reached the edge of the ditch. The leading part of the tracks began extending out into the open space. The engine roared like a wounded animal as the driver frantically tried to reverse the massive twenty-five-ton vehicle, but it was too late.

Slowly, incredibly slowly given the weight involved, the Panzer toppled forward into the anti-tank ditch, the barrel of the cannon striking the ground on the far side as it did so. Dawson clearly saw the barrel bend upwards as the front of the vehicle vanished from sight, to crash down into the ditch with an echoing thump and a sudden flurry of earth. The heavy tank settled with its rear high in the air, the front buried deep in the ditch. For a few seconds nothing happened, then the driver ran the tracks in reverse for maybe ten seconds, the engine roaring, which had no effect upon the tank's position whatsoever. Then he must have realized it was a point-less exercise, and switched off the engine. There was no way that Panzer was going to move again without very heavy lifting equipment. And even when it was out of the ditch, the Germans would still have to change the barrel on the turret before it would be battle-ready.

'Bloody hell,' Dawson muttered. 'Scratch one Panzer. Not a bad result from one easy rifle shot.'

He took a final look round, then shouldered the Mauser and backed into the wood. A few seconds later he rejoined Sykes, who was leaning against the side of the *Topolino*, holding the Schmeisser machine-pistol ready.

'OK?' he asked Dawson, as the corporal approached. 'Where's the Panzer? Stuck on the other side of that anti-tank ditch, I suppose?'

Dawson grinned at him. 'More stuck *in* it, actually.' He quickly explained what had happened when he'd taken out the commander of the Panzer.

'I heard your shot,' Sykes said. 'I wondered what you were up to. Bloody well done, Dawson.'

'I was just lucky, really.'

'Men like you make their own luck, Dawson. If you hadn't been with me on this little jaunt, I'd be dead. We both know it.'

Dawson nodded, then turned to more important matters. 'So you reckon we've crossed the border, sir?' he asked.

'I don't know for certain, but most probably, yes. I can't think of any good reason why the Belgians would have constructed an anti-tank defence on their side of the French border. It only makes sense that it's a French-built ditch designed to stop a *German* invasion coming through Belgian territory, just the same as they did in the Great War. So I think we left Belgium somewhere in the field back there, on the other side of that ditch. Now we're in France. And we should probably get moving. I know you stopped that Panzer, but the Jerry infantry won't have any trouble crossing that anti-tank ditch. They're bound to start heading this way as soon as they do.'

'Right you are, sir,' Dawson said, and walked around to the driver's door of the now very battered and bloodied Fiat. Before he got into the car, he tapped it gently on the roof with the flat of his hand and looked across at Sykes.

'I know I wasn't very impressed when that Belgie colonel gave us this car,' he said, musingly, 'but it's done a blinding job of getting us out of trouble. If we'd had a big heavy staff car like I was expecting, it'd be stuck at the bottom of that ditch by now. We'd either be dead or prisoners.' He ran his hand around the hole that the shell from the Panzer had blown through both sides of the back of the Fiat. 'And if this had been made of proper steel instead of this Italian cigarette paper, that shell would have exploded when it hit and blown us to pieces.'

Sykes nodded. 'You're right. They call it a "little mouse", but actually it's a hell of a car.'

They climbed back into the *Topolino*, and Dawson started to thread the little car around the trees and bushes, making slow but steady progress through the forest towards the south, heading deeper – they hoped – into French territory. As before, Dawson had to keep the Fiat heading more or less downhill, but that was no problem. They'd reached virtually the highest point in the area, so the only way they could go from there was down.

Within quite a short distance the trees started to thin out, and the forest was replaced by open ground and cultivated but apparently abandoned agricultural land. In a few minutes Dawson was able to leave the rough ground in favour of another track, which offered a slightly better driving surface. It was a mixture of gravel and hard-packed earth. No doubt in the winter it would turn to mud – the deep hoof marks of cows or oxen at the edge of the track showed that clearly enough.

The track meandered down the hill and, just as they'd found in the border area on the Belgian side of the frontier, the countryside was deserted. The sense of emptiness persisted until just after the track met what could best be described as a lane, which was wider and had a rather better and much smoother surface. A couple of minutes after Dawson turned the Fiat onto it, and had driven around the first bend, he and Sykes found themselves confronted by a road-block about a hundred yards in front.

There was no possibility of driving around this one.

CHAPTER 38

12 MAY 1940: FRANCO-BELGIAN BORDER REGION

A heavy wooden trestle blocked the entire width of the road. Mounted on one side of it, and pointing directly at the approaching Fiat, was a machine-gun on a bipod, with two soldiers manning it. Grouped behind the central section of the trestle were another half dozen troops, long-barrelled rifles aimed up the track.

'French troops,' Sykes muttered. 'Time for a white flag,' he added, and pulled a large and rather grubby handkerchief out of his pocket. There was no glass left in the Fiat's windows, so he simply stuck his arm out of the opening where the side window had once been, and waved his sign of surrender.

'Are you sure these are Frogs?' Dawson asked quietly, slowing the *Topolino* to little more than walking pace as they got closer to the road-block. 'That machine-gun looks a bit like a Bren to me, with that vertical magazine.'

'I'm quite sure they're French,' Sykes replied. 'It's not a Bren, though you're right – it does look a lot like one. It's actually a MAC FM 1924/M29, a bloody good weapon. And those rifles are Berthier M1916 models.

348

They're a hangover from the Great War. We're not facing front-echelon troops.'

'What do you mean?'

'The new standard weapon for the French forces is the MAS 36, but production has been so slow only the most elite sections of the army have been issued with them. So these men are probably members of one of the twenty-six divisions of the French Second Army, which I think is under the command of a general named Prételat. Right now, "Second Army" also translates as "second rate", because they're mainly reservists. The French have stuck them here because they think the Ardennes Forest is enough of a natural barrier to stop the German armour.'

'Which isn't true,' Dawson said. 'There's a bogged-down Panzer up on the top of that hill to prove it.'

'Exactly. So all we have to do is convince these soldiers that what we're saying is true and persuade them to let us drive past. Then get the hell out of here before half the German army sweeps over that hill behind us.'

'Yeah, right,' Dawson muttered, and braked the Fiat to a stop about twenty feet short of the trestle blocking the road.

'So what now?' he asked.

'You stay here and keep both your hands on the steering wheel, where those soldiers can see them. I'll get out and talk to their officer. I can manage those few steps.'

Sykes pushed open his door, lowered his feet to the ground and stood up, still waving his white handkerchief, and made his way, walking stiff-legged and obviously in pain, towards the barrier. As he reached it, a French officer, immaculately dressed, walked around the end of the trestle to meet him.

Dawson watched with interest as the two military officers greeted each other, as military officers always do, with salutes – Sykes's version somewhat weary and casual, the French officer's response sharp and snappy. The two men moved out of earshot of the soldiers manning the barricade and stood close together, talking quietly, Sykes punctuating his explanation with frequent and eloquent hand gestures towards the hill that extended up to the north, behind the Fiat *Topolino*.

It looked to Dawson as if Sykes was having a tough time convincing the French officer of the truth of what he was saying, because the man kept shaking his head in apparent denial. But the major was persistent and forceful, and finally turned and gestured to Dawson to drive the car over to where he and the French officer were standing.

Dawson eased the car down the lane and stopped next to the two men.

'Stay in the car,' Sykes instructed through the blown-out window, then stepped to the rear of the car and pointed to the shell hole driven through both sides of the car. He launched into rapid French, the only words of which Dawson understood were 'Panzer Trois', and the French officer finally nodded.

He turned towards the heavy trestle barricade and issued an order, and the soldiers behind it lowered their weapons and began to slide the barrier to one side.

As soon as there was a big enough gap, Sykes nodded to Dawson and motioned him forward. The corporal slipped the Fiat back into gear, drove it past the barricade and then stopped, waiting for the major to join him.

And a few moments later Sykes appeared beside the passenger door, still talking to the French officer. Then he shook hands with the Frenchman and got back into the Fiat.

'OK, Dawson,' the major said. 'Get us out of here.'

'Did he believe you?' Dawson asked.

'I'm not entirely sure. He seemed to think the worst-case scenario was that the Germans might manage to get a handful of infantry troops through the Ardennes Forest. He certainly didn't believe there could be Panzers within a couple of miles of where he and his men have been stationed. That's why I showed him the shell hole that's providing us with some fresh-air ventilation in the back of this car.'

Dawson lifted his foot off the clutch and the *Topolino* moved away, gathering speed slowly down the lane.

'So where to now, sir?'

'Keep heading south,' Sykes said. 'According to that officer, we're due north of a town called Rocroi, which is marked on my map, oddly enough. So just keep going downhill, and there should be a main road heading west somewhere in front of us.'

Dawson changed up a gear, and at that moment the hillside behind them erupted with machine-gun fire, interspersed with the deeper bangs from heavier weapons, maybe artillery pieces, and the cracks of exploding mortar bombs and grenades. One mortar bomb landed in the lane a few yards ahead of them, and another behind, but not close enough to injure them or damage the car. Dawson twitched the wheel, starting to weave from one side of the lane to the other, making use of all the width to try to avoid becoming an easy target.

'Is that the bloody Frogs firing at us?' he demanded, as Sykes swivelled round in his seat to look back up the lane.

'No. They're firing up the hill. I think those two mortars were just strays, badly aimed. Those are the German troops mounting their attack on the French positions.' Sykes turned back to face the front of the car again. 'Fast as you can, Dawson. Just put as much distance as possible between us and the French line, because the Jerries are going to break through very quickly, in my opinion. We can't get caught by them now, not after all we've been through.'

Dawson accelerated obediently, the little Fiat bouncing from side to side as its speed increased.

They rounded a corner, and almost ran into a group of fully armed French troops, heading up the lane towards them.

'Stop!' Sykes shouted, as Dawson hit the brakes.

As the Fiat stopped, Sykes opened his door and leant out, shouting out something in French to the officer who seemed to be in charge of the soldiers.

Dawson stared through the windscreen at the French troops who were passing the car. The thing that struck him most forcibly was their age. They all seemed old – very old – to be soldiers. They were men in their fifties, maybe even their sixties, making a stark contrast to the average age of the personnel in the British army. Reservists they undoubtedly were – Sykes had already told him that – but to Dawson the word 'retirees' might have been more appropriate. Against the German front-line troops who were no doubt already streaming down the hill towards them, they would probably prove no more than an irrelevance, and certainly not a viable defence against the invasion.

Another mortar shell screamed out of the sky and exploded with a flat crack just to one side of the lane, behind a part of the hedgerow and near the far end of the column of troops. The shrubbery helped reduce the effect of the weapon, but even so shards of shrapnel speared into the rear ranks of men, causing painful and debilitating flesh wounds. The injured soldiers yelled in pain, dropping their weapons, while their companions dived for cover.

'Sir,' Dawson shouted urgently, 'we need to move, get out of range.'

Sykes dropped back into his seat. Dawson quickly weaved the car around the disorganized and scattered groups of soldiers, and accelerated again once he was clear of them, driving the car as fast as possible down the lane.

'That wasn't a stray round,' he said. 'The Jerries are targeting the reinforcement troops, as well as the men manning the barricades.'

'You're right,' Sykes agreed.

'I don't feel good, running away from a fight,' Dawson said. 'Leaving that bunch of pensioners to try and stop those Jerries.'

'Nor do I, Dawson, but the reality is that there's nothing we *can* do. We've got two Mausers and a Schmeisser. If we were driving a tank, it would be a different matter. The best thing we can do to help the

French – and us, obviously – is to get ourselves to safety and get this demolition charge properly examined by experts, and that means somebody in Britain. This is one of those cases where we serve the greatest good of the greatest number by *not* getting ourselves involved in the battle, but by running away from it. I don't like it, but that's the truth of this situation.'

Dawson nodded and concentrated on keeping the Fiat moving as fast as possible. The noise of the escalating battle behind them was getting louder as more and more weapons – French as well as German – began firing. The yammering of machine-guns and the rattle of rifle fire were almost constant. Dawson thought he could detect the throaty roar of big petrol engines, and that meant Panzers.

'It won't take the Jerries long to break through, will it?' Dawson asked after a couple of minutes.

'No. The Germans have the advantage of surprise, they're almost certainly better armed, trained and equipped, and they're facing reserve troops. I'd be amazed if by tonight they hadn't broken through the French lines and then completely destroyed the fighting capability of the French troops here. It'll be a short and bitter fight, but as far as I can see there'll only be one possible outcome.'

'The Germans will fuck the French,' Dawson said shortly.

'In a nutshell, yes,' Sykes replied. 'And what's going to happen here, in this place, will probably happen all over France. Just as they did in the Great War, the Germans will crush the French. Only this time around, it won't take them anything like as long.'

'Just as well the Frogs have got us to help them, then.'

Sykes laughed shortly. 'I wish I could believe that,' he said. 'We're not exactly the best-equipped fighting unit in the world at the moment. I have a horrible feeling the Germans are going to push us out of France and Belgium, probably very quickly. The only thing that'll stop Adolf and his booted hordes from tramping through London within the year will be the English Channel. That narrow stretch of salt water is a barrier even the Germans are going to find very hard to cross. Right now I think that's about the best defence Britain's got.'

Dawson came to a T-junction, stopped the Fiat and glanced both ways. They'd reached another lane, a little wider than the one they'd followed down the hill, but still fairly narrow and lacking a decent hard surface.

Sykes followed the corporal's glances, looked at the map, which apparently provided little inspiration for him, and then up at the sun. Finally he muttered: 'This road junction isn't marked on the map, so you'd better turn right, I suppose. That's more or less west, I think. And keep your eyes open for a signpost or anything that'll tell us where the hell we are. We need to get to Rocroi.'

Dawson turned the wheel and headed off along the lane, the sound of the battle now starting to diminish behind them. There were a number of side turnings off the lane, but they all looked narrow and possibly only went to isolated dwellings or perhaps even groups of fields. Dawson ignored them.

The lane curved sharply to the right, and then started to climb gently – a slope the little Fiat was able to cope with. Even so, Dawson had to coax every bit of power out of the engine to keep them moving.

'That's the top of the hill coming up now,' Sykes said, pointing ahead. 'It should be easier after that.'

The major was referring to the gradient, and in that respect he was absolutely right. The Fiat would have made much quicker, and much easier, progress travelling downhill. Unfortunately, that wasn't going to happen – at least, not in the direction the car was heading.

As Dawson nursed the *Topolino* to the crest of the hill, he suddenly hit the brakes and slammed the car into reverse. He wrenched the steering wheel hard over and drove the Fiat backwards into the hedge that bordered the lane, then span the wheel in the opposite direction to drive the car back the way they'd just come.

And the reason for his violent action was that just over the brow of the hill, no more than fifty yards away, sat another Panzer III, completely blocking the lane. Behind the tank, at least a dozen German soldiers stood, all heavily armed.

The only reason the Fiat wasn't already scrap metal was that the Panzer's turret and main weapons were pointing in the opposite direction. Dawson's actions had got the *Topolino* out of sight before the turret could be swung round to point at it. But they had been seen by the Germans, Dawson was sure of that, both by the soldiers and the tank crew – the movement of the turret confirmed that.

They may have got away from one scrap between the French and the invading Germans, but now it looked as if Dawson and Sykes were going to have to fight their own private battle, heavily outnumbered and ludicrously outgunned.

CHAPTER 39

12 MAY 1940: FRANCO-BELGIAN BORDER REGION

'Fuck it,' Dawson muttered. 'What the hell do we do now?'

He was driving the Fiat back down the hill they'd just climbed, trying to put some distance between themselves and the Panzer. But he knew they couldn't keep on going in that direction, because that would take them back into the thick of the fighting between the invading Germans and the French Second Army reservists, who by now might well be in full retreat.

'We get off this road,' Sykes ordered, checking behind them for any sign of the Panzer or the German soldiers. 'Take any right turn that looks well used. And be quick. That tank's right behind us.'

Sykes was right. The sudden appearance of a massive dark grey shape in the Fiat's rear-view mirror caused Dawson to twitch. The Panzer had just appeared at the crest of the hill. They could expect a shot from its cannon – or a burst from the twin forward-facing machine-guns – any second.

He saw the entrance to a narrow track about ten yards ahead of them, hit the brakes and turned the wheel. The back wheels of the Fiat hopped across the uneven surface as the car skidded sideways, Dawson fighting the turn all the way. The moment the front of the Fiat lined up with the entrance to the track, he floored the accelerator. The back of the *Topolino* hopped as he fed all the limited power of the engine to the rear wheels, driving the Fiat forwards.

The instant the little car left the track, there was a thunderous crack from behind as the Panzer's gunner fired a round from the 1.5-inch cannon, and there was a heavy explosion from the left of the car as the high-explosive shell hit something solid and detonated.

'That was too fucking close – again,' Dawson muttered as the car shot down the track. He was fighting for control, trying to keep the vehicle moving as quickly as he could and at the same time avoiding the worst of the potholes and other obstacles.

The cannon fired again, the gunner shooting blind, guessing at where his target might be. Luckily for Dawson and Sykes, he didn't guess very well, the cannon shell missing the car completely, though Dawson had no idea whether it went in front of them or behind.

'If we're still on this straight section when that Panzer reaches the end of this lane, we're buggered,' Sykes said. 'He'll see us and at that range he won't be able to miss.'

'I know, I know. As soon as I see anywhere we can go . . .'

An open gate loomed up on their right-hand side and Dawson turned the Fiat towards it, aiming for the centre of the opening. He over-cooked it slightly and the left rear wing of the car crashed into the gatepost. Dawson hit the brakes and stopped the vehicle immediately – the

Fiat was their only way out of the mess they'd found themselves in, and if they blew a tyre, that was it because, thanks to the earlier shot from the other tank, they had no spare wheel. Stopping to check on the damage, with a Panzer III only a few dozen yards behind, wasn't Dawson's idea of good timing, but he had absolutely no option.

Dawson leapt out and ran round to the back of the little car. The wing had been split by the impact and bent inwards, and two jagged edges of the ripped steel were pressing on the tyre. There was already a gouge in the rubber of the sidewall, and Dawson knew that if they'd driven on for even a few more yards, the steel would have carved its way through the tyre and blown it.

The remedy was simple. He reached down, grabbed the edge of the twisted wing in both hands and pulled it away from the tyre. The torn edge of the thin steel was razor-sharp and the metal cut into his hands, but Dawson ignored the pain, because already he could hear the noise of the Panzer's engine as the tank accelerated down the track towards them, crushing undergrowth and hedges as it approached.

He shifted one section of the ruined wing, then grabbed the other part of it and repeated the treatment, again feeling the steel cut into his palms and fingers as he did so. He quickly checked what he'd done, making sure that nothing else could touch the precious rubber of the tyre, then ran back to the driver's seat.

'Quickly, man,' Sykes muttered, as the corporal sat down.

Dawson slammed the gear lever into first and the Fiat lurched across the field. No crops had been planted, which was a blessing, and the surface was just rough, grass-covered ground, mainly level, but with a slight down-slope at the far end, where the illusory safety of another wood beckoned, perhaps a hundred yards away. The *Topolino* lurched and bounced across the uneven ground as Dawson wound the speed up as much as he dared.

'If we can just make it into the trees,' he said, 'at least the gunner in that fucking tank won't be able to see us.'

'You drive, Dawson. I'll pray,' Sykes replied, his whole attention focused on the field behind them, and the gate they'd driven through. He was clutching the Schmeisser machine-pistol in his hands, though against the armour plate of the Panzer it would be a completely ineffective weapon.

'Where is it?' Dawson asked. The Fiat was bouncing about so much that the rear-view mirror was useless, just showing a blurred kaleidoscope of images.

'I can't see it yet,' Sykes said. 'Wait. Yes, there it is, just about to turn into this field. We've got maybe ten seconds before he's through the gate and able to fire. And he'll have a clear shot at us.'

'Why is it,' Dawson asked, 'every time we see a bloody tank it starts chasing us and shooting?'

'Two reasons, I suppose,' Sykes replied, still staring backwards across the field. 'First, we're probably the only enemy motorized vehicle they've seen and this car's a nice soft target. No armour, and no big gun we can use to shoot back at them.'

'And the second reason?' The bouncing of the car intensified as Dawson struggled to coax every last bit of power out of the tiny engine. The wood loomed ahead of them, but still about twenty-five yards away. It was going to be close.

'Probably the oldest motive in the world,' Sykes replied. 'Revenge. The German forces use radio far more than we do. All their tanks are fitted with sets. By now, every German tank commander in the area is going to know that two men in a Fiat *Topolino* on Belgian army plates were responsible for the loss of a Panzer III and the death or at least the serious wounding of its commander. And they aren't going to like that one little bit.'

'What – you mean it's personal?'

'Maybe. I don't know. Now stop talking and get us out of sight. That gunner will fire at any—'

But Sykes's words were drowned out by a shattering explosion of noise. The Fiat lurched sideways as a cannon shell slammed into it, and both men felt the massive concussion as the projectile passed right between them and out through the window opening on Dawson's side of the car. Yet again, the metal of the rear section of the *Topolino* had proved too thin to trigger the high-explosive warhead, which detonated somewhere over to the left of the wood. There were now three shell holes in the back of the tiny car.

For an instant, Dawson lost control of the vehicle, letting go of the steering wheel and clapping both hands to his ears as the shockwave hit him.

He shouted something to Sykes, but the major just shook his head – both men were still deafened by what had just occurred, and neither could hear the other, or any other sound, for that matter.

The Fiat lurched to the left. Dawson grabbed the wheel again and aimed the vehicle at the trees. But this wood was very different to the previous ones they'd driven through. For some reason there was heavy undergrowth all around it, and between the trees right in front of them. There were no gaps Dawson could see.

But he realized he didn't have any option. If they stayed in the open, the next shell from the Panzer's cannon would either hit them or some part of the car solid enough to trigger the explosive – the German gunner clearly already had their range. In either case, they'd be dead. The wood offered them their only possible chance of survival. So Dawson took it.

He picked two of the trees that seemed to be fairly widely separated, and aimed straight at the undergrowth between them.

'Hang on,' he yelled at the top of his voice, though he still had no idea if Sykes could hear him or not.

But the major visibly braced himself as the Fiat turned. Even if he hadn't heard Dawson's warning, the corporal's intentions were abundantly clear.

Still travelling at about twenty miles an hour, the front of the *Topolino* smashed into a patch of heavy undergrowth that was nearly as tall as the car itself. The front wheels bounced into the air and then crashed down again, flattening bushes and shrubs as the Fiat ploughed forward. More bushes loomed ahead, and Dawson kept his foot down on the accelerator pedal, trying to keep the speed up because the one thing he daren't do was get stuck among the bushes: that would seal their death warrant just as surely as a shell from the Panzer.

They passed between the two trees, the Fiat rocking and bouncing. There was another explosion, this one from the trunk of the tree on their right, as the gunner in the Panzer fired another round. Fragments of the shell rattled and bounced off the metal at the back of the car, but none of it penetrated – at least the steel was thick enough to prevent that.

Then they were through the bushes and shrubs. Dawson instantly shifted his size-twelve boot from the accelerator to the brake pedal and mashed it down hard, because there were three trees right in front of the car, and no way the Fiat was going to be able to drive between any of them – the gaps were just too narrow.

The Fiat's tyres slid over the loose and uneven surface. Dawson realized immediately he wasn't going to be able to stop.

Sykes braced his arms against the dashboard. 'Dawson!' he shouted.

'I know, I know.'

Dawson wrenched the steering wheel over to the right. The Fiat changed direction violently, the right-hand-side wheels actually leaving the ground, and the vehicle threatening to roll over. He span the wheel anti-clockwise, forcing the *Topolino* straight. The car crashed down onto all four wheels again, the suspension squealing, banging and protesting. Then the left side of the car slammed into the trunk of one of the trees. Metal screamed and tore, the car bouncing off the tree before finally sliding to a noisy halt. They were safe, for a few minutes at least, but the Fiat wasn't going anywhere soon.

'Have you actually got a driving licence, Dawson?' Sykes demanded somewhat icily as the corporal switched off the engine.

Dawson grinned at him. 'Now you come to mention it, sir, no I haven't. When we first met, you asked me if

I could drive, which I can, after a fashion. You never actually asked me about a licence.'

'My mistake, obviously.'

Dawson grinned again, and kicked the door open because it had jammed shut. Instead of opening, it just fell sideways to the ground, both the hinges smashed. He climbed out of the car to inspect the torn and twisted metal on its left-hand side, then ran across to the edge of the wood.

What he saw wasn't encouraging. The Panzer had stopped about a hundred yards away, more or less in the middle of the open field, the crew apparently waiting for something. And it didn't take much guesswork to deduce exactly what the tank commander was expecting to happen. Some distance behind the Panzer, at the top of the hill, grey shadows started to materialize as the German troops they'd spotted on the road came into view and began advancing towards him.

Dawson guessed that the tank commander was going to order the soldiers to enter the wood – the Panzer was obviously far too big to manoeuvre between the trees – to flush out the Fiat. Then the tank's gunner would be able to take his time in blowing them to hell. He counted at least a dozen soldiers in total, all of them, as far as he could tell, carrying Mauser carbines. Even ignoring the Panzer – which was difficult enough to do as it sat, engine rumbling and the turret occasionally traversing left and right as the gunner looked for a target – in the middle of the field, he and Sykes were outnumbered about six to one by the soldiers.

Dawson had no idea what to do about them – or about the Panzer.

CHAPTER 40

12 MAY 1940: FRANCO-BELGIAN BORDER REGION

Dawson heard a rustling behind him and immediately swung round, raising the Mauser. Major Sykes loomed up out of the gloom, still walking with difficulty, but he was walking, and carrying the other Mauser carbine.

'It's me,' Sykes said. 'What's the situation? And don't just tell me we're fucked. I already know that.'

'We're fucked, sir. The Panzer's sitting out there waiting for us to show ourselves so it can blow us to buggery. There are about a dozen Jerry front-line troops heading our way, to drive us out of the wood. And that car isn't going to move for a while. I'll have to try to straighten out some of the damage before we can use it.'

Sykes looked across the field at the waiting Panzer, then at the German soldiers who were slowly approaching, moving quickly from one piece of cover to the next, and then waiting for their comrades to catch up.

'We do have one advantage,' the major said thoughtfully, after a moment.

'What's that?'

'We're hidden in this wood. They're out there in the

365

open. We can see them, but they can't see us, otherwise they'd already be shooting.'

'Yes, but if we start firing at them, that Panzer will open up with its cannon or machine-guns and we're done for.'

'Not necessarily. These trees will stop anything they can fire at us. What we have to do is separate – which means you walking away from here because I can't move much further – and find a bloody great thick tree trunk to hide behind, and then we try and shoot down as many of those Jerries as we can. If we can take out three or four of them, maybe the others will push off.'

'Yes, but . . .' Dawson started, then lapsed into silence.

'If you've got any better ideas, I'd like to hear them,' Sykes said.

Dawson shook his head. 'No, I haven't. Right, I'll go that way,' he said, pointing to the east. 'What about a signal to start firing?'

'I don't think it'll make any difference, do you? I'll give you a couple of minutes, then I'll start, so don't go too far.'

'What about that bloody Panzer?'

'Their gunner can't see us either, otherwise we'd already be dead, so forget about it. Just concentrate on the soldiers. This is our only chance of getting out of here.'

'Right,' Dawson said again, somewhat uncertainly. Then he nodded and strode away, vanishing from sight almost immediately in the heavy undergrowth.

He walked for about fifty yards, stopping every few steps to check that the approaching enemy soldiers were still in view, then ducked down beside a massive old oak that looked as if it would stop absolutely anything. There was a bush growing beside the tree which provided even more cover, but there was a clear space under its lowest branches, maybe a foot high, which would allow him a clear view of the field – the field that was about to become a killing ground.

Dawson lay prone, wrapped the Mauser's sling around his left arm and braced his elbows well apart, to provide the most stable rest possible for the rifle. He knew the weapon was already loaded – every time he'd picked it up he'd checked that – so he just slipped off the safety catch, aimed the muzzle towards the field and started looking for a target.

But before he could fire, Sykes's rifle cracked over to his left, and a German soldier about 150 yards away suddenly crumpled to the ground and lay still. One down, but that still left about eleven to go. And the remaining soldiers weren't going to be easy targets. When Sykes fired his weapon, all the other soldiers had dived for what cover there was, confirming Dawson's belief they were front-line troops. As he looked up the field, he saw immediately that none of them were still in sight.

But that didn't mean they were safe, because he'd watched one of them dive behind a low section of the hedge. Dawson could even see a part of the man's grey uniform through the foliage. That was enough for him. He sighted the Mauser where he guessed the soldier had to be hiding, and squeezed the trigger. The rifle kicked sharply against his shoulder. And beside the hedge, an indistinct figure rose up for an instant, then tumbled backwards to lie on the ground.

Then Dawson saw a slight movement on the Panzer

and guessed exactly what was about to happen. He pulled back the Mauser and turned around, into a sitting position with his back to the massive trunk of the oak tree.

Immediately, the cannon on the tank fired, the high-explosive shell screaming into the wood and detonating against something solid. It wasn't an aimed shot, because Dawson knew he and Sykes were invisible to the Germans – the thick undergrowth ensured that – but just intended to make them keep their heads down while the soldiers advanced closer towards them.

And to reinforce that uncompromising message, the gunner in the Panzer then opened up with the twin turret-mounted MG 34 machine-guns. Dawson stayed exactly where he was as a stream of 7.92-millimetre bullets ripped and tore at the vegetation around him, and thudded into the oak tree. Then the gunner swung his weapon, traversing to the west, towards Sykes's position. He just hoped the major had been quick enough – and mobile enough – to get himself behind a tree before the bullets reached him.

The noise of the firing was thunderous, and the German gunner knew his stuff, because he then swung the weapon back in the opposite direction, back towards Dawson, raking the edge of the wood with a lethal fusillade of bullets. Again Dawson cringed, but the moment the man's point of aim shifted, he again dived to the ground and brought the Mauser to bear.

As he'd guessed, as soon as the gunner had opened up, the German soldiers had broken out of cover and started heading across the field again, moving tactically, in short, weaving runs from one dip in the field to another. The problem they had was that there weren't that many places they could hide in the field, which was largely open, studded here and there with stunted bushes and with just a few hollows and dips big enough to conceal a man.

Despite the continuous machine-gun fire, Dawson took careful aim at one of the closest of the approaching soldiers, and was about to fire when a sudden thought struck him. The noise of the twin machine-guns was probably loud enough to drown out the sound of a single shot from the Mauser, but if he killed one of the leading soldiers, the Germans would know at least one of their enemy was still shooting back.

He shifted his point of aim, picking a German right at the back of the approaching patrol, waited until the man reached one of the bushes, and then fired. The bullet slammed into the German's body and tossed him backwards, his weapon dropping to the ground. But none of the other soldiers reacted in any way, so Dawson knew they hadn't heard his shot.

He flattened himself behind the tree once again as the machine-guns in the Panzer sent another fusillade of bullets in his general direction, then turned back to the field, looking for another target.

The soldiers were still advancing, apparently unaware that another of their number had been killed or seriously wounded. Dawson picked out another soldier, again right at the rear of the group, took careful aim and squeezed the trigger. Again the Mauser kicked against his shoulder, but at that instant the German soldier moved, and the bullet took him in the arm, not the chest. Even from his hidden position in the wood, and even over the sound of the machine-gun fire, Dawson could hear the man's sudden howl of agony.

Immediately one of the enemy soldiers shouted an order, and the Germans scattered, diving for whatever cover they could find. And then what had worried Dawson from the start happened. One of the Germans, maybe the patrol leader, obviously realized just how exposed they were advancing down the field towards the wood, and that the Panzer offered them an absolutely impregnable bullet-proof shield.

Dawson heard a shouted order. The remaining soldiers jumped up out of the positions where they'd gone to ground and started running towards the back of the tank.

Dawson aimed quickly, picking out one of the running men, and fired. His bullet missed the soldier he was aiming at, but another Jerry ran behind the man just as he fired, and the bullet sent him tumbling, to lie writhing in agony on the ground. A lucky shot.

But, as he reloaded, the last of the German soldiers skidded out of sight behind the Panzer, and Dawson knew that now they really were in trouble. He'd accounted for four of the enemy soldiers, three probably killed and one wounded and out of commission. He knew Sykes had got one as well, hopefully two or three, so between them they'd reduced the enemy's strength by about a half, if they'd counted right and the patrol had consisted of about twelve soldiers to begin with. But that still left roughly half a dozen German soldiers facing them, and the Panzer III, about which they could do nothing.

And now Dawson could hear the engine note of the

tank changing as it started moving forward, heading slowly down the field towards the wood, the German soldiers invisible somewhere behind its lumbering grey bulk.

The German plan was as obvious as it was inevitable. The tank would rumble on across the field until it reached the edge of the wood. As soon as it was close enough, the German soldiers sheltering behind it would split on both directions, charging into the wood to hunt down him and Sykes. If they were really lucky, they might manage to take out one or two of them each, but that was the best they could hope for. And then the remaining enemy soldiers would kill them. It was as simple as that.

Dawson knew they were as good as dead.

CHAPTER 41

12 MAY 1940: FRANCO-BELGIAN BORDER REGION

The Panzer rumbled on, the main gun remaining silent without a target to engage. But the twin coaxial machineguns kept up a steady barrage into the wood, the turret traversing left and right as the tank approached the line of trees.

For the first time since he'd arrived in Belgium, Dawson felt completely helpless. He couldn't even see any of the German soldiers behind the tank, far less shoot at them, and loosing off a round from his Mauser at the Panzer would be completely futile – he doubted if the crew would even hear the impact. What he and Sykes needed was some kind of anti-tank weapon. That, or a miracle.

Miracles seemed to be in short supply, but Dawson suddenly realized that they did actually have an anti-tank weapon. Or, to be exact, something that might function as one. The upper half of the German demolition charge was, he was quite certain, packed with plastic explosive, and he even had the detonator that screwed into the top of it.

What he couldn't work out for a few seconds was how

the hell he'd be able to get it into position, because if it was going to work, the charge would have to be virtually touching the Panzer, and preferably its underside, where the armour plating was thinnest.

Then inspiration came. Dawson backed away from the oak tree, checking where the machine-gun was aiming, and then ran back through the woods, trying to ensure he kept as many tree trunks between him and the Panzer as possible. In a few seconds he reached the battered Fiat *Topolino*, pulled open the door and grabbed the top half of the demolition charge. He pulled it out, then reached back inside for the detonator. Slipping that into his battledress pocket, he shouldered his Mauser again, picked up the charge and stumbled – the charge was heavy, cumbersome and awkward to carry – back towards the edge of the wood.

He stopped, panting, beside a big tree and checked the lie of the land. The Panzer driver hadn't got that many options. He needed to get the nose of the tank through some of the undergrowth to give the soldiers following behind the best possible chance of entering the wood without being shot, and the trees were growing so close together that there were only a couple of places where he could achieve that.

The tank was now under fifty yards away, still advancing slowly to allow the German soldiers to keep up and keep hidden behind it, and the driver was obviously aiming for a spot between two large trees about fifteen feet apart, a short distance over to Dawson's left.

He stepped out from behind the tree and struggled over towards the gap. As he did so, the machine-gun opened up again and started spraying the wood directly in front of him, firing blind. There was only one thing Dawson could do.

He dived full-length on the ground, with his head pointing directly towards the weapon, and pushed the demolition charge in front of him as well, hoping as he did so that he'd been right about the stability of the plastic explosive he'd guessed was inside it.

Bullets ripped through the undergrowth in front of him, and a couple hit the demolition charge, striking the heavy object with solid thumps that pushed the charge a couple of inches back along the ground towards Dawson's head. But it didn't detonate.

Another bullet clipped the edge of his right boot, driving a red-hot furrow through the skin on the outside of his ankle. Dawson grunted in pain but didn't move.

Then the gunner shifted his aim slightly, the stream of bullets tracking over to his left. Dawson stood up, wincing as he put weight on his right leg, and limped forward again. He stopped to check on the position of the Panzer. It was now heading straight for him. He nodded to himself, knelt down and started burrowing through the undergrowth towards the edge of the wood, directly into the path of the twenty-five-ton vehicle, dragging the demolition charge along.

He crawled right to the edge of the layer of undergrowth, thrusting his body forwards. He checked on the position of the Panzer again, to make sure it was still heading directly towards him. Then he stopped moving, took the detonator out of his pocket and carefully screwed it into the top of the charge.

Then he looked ahead again, estimating the size of the gap under the tank. It looked to him as if the underside of the Panzer would just clear the top of the detonator.

'Bugger,' he muttered, and looked around. But the ground was level, and there was no way he could raise the weapon any higher.

But there was one thing that might work. Dawson took a length of cord from his battledress – one of several non-standard bits of kit he'd found useful in the past – and tied the end of it around the top of the detonator. Then he made yet another check, a final check, on the position of the Panzer, and backed out of the undergrowth, unrolling the ball of cord as he did so.

He retreated in a straight line. For his plan to work, he had to be able to see the moment the body of the tank moved over the demolition charge. Then the cord ran out. Dawson muttered in irritation: he was in an open area and the instant the tank nosed into the wood he'd be visible to the crew, and especially to the gunner. He picked up a stone and placed it over the end of the length of cord to anchor it. He retreated further, behind a tree, and leant his Mauser up against it. He wouldn't need the rifle for the next few minutes, and carrying the weapon would only encumber him.

Dawson checked that he could still see the demolition charge. The dull-grey semi-spherical – or whatever the correct name was for that particular shape – was clearly visible hidden in the undergrowth. As was the Panzer III, now only a matter of a few feet from the edge of the wood, still moving slowly straight towards him.

'Come on, you bastard,' Dawson muttered, checking he could still see the end of the cord, in the clearing just in front of him.

The tank continued forward until its tracks were just brushing the edge of the undergrowth that marked the limit of the wood. And then it stopped, maybe six feet clear of the demolition charge.

'No, no,' Dawson said, staring at the sight in anguish. 'Come on, damn it. Keep coming.'

He checked behind the Panzer, wondering if the German soldiers were now making their move. But there was no sign of them. Presumably they were waiting for the tank's gunner to clear the area before they moved in to mop up everything.

The Panzer's turret swung left and right, as the gunner apparently looked for a target. And his only option, Dawson realized in that instant, was to give him one. He grabbed the Mauser, stepped out from behind the tree and fired a shot directly at the tank, not bothering to aim. The bullet slammed into the armour plating below the turret, and immediately the twin machine-guns swung round to point at him.

Dawson ducked back behind the tree as the firing started, bullets ripping the bark from the trunk behind him. Then it stopped, the German gunner recognizing that his target was safe until he moved again.

Dawson risked a quick glance around the trunk of the tree. The Panzer driver was inching the tank forward, perhaps trying to give the gunner a better angle to shoot from.

But whatever the reason, it was enough. The hull of the tank had just moved directly over the demolition charge.

Dawson dropped the Mauser, lurched around the side of the tree and dived for the end of the cord. His fingers closed around it and he gave a sharp tug, then ran back to the tree he'd been using for shelter, just as the machine-guns opened up again. He crouched down and clasped his hands firmly over his ears, pressing as hard as he could.

The detonator, from what he could remember of the scene they'd witnessed at Eben Emael, had about a ten-second fuse, and Dawson silently counted down the numbers in his head. He reached zero, but absolutely nothing happened. For another couple of seconds he did nothing, then glanced around the tree trunk.

And as he did so, a colossal explosion ripped the air apart. Even with his hands over his ears, Dawson was deafened. The effect on the Panzer was nothing short of catastrophic, despite most of the energy from the charge being directed downwards – that was, after all, the purpose of a shaped charge. The turret blew off the tank, rising upwards a couple of feet before its massive weight forced it to crash back onto the body of the Panzer again. For a moment, it almost looked as if it had miraculously reattached itself, but then it slowly toppled sideways off the top of the tank, to land on its side with a crash beside it, before toppling over, upside down.

A column of flame shot out of the turret ring, the location on the top of the vehicle where the turret had been attached, but no sound came from within the wrecked vehicle. Dawson guessed that the explosion would have killed the entire crew instantly. The fire grew in intensity, the flames leaping higher, and Dawson guessed there'd be explosions following quickly once the flames started cooking the ammunition.

But that still left the German soldiers who'd been

behind the tank. He and Sykes weren't out of the woods yet, in either sense of the expression.

Dawson grabbed his Mauser and ran through the trees over to his right, trying to widen the angle so that he could get a shot at the enemy soldiers

He heard a single rifle shot from somewhere to his left and guessed that Sykes had survived the blast and was doing his bit to eliminate the threat.

Dawson reached the edge of the wood, stopped beside a tree and peered around it, raising his Mauser. But after a few moments he lowered the weapon. It looked as if the blast from the demolition charge had been funnelled under the tank and had killed the soldiers following the Panzer, because six unmoving shapes lay sprawled behind the burning vehicle.

Which begged the question: what had Sykes been firing at?

But that could wait for a few moments. Dawson strode across the field to the bodies, just to make sure.

He'd seen his fair share of death, both since the start of the war and in his previous life as a demolition specialist, but none of that prepared him for what he saw in that field. The Germans had almost literally been ripped apart by the blast, eviscerated, limbs torn off, their exposed skin flayed off. The only consolation was that at least it would have been a quick death. None of them would have suffered.

Dawson shook his head and walked back into the wood to find Sykes.

CHAPTER 42

12 MAY 1940: FRANCE

'Well, you buggered that up good and proper, didn't you?' Sykes said, when Dawson reached him. 'We've risked life and limb to get that German demolition charge back to our lines, and now you've gone and blown it up.'

Dawson shook his head. 'Nope. That was just a big lump of plastic explosive fitted with a detonator. The important bit is the section that fits under the plastic, and that's still in the back of the Fiat.'

Sykes smiled. 'I know. I was just making a joke. That was bloody good work, Dawson. I was sure that Panzer would do for us. Now it's just a pile of scrap metal. A burning pile of scrap metal, actually. Did you check the soldiers who were behind it?'

Dawson nodded. 'All dead. Blown to pieces by the explosion, in fact. So who were you shooting at?'

'I think you must have only winged one of them earlier, because I saw him coming down the hill just after you blew up the tank. He was still carrying his rifle, and I reckoned that showed hostile intent, so I shot him.'

'So now what?'

379

Sykes looked up at him from his prone position beside the tree. 'I can cover the field from here, just in case anyone else decides to come down and take a look at what's left of that Panzer. You'd better see if that Fiat's still driveable. If it isn't, I don't know what we're going to do for transport.'

'It should be OK, I think. Just a few bent panels, with a bit of luck.' Dawson slung the Mauser over his shoulder and walked away, back into the wood.

The Fiat looked a mess. The entire left side of the car was scratched and battered, with massive dents in every panel. But both tyres were still inflated, the steering wheel turned the front wheels and the back wheels seemed to be straight. Dawson had to lever the remnants of both the front and rear wings away from their respective wheels, but as far as he could see, that was all he needed to do. The driver's door lay beside it, where Dawson had kicked it off.

And there wasn't time to hang about. He knew they were probably only minutes ahead of the German advance, and what they needed to do was get somewhere else – almost anywhere else, in fact – as quickly as possible.

Once he was sure that the car would start and run, Dawson went back to where Sykes was lying and helped the major hobble over to the Fiat and get inside.

'Which way?' Dawson asked, once he'd started the engine and got the car moving. 'Back up to the road?'

'No. Too much chance of running into a bunch of Jerries. Follow the edge of the wood over to the west. I thought I saw a gate at that end of the field when we were driving down it with that Panzer chasing us.

Though I might have been mistaken. My mind was on other things at the time.'

Dawson turned the Fiat and nosed it out of the trees, and then turned left, as Sykes had instructed. The little car bounced along the edge of the field, following the curved line that marked the edge of the wood.

Suddenly, a rattle of firing burst out from somewhere behind them. Sykes swung round to look behind, raising his Mauser.

'I don't see anything,' he muttered.

Then another series of bangs, much louder, rang out. Dawson guessed what was happening.

'That's the Panzer,' he said. 'That'll be the ammunition cooking off. First the machine-gun stuff, and then the rounds for the cannon.'

A few seconds later, Sykes spotted what he was looking for. 'There,' he said, pointing ahead.

In the far corner of the field was a five-barred gate, wide open and hanging drunkenly from a wooden post.

'Maybe it leads to a lane or a track,' Sykes said. 'Let's face it, if there's a gateway, logic suggests there has to be something the other side of it.'

And there was. Dawson drove the Fiat through the opening and found himself on a fairly wide but unmade track, meandering in a south-westerly direction. They had no idea where it went or what was at the end of it, but it was taking them more or less the right way, so they followed it.

They saw nothing and nobody – military or civilian – until they'd joined a much better road heading almost due south, and entered the village of Rocroi. There, a road-block manned by a joint force of *gendarmes* and French army reservists stopped them.

Sykes identified himself and Dawson, and explained the situation to the senior NCO there, with almost the same lack of comprehension as he'd met with the officer near the Belgian border. He must be mistaken, the NCO kept insisting. The Ardennes Forest was an impassable barrier to armoured vehicles, and certainly no tank would ever be able to get through it.

'Well, you tried, sir,' Dawson said, as he started the little Fiat again and steered it down the road out of the village. 'It's their problem if they don't believe you.'

'I know, Dawson, but it's really frustrating. How's your foot, by the way?'

'Bloody sore and getting stiff, but I can manage for the moment. Did that Frog tell you where to go?'

'I'm sure he would have liked to,' Sykes replied. 'Anyway, we're heading for Reims, because, according to him, there are some British troops stationed there. I didn't know that, and I've no idea where he got his information from, but Reims is probably as good a destination as anywhere else. At least it's away from the border area.'

'How far away is it?'

'About sixty miles or so. You reckon this thing will hold together that long?'

'This beautiful car, sir, will hold together as long as we want it to.' Dawson patted the dashboard affectionately, then glanced round at the bullet-riddled interior, and the bits of twisted metal that had originally been the two front wings.

Just over two hours later, Dawson braked the Fiat to a stop at another road-block, but this one was manned by men wearing an entirely different colour uniform than those they'd got used to seeing over the previous few days.

'Bloody hell,' the NCO at the barricade said to the soldier standing beside him, looking with disdain at the *Topolino* as it drew to a stop in front of them. 'It's a couple of lost fucking Belgies, and they're driving the biggest piece of shit I've ever seen on the road.'

'You watch your mouth, Sarg,' Dawson said, levering his massive frame out of the driver's seat and standing in front of him. 'This piece of shit, as you put it, has saved our bacon more times than I can count over the last couple of days.'

'You're British army?' the NCO asked.

'Of course I bloody am. Now stop standing there with your fucking mouth open catching flies and take us to your CO. My mate wants a word with him.'

'You watch your mouth, Corp. And your mate,' the sergeant sneered. 'Who is he, then? Another bloody lost corporal?'

'Not exactly,' Sykes said, clambering out of the other side of the Fiat, his major's pips barely visible on his tattered uniform, but his voice and manner marked him unmistakably as an officer.

The sergeant looked at him for a moment, then saluted briskly, his manner changing instantly. 'Sorry, sir. Didn't see you in there.' He switched his attention to the soldier standing next to him. 'Lift that bloody barrier, then. Get a move on.'

A few minutes later, Sykes – with Dawson assisting him – walked into a large tent that seemed to be full of British army officers, all concentrating on a large map pinned up at one end, and listening to a major delivering a briefing and using a pointer to indicate positions and places.

'We'll probably soon be given orders to head west, to reinforce the BEF in Belgium, because the French are quite sure the Germans won't be able to break through here,' he was saying, resting the end of his pointer on a large patch of green on the topographical map. 'They believe the Ardennes Forest is too formidable a natural barrier to allow significant enemy troop movements, and the terrain is certainly impenetrable to armour. So we probably won't be seeing any Panzers around here that we can kill.'

There was a polite laugh at this remark, which ceased abruptly when Sykes spoke.

'The French are wrong, and so are you,' he said quietly.

Every officer in the tent turned to look at him. A small, slight figure, wearing a filthy uniform and no cap, unshaven and haggard, one leg of his trousers black with dried blood, supported by a vast corporal with a face that could have been carved out of granite, his uniform in a similar state and a Schmeisser machine-pistol slung across his chest. In his other hand he held a large, grey-painted circular object.

'What? And just who the hell are you two?' the major demanded.

'Sykes. I'm a major in the Royal Scots Greys. And I say again – the French are wrong.'

'How do you know?'

'I know because we've just crossed the border from Belgium and gone right through the Ardennes Forest.

We saw plenty of German troops up there, plus one Panzer Four and a couple of Panzer Threes. In fact, we destroyed one of them and pretty much wrecked another, or rather Corporal Dawson here did.'

'I don't believe you.'

'Do I look like I care what you believe? I'm telling you what we saw and what happened. If you're too stupid to take note of it, that's your problem.'

'Just a minute.' The senior officer in the tent stepped forward. 'Just calm down, both of you.' He turned to Sykes. 'I'm Lieutenant-Colonel Watling. You say you crossed the border into France from Belgium. What were you doing up there? As far as I know, your regiment hasn't been sent into Belgium.'

'We were sent to Eben Emael,' Sykes said, 'just the two of us, to assess the strength of the Belgian static defences.'

'We heard that the fort surrendered, after the Germans attacked it,' Watling said.

'I know. We watched the Germans do it.' Sykes outlined what had happened since the German gliders landed on the roof of Fort Eben Emael. 'And that's really why we're here now. We managed to obtain one of the German demolition charges, the ones they used to destroy the cupolas on the fort.'

'Obtain? How?'

'We nicked it, sir,' Dawson said shortly.

'I see. And you have this device with you?'

'Exactly, sir. Or, at least, we've got the lower section – that's the bit Dawson's holding now – and we think that's the most important bit. He used the other part of the weapon – the explosive charge – to blow up a Panzer Three just this side of the French border.'

Watling looked appraisingly at Dawson, and nodded. 'So you need to get that piece of equipment back to Britain, where some of our boffins can take a look at it?'

'Yes, sir.'

'Right, we can have it sent back to our lines, I suppose. This is a reserve armoured unit under the command of General Hobart, so we've mainly got tanks and armoured cars, but we've a few trucks and cars as well.' Watling looked closely at Sykes, who was swaying slightly despite Dawson's supporting hand. 'Or maybe an ambulance might be more appropriate in this case. I presume you'd both like to accompany the weapon back to Britain?'

Sykes nodded. 'It might help if Dawson and I could explain exactly what we saw the Germans do with it. And after all we've been through to get it this far, I'm not prepared to let the weapon out of my sight.'

'I can understand that. Very well, I'll organize an ambulance – or some kind of vehicle, at any rate – to take you two back to Blighty. In the meantime, get yourselves cleaned up, find something to eat, and then get some rest.'

'Thank you. One final thing, sir,' Sykes said. 'I haven't been able to contact either my unit or Dawson's since we left Eben Emael. Could you signal my CO and let him know we're both OK and let him know what happened to us?'

Three hours later, washed, shaved and wearing clean uniforms, Sykes and Dawson emerged from their respective mess tents having sampled slightly different versions of the same tinned beef stew and headed over to where a truck waited, a driver already in the cab, smoking.

Sykes was walking slightly better, but still with a pronounced limp.

'You OK, sir?' Dawson asked.

'I'm better, certainly. Are you ready?'

Dawson glanced into the back of the vehicle, making sure that the demolition charge was there, then nodded. 'You ride in the cab, sir,' he said. 'I'll stay in the back, with the charge.'

Dawson lifted the Mauser and Schmeisser machine-pistol into the truck – he'd refused to surrender either weapon – then gave Sykes a hand to climb into the cab. He was on his way to the rear of the vehicle when a young lance-corporal ran over to him.

'Major Sykes?' he asked. 'You know where he is, Corp?'

Dawson nodded and pointed up at the cab, where Sykes was leaning out of the window.

'I'm Sykes. What is it?'

'Signal for you, sir.' The lance-corporal passed up a piece of paper and Sykes read the message quickly, then read it again, more slowly.

'Good news and bad news, Dawson. We've been authorized to accompany the German device as far as Calais, and I'm to take it across the Channel. But for some reason your peculiar talents are in demand again, and you're to stay here in France. There's another job someone would like you to do. You'll be briefed when we get to Calais. Sorry about this.'

'It's OK, sir,' Dawson said. 'It's not your fault. I'll go and get in the back.'

The big corporal turned away and trudged to the rear of the lorry, heaved himself up into the loading area and then tapped twice on the back of the cab to show that he was on board and ready to leave.

The driver engaged first gear and pulled away.

Dawson crossed to the rear of the truck, sat down and peered out of the back as the British army camp started to recede into the distance. He reached down, unlaced his boots, and sighed with pleasure as he pulled them off his tired and aching feet. Then he looked out of the back of the truck as it gathered speed, and shook his head.

'Fucking army,' he muttered. 'I hate the fucking army.' He lay down on the bouncing steel floor on a pile of sacking, pulled a rough blanket over him and almost instantly fell asleep.